D0587145

Enterprise Logs

STAR TREK®
Enterprise Logs

Conceived by ROBERT GREENBERGER
Edited by CAROL GREENBURG

POCKET BOOKS
New York   London   Toronto   Sydney   Singapore

This book is a work of fiction. Names, characters, places and incidents are products of the authors' imagination or are used fictitiously. Any resemblance to actual events or locales or persons living or dead is entirely coincidental.

An *Original* Publication of POCKET BOOKS

POCKET BOOKS, a division of Simon & Schuster Inc.
1230 Avenue of the Americas, New York, NY 10020

This book is published by Pocket Books, a division of Simon & Schuster Inc., under exclusive license from Paramount Pictures.

ISBN: 0-671-03579-7

First Pocket Books trade paperback printing June 2000

10 9 8 7 6 5 4 3 2 1

POCKET and colophon are registered trademarks of Simon & Schuster Inc.

Cover design by David Stevenson

Printed in the U.S.A.

Contents

Introduction

"Don't let them promote you . . . don't let them transfer you . . . don't let them do anything that takes you off the bridge of that ship. . . . Because while you're there . . . you can make a difference."

—Captain James T. Kirk, *Star Trek: Generations*

The *U.S.S. Enterprise* has been a part of America since the Revolutionary War and, thanks to Gene Roddenberry, has ensured the name's place in Earth's future. What other fictional creation could possibly be so firmly entrenched in our culture? After all, the *Enterprise* model proudly hangs in the National Air and Space Museum in Washington, D.C., and the first space shuttle was named *Enterprise* by popular demand. Recently, the public voted for *Star Trek*—depicted by the *Enterprise*—to join the fifteen stamps symbolizing the 1960s.

"My feeling was that if you didn't believe in the spaceship . . . if you didn't believe you were in a vehicle traveling through space, a vehicle that made sense, whose layout and design made sense . . . then you wouldn't believe in the series," Gene Roddenberry said in *The Making of Star Trek*. Without an identifiable ship, its captain and crew would be irrelevant. As important as the captains within these pages are, so too is the vessel they command.

Originally calling it the *Yorktown*, Roddenberry quickly renamed the ship *Enterprise*—why is undocumented, but one could argue the name alone conjures up man's spirit and in one word sums up the nature of the captain.

As Roddenberry developed *Star Trek* for NBC, he projected our cultural development several centuries into the future. Having overcome great difficulties, mankind ultimately reached out to the stars. To do so, they needed starships capable of jumping between solar systems, far from Earth. In order to ensure the crew's completing their mission, each ship needed to be captained by a strong individual, one who could think for himself and act in the best interests of the United Federation of Planets. While there have been many lauded captains in Starfleet's history, those who have commanded the *U.S.S. Enterprise*, from Pike to Picard, seem to rise head and shoulders above the others.

Of the twelve *Constitution*-class vessels that were Starfleet's vanguard, several met with terrible fates. But the *Enterprise* endured, garnering a reputation as flagship for the fleet. Much has to do with the man at the hub of the bridge. Although Roddenberry got his inspiration from Captain Horatio Hornblower, a fictional hero of his youth, he molded the image of captain to suit his actors. There's a lot of Hornblower in Jeffrey Hunter's Pike, but it's mixed with a dash of Hamlet. William Shatner's Kirk, though, was brasher, faster to act. Still, Shatner should be credited with making certain the writers did not ignore the humanistic side of Kirk, which allowed him to temper the well-known cliché of the bed-hopping captain with the protrayal of a man upholding Starfleet's ideals and keeping his ship and crew safe.

Captains who have followed Kirk have ghosts to live up to. In Starfleet's early days, the rules were still being defined. Pike was known for his bravery, but Kirk was known for his "cowboy diplomacy." How did these predecessors influence the command styles of Harriman and Garrett? Jean-Luc Picard had twenty-two years of commanding the *Stargazer* under his belt by the time he first stepped aboard the *Enterprise*. Could he not stop and wonder what his "ancestors" would do in his place? Meeting Kirk no doubt changed his view on command, no matter how slightly.

The lessons learned by one captain from another have been exhibited throughout Starfleet's history. Spock certainly learned well from both Pike and Kirk, and the way Hikaru Sulu evaded Captain Kang in "Flashback" was certainly a Kirk-style maneuver. Even Captain Janeway has admitted some admiration for those legendary commanders, although her style is unique unto herself.

While Pike may have had his moments of self-doubt and Kirk witnessed the deaths of those closest to him, they managed to put aside their personal demons and remained in command. Other captains encountered along the way have been less fortunate. We've seen them devastated (Matt Decker), we've seen them mad (Garth), and we've even seen them traitorous (Ben Maxwell). It should be noted that the question of including Edward Jellico in this collection was hotly debated. After all, he commanded the *Enterprise* for several days during the popular two-part episode "Chain of Command." However, he commanded briefly and was rather unpopular, and were we to include him, we'd have to include everyone who temporarily held command of the *Enterprise*. (Even Dr. Crusher. Even Khan.)

A word about those who tested the captains' mettle. There are many different ways to command a crew, and one must respect the skills of one's opponent. Kirk certainly held the Romulan commander in some regard in the classic "Balance of Terror." The Klingon captain Kor on more than one occasion showed his dedication to honor and duty, dying in a blaze of glory that no doubt inspired countless songs among his people. General Martok clearly demonstrated an understanding of command that earned him first Worf's respect, and then leadership of the Klingon people.

To command a starship takes resolve, courage, and the innate ability to handle the unexpected. As seen in the following stories, the captains approach problems differently—some with humanity, some with daring, some with cunning—but all do it with pride. The nine authors that follow showcase those different elements, most choosing to focus on the captain apart from ship and crew, others focusing on the captain and his relationship with his crew. The insights gleaned from these stories will no doubt allow readers to come away with some idea of why these people are noteworthy figures. Adding some gravity to this volume are two stories based on the first two captains of the *Enterprise*, taken from the pages of history.

From 1776 through the twenty-fourth century *Enterprise* captains have excelled through a mixture of dynamism, practicality, and a heavy dose of humanity. Sit back and enjoy the adventures.

—ROBERT GREENBERGER
Fairfield, CT
January 2000

Captain Israel Daniel Dickenson
The Sloop-of-War *Enterprise*

"In every revolution, there's one man with a vision. . . ."

Captain James T. Kirk, *Star Trek*

DIANE CAREY

Diane knows a little more than most of her colleagues about ships and the rigors of command. In addition to being an accomplished author of science fiction and historical fiction, she is also a seafaring type, preferring older vessels. In fact, Diane braved the lash of early winter, crewing aboard the 1893 Schooner *Lettie* G. *Howard* and arriving at New York City's docks. She stopped rigging and cooking just long enough to complete the following story.

This summer, Diane adds her own vision to the *Star Trek* universe with a new series of novels, starting with *Wagon Train to the Stars* and introducing one and all to the *U.S.S. Challenger.*

Diane's contributions to *Star Trek* extend back more than a decade, including the giant novel *Final Frontier,* which gave readers a glimpse at George Kirk, father to James. She has written six Original Series novels, four novels set during *The Next Generation* (including the first original story), six adaptations and one original *Deep Space Nine* story, and two *Voyager* novelizations.

With her husband, Greg Brodeur, Diane continues to whip up exciting stories, and shrewd readers will detect the loving attention paid to the starships, making them vital characters along with their crew.

Diane adds:

Special thanks to Captain Austin Becker and the Sloop-of-war *Providence* of Rhode Island, replica of John Paul Jones's fighting ship, for their help and good works in preserving Revolutionary War history.

My admiration and gratitude also go to Captain Erick Tichonuk, First Mate Len Ruth, and all the crew at the Lake Champlain Maritime Museum of Basin Harbor, Vermont, for their hospitality and advice, and their faithful tending of the replica Gunboat *Philadelphia.* The original *Philadelphia* resides at the Smithsonian Institution in Washington, D.C. Another of Benedict Arnold's gunboats, believed to be the *Spitfire,* has recently been found at the bottom of Lake Champlain. As a sailor of historic ships, I convey my applause to the team recovering this national treasure, and hope she soon rises to receive the tribute she deserves.

The Veil at Valcour

"Are the Americans all asleep and tamely giving up their liberties?"

Benedict Arnold, 1775

Dawn, October 11, 1776

"That's the signal gun! Row for it, men! Royal Navy in sight! Heave! Heave!"

Frosted orange leaves roared across the chop. Wind snatched away the coxun's orders. Beneath me a dirty bateau clawed upward, punching through whitecaps against a bitter wind. An hour ago the wind had been at my back. Now, scratching down the Adirondack hemlocks and spruces, it chipped at my nose and cheeks and froze the moisture in my eyes.

"How near are we? Will we see the Continental Navy soon?"

"Heave! Few minutes. Hard over, larboard! Heave!"

Black lake, black land—the large double-ended bateau muscled up on its right side as if hauled by a winch! I let out a strangled shout and became intimate with the gnawing water at my left elbow. Everything was so black, so dark, that I entertained a brief crazed fear that the men in this boat were the only Americans here and we would face the British ships all alone.

The coxun's fingers dug at my collar as he pulled me back to my seat. "Keep a grip on them fascines there, your honor."

"What happened?"

"Tiller's over. We're coming into the strait."

"It's the devil's own dark! How could you know to turn?"

"Wind dropped. We're in the lee of Valcour Island. We'll meet up with the American navy any minute."

While the boat hurled itself vertical on the unhappy chop, then skated sickeningly downward, I sat upon a prickle of hardwood saplings, twice as long as I was tall, stripped of every branch and tightly bound into nine- or ten-inch bundles so that they were almost tree trunks again. Five of these bundles, a great weight indeed at nearly two hundred pounds each, were strapped across the bateau's wide beam, and caused the boat to wobble and struggle horridly. Along with those, piles of evergreen boughs with warty bark and needles assaulted my legs with every shiver. What could a navy want with trees?

I strained to see into the darkness, but might as well have had a mask over my eyes. The shore of New York, on our left until now, remained invisible. Around us, Lake Champlain was deeply cloaked.

Then, out of the night, came a voice blasting on the wind. "Hands to the tops'l sheets and braces! Bring the tops'l yard abeam! Don't worry, boys, we possess the caution of youth! Other words, none!"

A huge dark mass surged out of the night, angling over my head as if I'd stepped onto a porch. Swinging in a wide arch came a thirty-foot wooden spear with four enormous triangular sails lancing the sky like great teeth. A ship's bowsprit, inches away!

"Oh!" I dropped back and kissed the water again.

Moonless night had hidden an entire ship!

The ship's sides were mounted with bundles of cut evergreens, a shaggy fence making the vessel into a giant bottlebrush. What an otherworldly sight! Camouflage?

"Hard over, Henry!" the voice again came as our bateau rowed abreast of the massive shuddering object. If the boat and the ship came together on the same wave, we'd be crushed. "Port brace, haul away! Lavengood, Thorsby, Barrette, man the bunts and clews. LaMay, show them the lines, quick, man! Barclay and Rochon, lend Hardie a hand! McCrae, your brace is fouled in the spruces. Don't hurt your hands. McCrae, do you hear me? Stephen!"

Black hull planks bumped the bateau. Bracketing his mouth, the coxun shouted up. "On deck! Heave us a painter!"

High above, a wall of angular gray sail snapped in anger. Then, *flap, flap . . . crack!*—the wind filled it! The ship heeled hard, bit the water, and leaped beyond us.

"Sheet her in and stand by! Larboard, slack your sheet! Clew the tops'l! McCrae, what do you think you're doing? Rochon, I said stand *by* on that sheet!"

That wind-muffled voice—did I recognize it? Or was it wishfulness after three cargo boats and two fishing smacks?

Just above me, a lantern flickered to life, dancing on the night. Its fiendish glow changed everything. Hemp ropes veined a hundred feet into the sky. Two great wooden strakes carried a huge sail that swung like a swan's wing.

From an unseen hand, a rope snaked out to the bateau, falling a foot from me. The coxun snatched it up, and twisted it to a cleat, and thus we wheeled sidewise toward the surging wooden wall.

"Is this the right ship?" I called. "I'm seeking Israel Daniel Dickenson, aboard the *Betsy*. Or is it the *George*? I've got conflicting information on the ship's name."

"We don't call our ships that way." The coxun grasped a spruce bow fixed to the ship and with superhuman power dragged the bateau close, and we skated an inch from disaster. "Get up there, man, before we're beat to splinters!"

As the bateau heaved upward, I stood and put one foot on the bateau's rail. "I'll break my neck!"

"Jump!" the coxun bellowed, "or you'll have seventy ton of sloop in your gullet!"

With one toe I pushed upward, hands scratching for a grip. Boughs rustled, my cloak and tricorn hat disappeared, and I was carried up and away, a fly clinging to a mule's black belly!

"Fend off!" the coxun called. Oars blunted the ship's sides. The boat roached away.

"Heaven help me!" With me riding her wet flank, the ship clawed forward and defied New York's western shore with her long bowsprit. Over me the hostile sail whistled. Above it, a smaller square sail crawled into a bundle and screamed on its yards. I saw all this in an instant—lines snapped, blocks creaked, water sprayed, boughs whipped, and the yard squawked like an enraged pelican trying to snap me up.

Again, that voice. "Hands to the larboard side, for God's sake!"

A force grabbed me from above. I lost my legs. My body went straight outward on the wind. Headfirst I plunged through the bundled branches and flopped face-first upon a tilted deck. Pressing my hands to the planks, I twisted to look up.

Above me, a narrow man-shaped shadow loomed. "Get those fascines over to *Philadelphia* and mounted on. Should've been well done by midnight. Give them to Blake, he's the mate. Or Captain Rue himself. Tell them to rig their canopy and hurry! The wind's from the north!"

I rolled over and choked, "Daniel! Thank Heaven!"

The shadow's shoulders lowered some, arms out at his sides. His head tipped forward. Against the bleak sky, shoulder-length unbound hair flew wildly. "Adam Ghent, that's not *you* on my deck."

He offered no hand to help me up. His unglazed anger was visible even in the dark.

But wait—the sky had lightened. As I drew to my feet and braced my legs, I could make out men around me doing feverish work, sawing, tying, hauling lines in a clutter of iron tools, round shot, wadding, tackles, blocks, piles of rope, and sponge rammers. A boy of about ten years used a bellows to keep a stone hearth glowing inside a formation of bricks. There were no uniforms. The men wore anything from muslin to buckskin, some with wool vests and tricorns or any manner of hat they could construct, and buff or black breeches. They didn't look like a navy.

I stood upon a deck that took up the front half of the ship. On my left was a snarly-looking black cannon. On my right stood a set of ladder steps leading up to another deck, a higher one, which scooped back to the stern. I could just make out more men up there, minding a huge tiller.

Through the shaggy fence of branches, I saw another ship on the water, almost as large as this one, with two quill-shaped yards jabbing the sky. Massive parallelograms of canvas carried her into a crescent of anchored vessels, a line of ghosts on a moorside vigil. All the boats wore beards made of bundled saplings.

"Who's that?" I pointed at the other sailing vessel.

"The Galley *Washington*," Daniel answered brusquely, "moving into defensive position. Lavengood, sheet in all you can get. By the saints, if we're not up another point! Good ship!"

To our right was the crescent of anchored vessels, the smaller ones with one mast each, the larger ones, others like the *Washington*, with two. "What are all these boats?"

Daniel flopped an arm against his thigh. "Why, this, brother, is the Continental Navy! Eight fifty-four foot gunboats, a cutter, two schooners, three galleys, and the sloop you're on. And sad you'll be ever to have laid eyes upon it."

"Why are they anchored? You're not meaning to have a battle this way—"

"The gunboats are flat-bottomed and square-rigged. They can't hope to maneuver upwind. We'll fight at anchor."

The sloop heeled fiercely and passed the ship called *Trumbull*, heading northwest, away from the place where we should be anchored.

"We'll be nicking *Revenge*'s sprit at this pace," a man at the tiller commented. He had a black bandana tied onto his russet hair and arms like tree limbs, and he used lines to control the heavy tiller with tackles.

"We'll make anchor with one more tack," Daniel said to him, "and come to our position on the broad reach."

"It'll have to be handy."

"Say it again, Henry, that the Fates hear you over the wind."

In defiance the wind screamed away his words. We cut past four of the gunboats, with their single masts drawing circles on the sky, sails bundled upon slanted yards. At the south of the bay, another sailing ship maneuvered in the cup of the crescent. "Who's that one?" I asked.

"*Royal Savage.* Quiet, Adam. Ready about! Keep a firm turn on the pins, men. Let's not have a repeat of that ugly little episode yesterday. Let go your jib sheets! Helm over, Henry!"

At the tiller, Henry and two other men suddenly shifted from one side of the ship to the other. Only now, as their cold-reddened toes squeaked on the wet deck, did I realize they were bare of foot. Some had tied cloth about their feet, but these men were wearing rags.

The ship's narrow body shuddered, came to an even keel, rocked briefly on the chop. The long bowsprit bit into the north wind.

"Starboard, haul away your jib sheets!"

The crew's heads disappeared and their elbows pummeled the air. The four triangular sails on the bowsprit whacked like wild horses, making a drumming sound, but the bow came around. The ship turned on a pin, the sails snapped full, and instantly we were faced back east, stabbing the bowsprit at Valcour Island.

"Prepare to haul that gaff down by hand," Daniel ordered. "The sail'll fight you. Hands to the cathead!" When some men looked confused, he added, "Show 'em, Henry. Barrette, man the aft anchor. Men, it's critical both anchors drop at the same time, understood?"

The man called Barrette smiled ruggedly and said, "I can forge 'em, Daniel. Bet I can drop 'em too!"

"Good man," Daniel said. "Otherwise we'll end up with our stern swung south. We must be broadside to the enemy. We're passing *Connecticut*—as we come abeam of *New York*, we'll strike sail and drop anchor. Almost there . . . wait . . . wait . . . ready . . . aft anchor, drop! Take in and make fast—quick, quick! Peak and throat halyards, lower away! Forward anchor, drop! Downhauls, haul away!"

I had only half a clue what he was up to, but the ship seemed to know. The big sail and the triangles fell into linenfolds, iron rings screaming on the cables, and the wind raced by without us. The anchor lines snapped with us between them. We were anchored in position, with a galley before us and the crescent of other boats behind, strapped across the bay between Valcour Island and the shoreline of New York.

Daniel faced his crew down on the gun deck. "Cockbill the tops'l yard. Clear for action, boys, ready every gun. Get that canopy up and the pine boughs on top of it! Get it over the forward guns if you can. Handily now! Wind's from the north!"

Around us, shivering, the men scratched to their work.

Eyes ferocious, lips flat, Daniel Dickenson finally turned to give me the attention he had avoided. "Come for last rites?"

"I brought a parcel from your mother." Rather clumsily, I climbed the nearly vertical steps, holding ropes that were fastened in the fashion of a handrail. Still Daniel had to clasp my arm and pull me to the upper deck. Bracing my legs, I fished through my coat, hoping the ride upon the ship's flank had not claimed the bundle. Good, here it was.

He did not take it. "You came from Connecticut to bring mail?"

My brother-in-law leered at me through a flop of brown hair beating his cheekbone. I scarcely recognized him. Four months ago he had gone to answer the call for experienced sailors and wrights, rosy-cheeked and well-clothed, umber hair bound at the back of his neck like a gentleman. The wraith before me was gaunt, waistcoat ratty, breeches patched, day coat completely missing. His hair was long and lusterless, gone dark as oak bark. Scratched, bare arms protruded from torn sleeves as if someone had dressed a cadaver. Upon his feet were Indian moccasins, worn to parchment.

"What happened to you?" I whispered.

"Camp fever," he said. "Typhoid, malaria, and four months round-the-clock toil to construct these gunboats and galleys, launching a new vessel by the week."

"Where are the riding boots I gave you? And the white linen shirt Eloise made?"

"Traded the boots to Indians for cornmeal in August. The shirt was burned off at the blacksmith's forge making the anchors. Glad I am to have this brown hunting shirt and waistcoat."

He stopped talking as two men came to his sides, one being the man from the tiller called Henry. They were the only two men not rushing to some task of preparation.

"First mate Henry Hardie," Daniel began, "and Doctor Stephen McCrae. My wife's brother, the parson Adam Ghent. What he's doing here is a mystery."

I bowed low, and would've tipped my tricorn if I'd still had it after my little ride. "Every navy needs a chaplain. I'm here to lead morning prayers."

"We only have one morning left," Daniel said cryptically.

The two other men said nothing. I knew how I must appear to them, with my blue wool coat and white neckerchief stuck with crumpled autumn leaves and pine needles, windburn russeting my thin ivory face, blond hair blowing into my eyes. Daniel had always likened me to a parakeet, his height but a third less his weight. Today, braced on many sides by the frosted Adirondacks, we stood on the deck of a fighting ship in a very strange equity, surrounded by fifty half-frozen carpenters, shipwrights, sailmakers, ropeworkers, ironsmiths, powderboys, and militiamen, and not one to bring me tea or buff my buckles.

"What is this boat we're on?" I peered up at the hundred feet of single mast. "Did you build this too?"

Henry Hardie tightened his folded arms. Under his black bandana, one eye tended to squint. "She's a Canadian provincial sloop they used to guard the lake for the redcoats. The General went and captured her from the British at St. John's last May."

"All of five years old," McCrae added, "and she's the grand dame of our fleet. Until today, she was the biggest ship on Lake Champlain."

"What's different about today?"

"Wind's from the north," Daniel blurted.

There was that phrase again. What could that mean? But instead, I asked, "Is this the *George*? I've heard several names."

"The General doesn't name our ships after people, like the King's admirals do. She's a Yankee sloop now."

"But I saw a 'sloop' on an embroidery once. It had three masts."

Hardie shifted his cold feet. "The British call any ship a sloop which has a single gun deck. Three masts is 'ship-rigged.' This girl's a 'sloop rig.' One mast."

"Congratulations, Adam," Daniel snarled. "You now know more about sailing ships than most of these men here."

"Come now," I shivered. "What should we call her, then? And shouldn't I present myself to the captain while we rest at our anchorage?" I made a little practice bow at the waist.

Behind Daniel, Hardie cocked a hip. The man called McCrae smirked ironically.

Daniel hung his arm around the gigantic folded sail with its two wooden strakes spearing back beyond the stern into the night. "This is the Sloop-of-war *Enterprise*. I'm captain. And this isn't an anchorage. It's a coffin."

Directly in front of the anchored sloop, the hogbacked scrub brush of Valcour Island wrecked the wind that raked down her spine, causing unearthly chop in the bay. While at anchor, we climbed down to the gun deck to get out of the frigid wind. Men around us began to huddle beside the sloop's twelve four-pounder cannons. Wordlessly they stacked hand-chilling iron balls upon shot racks.

Out there, on the bay, the line of little ships clinked and wobbled, held in place by a complex of cables and anchors. On a few of the ships, like this one, men were mounting canvas canopies and thatching them with evergreen boughs, releasing a Christmastime aroma through the pitch and black powder.

So this was the Continental Navy. What a thin line indeed we made.

Bracketed by his two friends, Daniel glared at me. "I charged you to stay in New Haven and take care of mother and Eloise."

"I'm caring for Eloise best I know how—by making sure her husband comes home safe. As for your mother, she takes care of herself."

I held out the bundle of burlap from Daniel's mother, no bigger than a holiday pudding, tied with twine, sealed by a dot of candlewax with a shank of cat hair pressed into it. Still he did not collect it.

"There she is," he commented dryly. "Hello, Mother."

"Let's open it, then." McCrae reached for the parcel.

Daniel slapped his hand down. "Are you mad? You've no idea what might crawl out of that."

"Get him, Henry."

At McCrae's order, Henry Hardie scooped Daniel's elbows from behind and dragged him backward while McCrae snatched the parcel from my hands.

"Here now!" Daniel bellowed. "This is serious! The Royal Navy's been spotted! We must prepare to receive them!"

Two more men, whom I would come to know as Lavengood and Thorsby, sprang to hold Daniel back while his possessions were pillaged. I was surprised at their insubordination. This was nothing like the stiffly proprietous British soldiers patrolling the Colonies. Especially the impudent young doctor—he surprised me.

"Won't take a moment." McCrae cut the string with a copper knife. On top of a cannon the parcel unfolded itself, spilling an odd collection of candles, twigs, dried flowers, and a fist-sized bag made of animal skin and stuffed full, dangling from a leather thong. "What's this bag?"

"It's called a crane bag," I explained. "Daniel's mother is somewhat of a—an apothecary."

"Doesn't smell like medicine." McCrae let Hardie smell it too, then the big bearded man named Rochon.

"She told me it's purifying incense," I explained. "Cedar, sandalwood, sage, rose oil, and salt is what she mentioned."

Rochon looked at Daniel. "Why would your mother send that?"

"Because she knows lake water stinks. Put that away!"

"Where did she find a crane to skin?"

"It's probably some poor quail she slaughtered. All of you, this is folly. There's a battle coming!"

Unbelievably, the crowd around the flap of burlap was growing rather than shrinking. Struck me that, for these men, there'd been a battle coming for months and they hadn't the energy to believe the moment had finally arrived. The distraction of a parcel from home, anyone's home, was too magnetic not to give it a minute or two of what little they could spare.

"Look at the tiny bell," Hardie said, pointing at the clutter now revealing itself. "And a black candle."

"And a green one," McCrae noted. "Does the color mean something?"

When Daniel wouldn't answer, I did. "She said that in olden times bells were rung to bless the souls of the dead."

Lavengood's face snapped up. "Does that mean she thinks we'll die?"

"No!" Daniel bellowed. "Pity's sake, Adam!"

"What's it mean, then?" Thorsby asked.

Daniel hesitated, shifted, and was finally released by the men holding him. Sagging, he admitted, "All right, well, it asks the favor of those on the other side of the Veil."

"What veil?" Hardie demanded.

"*The* Veil. Between this world and the other. It's a superstitious woman's folly! You can tell by the ingredients she's living in a dream!"

"Can you?" McCrae opened the crane bag and, shielding it with one hand, spilled the contents onto the frame of the cannon truck. "Here's blue flower."

"Monk's Hood," Daniel fumed. "Just a plant in her garden!"

"What about these others?" McCrae asked.

"She embarrassed me all my childhood with her nonsense!"

Hardie peered curiously. "What can it hurt to tell us, Daniel?"

A flash of empathy raced through Daniel's dark eyes at the men's hunger for distraction. Making a grumble in the bottom of his throat, he took a step closer, but did not touch the contents of the little pile, as we all used our bodies to made a windblock to keep the bits from blowing away.

"Nightshade," he reluctantly began, "dried white rose . . . devilvine and foxglove—there, you see how silly she is? All this is from her moonlight garden. It's coming into morning! The battle will occur in broad daylight."

"Could she have an idea about the night?" I asked. "Perhaps your enemy fleet will arrive after dark."

He threw his arms wide. "Feel that wind? They've got it at their sterns! They'll be here any time. She had no idea I would engage the British at all, yet she sends me a bag of moon-ruled herbs. Once the enemy fleet passes south of the bay mouth, *Royal Savage* will go out and lure the British upwind into Valcour Bay and we will fight under a cold noon sun, *if,* with God's grace, they don't already know where we are and try to come in from the northern strait. Either way, we fight under the sun. So much for the moon."

McCrae held up a sprig. "Is this a moon flower too? And pinecones and acorns. What's this one?"

"Dried apple. Cedar, hemlock, rowan—tree magic! She's sent the whole forest! And here I am on the water!"

"Here's a stone," Hardie pointed out. "White one."

"Moonstone," I told him. "She said it was for rising above trouble. The St. John's wort is for invincibility. The thistle and staghorn are for protection too."

"We'll take it," LaMay sputtered. The other men grumbled an ironic laugh.

I turned to Daniel. "What does it all mean when it's put together? You might as well tell us, for the entertainment value."

The men nodded and rumbled encouragements.

Spearing me with a terrible glower, Daniel shifted his weight on the bucking deck. "Uch, all right. . . . It's a charm of concealment."

The men seemed to like that. Daniel seemed to hate it.

"She said she wanted to make a flying potion," I told him, "but that you always refused it before."

He pressed one hand to his forehead. "It's not that you fly, my friend, it's that you *think* you fly." He clapped his hands once, sharply. "Men, get to your guns! Load up! Grease the trucks! Pile the shot on the starboard racks. The enemy's been spotted, save your souls! Get cracking before we freeze in place!"

The men splintered off. Daniel stomped down the deck, scooped up a line, and began to coil it. I was left shivering in the waist of the sloop. Around me the ship creaked and rolled upon the bay's chop. Above, the morning sky lightened, but an ugly light.

After gathering up the crane bag, candles, bell, and the other contents of the burlap bag, I waddled after him. "Daniel, it's injudicious of you to scoff at your mother this way."

"In what manner should I do it, then?"

"Don't be cranky. These fears aren't trivial for her. She's told me she's had them since the day you were born. Please pay them some attention, for my sake? I've come so far."

"You entertain too easily a woman's fears."

"But what is the symbolic message of these things she sent? I'd like to know, in a professional capa—"

"You're a chapel minister! Why would you care what a thistle means to a pagan?"

"She says this is a critical time for you. She read signs—"

"Signs?" He slammed the coiled line to the deck and started stacking round shot. "Birds flying backward? Water running uphill? Butterfly eggs turning black? Do you see that schooner out there? They've just spotted our enemy. I have reality to deal with."

Pausing, I changed my tone of voice. "I came also because of signs I've seen myself. Daniel, I grieve to tell you . . . George Washington has evacuated Long Island and New York."

A shot slipped from his hand and thumped hard to the hollow wood. It rolled away. Daniel was suddenly still. So were many men within sound of our voices. The change was sobering.

He did not look at me, but gripped a swivelgun on the ship's rail as if to steady himself. "That's . . . grim news, brother."

Nearby, Hardie pulled his bandana lower on his forehead. "It means we could be caught between an advancing army either from Canada or also up the Hudson."

Apparently I had put a crushing burden upon my brother-in-law. Daniel pressed his hands to the swivelgun and closed his sunken eyes. "Then we must not go ashore. If our ships sink, we must sink with them. Henry, send LaMay in a boat to the *Congress*. Tell the general."

Hardie swirled off, snapping orders to some other men.

Daniel straightened, suddenly aged. He gripped the rough-cut branches that were bound to the sides of the sloop and gazed at the southerly mouth of Valcour Bay. There another ship, a schooner, was fighting for control of the wind as she exited the bay. *Royal Savage*, he had called it. I wondered why a Colonial ship had an English name, but decided not to ask.

"You shouldn't have come, Adam," Daniel uttered. "You've boarded a dead ship, in company of a dead crew."

I shrugged. "God will be with me."

"You'll only be distracting him from the rest of us. We're set to stew in this freshwater cauldron." He drew a ragged breath. "This morning smells of winter. Midnight's necromance never wicked off. And we possess only the water now. . . . Pray we hold it."

"Oh, there's more than water here," I pointed out, trying to lighten his mood.

He looked at me. "What do you mean?"

I fingered the bare-wood fascines flanking the sloop's rail, sticking high into the air like fortress walls. "Earth," I said. As the cold breeze snatched at the branches, I brushed them. "Wind. Water, obviously . . . and fire." I patted the stone-cold body of the swivelgun. "The four natural elements of power your mother speaks about."

He shook his head in dismissal. "Mother visits again. I wish you'd left her home, Adam."

"Daniel!" Hardie called. "*Congress* is headed back to position. General's boat's coming alongside."

"Oh!" I cried. "May I meet him? I've heard all about him!"

White stockings aflash, I scrambled after Daniel as he descended the steep ladder to the lower deck. A rowboat, smaller than the bateau I had occupied, drew up to the ship's side. In it were two oarsmen and an officer in a Colonial blue coat and tricorn.

"General!" I called. "Honor to meet you, sir! May I shake your hand?"

Hawk-eyed and hawk-nosed, black of hair and burly with residual power in his shoulders and hands, the general was a robust man of about thirty-five years, with burning blue eyes. He scowled up at me and Daniel from beneath his tricorn hat. "Who are you?"

"Parson Adam Ghent," Daniel grumbled. "My wife's brother."

"You haven't just arrived, Reverend, in the middle of mayhem?"

"I have, sir. And pleased I am to congratulate you for your conquest of Fort Ticonderoga! Everyone in New Haven is proud of its native son!"

The general grimaced. "Mmm, seems to have slipped the notice of the Continental Congress somehow. Why have you come?"

"To bring a parcel from Daniel's mother, and the unwritten love of my sister. His mother has some requests of him."

"You must pause to pay your mother attention, Dickenson," the general said right away. "But listen first—our enemy is hull up on the northern water. The Royal Navy has toted a two-hundred tonner across the land in pieces and reassembled it. A full-rigger, twenty-four pounder cannons. Our scouts on the *Revenge* report counting no less than twenty-four gunboats, a radeau gun barge, and a goodly number of Indians in canoes. That's three times what I expected, all crewed by able seamen, commanded by Royal Navy officers. Us, we have a wretched crew of green ships and green men who don't know a halyard from a garter snake. Waterbury wants us to retreat. I've come to tell you and every captain that I have no intention of retreat, not before we've even touched off a gun. Why does he think I built this fleet? This north wind is our advantage. We must be clever!"

Henry Hardie leaned through the branches. "We could up anchor and run out suth'erd of them while we have the chance, perhaps engage them under sail as we run toward Ticonderoga."

"We can't outsail the Royal Navy on open water," Daniel told him. "Quarters in this bay are tight. Their mastery of the sea will serve less in a pond. We're small targets, we have that on our side. And, bless it, the weather gauge."

"I thank you for your support, Captain," the general said. "It is our plan that the *Royal Savage* should lure the British ships south of the bay before the British discover we're hiding here. I hoped they'll recognize her as one of their own which was captured, and it might make them lose reason and pursue. Then, being a schooner, the *Savage* will be able to pinch back up and join us while the British fall south."

The general turned, almost wistfully, and looked at the narrow strait leading out to Lake Champlain.

"That's my hope," he added, "but hope must be braced with spirit. We must show 'em here and now what we're built of. The British don't think we have the mettle to be a nation. They don't think we'll fight. We're Colonists in a fleet of rowboats, but the King's navy would not face us until they had their two-hundred tonner ready to sail. They dallied an extra month to ready that ship. So who is afraid to fight? It comes down to their pride against our stubbornness. Today is the day we will make England understand we mean to be a nation independent. This is it, my friends—the United States Navy's first engagement! May we prevail! Bless you all!"

With a snapping motion, he gave the order to shove off. The rowboat lurched away on a rising wave.

Daniel watched them go. His expression told nothing.

I clapped a hand to my chest. "My goodness, he is infectious! Did you see those eyes?"

"If we have a navy," Daniel said, "that man built it. He's the one who warned that the British could use Canada as a platform from which to strike at us. He predicted Lake Champlain might be used by the enemy to stab downward from the Richelieu River into the heart of the Colonies and split us apart. That would've been the end, before we even had a beginning. He was the only one who saw it, and he has knocked together this little fleet in a matter of weeks, to defend the lake today."

Leaning sideward against the fascines, Daniel gazed after the tiny rowboat wretching away from us, heading westward toward the gunboat *New York*. He watched the man in the tricorn hat.

"He has some tyrannical ways and suffers indignity poorly, but if I stay, it is only because of him. If I fight, it is because he showed me why. If the United States are ever to become a nation, it will be due to the mighty spirit of General Benedict Arnold."

"There they are!"

The wind off Valcour was unsteady, causing not swells but an unhelpful chop. A diabolical presence appeared at the mouth of the bay—a honeycomb of English gunboats struggling under sail, coming two by two and three by three, and then bigger ships with sails puffed full, yards swinging as they tried to turn. All these, all at once, attempted to claw into the bay against the wind.

I snatched Daniel by the arm. "How can I help?"

"It's too late to train you to a gun. Help McCrae."

"What's his work?"

"Stephen is the only doctor in the fleet. *Enterprise* is the medical ship. You thought I was making a joke about last—"

From the trees on the island came an unexpected *pop*, and two seconds later the fascine next to my shoulder shook. Mauled by splinters and needles, I staggered on the bucking deck and fell to my knees, my mouth full of wood spray. What had knocked me down?

"Adam!" Daniel scooped me up and checked for blood, but my only injuries were scratches.

"Indians!" Henry Hardie pointed onto the high cliffs of Valcour Island. "They've landed Indian snipers on the island with muskets! Keep your heads down, men!"

Daniel swung around. "Lavengood, take the forward swivelgun to 'em. Lather 'em with grape!"

Now I understood the bound saplings made fast to the ship's sides, and the canopy layered with pine boughs. Beside me, the fascines stood firm, except the very top of one was now partly shredded. That musket shot would've happily cut through my chest, but instead sheared across the top of the fascine. All that had struck me was the concussion and some splinters.

"Look!" I pointed at the mouth of the bay, where I saw a huge cloud of square white sails.

"That's their full-rigger," Daniel said, still holding onto me in some kind of possessed preoccupation. "*Inflexible*. She'll have sixteen or eighteen twelve-pounders. Each of our gunboats only has one twelve. If she comes up, she will annihilate us."

Though we held our breaths, the big ship moved sideways against the wind, scuttling farther south, never turning toward us. Back and forth it tacked with obvious effort, courting the mouth of the bay but never coming in.

"They're stuck downwind!" Daniel gasped. "Bless the wind!"

As the men cheered, Rochon pointed at another lick of sail just barely showing through the mouth of the bay, struggling on Lake Champlain. "Their gun raft can't come back up either! Their biggest ships are stuck down!"

"The lake's too narrow for ships that size. They haven't tacking room. Good thing—we're hopeless of counterbalancing the presence of a two-hundred tonner. She might be even more, by the look of her. Might be three hundred, war loaded."

I saw the truth in Daniel's eyes, that sinking and desperate awareness of complete overwhelm. As the British ships came and came and kept coming, we gradually swallowed the terrible spoonful—we were inferior in almost every way, insufficient against the numbers and quality of both ships and seamen. We faced trained officers who thought themselves our ruling class, who had the privilege of a king's navy to command. They possessed the whip hand. We were but Colonial thimbles bobbing purposefully on the white chop.

Rochon blew on a guttering linstock to keep it lit. "Here comes a schooner. What's its name?"

"The *Carleton*, I think," Daniel said, "if our scouts got it right. Do they mean to take us on alone?"

"I can see her guns. Look like sixes to me."

"Let's make our fours speak well to them. Fire at will, Joe!"

"Welcome to America, *Carleton.*" Rochon's burly body took a single step forward. "Fire in the hole!"

Some of the men had the sense to block their ears. Sadly, I was not one of these. Again I was jarred to my knees, this time by the sheer stupendous noise. Never had I heard such a noise, and I was once nearly struck by lightning! A second later, the tremendous boom echoed off the rocks of Valcour Island and assaulted us a second time.

Around me, many men were huddled in shock. They apparently hadn't heard a loaded cannon go off either, nor had they smothered in the gassy cloud of gun smoke.

"Get up!" Daniel raged. "Load, aim, and fire! Worm and swab and do it again! Doubleshot ball and canister! We're not here to save ourselves! Give me that schooner's rigging for breakfast!"

His conviction drove away our terror and charged every man. Better get used to it. I stumbled up.

Scarce a second later, head-splitting cannon blasts rang from all the other Colonial ships, and the brawl was on.

The Schooner *Carleton* was the only English ship that got anywhere near us. It now began a savage response. Hot shot bounded through the air. Their first ball struck the Gunboat *Philadelphia* right in the middle of her canopy, ripping most of it away. Then a full broadside brutalized many more of our ships. In minutes Valcour Bay was shrouded in acrid smoke.

But the wind was from the north. Bless the wind—the Crown's big ships, which they had carted from the St. Lawrence, were useless to maneuver up the narrow strait at the mouth of Valcour Bay. Finally, in a tantrum of sheer muscle, the twenty or more British gunboats dropped their sails and rowed themselves into a raggedy string across the bay behind the *Carleton*, manned by feral sailors ashamed that they had to row. Once in position, they tore into us. The inhumanity began in earnest.

Fiendish with desperation, we returned savagery for savagery. There were no calls for heads down, take care, step cannily, no concern for the injuries or death being suffered. Something completely else was at work. These men were willing to lose limb and life. Half-frozen all night and now sweat-greased under cannonfire, they cared nothing for their comfort. They were fighting not to live, but to live in liberty. It made all the difference.

The casualties began to arrive almost immediately, ferried in rowboats heaped with bloody moaning bodies. I did what I could, hauling the wounded aboard, giving a shot of rum, holding them down while a grim Stephen McCrae took his capital knife, saw, curved hooks, and ligatures to their bones, flesh, arteries, veins, ligaments . . . then it was my job to cauterize the wounds with hot tar—if time allowed. The first one made me ill. The fifth made me cold. Over the side went arm after leg after foot after hand, until the shot-dimpled water around us ran red, decorated with a piteous stew.

And then, a boy of seventeen heaved back and died in my arms while his leg was being cut off. At first, I didn't realize he was gone. In the middle of my prayer, McCrae pressed his hand to mine and said, "He's done for this world, Parson. Put him overboard."

Somehow I was efficient about it. I heaved the corpse headfirst into the bubbling water. "God be with you, fellow."

This was the first day in my life I had ever put my hand on the dead. What it did to me, I cannot describe, except that in a few hours' time I went from a country minister flinching at a muzzleloader's pop to a flint-hearted veteran unaffected by the blare of a cannon two steps from me. Hundreds of howling Indians peppered us with musketshot, but I soon learned to trust Benedict Arnold's wooden barriers. Though mangled friends writhed all about me, I can only say my mind began to shut down. My hands worked independently of thought. My brain dully registered the shouts of Daniel and Hardie, the only two seasoned sailors aboard, helping the other men to aim the cannons to some effect.

Though my head was mostly down to my work, I registered the progress of the battle through individual cries that made it from ear to brain through the cannons' crash. . . .

"Royal Savage *is aground on Valcour! They're abandoning ship! Send a boat for them before those Indians kill them all!*"

"*Look at Arnold running about aiming the guns on* Congress *himself. I wish I had his guff.*"
"*He's the only one aboard who knows how.*"

"*They've boarded* Royal Savage. *They're turning our own guns on us. Thorsby, train the tackles on the forward gun to fire on them.*"
"*I rerigged the* Savage *with my own hands.*"
"*She's not ours anymore.*"

"*Quoin that gun down, LaMay! You're overshooting! Go for the Carleton's rigging!*"

"*Men, watch yourselves! Their grape is cutting straight through the fascines!*"

"*What's that explosion?*"
"*Gunboat! We hit the ammunition locker!*"
"*Great Lord Almighty . . .*"

"*Carleton's cable spring's shot away! She can't stay broadside! Rake her for all you're worth when she swings to her anchor!*"

It wasn't until nearly five o'clock that McCrae and I stole a moment to look up.

What a sight—all around us the Continental ships were in shreds, fascines shattered by grapeshot, rags dripping where sails had been. The British *Carleton* lay tattered, many casualties making colored dots on her decks. There wasn't a sail flying. She was unmaneuverable, taking volley after volley from our cannons. The sight was tantalizing. We might not win, but we were not losing!

I choked on cannon smoke and blinked stinging eyes at the

schooner, where a young officer in a blue uniform was crawling out onto the bowsprit, right in the midst of heavy fire.

"Looks like a midshipman." Henry Hardie squinted his watering eyes. "Other officers must be dead. Poor boy's probably found himself in command."

"He's doing something!" I cried, pointing.

"Getting their jib up," Joe Rochon described. "Gotta give'm credit, if he lives."

Gradually the triangular sail farthest out crawled upward and took some wind. The enemy schooner wobbled, then moved with some purpose, using the wind to turn her bow away from us. The boy on the bowsprit cast a line to one of the English gunboats, which mightily began to tow the schooner out of direct fire. Retreating!

So they had saved their ship, but we had forced them to fall back. We had forced them!

I grew up seven years in seven hours. I had thought battles went an hour or two. But here, from noon until sunset the two forces pounded each other. To our credit, we never folded. Not until dusk did the *Inflexible* finally crawl upwind enough to get in range. She loosed the malevolence of five broadsides at us, a barbaric way to behave, when one thought about it. The result was much destruction in our line and the further ravaging of the unfortunate *Philadelphia*. It seemed they were aiming for *Washington* or *Congress*, but kept striking the gunboat. Rochon said he thought the British assumed Benedict Arnold must be on one of the galleys, and they were right. Arnold's ruthless drive kept us all firing away. We knew he would never quit, so we never considered quitting, and we hammered *Inflexible* back to seven hundred yards. When darkness came, even the mighty three-master had to cease fire, unable to aim. After a few last impudent pops, silence spread quickly. When night enclosed us, the struggle waned in a pathetic kind of draw.

For fifteen ships against fifty-three, that was a kind of victory, wasn't it?

Soon we stood on the half-shattered deck, Daniel, Hardie, Mc-Crae, and I, gazing south. A great mesh of darkness shrouded the bay, which now was flat as a pool of ink. Many wounded rested below, some slipping away. We could not help them more.

On the land, Indian fires glowed through the trees, and on the shore of Valcour Island, the British had set our *Royal Savage* ablaze. The ship burned furiously. Earth, air, fire, and water.

"So different," I murmured, standing beside Daniel. "Even the water. It seems to accept the dead with almost human arms. Your mother said this was the time of year when the gate stands open and the Veil between worlds is thinnest. I think she's right."

Daniel sighed. "This is the autumn equinox. Oh, yes . . . I can see her standing in a circle of salt like an idiot, hair unbound, cheeks reddened with roan, brows darkened with acorn mash. . . ."

"Here." Exhausted, I drew a folded and sealed paper from my breast pocket. "She told me to give it to you at a key moment. I believe this moment qualifies."

Hardie looked over my shoulder. "More bird skin?"

Daniel opened the envelope, then parted his lips to answer. For a moment he seemed to see his mother's face in the petals. A sorrowful grin tugged at him. "Moonwort . . . her lasting love."

No matter how he might rave against his mother, a sentiment arose which he could not banish. I had timed this right.

"Accept her, Daniel," I said, "for my sake."

He looked up. "What've you to do with it?"

"Only that I've been . . . thinking, lately, of leaving the clergy."

This seemed to distress him more than the enemy presence. His eyes creased with concern. "Adam, why?"

My throat tightened. "Your mother's convictions made me question my own. They seem to be stronger than mine. I am supposed to believe in the miraculous, yet I have never seen it. Seven men died in my arms today, and I still found only confoundment. A minister should never have questions."

"We all have questions," he said gently. "Put aside your doubts.

Tonight is no time to give up anything which comforts us."

Seizing the opportunity, I said, "Glad you agree. Put this on." I raised my fist, from which dangled the leather thong with the crane bag on its end, which I had cherished throughout the day.

Nearby, Rochon, Thorsby, and LaMay plugged a hole in our hull, but kept an eye on us. McCrae took a moment to bind Lavengood's bleeding thigh with an oily rag, but he was listening too.

"Since you were born," I continued, "your mother has shouldered the premonition that her beloved son would die—"

"In water, yes," Daniel snapped. "All my life she pushed me away from every well and horse trough, wouldn't let me swim, bathed me with a cloth and bucket—she even did her laundry in a bread kneader!"

I raised a finger in his face. "The Commandment charges, 'Honor thy mother,' not 'Honor thy mother if you approve of her ways.' Instead you ridiculed and tormented her. You swam in the pond. Went riding in rain. Rode in a canoe. Joined the merchant mariners. You became a privateer, all to mock something that embarrassed you. This is your first battle at sea, and she thinks this is it. She begged me to come here."

With a wave of his hand he dismissed what he heard. "I come from a long line of silly fools, many who died at the stake from just this kind of trouble, more who suffered rejection later. My mother is one of these. The whole New Haven community avoids Mary Dickenson. As a boy I watched her suffer loneliness because of her twigs and stones. I was in torment to see her friendless. Only when I married Eloise did she have a companion, a little acceptance. If I die tomorrow, I will die with many men whose mothers saw nothing written in their bobbinlace."

"If you die," I attempted, "do you want me to go back and tell Mary you refused to do this last harmless thing for her? Is that the memory you want her to hold the rest of her life?"

Upon that challenge, I lay the crane bag on the rail beside the smoldering swivelgun, and draped the thong over it. I would not pick it up again. Either he would, or no one would.

He gazed at the bag. "Shall I shun a black cat and avoid the companionway ladder? I've flouted her superstition all my life. You want me to accept it today?"

"I want you to accept that there are forces older and larger than ourselves at work in you. I want you to accept God and accept yourself. Whether you are the end of a line of spiritual channelers I cannot say, but I have seen traits of heightened perception in you. You see things others miss."

"Noticing details is not supernatural. I simply pay attention."

"It's part of what makes you a good captain," Hardie commented. Was he agreeing with me? Or was he simply amused?

"All you have to do is survive the premonition," I finished. "Find a way not to die in the water. Once you're through it, the premonition itself will die. That's what I think."

Daniel pointed at the bag, giving me a quizzical sidelong glance. "If I put this on, the British will not be able to see me or shoot me?"

It did sound silly. I smiled. "Your mother thought so."

"What will the men think," McCrae charged, "when they see their captain wearing a talisman? This talk is blasphemous! They'll be afraid, lose their confidence—"

"Why, doctor?" I challenged. "Do they lose confidence when they see a holly wreath or mistletoe at Christmas? I am a man of God. I've looked into this, and it is not what the witch-hunters say. The old religion is what God let us have for comfort until He could reveal his Word to us. If only Daniel will accept God's tapestry, he can have peace with himself."

The deck fell quiet. Each man became a separate force, alone with his own doubts, demons, and fears.

Perceiving the distress around him, Daniel murmured, "Not the best time for a sermon, Adam." But the acrimony had gone out of him. He seemed suddenly exhausted.

"Put it on, Daniel," I said, "just to keep peace aboard."

Hardie straightened up. "Yes, Daniel, put it on."

"Throw it overboard," Stephen McCrae countered.

The little bag of stuffed bird skin lay beside the swivelgun. Leaning forward toward Daniel, I spoke with subdued honesty. "You need not destroy your mother in order to prevail yourself."

He stared at me, his eyes unrevealing, for long seconds. Something about this last statement made an impression.

"Henry," he announced, "if I vanish, you'll have to take command."

Hardie threw his head back and laughed, the first sound of merriment we had heard. Taking this for a trigger, Daniel snatched up the crane bag and draped the thong over his head. The bag dropped into place on his filthy waistcoat, right over his heart.

He spread his hands. "There. I'm invisible!"

The men laughed. He did seem funny, standing there caked with gunpowder, the little bag hanging around his neck. "Henry, since I've disappeared, will you please send the men back to the repairs? We'll be fighting again come morning light. Let's not sink before then. Start hammering."

"Very well. Let's go, men. Work, work."

His eyes crinkling, Daniel turned to me. "Are you happy now? This'll keep me from dying in the water because I'll catch it on a block and hang myself."

"Boat on the lee side!" someone called.

As we turned, a hard clunk on the larboard side broke our communion. A moment later a powder-burned man with a nightcap of dark hair and a beard swung aboard and came to Daniel. "Arthur Cohn reporting from General Arnold, Captain. *Philadelphia* has just slipped under. She's gone. *Congress* has twelve holes in her. She and *Washington* both have water coming on. On *New York*, every officer but the captain is dead. Our ammunition's almost exhausted. Even if we wanted to keep fighting come morning, there's trifle to shoot with. The general's going from ship to ship, surveying damage. He says he'll entertain all suggestions from his captains but surrender."

Daniel's face turned grim. Hopelessness set in deep.

"My compliments to the general," he murmured. "I regret to have no suggestions."

Cohn simply nodded and stumbled back to his rowboat, to go to the next in our line and spread this blighted news.

Sympathy for Daniel pierced us all. How daunting must it be for a captain to have no answers when his men are looking to him?

Sullen, he moved away from us to the bow of the sloop, climbed onto a gun truck, leaned forward over the flop of staysail, and simply gazed north, as if to implore the dying wind for one more favor. There he stood alone, and everyone stayed away from him. The sloop creaked around him, her draped headsails licking at his legs like pet dogs trying to ease his anguish.

"We'd better pick up the *Savage*'s survivors," Hardie muttered. "Can't let them be slaughtered by real savages."

"Send them to the *New York*," I suggested. "She needs a crew."

They all looked at me. Had I said something wrong?

"Fine idea, Parson!" Hardie lauded. "Mighty fine. Go tell your brother. Get his permission."

Beyond much more than a nod for their approval, I wearily trudged to the bow.

"Sorry to interrupt," I began, framing my words carefully, "but we've had an idea about *Royal Savage*."

Daniel didn't respond, but continued looking northward, into the darkness, his hands clutching the sail canvas. His gaze etched the night.

"Daniel?"

In the faint dust of moonlight from beyond the clouds, his face was chalky, as if someone had sculpted him upon the sky.

I moved closer. "Daniel? Are you all right?"

He continued to stare north. "Shh . . . can't you smell it?"

"Smell what?"

"The miracle you wanted!" He jumped down from the gun truck

and gave me a cheery shake, then called, "Henry! Signal the general's rowboat. Get him over here!"

"General, my compliments. We have a chance to get away."

"Surrender?" Benedict Arnold looked up at Daniel from his rowboat. "I spit on you for that, sir. Are you afraid to die?"

"No, sir, no, not surrender. Imagine this!" As the crew gathered around us, Daniel's enthusiasm brightening his eyes. "Dawn touches the spine of Valcour . . . the lake turns from black to gray. The British gunners light their linstocks, officers tighten formation . . . the fog parts . . . but the bay is empty. Like wraiths, our ships have dissolved with the mist. The night is gone. Precious hours lost. They scout the sound, but we've disappeared. The Royal Navy is deprived of its decisive victory. Imagine their rage, their confusion!"

"Make your point quickly, Sir, I have ships to repair."

"Our duty is to show England that this is a war. We did that today. Tonight, our duty is to show them that the Colonies survived. You pointed out to me that they always choose strength over time. General, let me ask this—what would you do to have an extra month at this time of year?"

Arnold's sharkish eyes flared beneath the tricorn. "A month in October is critical in these northern lands. Ticonderoga is garrisoned with ten thousand patriots and will take an extended siege for the British to break. If they lay siege, they'll have a bitter winter-long experience for which they're ill-prepared. If they elect not to storm Ticonderoga, they'll have to give us Lake Champlain until next summer."

"A year to prepare our Continental defenses. General, I can give you that year this very night."

Arnold paused. The rowboat rocked, bumping the sloop's shattered gunwales. "How?" he asked.

Daniel leaned over. "*Royal Savage* may yet prove a patriot. A burning ship is a seductive sight. And listen—do you hear the British hammers and saws? They're busy making repairs. We're trapped, and

they're overconfident. This gives us time to prepare the sweeps and
tholepins, shroud our lanterns, confer with our captains, and make
the men understand. With a light in the stern of each ship, we can
hug the shoreline and follow each other out, right under their noses."

General Arnold paused, his blue eyes fixed unforgivingly upon
Daniel. Slowly a picture transferred from Daniel's mind to his. "What
will prevent their seeing us move? It's a clear night."

Daniel's conviction was undeniable. "A fog is rising."

"Fog? There's not a wisp!"

"Believe me, it's coming. It will hide us. We need not destroy them
to win, General, we simply need deprive them of destroying us and we
will have won." Daniel looked at me now, a change that startled me.
He placed a meaningful hand upon my arm. "The new needs not destroy the old in order to prevail."

But Benedict Arnold no longer attended the communication between Daniel and me. He was off in his own mind, a plan spinning to
life behind his eyes. "Hooded lanterns . . . a man to guard each light
from the British eyes . . . grease every running block and sheave, bind
the anchors and chains, grease the locks—or better, we tear our shirts
and muffle the sweeps with cloth."

"Cloth is better, yes."

"Yes!" Abruptly General Arnold smacked the side of *Enterprise*
with the flat of his hand. "Colonel Wigglesworth can lead the way in
Trumbull. I'll call a council of war aboard *Congress* upon the half hour.
Spread the word—quietly!"

When long fingers of mist came bleeding between the anchored Continental gunships from the north strait, we were ready. The fog rose so
thick and white that we could scarce see our own bowsprit. Embrac-
ing the new plan, the patriot fleet quietly retrieved our anchors, put
out long oar sweeps muffled with cloth, and lit lanterns on our tran-
soms, shrouded so they could be seen only from dead astern. Thus
began the ghostly row.

With *Trumbull* leading the way, we skimmed down the New York shoreline. Speaking not a word, huddled deep in our hulls, the spirit squadron smoked out onto Lake Champlain under the very noses of the Royal Navy. The British, preoccupied with repairs and watching the *Royal Savage* burn through the fog, never saw us.

For hours we rowed like that, in silence. Finally the order came to put up our tattered sails and try to make our way south. We were well away from Valcour Island, and the British were guarding an evacuated bay.

Daniel found me huddled in the stern of *Enterprise*, catching what little warmth I could from the lantern whose shroud I was tending. Astern of us, the gunboat *Spitfire* was only a smudge in the darkness.

"We did it," he said as he knelt beside me. "They'll be raving mad in the morning. They'll waste time searching for us. They can't come south until they're sure we're not at their backs. Meantime, we'll put in at Schuyler Island and make repairs."

"Brilliant, Daniel. You see? You try to resist the spirits running in your blood, but you can't help but perceive things. You knew the Veil was coming. When it arrived, we were ready."

He surveyed me in a mystical way. "The new and old ways find transition in you, Adam, not in me. You're the one who had enough courage to embrace both ways. You are the Veil between old and new."

Draping an arm around my shoulders, Daniel leaned against the *Enterprise's* shot-pocked taffrail and gave the ship an affectionate pat. Then he plucked a sprig from the remnant of pine branch that had fallen on the deck from the wrecked canopy, and ran it across his lip to take whatever aroma still lingered.

"Do you think," he asked, "mother would like me to bring her a branch of Valcour hemlock?"

Beneath his warmhearted embrace, I smiled. "And we can be home for Halloween."

The young officer who climbed out onto Carleton's *bowsprit under fire was nineteen-year-old Midshipman Edward Pellew, later to become Vice Admiral Pellew, Viscount Exmouth, distinguished naval commander during the Napoleonic Wars.*

At dawn on October 12, the Royal Navy discovered Valcour Bay mysteriously evacuated. *After a fruitless delay hunting for the rebel fleet, they chased the Americans down Lake Champlain.* Israel Daniel Dickenson, Dr. Stephen McCrae, and the Enterprise *sailed south with Benedict Arnold's tiny fleet and were forced to engage the British a second time with great loss, destruction, and capture. Still Arnold refused to fold. The Americans scuttled several vessels, burned them, and defiantly left their flags flying to show that this was no surrender. They escaped overland, carrying their wounded, and joined the* Enterprise *sloop,* Schooner Revenge, Galley Trumbull, *and the* Gunboat New York *at Fort Ticonderoga, the only surviving ships of their squadron.*

The Battle at Valcour Island displayed to the British that the Americans would fight. They now had a taste of what they would face during a siege of Fort Ticonderoga. Thinking twice, they went back to Canada. The long winter months gave the Americans nearly a year to reinforce.

Though Benedict Arnold had displayed unprecedented leadership, the Continental Congress denied him a promotion, partially because several men from Connecticut had already been promoted.

Had the British punched down Lake Champlain without obstacle, the Crown forces would have sliced the Colonies and easily broken them. We owe a second look to the unyielding Arnold, who gave our nation its one and only chance, as well as our thanks to the heroic Captain Dickenson, who set a fine precedence for all Enterprise *captains to come.*

**Let me die in my old American uniform,
the uniform in which I fought my battles.
God forgive me for ever putting on any other.**

Benedict Arnold, in England
shortly before his death, 1801

Captain Osborne B. Hardison
U.S.S. Enterprise

"Command requirements do not recognize personal privilege."

Commander Spock, *Star Trek*

DIANE CAREY

When this project first came up, Diane was originally scheduled to write the Captain April story. After all, she has written more about him than any other author, so it seemed natural. However, Diane also really wanted to write the two historical stories, the ones that inspired Gene Roddenberry to select *Enterprise* as the starship's name. It wasn't hard to see the logic of letting the sailor write about what it was really like on those famous ships.

Diane wants readers to know:

This story is dedicated with supreme respect to Hector Giannasca and Joe Liotta, veterans of the carrier Intrepid, *whose hospitality I will always cherish, and to all the men who served the United States in the Pacific during World War Two, including my dad, Frank Carey, United States First Marines, veteran of the cave warfare on Peleliu Island.*

For those of us less versed on naval warfare, Diane thoughtfully provides us with a glossary.

AA—Anti-aircraft

F4F-4—Grumman "Wildcat" fighter plane

TFB-1—Grumman "Avenger" Torpedo Bomber

SBD—Douglas "Dauntless" Scout Dive Bomber

LSO—Landing Signal Officer, responsible for flagging in all landing aircraft

TF-16—Task Force 16, comprising fleet carrier *Enterprise*, battleship *South Dakota*, cruisers *Portland* and *San Juan*, and eight destroyers

TF-17—Task Force 17, comprising fleet carrier *Hornet*, cruisers *Northampton, Pensacola, San Diego*, and *Juneau*, and six destroyers

Imperial Japanese Third Fleet—fleet carriers *Shokaku* and *Zuikaku*, light carrier *Zuiho*, battleship *Kirishima*, four heavy cruisers, one light cruiser, and twelve destroyers.

Imperial Japanese Second Fleet—fleet carrier *Junyo*, battleships
Kongo and *Haruma*, six heavy cruisers, one light cruiser, and
twelve destroyers.

U.S.S. Enterprise, Carrier Vessel 6
Captain Osborne B. Hardison commanding.
Rear Admiral Kinkaid, OTC, combined Task Force 61

World of Strangers

"If you get back to the ship and into the groove, we'll get you aboard!"

Cdr. "Uncle" John Crommelin
Flight Deck Crew Commander

October 26, 1942. Combat conditions, general quarters.

0949 hours "Message from Admiral Kinkaid to ComSoPac, Sir."

"What's he say?"

" 'Hornet hurt.' "

"She sure is. Look at her . . . pitiful column of bluish-black smoke twelve miles away. Made me sick to watch those strikes light up the morning. If her AA guns were as good as ours, she might've fared better."

"Now we're heading the other direction. All the men are pretty depressed at leaving *Hornet* behind."

"We've got to protect the *Enterprise* now. She's the only flattop left in the South Pacific. We'd better clear that flight deck if we're going to land *Hornet's* aircraft as well as our own. Have Lieutenant Commander Thomas take a strike force of ten VB-10 crews to locate and strike the Japanese vanguard, then make for Henderson Field. That'll get planes off and do some good at the same time. Get them off quick, around ten-hundred, if possible."

"Yes, Sir."

"Then suggest Admiral Kinkaid turn Task Force 16 right two hundred degrees, heading southwest so we don't open the range too far for our returning fighters. Have Lindsey and Daniels shut down long enough to respot the flight and hangar decks, or we'll have Avengers sitting on top of Dauntlesses with Wildcats in their cockpits like some kind of dumped-over pushcart."

"Ah . . . aye, aye, Sir."

"Hold on, hold on, Mr. Whaley."

"Yes, Sir?"

"Thomas with ten VB-10's, ten hundred. TF-16 right to two hundred degrees. Respot."

"Thank you, Sir—thanks."

"That's okay, Ensign, we're all shook up. Carry on. And have somebody find Lieutenant Kines for me."

"Right away, Sir."

1046 hours "Captain, here's Mr. Kines, Sir."

"Captain Hardison, I didn't mean to abandon you. There was a problem on the waterline."

"Hopefully I won't need a lieutenant to baby-sit me much longer, Roy."

"Understandable, Sir. Most captains have a day or two to get used to all the names and faces before they have to drive around in heavy combat, never mind up against four enemy carriers."

"If things keep on like the past five days, I'll never get to step off the nav bridge. I'll have to start peeing in a coffee can instead of the h—"

"Sir, torpedo tracks! Three kanyos coming from starboard!"

"Point at them."

"There, Sir, white wakes!"

"Right full rudder. Swing inside them. Comb the wakes over."

"Bridge, emergency right full!"

*   *   *

1048 "Bow's swinging, Sir . . . torpedoes are pressing off to port . . . we missed them."

"Reverse rudder to swing hard to port. Destroyer *Smith*'s coming up on our port quarter. She's got damage. Let's not hit her."

1049 "Sir, lookout's got another fish, eight hundred yards dead ahead!

"Hard right rudder!"

"Goddamn . . . sorry, Sir . . ."

1115 "What's the condition on the flight and hangar decks?"

"Sir, Crommelin's flight deck team's striking some SBDs below to make room on the flattop, but we can't unjam number one elevator. It's stuck in the up position. Number two was jammed down, but they've got it working again, so Lindsey's cleared the flight deck for business."

"He's ready to start boarding those *Hornet* planes? They've got to be almost out of fuel."

"Yes, Sir, Jim Daniels is about to start waving them in. He wants the ship to stay into the wind. Those boys in the air are pretty shaken."

"Hell, yes, their home base is sinking. Do whatever Daniels wants. He's in charge now. He and Robin Lindsey are the best LSOs, I think, on the whole planet. If they can't pack a deck, nobody can."

"Yes, Sir."

"This isn't good at all . . . with the *Hornet* gone, if we fail to hold Guadalcanal, the Japanese grip on the Pacific will prevail, and we'll have a twenty-year nightmare ahead of us."

"Captain, excuse me. Mr. Griffin says radar is registering a large group of planes twenty miles off."

"*Hornet*'s flyboys?"

"They may not be friendly, Sir."

1119 "What was that problem on the waterline that distracted you, Roy?"

"Boat coming up to us, Sir, from the *Hughes*."

"A boat? While we're at twenty-eight knots?"

"They didn't want to use the radio. We boarded a petty officer with a Marine guard and a Japanese prisoner. I've got them on the fantail, but I wanted to check before I brought them to you."

"Roy, I've never heard anything like this before. What are you talking about?"

"I don't know how to say this, Sir, but the Jap is demanding to speak to you."

"You know better than that."

"Yes, sir. Except that he . . . Sir, he asked for you by your first and last names. Captain, how could a Japanese gunner possibly know you'd taken command here? He has a message for you—would you like to hear it?"

"Yes, I sure would!"

"He says, 'Tell Captain Ozzie B. that Snow Boy wants to talk to him.' Does that make any sense at all?"

"Oh, my . . ."

"Everything all right, Sir?"

"Uh, hmm . . . why don't you . . . come ahead and bring that man up here. I'll speak to him."

"Yes, sir. I'll be right back. Oh, and, you won't need a translator, Sir. The Jap speaks perfect American."

1120 "That's because he's an American. . . ."

1120:30 Enterprise Radar Officer Jack Griffin:
    "*Bandits above the clouds! All planes in air stand by to repel attack approaching from north. Above the clouds . . . above the clouds . . .*"

1121 "Dive bombers!"

1139 "Those were some terrific evasive maneuvers, Captain. I have to be honest, Sir, I didn't think an aircraft carrier could twist like a snake!"

"Tell me what's happening on the flight deck, Mr. Whaley."

"Crommelin's packed fifteen to twenty F4Fs and SBDs on the forward deck, as you can see. With number one elevator frozen, he doesn't dare take the time to strike them below, now that the landings are commencing again. LSOs got their hands full."

"Too bad those SBDs don't have folding wings. Keep the ship firmly southwest, right into the wind. Clear the LSOs to start bringing aircraft on board. Those boys in the air have got to be watching their gauges sputter."

"Unless you counter this, LSOs going to give priority to the planes with injuries aboard."

"Suggest that he land ours and *Hornet's* CAP fighters first. They've got to be running on reserve fuel by now. Gonna have a lot of wave-offs, trying to clear the arresting gear that fast."

"Yes, Sir, we probably will."

"Any sign of Mr. Kines with our guest?"

"I'll go look, Sir."

1140 "By damn, that Daniels is a daredevil! He's landing planes while the number two elevator's lowering! That's one congested flight deck. The SBDs are right abreast of the island. Half a carrier left to land on . . ."

"Yes, Sir, Daniels has landed over sixty planes, some bad shot up. I think Lindsey's taking over now."

1200 "Almost no arresting wires left now. Look at that deck. Looks like a parking lot at a Crosby concert."

"Sir? Mr. Kines is back . . . with . . ."

"Thanks. Go ahead and keep an eye out down there for me, Whaley. Okay, Roy, what've you got here?"

"Captain, this is a Japanese gunner picked up by the *Hughes* last night. His name is Yukio Suzuki, age thirty-two. He's got a broken arm and a bad bruise on his head. Apparently had to ditch."

"Sit him on the deck over there. He'll have to wait. The TBFs are running out of time."

* * *

1235 "Give me the numbers, Whaley."

"Sir, we've accomplished the near-impossible. We've landed forty-seven planes in forty-three minutes, under fire, with only five F4Fs ditched and no SBDs. Lindsay looked like he was directing an orchestra, bringing 'em in one by one, slow and safe. Even after you told him to knock it off, he kept bringing them in. Daniels bet him a dime for every plane he could bring in on the number one wire."

"How much did Lindsey make?"

"Made a buck."

"I'll double it."

"Swede Vejtasa was the last one to come aboard. They had to chock his tires right at the wire. No room left at all."

"I'll have to congratulate Lindsey and Daniels and Crommelin tonight for a hell of a job. Remind me, Roy."

"Will do, Sir."

"Ensign Whaley, inform Admiral Kinkaid of the ship's status and suggest TF-16 change course to 123 degrees . . . resume our retreat. Roy, what's the story on the lower decks?"

"Oh . . . Sir, mighty horrible. We've got dead and dying all over the hangar deck. One man with no legs and one arm left dragged himself over the side. We just let him alone and he went over on his own. We've had two hundred forty killed in Task Force 61 ships. Planes on board number eight-four, counting inoperables and spares. Pilots are, well, tired and disheartened, Sir."

1540 "Captain, Admiral Kinkaid advises we're now sailing beyond the range of Japanese strikes and we're protected by a dozen fighters."

"What about TF-17?"

"Unfortunately, Sir, seems—seems nobody's guarding them. *Hornet's* dead in the water. Admiral Kinkaid's informing Admiral Halsey that *Enterprise* is pretty severely damaged, as well as the other ships in the task force. If you have any amendments, I suggest you make them now, Captain."

"We'll take care of ourselves. Pray for the *Hornet*. Let's hope the Japs let her escape."

"We're all praying, Sir."

"Okay . . . well, Mr. Yukio Suzuki . . . that's right, stand up. I'm ready to talk to you now. Mr. Kines, get that man on his two feet. Plant him right here, please. Dismiss everybody off the nav wing but you and the Marine, Roy."

1542 "You look up at me right now. Start talking."

1542:10

1542:30 "Okay, if you won't talk, then I'll start. When your messages stopped coming, the War Department came and asked me what I thought happened to you. I told them you must be dead. I figured that was the only thing that could make you go silent. The Japs killed you because they found out. What are you doing in the Philippines?"

"Fighting for my people."

"Which people?"

"The Japanese people."

"Uh-huh. You tell me what you're doing here."

"I won't speak in front of them."

". . . Roy, you and the guard are dismissed to the bridge for a couple of minutes."

"Captain, I can't let you do that."

"It's a direct order."

"I don't care if it's the Eleventh Commandment."

"Mr. Suzuki here's an old friend of mine. Nothing's going to happen, understand?"

"No, Sir, I don't."

"Mmm . . . How about if you take the guard's sidearm and you stay and he steps onto the bridge?"

"Crocker, hand me your sidearm. Dismissed. Go into the nav bridge. Close the door. Go ahead, Sir."

"Thanks, Ray. Okay, Luke. Will you talk now? In front of me and Lieutenant Kines?"

"In front of you and him only . . . yes. I will talk."

"Captain, you know this man?"

"Sure do. This fella is Luke Suzuki, a kid from my neighborhood back home. I did some work for his parents, and I used to watch this sorry excuse when the parents weren't home. About—what is it, two years ago?—I talked him into working as a translator for the Japanese, undercover for Naval Intelligence. Four months ago, suddenly, the messages stopped. Y'know, Luke, I thought you died. I thought I got my favorite rug rat killed by talking him into being an agent for our side. You know what that did to me? Now I find you out here like this. You know what my stomach's doing right now?"

"I don't care anymore about you. I discovered where I belong. I serve the empire that bore me."

"Manure. You're as American as I am. You're a Presbyterian kid from Iroquois Street, you do a mean Jack Benny, and you danced to 'In the Mood' at your wedding. Don't give me any propaganda, Frankensteinito, I used to wipe your little square butt. I've had a hard couple of days here. You tell me right now what's making you tick, or I'm calling that Marine and he's going to pitch you overboard. And if you think I'm kidding, remember that I already thought you were dead once. Twice wouldn't hurt that much."

1542 "I'm not American anymore. What difference does it make who you fight for? Both sides are the same."

1551 "If we're dislodged from Guadalcanal, the Japanese will have an airstrip with which they can keep a grip on the whole South Pacific. Doesn't that do anything to you, Luke? What about your parents? What about Kuniko and Ricky? You want your wife and son living under Hirohito's rule?"

"What difference? They're living under the same thing now."

"Luke, I'm very busy . . ."

1552 "I listened to you. You talked me into working undercover. You talked about important things, how a world of America and the west was better than a world of Hirohitos and Hitlers and Mussolinis. I listened and I went. But you were just following orders. There isn't any difference. One tyranny is the same as another. I might as well be part of the tyranny that looks like me."

1552:30 "Because of you, I worked seventeen months for the Japanese, translating messages and news reports from the west, all the time funneling information back to the U.S. War Department. All the time hearing your words in my head. I intercepted and relayed critical information. I stopped other information. Twisted facts. Anything I thought would help. Ricky learned to walk when I wasn't there, because I was spying for America. For him. You said it was for him."

"That's your excuse for treason? Every man in the South Pacific is away from his family. Including me!"

"No! I was proud to go!"

"Make sense, then!"

"You know how America paid me back?"

"Watch it! Back off!"

"Roy!"

"Just watch it when you get close to our captain, pal!"

"It's all right, Roy, he won't hurt me. Stand down."

"I'm not going to let him threaten you, Sir."

"That's not what's going on here. Stand back. Go ahead, Luke, keep talking."

"Move him away from me."

"Back off, Roy. All right, talk. Hurry it up."

"One day I was . . . I translated a news report out of San Diego. The U.S. government is rounding up Japanese Americans and herding them into camps in Arizona. I checked it out. My parents, my uncles, and my wife and Ricky were thrown in there! My mother was born in Seattle, for Christ's sake! Because of you, I was sitting in Tokyo, working for Naval Intelligence, instead of with my family. They're prisoners. Like dirty dogs or something. I thought America was the place where that couldn't happen. You wanted to know, Oz? Now you heard it, same as I did crackling over my set. On that day, I became Japanese."

1553 "They're just afraid, Luke. It's war. People are scared. Their sons and husbands and daddies are out here dying. Back home, they feel helpless. They don't know what to do, so they're doing crazy things. Giving in to their fears."

"I understand fear. But you're lying to me again."

"What do you mean, I'm lying?"

"If it was just fear, they'd be rounding up people of German descent on the east coast. Wouldn't they? But they're not doing that, are they? Because Germans look like you."

1553:20 "It's true, I talked you into going. I believed every word I said. You had the look, you had the language, and it was the right thing to do. Freedom needed defending. It still does."

"Freedom without dignity is nothing. Freedom in shame? What good is it? America showed me how to act. I might as well side with my group."

"Sure. Why not?"

"Aren't you going to argue with me? No big words?"

"Why should I? It's natural. I don't like you, and you don't like me, and we don't like that Jew, and he doesn't like that Negro. It's wired into us. We're more comfortable around people who look like us. It's something God gave us so we could survive. Whales go with whales, dogs and cats don't like each other, birds flock, fish school, seals raft, deer herd. It's survival. Humans are the only ones who try to fight it. It takes practice, though. We do okay for a while, then we get a Hitler or a Hirohito who wants to set us back. I'm fighting against getting set back."

"Why should you?"

"Why should I fight?"

"Yes. Why bother?"

"Because I took a shine to a little Japanese kid on my street who thought the morning sun rose in me. It made me feel like a million bucks to have that little face grinning up and worshipping me. Okay? Simple answer? If I didn't know you, all I'd see out there is a yellow horde."

"Because of me?"

"That's right, idiot. You're the one who keeps me from looking at all those dive bombers like one big amber blur. Even though, at times, I have to admit it would help. Sure, side with your own kind. If you're a salmon."

1556 "My family shouldn't have to suffer this embarrassment. They're American citizens, same as you."

"The folks back home are scared. They're reacting in a bad, inexcusable way. But switching sides is not the way to fix it. You better screw your head on straight, kid. The Japanese are moving as a racial bloc in a Machiavellian power-grab. They intend to fight to the last child. They're training eight-year-olds to fight. Did you know that? How long till Ricky is eight?"

1558 "You want to talk about indignity? In ten minutes *Hornet* took two torpedoes, two planes, and two bombs. *Enterprise* took two hits and a near-miss. Twenty-four dive bombers scouring us out of the sky. If our AA wasn't superior, you'd be floating around on a scrap heap. Indignity from sitting in a camp? You know, I've only got so much sympathy to spread around. I've had forty-four killed and dozens of wounded and damned near shook this ship apart with violent maneuvering to squirm away from torpedoes, men crammed into sweaty ready rooms waiting for the next explosion, boys stuck in their planes on the deck while other planes crash into them on landing—"

"My family!"

"I know your family! Your family are some of my best friends. What's happening to them smells to high heaven, but this mess smells higher. At least blame the right people!—oh, hell with this. Come here, you little bastard. Just get a little closer to the edge of the *balcony.*"

"Captain!"

"Get away from me, Roy! Come here, you spineless punk. You see that F-25 over there with the aileron stuck in the upright position and the whole right side pocked with bullet holes? That's a fella named Souza from the *Hornet.* He had to make an emergency landing on our flattop because his own carrier's over there sinking, taking God knows how many men down with her. All her planes were stranded in the air, watching their gas gauges drop, while our Landing Signal Officers crammed planes onto this ship, and me up here executing maneuvers no aircraft carrier was built to make. You ever tried to dodge dive-bombers with eight hundred feet of ship shuddering under you? You ever laid out on a bloody deck in a puddle of burning fuel? Discomfort? Shame? Embarrassment? Indignity? You're a measly soft-bodied worm!"

"You have no right to call me names! I don't work for you anymore!"

"I'll call you what I please! I've got a ship full of survivors who watched their buddies ditch and crash and burn and drown. Indignity? It's ugly what's happened to your family, but it's not quite as ugly as crashing your plane into a black sea or dragging your own carcass over the side because your lower body's blown away. Arizona? You might as well talk about mail call on the moon!"

"Captain! Sir, maybe I ought to get this creep off the bridge wing."

"Leave him where he is. In fact I'd rather you get off."

"Sir, we had that conversation!"

"Just stand outside of that hatch for a few minutes."

"Sir, you've got a responsibility as CO to safeguard yourself."

"I'll be fine, Roy. Anyway, after today I'll know whether or not I should bother to keep fighting. If two friends from the old neighborhood can't work this out alone, what chance does a world of strangers have?"

*   *   *

1562 "All right. I've got my Lucky Strike and I'm calm again. But I can change. You know, Luke, you caught me on a real bad day. Hundreds of boys died over the past five days. Those men are out there giving up their young lives, and it's not very nice for them, the ways they're dying. It's perfect purgatory out there. They're not going through it to take over the world. They won't be conquering somebody's country when it's over. You can't say the same thing about the Japanese or the Germans."

"I don't want to hear this. I listened enough to your talking me into things."

"What'd you come here for, then? Obviously you went to a lot of conniving to get on my carrier. What do you want from me?"

"I came . . . I want . . . I want you to call the government. Get my parents and my wife and son and uncles out of that camp. You can do it. When I found out you were taking the *Enterprise*, I knew you had the power. They'll listen to you, Ozzie! The government will listen!"

"Probably."

"When you call, they'll find my family and free them."

"I don't know. I don't know . . . there's something wrong with that. You're out here switching sides, fighting for the enemy—I sent you out to do good business for our side, and I find you out here in the middle of the Pacific, telling me you're Japanese now. Why don't you have a cigarette while I think about this?"

"Will you get my family out? I'll work for whichever side you want, if you get them out!"

"Come at a pretty low price, don't you, pal?"

"My family isn't a low price. I don't care anymore which side wins. I was betrayed."

"Yeah, you were. But it's just fear and resentment at work in Arizona. It won't last. You're looking through the carnival mirror of a war. You know, Japan made the biggest mistake of its history when it attacked Pearl Harbor. A lot of innocent people got sucked into the vacuum. Okay, be mad at the Americans who put your family in a camp, but be more mad at the Japanese, who started all this."

"I *am* Japanese. Look at me. My face. My hair. I grew up thinking I was an American. Everybody said I was. My mother was, and my father couldn't remember anything else. I never looked at you and thought you were a Yank. I thought I was an American, we were the same, you and me. But now I know everybody looked at me and thought I was a Jap. I'll never be an American. This proves it."

1564:10 "Luke, I think if you'd showed up five days earlier, everything would be different for you. But seeing you here today, after what we've been through at Santa Cruz . . . nah, I can't think the same. I'm not calling anybody. Your family will just have to cool their heels in Arizona."

"You won't call?"

"I won't help you."

"They love you like a brother!"

"And all these boys suffering on my lower decks, dying in the sky and out in the water, they love each other like brothers too. You think those boys from *Hornet* are going to give up and desert because *Enterprise* AA was better than theirs? That's not fair, right? It's not fair that some rich boys in the states get desk jobs on the mainland and these men are all out here in the ocean and jungles because they're farm boys from Alabama. So I guess all these boys ought to ditch the effort. Refuse to fight anymore. Hell, everything's unfair. Yours is a big unfairness. You think I don't know where your folks are? You think I haven't been tempted to use my pull to get them out?"

"You knew where they were?"

"I knew since last June."

"You left them there?"

"They're paying a price. It shouldn't be happening. Did you know that some Japanese-Americans really are using their citizenship to spy on the U.S.?"

"That's not true."

"Yes, it is. Your family is taking the hit from other people's actions. It shouldn't be happening. But if I went to them, they wouldn't say their son should abandon America. We've got to save the country first and fix this other stuff later. What do you think your mom and dad would say if I got them out and told them Lukie was working for the Empire?"

"No, don't tell them anything! I don't want you to say anything to my father. I'll talk to him myself."

"What if you get killed? Figure your chances of survival are any better than any of the rest of my boys? And you might as well get used to hating me, because I won't call to get your folks out.

"I won't call. I won't call, because of all the other people who'd be left in those camps. If we want them out, we have to get this war over sooner. You'll have to pick for yourself whose side you're on. Lieutenant, permission to get this man off my aircraft carrier."

"Aye, Sir. Sir—"

"Yes, Roy?"

"Captain—I'm not sure I understand, and I need you to be absolutely clear. You want us to execute an enemy prisoner without process? Dump him over the side at twenty-eight knots? I'm not saying I won't do it."

"No. No. Listen. I want you to put him in an inflatable, fuel him up and get rid of him. He's not an enemy prisoner. He's a born and bred U.S. citizen working undercover for our side. It's our duty to send him back. He's going to go back and do the right thing, aren't you, Luke?"

"You're sending me back?"

"You can rendezvous with the Japanese task force, if you can find them."

"What would I tell them if I'm in an American boat!"

"Lies. What else does a spy do? Go back and do your job. Just do it with the right colors. Quit looking at people by the slant of their eyes. And your family, never mind them. It'll be tough on 'em for a while. It's not exactly a Chattanooga Choo Choo for anybody out here. Your family's enduring their part of the discomfort for the privilege of living in America. They won't be dying in a cold sea or crashing into your buddy's plane on a crowded flight deck or suffocating in a pool of gas. They're just paying their percentage of this big bill. They're tough. They're Americans. Roy, go on and take this man away. Lose him on the water somewhere."

"It'll be my pleasure, Sir."

"Luke, I'll see you when it's all over, if both of us live. We'll decide later what's going to be said to your dad. And to your little son. See you on the next corner, Snow Boy."

After the battles of Santa Cruz and Guadalcanal, the Japanese grip on the South Pacific began to slip and was never recovered. Desperation eventually led to the horrors of kamikaze attacks.

The Enterprise *was the finest example of World War Two fast multipurpose carriers and fought nearly all the great carrier battles, including Midway, Wake Island, Marcus Island, Guadalcanal, and Okinawa. She was one of the first U.S. ships fitted with CXAM radar, and gained a reputation for effective use of her formidable 40mm quadruple anti-aircraft guns. She was the first carrier to receive a Presidential Unit Citation, May of 1943, and was badly damaged by a kamikaze on May 14, 1945. The war ended while she was being made ready to fight again.*

Captain Robert April
U.S.S. Enterprise

"Just remember it's you they draw strength from. They look to you for guidance . . . and for leadership. Help them. Show confidence in them."

Commander Deanna Troi, *Star Trek: The Next Generation*

GREG COX

No stranger to the *Star Trek* Universe, Greg contributed the best-selling trilogy *The Q Continuum*, which gave us a long look at Q and his checkered past. Since it was so well received, Greg has been invited back to write another trilogy, this one set during the Eugenics Wars of the late twentieth century.

In this story, Greg goes back to a somewhat later era to chronicle an early mission for Captain Robert April and the *Enterprise.* April made one appearance on the animated television series, but ever since his inclusion in Stephen E. Whitfield's *The Making of Star Trek,* he's been acknowledged as the starship's first commander.

Greg has also explored the Marvel Universe, where he authored an *Avengers/X-Men* trilogy, as well as two solo adventures featuring Iron Man. Elsewhere in the realm of licensed characters, he has penned *Battle On!: An Unauthorized Look at Xena: Warrior Princess.*

For the Sci-Fi Channel, Greg happily contributes scads of trivia questions for their Web site.

Cox lives in New York City, where he works as a Consulting Editor for Tor Books. He thanks colleague Diane Carey for fleshing out Captain April and his crew in her novels *Best Destiny* and *Final Frontier.*

In addition, he would like to dedicate this story to the memory of John Colicos, who first brought the ruthless Commander Kor to life.

Though Hell Should Bar the Way

Captain's Log, 10th of October, 2246.

An outbreak of fungus has destroyed the crops on Tarsus IV, threatening an entire Federation colony with famine. As the largest and fastest starship in the sector, the Enterprise *is the only ship that has a chance of delivering vitally-needed supplies to Tarsus IV before this unanticipated disaster achieves catastrophic proportions. . . .*

"How are we faring, Helmsman?" Captain Robert April asked, leaning forward in his command seat. On the viewscreen before him, starlight streaked past at unprecedented speed.

"Warp factor 7 and holding," the stocky young man at the helm controls reported, his eyes darting between his instrument panel and the view ahead of the *Enterprise*'s prow. Lieutenant Carlos Florida did not bother to conceal the excitement in his voice; it wasn't every day he got to break Starfleet speed records.

Captain April nodded in approval. "And how's our fine ship bearing up under this truly exceptional velocity?"

Lieutenant Michelle Roberts reported from the engineering station to the captain's left. "Some minor fluctuations in the forward deflectors, Sir, but nothing we can't compensate for."

"Outstanding," April responded. Despite the dire nature of their mission, he felt a surge of more than justifiable pride at his ship's speed and resilience. The *Enterprise's* standard cruising speed had never exceeded warp 6, but it did his heart good to know that the freshly crowned empress of the fleet could pull out all the stops in an emergency. "Steady as she goes, then," he instructed the bridge crew. "Let's keep on making excellent time, shall we? A great many hungry people are depending on us."

He settled back into his seat, tucking his hands into the snug pockets of the wooly cardigan he wore over his gold command tunic. The well-worn sweater was a sartorial eccentricity that his devoted crew had long since grown accustomed to, one that gave him a professorial air quite in keeping with his benign, fortyish features and twinkling brown eyes. His distinct Coventry accent only added to the almost Dickensian persona of Robert April, founder of the Federation's interstellar exploration program—and first captain of the *Starship Enterprise*.

April took a moment to savor the elegant lines and sleek, streamlined design of the bridge. Slightly more than a year into the ship's maiden voyage of discovery, the nerve center of the *Enterprise* still looked as bright and shiny as it had on the day the *Constitution*-class starship had first soared free of her berth in spacedock. The blue-matte walls of the bridge remained fresh and unscuffed, while the gleaming parrot-red rail surrounding the command deck had not yet lost any of its original luster. Lighted instrument panels blinked and sparkled amidst a constant buzz of electronic activity. *Warp factor 7*, April marveled, imagining that he could feel the full force of the *Enterprise's* mighty engines thrumming all around him, despite the vessel's state-of-the-art inertial dampers. *Good heavens!*

The *Enterprise* sped through the vastness of space, crossing light-years every second. *What a remarkable achievement this ship is,* her captain thought. *A sublime testament to human ingenuity and aspiration.* Not for the first time, Robert April vowed to return the *Enterprise* to Starfleet intact once his five-year mission was completed.

But first there were those starving colonists to look after. "What is our estimated time of arrival in the Tarsus system?" April asked.

"Approximately forty-eight hours," Ensign Isaac Soulian informed him from the navigation station. Soulian double-checked his estimate against the course plotted on the astrogator panel between him and the helm. "Give or take fifteen minutes or so, depending on the amount of interstellar debris in our path."

"Understood," April stated. "Thank you, Isaac," he added, with characteristic informality; despite his rank, the captain was seldom one to stand on ceremony.

Forty-eight hours, April reflected. Literally two full days, at least as days were reckoned on Earth. Sometime soon, he realized, the brightest minds in Starfleet were going to have to figure out a new way to reckon time in space, maybe even one that took into account the relativistic effects of warp travel. April made a mental note to himself to propose just such a system of, well, "stardates," the next time he briefed Starfleet Command.

In the meantime, plain old hours and days lay between Tarsus IV and deliverance. April wished there was some way to get to the embattled colony even sooner—the ship's cargo holds already contained the provisions desperately needed by the colonists—but knew he couldn't safely spur the *Enterprise* any faster than she was already going. Forty-eight hours would have to do.

The hard part is going to be the waiting, he thought, regretting keenly that there was nothing else he could do for the famished colonists at this very moment. He briefly considered checking on the situation in sickbay, but knew that wasn't necessary; his chief medical officer, who also happened to be his wife, was already hard at work readying the sickbay to treat the most severe cases of malnutrition. *No need to bother Sarah while she's busy,* he concluded reluctantly, *even if I wouldn't mind her company just now.*

"Captain!" Ensign Soulian called out. The urgency in the young Lebanese officer's voice caught April's attention at once. "Alien vessel approaching."

April sat up straight, peering at the viewscreen. *Who the devil could this be?* As far as he knew, there were no other Federation starships in the vicinity; that was the whole problem, as far as Tarsus IV was concerned. "Onscreen," he ordered. "Full magnification."

An involuntary gasp escaped Lieutenant Florida's lips as the alien spacecraft came into view. April knew how the young helmsman felt; there was no mistaking the ominous outline of a Klingon battle cruiser.

It was deceptively fragile in appearance, the bulbous prow of the warship separated from its aft warp engines by a single tapered concourse. According to Starfleet Intelligence, however, the D-6 battle cruiser possessed formidable shields, plus comparable firepower—as the Federation had learned the hard way at Donatu V.

"Red Alert," April ordered at once, placing the *Enterprise* at full emergency readiness. Flashing red lights, and a low-pitched siren, added to the tense atmosphere upon the bridge. "Blast," the captain muttered to himself. "Why Klingons? Why now?"

First encountered by Starfleet only a few decades ago, the Klingons had already proven to be as much a threat to the Federation's outward expansion as the Romulans had been before them. No surprise then, April surmised, that the Klingon Empire would welcome the failure of an isolated Federation colony like Tarsus IV; it even occurred to him that the mysterious fungus that had devastated the colony's harvests might have been covertly planted on the planet by the Klingons themselves. *Lord knows,* April thought, *they're ruthless and cunning enough.*

He heard turbolift doors whish open behind him, followed by the impatient footsteps and indignant voice of his first officer. "All right, all right, what's all the commotion about?" Lorna Simon demanded, right before she got her first glimpse of the metallic blue battleship on the main viewer. "Oh, I see."

A less effective organization than Starfleet would have retired Commander Simon years ago, but April was grateful that the veteran officer had stuck with starship duty well into her sixties. Short, round, white-haired, and with a penetrating gaze that showed no lessening in alertness despite her advancing years, Lorna Simon always reminded the captain of the sort of tough, no-nonsense grandmother that no one could ever put anything over on. April couldn't think of anyone he'd rather have at his side at a sticky moment like this one.

"Seems like we have some unexpected company, Lorna, m'dear," April commented as his first officer dropped her arthritic bones, wrapped in a blue tunic and black slacks, into the science station at starboard.

"Gate-crashers is more like it," Simon replied acidly. The stiffness in her joints did not stop her from immediately initiating a full-range scan of the oncoming vessel. "Last I heard, this was Federation territory."

"This far into deep space, I'm afraid that possession truly is nine-tenths of the law," the captain observed philosophically. On the viewscreen, the oncoming battle cruiser was growing larger by the minute. "I don't suppose there's any way we can simply evade them?"

"Negative, Sir," Ensign Soulian answered. "The Klingon ship is on a direct intercept course, and one that puts them exactly between us and Tarsus IV."

"Right," April acknowledged. The untimely arrival of the enemy cruiser was sounding less and less like a coincidence. "You might as well drop out of warp, Carlos," he instructed the helmsman, "while we find out what this is all about." He watched the streaks of starlight upon the viewer collapse into discrete and distant points of light as the *Enterprise* slowed to impulse power. "Let's just hope our Klingon friends aren't feeling particularly belligerent today. We have more important things to do right now than rattle sabers at the competition."

His light tone concealed a deeper frustration. Robert April thought of himself as an explorer, not a soldier, and it was a source of lasting regret to him that the harsh realities of galactic politics had required Starfleet to take on a military capacity along with its more idealistic goals. In a better universe, he believed, magnificent starships like the *Enterprise* would be solely instruments of peace and discovery, not part-time weapons of war, and yet here even a rescue mission threatened to turn into an all-out battle. The sheer waste and folly of it all appalled him.

"Claw," he addressed his communications officer, an imposing Apache whose full name was Spirit Claw Sanaway. "Hail the commander of the Klingon vessel. Explain that we're on a mission of mercy."

"Yes, Captain," Sanaway confirmed. His deep voice sounded almost Klingon in its timbre; April hoped that this accidental commonality would help them communicate with the Klingons aboard the battle cruiser.

Lorna Simon looked dubious. The wrinkles upon her weathered brow deepened as she squinted at the main viewer. "Why do I have the feeling that those Klingons aren't going to be impressed by our altruistic intentions?"

Despite his determination to avoid an armed encounter if that was at all possible, Captain April feared his first officer's prediction would prove all too accurate. If there was a Klingon word for "mercy," he had never heard of it.

Aboard the Imperial Klingon attack cruiser *Kut'luch*, Captain Kor could not believe his good fortune. A Federation starship, alone and vulnerable! A youthful Klingon only recently appointed to his first command, Kor was eager to make a name for himself, and he could think of no better way to do so than to successfully challenge a powerful Starfleet vessel.

Kor stood proudly upon the bridge of his warship, which he had balefully named after an assassin's blade. Dim, purple light—the color of spilled Klingon blood—shone down on him through the metal grillwork of the ceiling, streaking the bridge with incarnadine shadows and adding a florid tint to his silver-and-black military uniform. A golden sash, stretched across Kor's stocky chest, proclaimed his status as the ship's undisputed commander. Shrewd, dark eyes swiftly assessed his crew's readiness for battle and found their status satisfactory. Stationed at their respective posts, the warriors under Kor's command were no less hungry for battle; the scent of their courage and anticipation enriched the musky, pressurized atmosphere of the bridge. "Visual!" he ordered in Klingon, impatient to look upon the face of his enemy.

The pale, pinkish countenance that appeared upon the main viewer was disappointingly mild in appearance. All humans were soft and spineless, Kor knew, at least compared to Klingons, but he had hoped for a somewhat more impressive antagonist nonetheless; the genial-looking human male before him, with his concerned brown eyes, fluffy chestnut hair, and nauseatingly sincere expression, reminded Kor more of a middle-aged librarian than a Starfleet commander. He could sense his crew's dashed hopes for a glorious battle. The human didn't even have a decent beard!

"This is Captain Robert April of the *U.S.S. Enterprise*," the human said. "We are engaged in a vital rescue mission that cannot be delayed. With all due respect, I request that you let us continue on our way without incident, unless you wish to assist us in our rescue operation, as a gesture of goodwill between our two peoples."

Kor blinked in confusion. What sort of greeting was that? Where were the threats and challenges, the boasts of one's prowess and weapons? Didn't these humans even know how to address a worthy opponent? Scowling, the Klingon captain let his dark face freeze into a stern and forbidding mask.

"I am Kor, captain of the *Kut'luch*," he said coldly, icy disdain in his eyes. He spoke in the human's own barbaric tongue, the better to demonstrate the efficacy of Klingon military intelligence. "You and your vessel will turn back at once, or be destroyed." He would have preferred to ask for the other starship's unconditional surrender, but his orders from General Korrd were clear; Kor's first priority was to ensure that no Federation vessel approached Tarsus IV, not to capture any stray starships. He could only hope that, Kahless willing, the *Enterprise* would dare to defy Kor's ultimatum, even though, sadly, he fully expected this Captain April to turn tail and run at the first blast of disruptor fire . . . if not before.

On the viewer, the human scowled, but his voice remained distressingly bland. "I'm afraid you have no jurisdiction over this sector," April pointed out, as pedantically as any hair-splitting Vulcan sophist. "I repeat, we are on a mission of mercy."

"Mercy is for weaklings," Kor replied contemptuously. "And do not waste my time speaking of 'jurisdiction' or any other legal nicety." He spoke to April as he would to a credulous child. "Here in the untamed reaches of the galaxy, you humans must learn, all true authority is a matter of arms—and the will to use them."

"I don't believe that," the human insisted, "and I never will." He leaned forward in his chair, as if to narrow the physical and philosophical gulf separating him from the Klingon commander. "Sentient beings are capable of better things, of a higher standard of behavior."

"It matters little what you believe," Kor stated, losing interest in his dialogue with the naive Federation captain. He longed for battle, not mere intellectual debate. "Our disruptors are locked on your vessel. You have two of your minutes to depart this sector; if you remain, your vessel and your crew will be obliterated."

April shook his head sadly. "Retreat is not an option, Captain. The lives of eight thousand colonists are at stake, and I'm not about to abandon those people now." His expression hardened, the stubborn set of his jaw seemingly at odds with the crinkly laugh lines about his eyes and lips. "I must warn you, Sir, that while the *Enterprise* will not fire the first shot, this ship can and will defend herself if necessary."

Kor lifted a bushy, angular eyebrow. Something in April's voice caught the Klingon commander's attention, and he regarded his human counterpart with new interest. No doubt the captain's warning was mere Federation posturing, and yet . . . perhaps April's blood was a more potent brew than he had originally assumed? For the first time since initiating communications with the Starfleet vessel, Kor let a sly smile raise the corners of his lips. Maybe this Captain April might actually provide him with the conflict—and the glory—he craved.

"Ah, Captain," Kor said wistfully, "how I wish I could believe you." He lowered his wiry, compact frame into the command chair at the center of the bridge. Glancing at the nearest chronometer, he saw that the *Enterprise*'s two minutes of grace were about to elapse. "Permit me to demonstrate that Klingons, unlike humans, do not bluff."

"End transmission!" he barked at his communications officer in Klingon, then thrust his fist at the gleaming Federation starship that reappeared upon the main viewer. "Fire at will!"

Kor's swarthy visage vanished abruptly from the *Enterprise*'s viewscreen. Robert April didn't need a full strategic analysis to guess what was coming next. "Brace yourselves, children!" he warned the bridge crew in typically avuncular fashion. "Looks like we're in for some rough weather."

A blast of white-hot disruptor fire lit up the viewscreen, momentarily overpowering the brightness filters. April blinked and looked away from the screen, but the glare quickly faded. "Shields are holding," Lorna Simon reported promptly, even before the initial glow of the disruptors had entirely dispersed, "but these greasy-faced hooligans mean business. That was no warning shot."

"No," April agreed. "Our Captain Kor doesn't strike me as particularly tentative in his approach." He realized that he had no choice but to retaliate; the Klingon Empire had to learn that the *U.S.S. Enterprise* was not easy pickings. "Carlos, return fire. Lasers at full intensity."

"Yes, Sir!" the helmsman complied. A binocular targeting scanner extended upwards from beneath a flap at the left end of the conn. Florida placed his face against the mounted viewer as the ship's short-range sensors fed him data on the range and composition of the enemy vessel. A second later, an incandescent crimson beam sprang from the *Enterprise's* forward laser banks to strike the forbidding battle cruiser at its prow. Scintillating bursts of green-blue energy flashed where the high-intensity, gamma-range laser beam broke against the Klingons' deflectors. "A direct hit, Captain."

"Brilliant," April praised the young officer, while concealing his deeper ethical qualms from his crew. There were nearly two hundred men and women aboard the *Enterprise*, he recalled, whose lives were now as much at risk as those of the famine victims on Tarsus IV. He owed his crew the best defense this spanking new starship could muster. "Hit them again, Carlos. Show them what this beauty can do."

The *Kut'luch* met the *Enterprise's* lasers with a blistering barrage of their own. Blinding discharges of raw, destructive energy strobed the airless gulf between the two warring ships. Savage pyrotechnics exploded in eerie silence, the polychromatic effulgence of the dueling lasers and disruptors bouncing off the burnished hulls of both vessels to create a dazzling light show that was more or less wasted on the lifeless vacuum bearing witness to the blazing, high-tech hostilities. *'Twould be a beautiful sight*, Robert April mused ruefully, *if it weren't so bloody senseless. . . .*

Kor grinned wolfishly as another shock wave rocked the bridge. His dark complexion glistened beneath the blood-purple radiance of the battle lights. The surprisingly robust defiance offered by the *Enterprise* set his warrior's heart pounding in his chest. The two ships were proving to be quite evenly matched, and April, that unprepossessing and seemingly innocuous specimen of humanity, a much more formidable foe than Kor ever could have hoped. *So much the better*, he exulted privately, gripping the hard steel armrests of his command chair. After all, the greater the foe, the more glorious the battle.

"Captain!" shouted the officer in Klingon at the auxiliary systems monitor, an upstart young warrior named Kruge. "Our aft shields are weakening at three positions."

"So?" Kor snarled back at him. "Are you suggesting we retreat?"

The scorn in his voice eloquently testified to what Kor thought of that proposition.

"No, Captain! Of course not! I only . . ." Kruge hastily redirected his gaze onto the instrument panel before him. His shaking hands did their best to look busy. "Attempting to restore shields, Sir!"

Kor smirked, enjoying the junior officer's discomfort; it was necessary to remind these unseasoned whelps that they were not yet captains in their own right. Kor's own first commander had abused Kor mercilessly—until Kor slew him in honorable battle upon that commander's own bridge. *Someday, I too will face such a challenge, from Kruge or his ilk*, Kor reminded himself, *but not today*.

A cascade of silver sparks erupted from an overloaded processor at Kor's right. A fraction of the fiery spray fell upon the back of his hand, singeing his flesh, yet the pain only increased his enthusiasm for the battle. "Arm fusion torpedoes!" he demanded.

Kor was the scion of a noble house; he knew that his enemies (and any Klingon with a drop of ambition in his veins had enemies) whispered that he had attained his rank through family connections and not by virtue of his abilities and valor. *Not after today!* he vowed. Defeating the *Enterprise* would silence his critics for good.

"Fire torpedoes!"

Aboard the bridge of the *Enterprise*, the overhead lights flickered momentarily, as precious power was diverted to the depleted deflectors. Captain April felt the ship's artificial gravity fluctuate, inducing a temporary sensation of light-headedness and nausea. *That simply won't do*, he resolved; he couldn't have his crew getting spacesick in the middle of combat. He hit the intercom button on his starboard armrest, opening a direct line to engineering. "Doctor Marvick, this is April. Stabilize that gravity!"

"We're doing the best we can," his chief engineer protested indignantly. Judging from the petulant whine in his voice, Laurence Marvick sounded personally offended by (a) the Captain's order, (b) the Klingon assault, or (c) all of the above. "You can't just subject a sophisticated mechanism like this vessel to such an extreme battering and expect every system to function at peak efficiency."

"The *Enterprise* is a starship, Doctor, not a piece of crockery." The captain spoke with more heat than he normally preferred to employ, but this exchange only convinced April of something he had already suspected for some time: he needed to replace Marvick at the first opportunity. Although unquestionably a brilliant engineer, and one of the *Enterprise's* original designers, the man was simply too high-strung for a mission in deep space. Marvick belonged in a research facility somewhere, not aboard a starship exploring the final frontier.

Unfortunately, replacing Marvick would have to wait until such time as they weren't being attacked by hostile Klingons. "I want you to listen to me, Doctor. This is not a request. I expect up to remain up, down to stay down, and gravity to adhere to strictly terrestrial standards. Am I making myself understood?"

The captain's stern words had the desired effect. "Yes, Sir," Marvick assented, with rather less temperament than before. "I'll see to it myself."

"Thank you, Doctor. April out." He clicked off the intercom and, within moments, felt gravity (and his stomach) settle back into place. *That's more like it,* April thought. Beyond transferring Marvick, he further resolved to have the gravity generators reinforced with additional shielding the next time the *Enterprise* docked at a starbase. This was the last occasion he wanted to worry about the ship's gravity during an emergency.

Assuming, of course, that we come out of this donnybrook alive and well. A grimmer scenario lurked at the back of his mind; he knew too well that, above all else, he could not let the *Enterprise* fall into the hands of the Klingons. The security of the entire fleet could be threatened if Klingon engineers were able to probe the captured ship for her technological secrets. As much as he cherished the lives of his valiant crew, April fully intended to destroy his astounding ship before surrendering her to the enemies of the Federation. *I can only pray it doesn't come to that,* he thought.

"The Klingons have armed their torpedoes," Lorna Simon announced suddenly, her gaze glued to her sensor readouts. Looking past the coruscating clash of the two ship's energy weapons, April spied an intense orange flash emanating from somewhere on the undercarriage of the battle cruiser's prow. That first flare was immediately followed by a second orange discharge.

"Incoming!" Florida blurted, yanking his head back from targeting scanner. His fingers danced rapidly over the weapon controls.

Accelerating rapidly to near-warp speed, twin torpedoes zoomed at the *Enterprise*. Diverted from their attack on the *Kut'luch*, the starship's lasers manage to intercept the first torpedo, causing it to detonate prematurely. The thermonuclear explosion expanded outward in the vacuum, and the resulting shock wave shook both vessels. The *Enterprise*'s duranium framework rattled audibly, and warning lights blinked on all over the bridge. The acrid smell of burning circuitry violated the ordinarily pristine atmosphere breathed by April and his crew. Lieutenant Roberts coughed loudly as she raced to put out an electrical fire beneath the engineering subsystems monitor. Scorch marks marred the front of her blue duty uniform. *If that's what a miss feels like*, April thought gravely, *what would a direct hit do?*

He found out soon enough, when the second torpedo evaded the lasers entirely. The Klingon missile exploded against the outer ridge of the saucer section, forcing the *Enterprise*'s already strained shields to absorb the full force of the atomic blast. April felt the floor of the bridge vibrate beneath the soles of his boots as the *Enterprise* yawed to starboard before leveling out once more. The whiplash motion tortured his spine, and the captain had seized his armrests with both hands to keep from being thrown from his chair.

"Shields down to forty-eight percent," his first officer reported. The blast had disheveled her hair, so that a snow-white strand fell across her furrowed countenance. She gave April a pointed glance. "I don't know about you, Captain, but I'm getting too old to get knocked around like this."

"Point duly noted," April said breezily, determined to maintain his crew's morale. Beneath his blithe manner, however, frustration chafed at his composure. Unlike Kor, he was fighting a ticking clock as well; every minute wasted in this pointless conflict brought the starving people of Tarsus IV closer to extinction. *I have to end this now, one way or another.*

"Carlos," he addressed the helmsman. "I want you to target everything we've got against the Klingons' portside warp nacelle."

"Everything?" Florida gulped.

"Lasers, torpedoes . . . the whole kit and kaboodle." It was a risky strategy, the captain knew. Not only would the *Enterprise* be left essentially unarmed afterwards, aside from the capacity to self-destruct; there was still a lot that Starfleet didn't know about the design of Klingon warships, and so the targeting computer could only make educated guesses at where to target their phasers and torpedoes—and hope for the best.

"Yes, Sir," Florida said. He hastily pressed buttons and flicked switches on his console, lining up an all-out assault, just as the captain requested. "Just give me a second, Sir."

For the first time, April found himself wishing that his wife had not joined him on the *Enterprise.* If this all-or-nothing tactic failed, he might have only a minute or two to say good-bye to Sarah before consigning them all to oblivion. *Sorry, old girl, maybe you'd have been better off becoming an Earthbound veterinarian, just like you planned in the first place, before I sweet-talked you into Starfleet.* Deep down inside, though, he knew that, despite the dangers involved, neither of them would have traded a single moment of their lives together—even if both ended here, countless light-years from Earth.

"Here goes nothing," Florida whispered loud enough for April to hear. The press of a single button launched a coordinated strike that left everyone on the bridge speechless. Lasers sliced through the vacuum at the aft section of the battle cruiser, joined by a staggering salvo of fusion torpedoes. Explosion after explosion illuminated the besieged Klingon warship, which jerked gracelessly beneath the cataclysmic impact of the *Enterprise's* unchecked firepower. A thick cloud of radioactive plasma and debris spread from the rear of the cruiser, obscuring April's view of the enemy ship.

He peered anxiously into the roiling conflagration, forgetting to breathe as he waited to catch a glimpse of whatever damage their reckless bombardment might have inflicted on the *Kut'luch*. After several long seconds, the luminous plasma began to disperse, permitting April to discern the charred and sparking remains of a wrecked warp nacelle at the rear of the Klingon battle cruiser. "Smashing!" April exclaimed.

His daring tactic had succeeded. Although undoubtedly still armed to the teeth, Kor's ship had been effectively stranded at sublight speeds. "Carlos," April addressed Florida, "prepare to go to warp."

"Aye, aye, Captain," the helmsman chimed. His broad face was flushed with excitement and relief. "Just give me a second to get the engines back on-line."

"With all deliberate speed," April urged him. Fierce disruptor blasts lashed out from the becalmed battle cruiser, followed almost immediately by a direct transmission from Kor himself.

"April!" the irate Klingon roared from the viewscreen, looking somewhat the worse for wear. His greasy black hair was a disordered tangle, while his mustache and beard appeared distinctly singed at their edges. Beyond Kor's head and shoulders, the bridge of the *Kut'luch* seemed even dimmer and smokier than before. April thought he heard frantic shouting in the background.

"Do not even think of retreating, human," Kor snarled. "This battle is far from over, and only a coward would flee the field of honor while his foe still held arms against him. I will grapple with you to the last torpedo, then with hands and teeth if necessary. I challenge you, April: Stay and fight like a warrior!"

A most eloquent and compelling exhortation, the Starfleet captain thought, *provided one thinks like a Klingon.* As it happened, though, he had very different priorities. "My apologies, Kor, old chap," he informed the other captain. "I know you want a battle to the death, but

I'm afraid I simply haven't time to oblige you." He nodded meaningfully at Spirit Claw Sanaway, and the Apache officer promptly cut off the transmission, no doubt sparing them all an impressive stream of Klingon invective.

Beneath Carlos Florida's able hands, the *Enterprise's* warp engines surged back to life, instantly propelling the entire ship far away from Kor and his barbaric dreams of combat and glory, at least for now. In his heart, Robert April somehow knew that this would not be the last time that the *Starship Enterprise* would be forced to wage war against the Klingons. But that was a problem for another day, maybe even another captain. . . .

Aboard the disabled Klingon vessel, Kor watched in fury as his enemy's ship warped beyond the range of his weapons and his anger. He lurched from his chair and marched toward the main viewer, which now showed nothing but empty space and a thinning cloud of plasma and debris. Silently, he spun around to glare at his bridge crew, daring each and every one of them to challenge his authority by making even a single remark about the inglorious outcome of his assault on the *Enterprise*.

But not even the overreaching Kruge was ready to take on Kor directly; like the other warriors present, Kruge kept his mouth closed and his eyes dutifully intent upon his instruments and monitors. *Just as well*, Kor concluded; he was in no mood to deal with any petty insurrections.

"Hah!" he barked loudly, so that all could hear him. "It is true what they say. All humans are cowards." His crew quickly muttered their assent, with varying degrees of sincerity, and Kor reclaimed his place in the captain's seat. "Inform the empire that we are in need of repair," he added in a conspicuously offhand manner.

For all his efforts to save face in front of his soldiers, inwardly Kor could not escape the certain knowledge that he had failed in his mission; the *Kut'luch* no longer stood between the *Enterprise* and the hunger-stricken planet the humans called Tarsus IV. Clenching his fists so hard that his palms bled, Kor was forced to admit that he had severely underestimated the Starfleet captain.

I will not make that mistake again, he vowed.

Light-years away from where the Klingons nursed their wounds and plotted vengeance, the *Enterprise* dropped out of warp as she entered the Tarsus system. Traveling at impulse alone, Carlos Florida deftly navigated past asteroids and gas giants until the bright blue orb of a Class-M planet appeared on the viewscreen.

Almost there, April thought, bent on delivering his ship's cargo of salvation to the beleaguered colony as expeditiously as possible. Urgently, he consulted the closest chronometer; it was a close thing, but he calculated that they'd arrived barely in time to prevent massive loss of life among the hungry settlers. *No thanks to the Klingons*, he conceded. Kor's craving for combat had cost the Starfleet team very nearly all their margin for error.

"Hail the planet, Claw," April instructed. "Let them know we'll be in transporter range shortly." The governor of the colony was a man named Kodos, the captain recalled. He was anxious to contact Governor Kodos so they could begin coordinating the rescue operation. *The sooner we can get some food to those poor souls, the better.*

To April's surprise, Lieutenant Sanaway did not immediately put him in touch with the planet on the viewer. "Claw?" he asked, glancing back over his shoulder at his communications officer. The big Apache had a hand pressed against his earpiece as well as a puzzled expression on his face.

"I'm sorry, Captain," Sanaway explained, "but Tarsus IV is not responding to our hails." He shrugged his massive shoulders. "I can't explain it, Sir. We're definitely within range for ordinary communications, visual and verbal."

April didn't like the sound of this. It was possible, he supposed, that this was merely some form of technical difficulty, but a chill came over him nonetheless. "Try the emergency channels, plus some of the nonofficial frequencies to boot," he ordered Sanaway, then turned toward his first officer. "Lorna, do me a favor and scan the planet for life-forms. Humanoid, I mean."

"Yes, Captain," she complied. April could tell from her voice that Simon was worried, too. *Something is very wrong,* he thought, feeling a terrible sense of foreboding work its way through his bones. *I know it.*

An uncharacteristic gasp from Lorna Simon alerted him that the matronly first officer had discovered something shocking. "Captain," she stated slowly, trying without much success to quell the tremor in her voice, "sensors report a little over four thousand humanoid life-forms on Tarsus IV."

"Dear Lord," April murmured. He knew as well as Simon that the known population of the colony was at least twice that number. "What in heaven's name happened to the rest of them?"

The answers came in swiftly after that, in the form of scattered audio reports from civilian transmitters, long-range evidence of mass graves beneath the planet's surface, and, eventually, heartbreaking eyewitness testimony from traumatized survivors and refugees. At first, April feared that the Klingon Empire had staged a sneak attack on the vulnerable colony, but the truth proved to be far more disturbing: The planet's elected governor, the thoroughly human being they were already calling Kodos the Executioner, was responsible for the atrocity that the *Enterprise* had arrived too late to avert. Not trusting relief to arrive in time, Kodos had executed half his people in a desperate, brutal attempt to guarantee that there would be enough food for those remaining. The governor himself, April was soon informed, committed suicide upon hearing of the *Enterprise's* timely arrival; his incinerated body had been reportedly found and identified by the first landing party on the scene.

April drew little solace from the news that the infamous executioner had joined his victims. Later, in their private quarters aboard the *Enterprise,* he shared his sorrow with his wife. "I don't even know whom to blame, Sarah," he commented, as they sat side by side on a treasured pre-World War III couch that April had once beamed up directly from a quaint little antique store in Bath. Reports, schedules, clipboards, and a seemingly endless list of fatalities littered the low, rectangular table before him. "Kodos, for resorting to such insane, draconian measures, or the Klingons for fatally delaying the *Enterprise?*" Clasping his wife's hand, he contemplated the tragic massacre documented in the reports strewn atop the table. "This sort of ghastly awfulness shouldn't happen anymore, not in the twenty-third century." An anguished sigh slipped past his lips. "I thought we'd evolved beyond this."

Dr. Sarah Poole April gently rested her husband's head on her shoulder. "Maybe someday, Rob," she said softly. Weariness echoed in her voice, matching the dark shadows beneath her moist, grape-green eyes. She had put in long hours since their arrival at Tarsus IV, supervising the medical end of the relief efforts. To her distress, she'd needed to convert two of the shuttle pads into auxiliary sickbays just to accommodate the many victims of shock and starvation. "Someday, but not just yet."

"Someday," the captain repeated, drawing strength from his beloved's evocation of a better day ahead. As always, it was his unshakable faith in the future that sustained Robert April through the hardships and suffering that still accompanied humanity on its bold pilgrimage to the stars. "That's right. It's not too late after all. Someday, maybe even sooner than we think, all this tragedy will give way to a more civilized era, with more than enough time for peace and discovery."

"And justice?" Sarah asked, looking away from the documents recording Kodos's crimes for posterity. A simmering anger edged out the exhaustion in her voice and eyes. "What about justice?"

"Yes, that too," April insisted. On one of the lists of survivors he noted again the name of James T. Kirk, the teenaged son of his good friend George Kirk; April had initially been horrified to discover young Jimmy among the refugees, but now it gave him no small measure of relief to know that, at the very least, his friend's son had lived through the massacre and could now be safely returned to Earth. Remembering Jimmy Kirk's brave face and courageous spirit, unbroken despite all the horrors the boy had endured on Tarsus IV, helped April muster the faith he needed to reassure both his wife and himself. "We cannot let the likes of Kor or Kodos kill our dreams and our ideals. No matter what, we must cling to the hope that someday, somehow, justice will be done."

And one day, it was.

Captain Christopher Pike
U.S.S. Enterprise

"Chris, you set standards for yourself no one could meet. You treat everyone on board like a human being, except yourself."

Dr. Philip Boyce, *Star Trek*

JERRY OLTION

There is more to being a captain than leading your men into battle. Author Jerry Oltion provides a change-of-pace look at Christopher Pike and his crew. While readers may be familiar with the early workings of this era—thanks to the award-winning "Menagerie" two-part episode of the Original Series—Jerry explores a little more of the crew's dynamic. And while the presence of the Klingons may be comfortingly familiar, much seems a lot more innocent than later generations of crew would experience. After all, April and now Pike are helping write the book, the rules for starship captains to follow (or in Kirk's case, break).

When not writing, Jerry has been a gardener, stone mason, carpenter, oil-field worker, forester, land surveyor, rock 'n' roll deejay, printer, proofreader, editor, publisher, computer consultant, movie extra, corporate secretary, and garbage truck driver. For the last eighteen years, he has also been a writer.

He is the author of over ninety published stories in *Analog, The Magazine of Fantasy & Science Fiction*, and various other magazines and anthologies. His work has won the Nebula Award, and the Analog Readers' Choice Award, and has been nominated for the Hugo Award. He has nine novels, the most recent of which is *Where Sea Meets Sky*, a *Star Trek* novel. He has two previous *Star Trek* novels, *Twilight's End* and *Mudd in Your Eye*. He and his wife, Kathy, also collaborated on a novel in the *Star Trek: New Earth* series.

Conflicting Natures

The air stank with the smell of burning bridge. Captain Pike tried to ignore the pungent aroma of fried electronics and concentrate on the damage report that Yeoman Colt had given him, but the smoke had put a tickle in his throat that gave him a dry, persistent cough. It also made his eyes water, and he found himself wiping at them as if he were crying over the damage done to his starship.

As well he might. The Klingon battle cruiser had attacked the *Enterprise* without warning, punching through the Federation starship's shields and overloading half its command consoles before Pike and his crew could return fire. The battle had raged for half an hour before they had managed to destroy the Klingon ship with a salvo of photon torpedoes, and there was practically no system on board left unaffected.

The bridge crew and an emergency engineering team were at work inside the equipment consoles. Sparks still flew as the workers cut away slagged components, adding to the general miasma in the air.

"Dammit, can't somebody get the environmental controls on line?" Pike demanded.

Lieutenant Burnstein, the chief engineer whom Pike called "Burnie" after an unfortunate incident with an infrared toaster, had his head and shoulders inside the helm console between Pike's command chair and the forward viewscreen. "We can fix the air conditioning or we can get this bucket of bolts back into flying shape," he said, his thick New York accent muffled from inside the console. "It's your choice, Captain."

Pike didn't like that choice. The *Enterprise* was supposed to be the Federation's top-of-the-line flagship, the finest example of multiplanet cooperation and technology available anywhere. It was barely nine years old, and he was only its second commander, after Captain April. The ship had been designed to be the shining light of freedom in the galaxy for decades to come, but here it sat dead in space after a single battle with the Klingons, and the repair crew couldn't fix the life support system and the helm at the same time.

He coughed again, stopping only when he ran out of air. He forced himself to breathe shallowly, and had just about recovered well enough to speak when Communications Officer Dabisch said, "Incoming message from Starfleet." Dabisch didn't seem to be having any difficulty breathing, but then he was a purple-skinned Gallamite with a transparent cranium and who-knew-what for lungs. Apparently there were trade-offs.

Pike used his breath to say, "Onscreen."

The forward screen lit up with the gray-bearded face of Commander Wilson, who took in the destruction on the bridge in a glance. "What in Cochrane's name happened to you?"

"We had a little disagreement with the Klingons," Pike said.

"It looks like you must have disagreed with their entire fleet. Do you need backup?"

Pike started to reply, but he coughed and had to hold his breath for a moment to stop it. When he could speak again, he said, "Thanks, but we've got the situation under control."

Wilson looked at the bridge again, then shrugged and said, "I hope so. But I somehow doubt you'll be up to hosting an alien observer anytime soon."

Pike suppressed a groan. Of all the duties he hated, escorting alien dignitaries was the one he hated most. It was also one of the most important, especially now with the Klingons building their own empire to challenge the Federation. Every new race could become either an ally or an enemy, depending on who treated them well and who treated them poorly.

He looked at the repairs underway around him. The *Enterprise* wouldn't be beautiful anytime soon, but it would be serviceable, and duty was duty. "Who, when, and where?" he asked.

Wilson let the faintest of smiles play across his face. He'd known Pike would volunteer, or he wouldn't have mentioned it. "They're called Eremoids," he said. "They're independent, reclusive, and touchy as hell. They're also sitting on one of the best lithium deposits in the Alpha quadrant, but our attempts to negotiate a mining agreement with them have been a total disaster. They've pretty much told us to get lost, but now one of them has suddenly asked to watch a Federation ship in action. He says he wants to see how humans work together to solve problems." Wilson chuckled. "Looks like he'll have a prime opportunity for that, eh, Captain?"

"True enough. And I suppose if we impress him enough, the Eremoids will reconsider our request for mining rights?"

"He hasn't promised anything, but it would certainly help our cause."

"All right, that leaves when and where."

"Starbase 7, as soon as you can get there."

Pike turned and looked over his right shoulder at Number One, who sat at Spock's science station while her helm controls were being repaired. Her thick, dark hair stood up in front where she had been running her fingers through her bangs in frustration as she helped to coordinate the repair work. "Travel time?" he asked her. Normally he would ask José Tyler, the navigator, for course and speed information, but Tyler's console was right next to hers and just as fried. Pike had sent him downship to help where he could until Burnie got his station on line again.

Number One consulted the sector map at the science station. "Three days at warp 6," she replied.

"What about warp 7?"

From under the helm console, Burnie said, "If you want warp 7, you'll have to do without lights."

That wasn't exactly what Pike wanted Starfleet Command to hear. He hid his annoyance behind an opportune cough. "We'll be there in two days. With our lights *on.*"

Wilson smiled knowingly. "Very good. Wilson out."

When the starfield replaced his image, Number One asked, "Captain, do you really think this is a good idea? Half our critical systems will still be under repair. This alien will be able to see inside access hatches without even bothering to—"

"We do have security protocols," Pike reminded her.

"Yes, but—"

"Lieutenant Commander. We also have orders."

"Yes, Sir." She turned back to her station, her cheeks growing red as she did.

He looked back to the damage report, but it took him a moment to concentrate on the words displayed there. He hadn't meant to slap her down quite so hard, but dammit, she'd been questioning orders. If the crew saw their second in command get away with that, it would erode discipline all through the ship. That on top of Burnie's casual attitude in front of Starfleet reflected poorly on Pike's leadership. Never mind that the crew had performed flawlessly in battle; they had let their hair down a little too far afterward, and those little lapses in discipline were what Wilson—and their new alien observer— would see if Pike allowed them to continue.

The smoke tickled his throat again. This was really too much. "I'm going to go down to environmental and see if I can help get this air fit to breathe." He stood up—and collided with Yeoman

Colt, who dropped the thick datapad she had been about to hand him.

"Yeoman, what have I told you about sneaking up behind me?"

She was new on board, a mere slip of a girl straight out of the academy and way too eager to please. As she picked up the pad and tucked a stray wisp of her strawberry blonde hair behind her ear, she said, "Yes, Sir. I mean you said not to, Sir. And I wasn't, Sir. But the turbolift door is right there and the gap in the handrail is right behind your seat, Sir, and—"

"I'm not interested in excuses; I'm interested in standing up without coming nose to . . . nose with my yeoman." He took the pad, noted that it was an updated—and much longer—damage report, and dropped it on his chair to read later. He could state in one word the condition of his ship: bad.

Two days later it looked a great deal better. The bridge crew were at their normal stations instead of beneath them, Burnie had retuned the engines for long-range travel, and the weapons systems were back on line and ready for more Klingons. The air was even breathable again, if still a bit heavy.

Captain Pike smoothed the front of his dress uniform as he waited in transporter room one for the Eremoid. Yeoman Colt stood at his left, and Number One at his right. The transporter tech activated the beam, and a moment later the alien materialized in the shimmering column of light. His luggage, a single large duffel bag, materialized beside him.

He was humanoid enough to trigger instinctive responses to his differences. Pike felt himself tense immediately when he saw the short, sharp horns curving upward from the alien's dark brown temples. Number One shifted uncomfortably beside him, perhaps at the newcomer's emerald green eyes set too wide apart in deep vertical slits, or at the pointed teeth he revealed when he smiled. Colt made no move, but when Pike glanced over at her he saw her nostrils flare and her skin flush. She had undoubtedly noticed the alien's well-muscled physique, made quite evident by the skintight black-and-gold body-suit he wore.

"Welcome to the *Enterprise*," Pike said, extending his hand. "I'm Captain Pike, this is Lieutenant Commander Lefler, my second in command, and this is Yeoman Colt. She'll be your guide while you are on board."

The Eremoid examined Pike's hand closely before reaching out with his own—six-fingered and equipped with sharp claws, Pike noted—and making a perfunctory handshake. "I am Verka," he said. His voice was deep and resonant.

"Starfleet Command tells me you're interested in seeing how humans behave in action. Is that true?"

Verka narrowed his eyes even further than before. "Of course it's true. If you're implying that I obtained my invitation under false pretenses—"

"No, no," Pike said hastily. "I just wanted to make sure I understood your needs correctly. Starfleet wasn't very specific about what exactly you were interested in seeing."

"As much as you will show me." He slung his bag over his shoulder. "Starting with my quarters, please."

"Of course. Right this way." Pike gestured toward the door, wondering once again if this had been such a great idea. He had hoped that a diplomatic mission would give his crew a chance to relax a bit, but he already felt as if he was walking on eggs and he'd just met the guy.

Colt and Number One fell in behind them as they walked to the turbolift. Verka noticed, and said, "Do females automatically defer to males in your society, or do you separate yourselves by rank?"

Number One hadn't been happy at being ordered away from her duty station to greet an alien visitor, especially when Colt had been given the job of actually getting to know him. "The corridor's too narrow to walk four abreast," she answered before Colt or Pike could think of a reply. The turbolift door whisked open, and after everyone had entered, she and Colt wound up near the door. "Do you require the lead position?" she asked.

"No," the Eremoid said. Then, after a pause, he added, "Thank you."

"We're putting you on Deck 4," Colt said. "The guest rooms there have a great view—provided you like to see the stars."

"I am familiar with them," Verka said. "I am most interested in seeing you." There was an embarrassed silence, then he added, "In action. In the plural sense. I mean. . . ." He suddenly clapped his free hand over his mouth like a child who had just spoken a swear word within earshot of his mother.

Pike had to fake a sneeze to disguise his laughter, but Colt said innocently, "It's all right. I know what you mean."

Verka slowly relaxed. "Good."

The turbolift deposited them on Deck 4 and they began walking down the corridor, this time with Colt and Number One in front. Colt turned sideways as she walked and asked, "Do women defer to men in *your* society?"

"The weak defer to the strong," he said. "Occasionally the strong defer to the intelligent, but that is less common."

Colt smiled. "That sounds a lot like us."

"Yet you somehow work together. Can you all be equally strong, or equally intelligent?" Pike looked to Colt, who couldn't have weighed over fifty kilos soaking wet, then to Number One, who could beat the ship's computer at three-dimensional chess while plotting a course through an asteroid field. The two were hardly equal in anything, except perhaps their mutual low-level irritation with each other, which they worked hard to keep from affecting their performance. "We're all equally dedicated to Starfleet," he said.

"Ah." The Eremoid shifted his bag from one shoulder to the other, but as he swung it around in front of him, the edge of it clipped Colt in the side. It was a soft blow, but she was already off balance from walking sideways; the impact knocked her backward, her arms windmilling.

Pike felt a flash of irritation at the alien, but he suppressed it immediately and reached out to catch his yeoman before she could fall.

He deposited her on her feet again, uncomfortably aware how close his left hand had come to grabbing her in an embarrassing spot. She seemed just as aware of it, smoothing out her shirt and pointedly not looking at Pike even as she thanked him, but they both forgot their embarrassment when they realized that the Eremoid had leaped just as quickly toward the wall and was holding his bag out as a shield.

The three humans stared at him uncomprehendingly until he lowered the bag. "You aren't going to attack?"

"What?" Pike asked. "Of course not. It was an accident. Wasn't it?"

"Most assuredly." Verka slowly stepped away from the wall. "Though I confess I don't understand what difference that makes. An offense is an offense, isn't it?"

"No," Colt said simply.

Verka cocked his head to the side. "No?"

"No. But if you're worried about it, an apology never hurts."

"Ah, yes. I have heard of this custom. I apologize for . . . what? Invading your space? Violating your person?"

"Upsetting your equilibrium?"

"That's it. All you did was make me lose my balance. Apology accepted. Would you like some help carrying that bag?"

He stiffened. "Hah! Just as I suspected. Saying this apology makes me weaker now. I take it back."

She laughed. "No, silly. Carry it yourself if you want; I was just trying to help."

"Silly? Is it silly to defend my honor? Is it silly to—"

"Here's your quarters," Pike interrupted.

"Ah."

The Eremoid ducked inside as the door slid open, then immediately whirled around and barred the way. Number One nearly bonked her nose on the alien's forehead, and Colt did pile into Number One's back. Number One turned and scowled at her, then turned back and took a half step into the stateroom.

"What are you doing?" Verka cried. "You said this was my room."

"It is," Pike said.

"Then stay out!"

"I'm the captain of the ship," Pike explained patiently. "I can go anywhere I like. So can Number One, and for security reasons I've given Yeoman Colt authority to watch over you at all times as well. But if you need time to yourself, we'll honor your privacy. All you need to do is ask."

Verka took a deep breath. "I see. On my world, a person's home is an absolute sanctuary. It's the one place we can go and be totally safe from harm. I am—I need such a place."

"Wouldn't you at least like someone to show you how to use the facilities?" Colt asked.

"I will puzzle them out myself, thank you."

"All right, but don't blame me if you get sucked out the waste port."

"Yeoman!" both Pike and Number One said in chorus.

"Sorry. No offense intended."

Verka attempted a smile. "Strangely enough, none taken." He took a step backward and set his bag on the floor. "Please, this is all very difficult for me. May I have some time alone?"

Pike wondered how smart that would be. The transporter would have filtered any weapons out of the bag or hidden on his person, but there were other ways to sabotage a ship if that was his intention.

And there were other ways to keep an eye on him, too. Pike said, "Certainly. We'll check on you in an hour." He turned away, ushering Colt and Number One away with him. Verka moved deeper into his room, and the door slid closed between them.

Pike immediately stepped up to the computer terminal on the wall only a few paces away. "Computer, keep watch on the Eremoid. Notify me immediately if he does anything suspicious. That includes trying to leave his quarters."

"Acknowledged," the computer said.

He led the way back to the turbolift. After they were safely on their way up to the bridge, he said, "He certainly is a prickly one, isn't he?"

"If Colt didn't keep irritating him, maybe he wouldn't be," said Number One.

Colt said, "Irritating? He's the one who's irritating. I've dealt with men like him before, and if you give them an inch, they'll take a light-year. You've got to show them you're not scared of them or they'll walk all over you."

"This is an alien," Pike reminded her.

She snorted. "No offense, Captain, but he's a *male* alien."

The door opened onto the bridge just as Pike said, "You don't treat *me* like that."

Everyone looked up. For a moment it seemed as if they were all trying to imitate Spock, but then the navigator, Tyler, snickered. Dabisch made the honking noise that he used for laughter. Even Spock arched an eyebrow.

Then Colt asked innocently, "Would you like me to, Sir?"

"That won't be necessary, Yeoman," he said, ignoring the sounds of distress as everyone turned away again. He sat in his command chair, then quickly got up and removed a datapad before settling back down.

"What's this doing here?" he demanded.

Number One joined Tyler at the helm. He heard Colt come up to stand behind him. "It's the latest progress report on our repairs, Sir. I left it there because that seems to be where you store them, and you were already getting dressed to meet our guest."

"Oh." Was that a subtle reminder that a yeoman usually helped the captain into his uniform? Pike had relieved her of that duty the moment he realized Starfleet had sent a young woman to replace his previous yeoman. In the months since then, he had come to wonder if he had made a hasty decision, but so far he had let the order stand despite her obvious displeasure at the unusual treatment.

He glanced at the datapad, but the intercom whistled for attention just then and Dabisch said, "Our visitor wishes to speak with you, Captain."

Pike punched the intercom button in the arm of his chair. "This is the captain."

"I—um—seem to have misjudged the plumbing," Verka said.

There was a loud sucking sound coming through the intercom along with his voice.

"I'll send someone right down," Pike said.

"I—I suppose that means I'll have to let them into my quarters?"

"If you want to keep breathing air inside the ship, yes."

"Very well. I will prepare for the . . . invasion." The intercom went silent.

Pike swiveled his chair sideways. "Yeoman, go storm his quarters and see if you can fix whatever he did. And this time try not to start an interplanetary incident."

"Yes, Sir." She rushed for the turbolift.

"Captain," Spock said. "I have been researching the Eremoid civilization, and I have found a startling detail."

" 'Startling?' Mr. Spock?"

"Indeed. There have been twelve previous attempts by Eremoids to visit alien societies, both in space and on starbases. In every case, the Eremoids died in fights with their hosts over what seemed to the hosts to be insignificant transgressions."

Pike sighed. "Why doesn't that surprise me? And we're lucky thirteen, eh?"

"The Vulcans have proven statistically that there is no connection between numerology and. . . ."

"I'm glad to hear that. All the same, I want everyone to be on their best behavior at all times. Understood?"

The bridge crew all chorused, "Yes, Sir."

"Good. And Tyler, wipe that silly grin off your face."

"Yes, Sir."

Colt returned a few minutes later with Verka at her side. "He decided to get started while we still allowed him on board," she explained.

Verka was carrying a large, boxy datapad. He took up a position at the handrail just to Pike's left and said, "Please behave as if I were not here."

Sure, Pike thought. That would be about as easy as nibbling at an angel food cake with a spider on it. But he only said, "Very well. Helm, take us out of orbit. Set course for the Gamma Gemini system. Time warp factor 6." Gamma Gemini was a new colony about seven light-years distant. Its fourth planet was a very Earthlike world and was receiving a heavy influx of colonists, whom Starfleet wanted to reassure regarding their protection from Klingon incursions. Any starship passing near was urged to check in and make its presence in the sector known. No one complained, least of all Pike; it was a good excuse for a little unofficial R&R under a blue sky.

The forward viewscreen showed a swirl of stars as Tyler and Number One put the *Enterprise* on course and engaged the warp engines. When the familiar white streaks of comets and space debris began their march across the screen, Pike leaned back in his chair and picked up the progress report. It was grim enough to distract him from the note-taking alien in his peripheral vision. The observation deck was still open to space, shuttlebay doors one and two were jammed in the down position, and a power failure in ship's stores had reduced the supply of fresh produce to apples and potatoes.

Pike punched the intercom button for engineering. "Burnie, what the hell happened in stores? We've got a couple tons of compost there because the power was out for seventeen hours."

Burnie sounded no happier than Pike. "You wanted warp 7 when the antimatter injectors were still out of alignment. The power had to come from somewhere."

"But my god, man, not the food supply!"

"We're going to Gamma Gemini, aren't we? Where do you think vegetables come from in this sector? We can restock there."

"That's my decision, not yours, mister."

"Right, Captain. Uh . . . request retroactive permission to sacrifice the food supply for motive power."

"Granted," Pike said. "But next time cut the running lights."

"Already did that, Sir."

"I see." Pike looked at the report again. Sure enough. It looked like Burnie had squeezed power from every system possible.

"Is that all, Captain?" Burnie asked.

"Yes. Good work." Pike switched off the intercom.

"Amazing," said the Eremoid.

Pike turned to see him scribbling on his datapad with a claw. "What?" he asked.

"How you averted that confrontation with both his honor and yours intact. I would never have believed it if I hadn't witnessed it myself."

"It wasn't a confrontation," Pike said. At the edge of his vision he saw Colt roll her eyes upward. "Was it?" he asked.

"Maybe not to you," she said.

"What's that supposed to mean?"

"If I were Burnie, I'd have gotten a little . . . excited by your tone of voice."

"Burnie? He and I—I mean—he's from New York! You have to talk like that to get his attention."

"Oh. Do they teach you that in officer's school, or is that something you picked up on board?"

"It's my astute interpersonal communications skills, Yeoman."

She leaned back against the handrail. "And how do you get my attention, Sir? Since I'm from Oregon, I mean."

Number One whispered something to Tyler, whose cheeks puffed out with the effort not to laugh.

"Do you have something to share, Number One?" Pike said.

"No, Sir." She stared straight ahead.

Pike glared at the back of her head. She knew he permitted a bit of informality among the crew, but this was ridiculous. So was Colt's question. What had gotten into everyone? He heard the scritching of claw on datapad. Ah. Nerves. Everyone was trying to keep from upsetting the Eremoid, so they were overcompensating with silliness. On top of that, it had been a trying week. Maybe it was time to blow off a little tension the good old-fashioned way.

"Why don't we have a little welcoming party for Verka on the recreation deck tonight?" he asked.

"No," Verka said quickly. "I couldn't possibly."

"You sure? That would be the quickest way to learn how we interact. With humans it's not all orders and duty, you know."

"No, I didn't know." Verka gritted his pointy teeth, then nodded. "I will attempt it, but please don't be offended if I must flee in the midst of the party. I am not used to groups."

"Understood. No problem." Pike leaned back in his chair, then turned to Colt and said, "Look, sunlight!"

Startled, Colt looked up through the clear observation dome, but there were only the white streaks of hyperspace. "Sir?"

"That's how I get an Oregonian's attention." To the Eremoid, he said, "I spent a winter in Portland once. Rain, rain, rain, for six months at a stretch."

"I see," he said, but it was clear he didn't.

The party started out well. There was plenty of Saurian brandy, and the chief of stores declared a keg of genuine Earth Guinness to be in danger of spoilage due to the power failure. The Eremoid stayed on the periphery with Spock, taking copious notes while people came by to tell him jokes, refill his drink, or answer questions. Number One began a discussion of music, which led to dancing, which Verka predictably refused to try. Pike wasn't exactly comfortable with the idea, either, but when Number One asked him to help her demonstrate for their guest, he couldn't very well say no.

Then of course she chose a slow waltz. Pike felt clumsy as a targ on ice, and Number One felt entirely too warm and soft in his arms, but he ignored the shouts of "Woo, woo, Captain!" from the sidelines and concentrated on not stepping on her feet.

Doctor Boyce was dancing with Yeoman Colt, which looked to Pike like Father Time standing beside the New Year on January 1, but they both seemed to be enjoying themselves. When the music ended, Boyce thanked Colt for the dance and then turned to Number One. "Mind if I cut in?" he asked Pike. "It's not every day an old geezer like me gets to dance with pretty women." Number One blushed, and

Pike said, "Watch out. He'll put his hands anywhere, then claim Marinthian muscle twitches made him do it."

Colt was still standing alone when the next song started. She caught him looking at her and cocked her head slightly. Hesitantly. Pike looked away, instinctively checking for an escape path, but stopped that motion in mid-glance. Why couldn't he dance with his yeoman? Why not indeed? He smiled and held out his arm just as she began to turn away; she did a double take and stepped toward him instead. *Let the Eremoid try to figure out what that meant,* Pike thought as he took her in his arms and they began to sway back and forth to the music.

The fistfight, when it came, didn't even involve Verka. Pike didn't see how it started; he had his eyes closed and was resting his cheek on the top of Colt's head as the song wound down. There was an angry shout from the back of the room, then a crash as something fell over. A second later, the room descended into bedlam, as everyone cleared away from Tyler and one of the engineers, who had each other in a headlock and were punching merrily at one another.

"Hold it!" Pike yelled, rushing toward them, just as Burnie waded into the fray from the other side, shouting "Hey! Hey, hey, hey!" Burnie grabbed the engineer and Pike grabbed Tyler, and they pulled the two apart.

"Calm down!" Pike said. "I said calm. . . ." Tyler flailed out with his left hand, accidentally clipping Pike on the shoulder.

"Attennnn-tion!" Pike yelled at the top of his lungs.

Everything stopped except the music, which continued to play softly as Pike said, "What the hell is going on here?"

"He said I couldn't plot a standard orbit around Venus," Tyler said.

"He was braggin' about how hot a pilot he was," the engineer said. "So I made a joke. Nobody can plot a standard orbit around Venus; it rotates retrograde. Period of one-hundred seventeen days. A standard orbit would drop you right into the Sun."

"Oh," said Tyler.

Colt, only a step behind Pike, laughed.

Pike turned to her. "You think that's funny? An officer strikes a crew member because he thought he was being insulted, and you think that's funny?"

She sobered right up. "No, Sir."

"What's the matter with this crew?" he demanded. "You're a disgrace to Starfleet. You . . ." he pointed at Tyler, resisting the sudden urge to make a fist and continue the motion straight into his chest "—are confined to—"

"Where's Verka?" Number One suddenly asked.

Oh, bother. He'd forgotten the alien. Watching, taking notes, and no doubt deciding it would be a cold day in hell before he would let these irrational humans have a mining claim on his planet. Pike looked over at the corner where the Eremoid had been playing wallflower, but he wasn't there.

"Verka?" he asked.

"Here," came a weak voice from down low. Pike pushed his way through the crowd toward the source of it and found the alien huddled beneath the buffet table.

"Are you all right?"

"Aside from being terrified, you mean?"

"Terrified?" Pike stood up. "Oh, for Christ's sake, Tyler, now see what you've done?"

"I'm sorry, Sir."

"Well you ought to be." Pike bent down again. "It's all right. Nobody's going to hurt you. My navigator just got a little twitchy, that's all. It's over."

"It's *over?*" Verka asked. "You mean you aren't going to start killing one another?"

"Over a stupid misunderstanding like that? Of course not."

The Eremoid peeked his head out from under the table. "I meant you. You called everyone a disgrace."

"They are. And in a minute I'm going to read them the riot act. But nobody's going to kill anybody. Come on out of there."

He helped his guest to his feet again. Verka looked at the

stunned crowd, still standing at attention, and said, "This is unbelievable. On my world, such a statement would have resulted in a massacre."

"You're kidding."

"You doubt my . . ." he clapped his hands over his mouth again.

"It's all right," Pike said. "No, I don't doubt your word. It just sounds pretty incredible."

Verka lowered his hands. "Your ability to survive so much conflict is equally incredible to me. My people have to avoid one another if we don't wish to fight. That's our only way."

"How do you *breed?*" Colt asked.

"Yeoman!" Pike said, but Verka grinned.

"Briefly," he said. "And seldom."

"Well, that explains a lot," said Doctor Boyce.

"Indeed it does," said Verka. "Occasionally a couple will bond closely enough that they can live together, but it happens so rarely that songs are sung about it when it does. I thought perhaps I would be one of the fortunate few, but my childhood lover had a brief liaison with another of my friends, and now none of us can speak to one another for fear of starting an argument that would kill us all."

"That's rough," Colt said.

"Yes, it is. I find that I still love her, but I can't risk going to her for fear of growing angry. I had heard that humans could actually survive such slights, so I came to see how it was possible. But now that I have seen it in action I am still no wiser than before. Why don't you kill one another?"

Pike frowned. Verka had come here for personal reasons? Starfleet had diverted the *Enterprise* to give him the VIP tour, hoping it would lead to mining rights on his homeworld, and what he was most interested in was learning how to get his girl back?

Spock had been standing quietly in the corner all this time. Now he said, "Perhaps I can provide a unique insight here. Vulcans suppress all emotion, but that doesn't eliminate conflict. In my own observations of humans, I have discovered that they often use aggression and anger as a way to say what they need to say to one another without actually fighting. Their relations are often better after such an outburst."

"Then these two who were fighting will continue to work together?"

"They'd better, or they'll be swabbing the decks together," Pike said menacingly.

"And you and Yeoman Colt will continue your courtship rituals?"

"Courtship rituals?" Pike asked, blushing from head to toe. "We were just dancing."

"On the bridge? I have observed countless instances there where you exhibited what I would consider . . ."

Of all the people to come to his rescue, he would never have expected it to be Spock, but the Vulcan held out his hand for silence and said, "There have been many inappropriate displays of emotion on board this ship since your arrival. Some can no doubt be attributed to fatigue, but I believe the frequency of these outbursts is beyond the norm even for a time of extreme duress." He held his hand closer to the alien's face. "If you would permit me . . . ?"

"Permit you to what?"

"I have limited telepathic ability. I believe you do as well. May I examine you to be sure?"

"Telepathic ability?" Verka said. "What? Are you insinuating that I'm somehow causing your bad behavior?"

"Yes," Spock said.

They stared at one another for a moment, the Eremoid with open hostility while Spock stood as impassive as ever, but Pike saw the Vulcan's nostrils flare and realized that he was fighting his own emotions as well. He was just better at it than the rest of the crew.

That was all the proof Pike needed, which was a good thing because the alarm klaxon wailed before he could order the Eremoid to let Spock examine him. "Red Alert," the computer said. "Red Alert. Colony vessel under attack dead ahead."

"Battle stations!" Pike said. "Let's go!" To the Eremoid he said, "Come with us, but stay out of the way."

Number One said, "Is that smart? If he's . . ."

"I want him where I can keep an eye on him," Pike replied. *And stun him unconscious if necessary*, he thought, but he prudently left that unspoken.

He led the charge for the turbolifts. When they reached the bridge, people rushed for their stations and the night crew scooted aside to let the more experienced officers take over. Dabisch put a tactical grid on the viewscreen, on which they could see half a dozen colony ships drawn into a tight ball, letting their shields overlap for extra strength, while a single Klingon warship swooped around and around them, firing its phasers in search of a weak spot.

"Photon torpedoes," Pike said. "Full spread. Target him as he makes a turn so he'll be at maximum distance from the colony ships."

"I'm on it," said Number One.

"Range, Mr. Tyler?"

"We'll be there in fifteen seconds."

"The colony ships are readying their own weapons," Spock said. "They can't shoot through each other's shields; they will have to drop them to fire."

Pike had hoped to catch the Klingon by surprise, but he couldn't let the colonists drop their shields. "Dabisch, warn them not to," he said. "Uncoded transmission. Tell them we'll be there in sixty seconds."

"Uncoded . . . Sixty seconds. Aye, Sir." Dabisch's hands flew over the communication keys; then he echoed Pike's words into his microphone.

Pike said to no one in particular, "We may have had to blow our cover, but with any luck, we didn't blow the surprise. How long now?"

"Seven seconds," Tyler replied.

"Ready on those torpedoes."

"Ready," Number One said.

"Colony ships are holding position," Spock reported. "Klingon cruiser is arming photon torpedoes."

"Too late," Pike said, grinning savagely. This was one Klingon who wouldn't harass any more colonists.

"In range," Tyler said.

"Fire!"

Number One stabbed at the control with her forefinger. The viewscreen flared with six brilliant points of light as they reached out to the Klingon ship. The first four impacted their shields, but the fifth scored a direct hit on the bulbous control pod in front, and the sixth penetrated the cruiser's wing-shaped body before exploding, turning the entire ship into an expanding cloud of plasma. Normally Pike would have felt at least a little dismayed at the loss of life, but not this time. The Klingons had asked for it.

"Check the colonists," he said. "Are they all right?"

Dabisch queried the ships. "No damage," he reported. "I have a Mister Hampton on the channel. He wishes to speak to you personally."

"Put him on."

On the viewscreen the remains of the Klingon ship gave way to an image of equal chaos: a young man sat at a control panel, a baby in his arms, while two toddlers ran shrieking across the frame behind him, pursued by a harried woman in a bathrobe. A small black dog barked at them all, but the man didn't seem to notice. "Thank you, Captain!" he said.

"Just doing our job," Pike replied.

"We appreciate it." The baby waved its arms and gurgled happily, banging its closed fist against the control console.

"Careful!" Pike warned.

The man glanced down, then back at Pike. "It's okay, he can't hit anything vital." An alarm beeped on his console, and he turned to the woman. "Honey, can you get that? I think the forward shield generators are overheating."

Pike squirmed in his seat at the sight of such a sloppy bridge, but amazingly enough, things seemed to get done. The woman—Mrs. Hampton, Pike assumed—slid into a control station behind her hus-

band and shut down the shields one-handed, all the while struggling
to hold her two- or three-year-old girl by the back of her shirt. Mr.
Hampton piloted the ship away from the others so she could activate
the aft shields and radiate the waste heat through their generators instead. When they finished, he looked back at Pike. "Are you going on
to Gamma Gemini?"

"That's our plan," Pike said.

"Good. Mind if our expedition tags along?"

"Not at all."

"Thank you. Give us a few minutes to catch our breath and we'll be
ready to go."

Pike would have doubted that a ship run in such a sloppy fashion
could be ready to fly in a week, but he was pleasantly surprised when
only five minutes passed and Dabisch said, "They're ready any time
we are."

"Then let's go," said Pike.

Tyler engaged the engines, and they were on their way again.

"That was incredible," said Verka.

"What was? The battle?"

"No, the way you handled it. You were practically at each other's
throats below, and here you worked together like protons and elec-
trons. And that family! The stress level in their ship must have been
incredible, yet they worked together as smoothly as you. I had heard
that humans could function in groups, but I never imagined you could
do so despite such powerful emotions. Anger, frustration, attraction,
and jealousy—none of it seems to matter." He looked from Pike to
Colt and Number One as he said that.

Colt turned red, and Number One laughed out loud when Pike
said, "Attraction? Jealousy? What are you talking about?"

The Eremoid clapped his hands over his mouth.

"Humans are notoriously unaware of their own interpersonal relationships," Spock said. He stepped toward Verka and held his hand
out toward his forehead. "As are you, it would seem. May I?"

Verka shivered, but he lowered his hands and said, "Go ahead."

Spock pressed his fingers to the Eremoid's temples and cheekbones and closed his eyes. A few seconds passed, then he lowered his hand and nodded. "As I suspected. You are a projective empath."

"Me? Empathic? Hah!"

"You are. And if all Eremoids share your ability, it is no wonder you don't get along. Your emotions would amplify each other in an uncontrolled feedback loop."

"That . . . certainly would explain things," said Verka. "But what can we do about it?"

Spock said, "You have already evolved coping mechanisms. Your custom of living separately, and your custom of banning others from your homes, keep you separated so you cannot kill one another even when your anger builds enough to make you want to do so."

Verka said, "But I don't want to live alone! I want to spend my life with my one true love."

Pike said, "Then you'll have to learn how to defuse your emotions before they can build up to lethal proportions."

"Yes, but how? I've seen you do it, but I still don't understand it!"

Pike felt himself growing frustrated, but he knew it wasn't an honest emotion. Nevertheless, he let it build to the bursting point, then shouted, "By giving yourself a release valve to blow off steam, you idiot! And a little self-discipline would do you a world of good, too."

He could have heard a pin drop. No one on the bridge even dared breathe—except the Eremoid, and he was too stunned to speak.

Then he found his voice and shouted back, "Idiot? Self-discipline? You're the idiot! Haven't you been listening to your own science officer? I *can't do that.* My people's empathic power—our empathic curse—makes every argument escalate into mayhem!"

Indeed, the bridge crew were all looking like they would like to blast the Eremoid into a smoking ruin right where he stood, and Pike felt the urge just as much, but he pitched his voice as softly and reasonably as he could manage and said, "Does it really?"

"Yes, it does!" Verka gripped the handrail beside Pike's chair with trembling hands.

"Even this one?"

"What?"

"Why haven't you killed me?" Pike asked.

The Eremoid stopped. He obviously wanted to, but not quite enough to actually do it. That realization stunned him so much that he lowered his voice and asked, "Because your anger doesn't amplify mine?"

"That'd be my guess." Pike waited a moment for him to calm down still further, then said, "Feel better now?"

"I . . . yes, actually, I do." He released his grip on the handrail. "You did that on purpose, didn't you? How did you know that would happen?"

"Experience. Experience you don't have. Spock was right when he told you that we humans sometimes use our anger as a way to say what's really on our minds without actually fighting. You've learned to avoid conflict entirely, but there can be value in conflict. You just need to learn how to use it to your advantage."

Verka slowly nodded. "He said your relations actually improve after you argue. Can this be true?"

"Well, what do you think of me now? Am I still an idiot?"

"Perhaps not," Verka allowed. "But you haven't solved my problem, either."

"No? What do you think would happen if you called your former lover an unfaithful homewrecker?"

"We would fight to the death."

"What if you did it from here?"

"What?"

"There's got to be a limit to your empathic range. I'm guessing we're well beyond it."

The Eremoid tilted his head, thinking it over; then he said wonderingly, "We could fight on purpose. Get it over with while we *can't* kill one another. But do you really think that would solve anything? Wouldn't we just kill one another the moment we get back together?"

"Maybe. Or maybe by the time you get together again your empathic ability will reinforce a more . . . appropriate emotion."

Verka nodded. "Perhaps. I—I believe it might be worth a try. If you will excuse me, I think I would like to handle this in the privacy of my quarters."

Pike laughed. "Good luck."

"Thank you." Verka turned away, and Pike made a mental note to warn the Federation to deal with the Eremoids from a safe distance from now on, but Verka turned back around and looked at Pike, Number One, and Colt. "Good luck to you three as well."

"It's not—I mean—you don't under . . ." Pike stammered, but Number One said, "Methinks the captain doth protest too much. Come on, Yeoman, let's go claw each other's eyes out over a drink."

She stood up from the helm, took Colt's arm, and the two of them stepped into the turbolift, walking sinuously enough to get themselves arrested on some planets. Number One turned sideways and leaned back against the turbolift wall, "Permission to leave the bridge?"

"Granted," Pike said. "Gladly." He rolled his eyes and turned back to the Eremoid. "See what you've started?"

"Started? Me? Are you insinuating—?"

"Never mind."

Captain James T. Kirk
U.S.S. Enterprise

"No man achieves Starfleet command without relying on intuition, but have I made a rational decision? Am I letting the horrors of the past distort my judgment of the present?"

James T. Kirk, *Star Trek*

MICHAEL JAN FRIEDMAN

There is little question that Mike is one of the busiest and most prolific authors in this collection. Word for word, he may be matched by Peter David, but no one has time to count their annual output for comparison. One reason for Mike's productivity is that he enjoys exploring the various aspects of the *Star Trek* universe; he always tries to find something new to say about our beloved characters. Here he stretches himself with his approach to Kirk, a character he has written on numerous occasions in both hard- and softcover.

In most cases, Kirk is always seen as the leader of the crew or as the Id in the Id-Ego-Superego triumvirate with Spock and Dr. McCoy. Here, though, Mike focuses solely on the captain in a situation that calls for a unique combination of his considerable skills. But Kirk being Kirk, there is of course a woman involved.

Mike has written original fantasy novels but has lately concentrated on writing the largest number of prose works based on licenses. His name can be found on books featuring Batman, Wishbone, the Silver Surfer, the X-Men, and in 2001, *Star Wars.*

While Diane Carey enjoys being part of a crew on older ships, Mike prefers the solitude of smaller, modern-day sailboats. On those rare occasions he can get away from his home, Mike can be found on the Long Island Sound.

While still trying to figure out how to program his VCR, Mike does find time to root for the New York Yankees and is Rules Committee chairman for the Federal League, another excursion into the world of fantasy—this time baseball.

The Avenger

Captain Jim Kirk looked at the dead woman's face. Her skin was pale even for a Draq's, her bronze hair spread out on her large, purple pillow like an exotic sea creature.

"Tell me what happened," he said.

Deffen Jakol, the heavyset, golden-haired commander of the Draqqi space station, heaved a sigh that tested the confines of his tight-fitting, dark blue uniform. Like all of his people, he had eyes that were oversized by human standards and his skin had a faintly lavender tint to it.

"Apparently," said Jakol, "she arrived in our station's bar sometime before eighteenth cycle last night. She spoke to several people, most of them males, and certain . . . overtures were made. For one reason or another, none of them came to fruition."

Kirk nodded. "Go on."

"Finally, at about nineteen cycles, she finished her last cocktail and left the bar. It seems she left alone, though no one there was entirely sure about that. A Pandrilite said he saw her in the corridor outside her quarters at about twenty cycles . . . but by his own admission, he was rather inebriated at the time."

"Then what?" asked Kirk.

"Then she came back here, to her quarters."

The captain looked around at the place. It was well furnished by Draqqi standards, purples and blues predominating in the choice of wall and floor coverings as well as in the plush, low-slung array of furniture.

The dead woman was wearing a translucent Draqqi sleeping robe with a delicately brocaded bodice. Kirk turned to the commander. "She dressed for bed before she was killed," he observed.

"So it seems," said Jakol.

"Do we have any idea how the murderer got in?"

"None at all," said the Draq. "Nor do we know whether she was surprised to see him. With all she had had to drink, it's possible she didn't even know he was there."

Kirk's gaze fell on the ugly dark spot on the woman's gown, which radiated from a point just above her bodice. "But we do know that she was stabbed," he told Jakol.

The commander frowned. "Yes . . . once, through the heart."

The captain looked up at the velvet-papered wall directly above the victim's corpse. There were five distinct characters scrawled there, written in the victim's blood. Kirk approached them.

He had been stationed on Draqqana for a couple of months early in his career, when he was serving as a lieutenant on the *Farragut.* And though a good ten years had passed, he was still able to read Draqqi without too much difficulty.

"Estheen," he said out loud. The captain mulled the word over for a moment. "Was that her name?"

Jakol shook his head. "No. It's a name, all right, but not hers. She was called Mani Begron."

"And you say she was a diplomatic envoy to the Iach'tu?"

"Yes," the commander confirmed. "And unfortunately, very much a key player in the peace negotiations."

Kirk swore beneath his breath. The peace negotiations were what had brought him back to this sector of space. His orders from Starfleet Command were to see them completed at any cost.

Nor was it difficult for the captain of the *Enterprise* to understand his superiors' resolve. Six years earlier, the Draqqi had been conquered by the Iach'tu and subjected to all manner of cruelty.

Had Draqqana been a member of the United Federation of Planets, it would never have happened. However, the Draqqi were a fiercely independent people. Even after they threw off the Iach'tu yoke of oppression, they refused to join the Federation.

Finally, a Dopterian ambassador gained the Draqqi's confidence and convinced them to sign a treaty with their enemies, arguing that it was only a matter of time before the more powerful Iach'tu were again tempted by Draqqana's ample resources. What's more, the negotiations had gone more smoothly than anyone had dared hope.

Until now.

Kirk had studied forensics like everyone else at the academy, but he was hardly an expert on why and how people murdered each other. His only real expertise was in getting the best out of a crew of more than four hundred men and women as they explored the vastness of space.

As a result, he felt very much like a fish out of water at the moment. But then, it wasn't the first time he had been compelled to exceed the traditional role of a starship captain.

Kirk considered the corpse again. "Can she be replaced?" he asked.

Jakol shrugged. "Not easily."

"Not easily at all," came a voice.

The captain glanced at the voice's owner. She was Draqqi, female and undeniably attractive, her dark eyes and darker hair a complement to her full, lavender lips and pale, perfect skin. The insignia on her uniform identified her as the station's security chief.

But to his surprise, Kirk didn't need any help identifying her. And judging by the look on her face, she didn't need any help identifying *him*.

Commander Jakol indicated his colleague with a gesture. "Captain Kirk, I would like to introduce—"

"Subcommander Orisa Jilain," Kirk finished without thinking.

Jakol looked at the captain, then at the security chief. "I take it you two know each other?"

Orisa nodded. "We've met."

Memories surged in Kirk's mind. Only one of them was unpleasant—the day he had said good-bye to her.

"We have indeed," the captain agreed.

Before Orisa could say anything else, they were approached by Kirk's chief medical officer. Doctor McCoy had beamed over with the captain to examine the murder victim and see if he could offer any insights.

He had never met Orisa, but he appeared to sense that there was something between her and Kirk. After all, McCoy wasn't just a trained psychologist—he was one of the captain's best friends.

"Got something, Bones?" Kirk asked.

"I sure do," the doctor said with a slight drawl. "The skin samples we took from under the victim's fingernails . . . cellular analysis shows they're not Draqqi, Jim. They're Iach'tu."

Kirk saw Jakol's mouth fall open. Orisa's expression was a melting pot of emotions, outrage not the least of them.

"Could there be a mistake?" she asked McCoy.

The doctor shook his head. "No mistake. I double-checked."

Orisa looked at him, the muscles in her jaw fluttering wildly. "I see," she said, her voice devoid of emotion.

McCoy regarded Kirk. "There must be surgeons in this system who could have made an Iach'tu look like a Draq."

"There are," Orisa confirmed, though she hadn't been asked. "Quite a few, in fact."

"And the rate of cellular degradation . . . ?" the captain wondered.

"Shows that she died early this morning," McCoy confirmed. "Just as Commander Jakol indicated."

Kirk absorbed the information. "And at least three planetary transports have left the station since then . . . so we can forget about the murderer still being around."

"I'd imagine," the doctor responded.

Orisa glanced at the corpse. "If it becomes known that an Iach'tu did this, the peace talks could be destroyed."

Jakol grunted. "Which could be the very thing he was hoping for when he committed his crime."

The security chief pondered her superior's remark. Finally, she said, "We need to catch the murderer and see him punished. And we need to do it as quietly as possible."

"So the talks can go on," the captain suggested.

"Yes," Orisa replied, her eyes cold and hard.

But it was clear to Kirk that she was speaking in her official capacity as security chief. Personally, it seemed to him, she wouldn't have minded a more violent resolution.

"I'm going to contact the authorities planetside," she said. "Maybe they can shed some more light on this."

Kirk agreed that that would be a good idea.

Orisa Jilain's office was small but efficient, three of its walls devoted to a collection of hexagonal screens that continually monitored her station's public areas.

The fourth wall was a transparent one. It gave Kirk a view of the station's main thoroughfare, where the captains of cargo vessels stood and conferred with the importers and exporters who were their employers.

For a while, Kirk peered at them through the transparent surface, his arms folded across his chest. Then he glanced over his shoulder at Orisa.

She was sitting behind a foreboding black workstation, plying her planet's security net for background information on Mani Begron. Her stern expression suggested to the captain that she didn't want to be reminded of what had happened between them.

He found that unsettling. The time he spent with Orisa had been a lot more than a casual affair. For a while, he had even considered the possibility of staying with her on Draqqana, spending the rest of his life with her.

But young as she was—a year younger than Kirk's twenty-three, in fact—she had had the sense to send him away. He would never have been happy staying in one place, on one paltry planet, and she knew that.

But he himself couldn't accept it. So they had met for the last time on the lichen-spotted stone bridge that connected the two halves of Draqqana City, and Orisa had begged the young lieutenant not to try to speak with her again.

Her eyes shiny with tears, her breath a frozen vapor, she had kissed him the way a snowflake kisses the ground. Then she had hurried away, her collar turned up against the wind and the cold.

And Kirk had stood there on the bridge, watching her, until the night took her away from him.

But now, as she sat and stared into her computer screen, she seemed like a different person—hard and businesslike. This wasn't the Orisa Jilain he had kissed that winter night. At her most stubborn, her most determined, she had never been like this.

Even when she told him she didn't want to see him again.

"Ah," she said, leaning back in her chair. "Finally."

"What is it?" the captain asked, coming around her workstation to look at her screen.

"As we discussed, Begron was a key player in the peace talks. In fact, she was the first delegate selected." Frowning, Orisa studied the screen, looking for something helpful. "When she was younger, she was a musician. She gave it up to become a lawmaker."

Kirk skipped down a little. "Never took a life partner," he read out loud, realizing only after he had said the words how awkward they might make his companion feel.

But Orisa didn't miss a step. "Was reputed to have a relationship with Third Minister Soren, though it was never substantiated."

"Incarcerated in an Iach'tu labor camp," said the captain.

"Who wasn't?" she asked.

Kirk looked at her. "Were *you?*"

Orisa didn't answer right away. Then she said, "That's ancient history. Let's move on."

But now the captain had an inkling as to what had happened to her—and why she had changed. "I'm sorry," he said earnestly.

"So am I," came Orisa's response. But it was mechanical, untouched by any real expression of regret.

He wished he had been there during the occupation. He wished he could have eased her suffering, or at least made the attempt. But he had listened to her and left her alone.

And now, Kirk thought, it was too late to do anything about it.

He scanned the rest of Mani Begron's file. "There isn't much else," he concluded.

"Unfortunately," Orisa commented. Then she went back to work, her slender fingers crawling over her input apparatus. "Maybe we need to try a different approach . . . check the database for violent crimes that exhibit the same basic modus operandi. . . ."

The captain wasn't terribly optimistic on that count. But in less than a minute, Orisa had come up with something.

"Felah Cuviq," she said, reading the words off her screen again. "Stabbed to death, just a couple of days ago. And on the wall above his head . . ."

Kirk felt a little chill climb the rungs of his spine. "The name Estheen was scrawled in blood."

Orisa looked up at him, the light from her screen casting a reddish glare on her face. "Felah Cuviq . . . you don't remember him, do you?"

He shook his head from side to side. "Should I?"

"He was one of the bureaucrats with whom your captain spoke when he offered us Federation membership. "The darkness in her eyes seemed to flicker for a moment, as if she were recalling something from those days. "And lately, he became a diplomatic envoy to the Iach'tu."

The captain felt his mouth go dry. "He was involved in the peace negotiations?"

"Yes," Orisa replied. "Even more so than Begron. He was the leader of the entire Draqqi delegation."

The implications hit Kirk like a tidal wave. "We're not just talking about a single incident anymore. Everyone in that delegation is in danger of losing his or her life."

"No doubt," she said. She thought for a moment. "Unfortunately, we can't postpone the talks."

Again, Orisa sounded as if she were saying what her position demanded of her, not what she felt.

"So we'll just have to find the Iach'tu who did this," she finished, "and see that justice is done."

Justice, the captain thought.

Orisa's voice had been controlled when she said the word, but he could perceive the underlying emotion in it.

"Are we talking about justice," he asked, "or vengeance?"

Orisa didn't flinch. "In this case, it's the same thing."

Kirk shook his head. "It's not the same thing at all—and we won't be doing Draqqana any favors by pursuing a vendetta. We need to be objective about this. Unemotional."

The irony of his speech didn't escape him. Usually, it was his Vulcan first officer who felt compelled to impart that sort of advice—and most often it was the captain to whom Spock imparted it.

Orisa's eyes narrowed. "Who's the security professional, you or I?"

He returned her gaze. "A professional should know when her feelings are getting in the way of her work."

She made a sound of dismissal. "That's easy for you to say. You didn't endure four years of bloody occupation. You didn't stand by helplessly and watch while your family and friends were destroyed."

Kirk stiffened. "Actually, I did."

Orisa looked at him askance.

"When I was thirteen," he told her, "I lived on a Federation colony world. There was a sudden, catastrophic food shortage, and the governor of the colony, a man named Kodos, had four thousand people put to death . . . so the rest could survive. Or so he told us.

"A few months ago, I ran into a theatrical troupe. A boyhood friend of mine suspected that the head of the troupe, who called himself Anton Karidian, was really Kodos. Shortly thereafter, my friend turned up dead.

"He wasn't the only one," said the captain. "I found out that at many of the troupe's stops, people had died under mysterious circumstances. Clearly, it was more than a coincidence.

"As captain of the *Enterprise*, I pursued my friend's theory about Karidian. And as time went on, I was more and more certain that he was right—that Karidian was Kodos—and that I would make him pay for all the misery he had caused."

"And?" Orisa prodded. "Was this Karidian the man you thought he was?"

Kirk shrugged. "He died before I could determine that for sure. But I found out who was killing people wherever the troupe staged a performance. It wasn't Karidian. It was his daughter, who believed her father was Kodos and was trying to protect him from his enemies."

She pondered the story for a moment. "And the moral?"

"If justice is blind, revenge is doubly so. I try not to worry about abstractions anymore. All I care about these days is keeping innocent people from getting hurt."

Orisa's dark eyes blazed. "When I was in that labor camp, the only thing that kept me going was the hope that someday I would see justice done. Now I have the chance to do that. Some old-line Iach'tu monster thinks he can spill Draqqi blood with impunity—as if we were still his slaves—and I'm going to show him otherwise."

The captain could see he wasn't going to make any headway with her. On the other hand, there was a lot more than her feelings at stake here.

"Look at it any way you have to," he told Orisa. "But be advised— I've got orders to see a peace treaty signed, and I'm not going to let anyone stand in the way of that—you included."

It wasn't easy for him to speak to her that way. Not after what they had had together. But as always, his duty came first.

Orisa didn't seem to mind his declaration. For the first time since they had been reunited, she smiled—but it wasn't a pleasant smile, not by any stretch of the imagination.

"Consider me warned," she said. "But you should be warned as well—when I lay eyes on the murderer, he'll be sorry he ever contemplated the idea of killing Draqqi."

On that note, Orisa dug into her people's database again. And this time, she came up with a *really* interesting bit of news. Their involvement in the peace initiative wasn't all Mani Begron and Felah Cuviq had had in common.

At one point during the occupation, they had been incarcerated in the same labor camp.

Kirk considered Yor Praddic in the bright sunlight that bathed the Draq's little garden.

Praddic was a handsome man with blue eyes and silver-gray hair. He was a member of the Builders Guild. He had two sons and a daughter, all of them by a wife who succumbed to a deadly disease months before the beginning of the Iach'tu occupation.

Most importantly, Yor Praddic had spent a year and a half in the Sadj Monh labor camp . . . along with Mani Begron and Felah Cuviq.

"We have a picture of the crime scene," Orisa said.

Their host looked discomfited. "Unfortunately, my stomach hasn't been very good since the occupation."

"It might help a great deal," Kirk told him.

The Draq sighed. "Very well."

Orisa brought up the image in question on the tiny screen of her handheld dataset, which reminded the captain of a general-purpose tricorder. Then she handed the device to Praddic.

He winced as he perused the little screen. "Seven gods," he breathed.

"You recognize the name?" Kirk asked.

Praddic looked up from the dataset and regarded him. "Yes. Estheen . . . she was a prisoner like me. It's been so long since I thought about her. . . ."

Orisa frowned. "And do you have any idea why someone would scrawl her name on a wall in blood?"

Praddic thought for a moment, his brow furrowed in concentration. Then he shook his head. "I'm sorry."

"What do you remember about her?" the captain asked.

Praddic sat down on a wooden chair and a wistful smile emerged. "She was beautiful, I remember that. Full of life. The camp was hard, the kind of place that could break you, but it never broke Estheen."

"Did anyone dislike her?" Orisa wondered.

Praddic shook his head emphatically from side to side. "All of us loved her . . . right up to the day she disappeared."

"Disappeared?" Orisa echoed. "What do you mean?"

Praddic shrugged a little sadly. "A guard asked her to come with him. That happened a great deal, guards taking people away for one purpose or another. Once in a while, the person they took didn't come back to the barracks. That was the case with Estheen."

"Do you have any idea why?" Kirk asked.

Praddic nodded. "There was a rumor that Estheen was pregnant with the child of another prisoner—a fellow named Idra, who had been tortured to death months earlier. It was never proven, of course, but the commandant didn't . . . take kindly to pregnancies." He looked away suddenly, tears standing out in his eyes.

Orisa put a hand on his shoulder. "It's all right, res Praddic. You've been very helpful."

He nodded, but he didn't say anything more. And since Kirk and his companion had no more questions for him, they left.

But Yor Praddic wasn't the only survivor of the Sadj Monh camp that they visited. There were three others.

Most of them provided the same information as Praddic. Some recalled a little more, some a little less.

Heenan Vonakh, a woman who dealt in precious stones, recalled that Estheen had a beautiful singing voice. Lurt Rebbis, a corpulent fellow who had suffered a stroke weeks earlier, said Estheen had disappeared shortly after his arrival in the camp, depriving him of the opportunity to get to know her better. And Nes Aavo, a prosperous clothing manufacturer, said the security net was in error; he had been imprisoned at Pelos Otryn.

That left Kirk and Orisa with only one place left to turn.

Iach'tu Prime was a dark sepulcher of a world, its cities a series of barely illuminated passages and immense chambers carved into mountainous piles of rock. Little grew on the planet's surface, which was why the fertile valleys of Draqqana had seemed so tempting to the Iach'tu.

It had taken the Draqqi government three days to secure what Kirk and Orisa needed—and even then, Iach'tu permission had been granted grudgingly, with a long and rigid list of parameters.

For instance, the *Enterprise* would be allowed within transporter range for only a few seconds. Kirk and Orisa would be beamed to a predetermined set of coordinates, from which point they would be blindfolded and escorted to their final destination. They would be prohibited from carrying weapons, portable sensors, or communications devices of any kind.

And they would have the equivalent of twenty-five minutes with the object of their desire, not a second more.

Jim Kirk regarded the Iach'tu who sat opposite him in the rough-hewn stone chamber, his craggy gray features thrown into stark relief by patches of luminous yellow lichen.

"Have they told you why we've come?" asked the captain.

Ussata Dornic shook his massive head from side to side, his lidless black eyes unblinkingly returning the human's scrutiny. "They have told me nothing," he grated.

"We're investigating two murders," Kirk explained. "The victims' names were Mani Begron and Felah Cuviq. Both of them were incarcerated in the Sadj Monh labor camp—the one you administered. We were hoping you might be of some help to us."

Dornic eyed him with an arrogance that belied his surroundings. "A Starfleet captain and a Draqqi station commander . . . doing the work of the planetary police? These must be unusual murders indeed."

"The victims were key contributors to the peace process," Orisa noted. "That's what makes them unusual."

The Iach'tu grunted. "The *peace process* . . . a quaint name for a remarkably onerous and demeaning activity. Why we would ever want to make peace with an inferior species like the Draqqi is beyond me."

The muscles writhed in Orisa's jaw, but she kept her emotions in check. "There was a name scrawled on the wall at both of the murder scenes. The name was Estheen. We understand she was a prisoner at the camp as well."

Dornic's mouth pulled up at the corners. "Estheen," he said, rolling the name off his tongue like a fine liqueur. "Yes, she was a prisoner there. A very popular prisoner, at that."

"What connection might she have with the victims?" asked the captain.

"I'm sure I don't know," said the Iach'tu. "And even if I did, why would I share my speculations with you?"

"Your government," said Orisa, "has agreed to reduce your sentence if you cooperate with us. I trust that's of some value to you?"

Dornic's tiny black eyes twinkled. "Ah. You've gotten my attention now."

"Tell us what you know of the victims," said Kirk.

The prisoner looked at him. "I remember them both rather well. They were incarcerated at Sadj Monh, as you say." His smile deepened. "What's more, I find it interesting that they should have played important roles in your peace process. One might even call it ironic."

"Why is that?" asked Orisa.

Dornic's expression hardened with something strangely akin to pride. "At my labor camp, they were informants."

The captain saw the Draq's face drain of color. "Informants?" Orisa repeated numbly.

The Iach'tu smiled at her discomfort. "Draqqi who spied on their comrades to obtain certain privileges. Certainly, you knew such people existed."

Orisa didn't answer him. "Were there other informants?"

Dornic appeared to ponder the question for a moment. "Quite a few, actually, considering how loudly you Draqqi tend to trumpet your virtues. As it happened, I found your people relatively easy to turn."

Orisa's eyes blazed and she bit her lip. Clearly, she was on the verge of lashing out at the Iach'tu.

"What were their names?" Kirk demanded, effectively preempting any unwanted displays of violence.

The prisoner gazed at Orisa a moment longer, deriving as much pleasure from her anger as he could. Then he returned his attention to the captain.

"There were three others," he said slowly and deliberately. "Heenin Vonakh, Lurt Rebbis, and Nes Aavo."

The captain glanced at Orisa, whose expression had changed to one of disgust. She and Kirk had spoken to these people only a few days earlier, and they had given no clue as to their treachery. Aavo had denied even having seen Sadj Monh.

Orisa turned to Dornic. "Aavo told us he had never heard of Estheen. He said he wasn't even incarcerated in your camp."

The Iach'tu made a bubbling sound deep in his throat—something akin to laughter. "Then he was lying through his teeth. He was there. He knew her. *Everyone* knew her."

It sounded like the truth. After all, Aavo and the other informants stood to lose everything if their duplicity came to light. But despite all that, none of them could have been the murderer. They were Draqqi—and McCoy had determined that the killer was Iach'tu.

"Our investigation of Mani Begron's murder scene shows the killer was one of your people," Kirk told Dornic. "Why would an Iach'tu decide to murder Draqqi informants?"

The prisoner scowled. "Why indeed?"

"We need a theory," Orisa told him.

Dornic regarded her. "Just as I need my sentence reduced. So rest assured, I will come up with one."

He thought a moment longer. Then his frown lifted. "There is *one* possibility," he concluded.

"And that is?" Kirk prodded.

"An Iach'tu named Sanda—though in all likelihood, he's dead."

"Tell us about him," said Orisa.

Dornic made a gesture of dismissal. "Sanda was a guard in my camp—a turncoat, like Aavo and the others. He worked against the Draqqi informants, on behalf of the prisoners—if you can imagine such a thing."

"I can imagine it," said the captain. "Go on."

The Iach'tu took a breath, then let it out. "Before Sanda could do much, he was exposed by my informants. I had him seized and sent back to Iach'tu Prime for sentencing. But before the vessel could reach its destination, it was attacked by so-called Draqqi freedom fighters." Dornic held his hands out. "All hands were reported lost—though Sanda's body was never found among the wreckage."

"Did Sanda have a relationship with Estheen?" Orisa asked.

The prisoner shook his head. "I doubt it. Mind you, he was probably taken with her. The majority of my guards were. But the notion of a liaison with an Iach'tu must have been unthinkable to her, no matter how much Sanda tried to help her people. Besides . . ."

"Yes?" said Kirk.

For just a fraction of a second, Dornic seemed lost in regret. Then his lip curled again and his air of disdain was restored.

"Estheen became pregnant—at which point I arranged for her to 'disappear' from my roles," he recalled. "So she must have had a lover in the camp—a Draqqi lover. As Commander Orisa will be happy to confirm, our species are incapable of cross-breeding."

The captain looked to his partner. She nodded.

"What did you do with the baby?" asked Orisa.

Dornic frowned. "As I recall, I gave orders to have it destroyed. It was Draqqi, and I had orders to discourage procreation."

Kirk saw Orisa swallow back whatever emotions were roiling inside her. Looking weary and drawn, she got to her feet and made her way to the door.

"Will that be all?" the Iach'tu inferred.

The captain got up as well. "That'll be all," he confirmed.

"Good," said Dornic. "And you'll be sure to let my government know how helpful I've been?"

Kirk considered the prisoner. "What did you do, anyway? How does an Iach'tu get thrown in prison for twenty years?"

Dornic shrugged. "I failed to remit the proper sum to the new government's tax collectors—an oversight I have had time to deeply regret."

The captain swore to himself. Then he joined Orisa at the door to the chamber and called for the guard.

Back on the *Enterprise*, Orisa went straight to her quarters and remained there. At McCoy's suggestion, Kirk gave her some time to be by herself. Then he paid her a visit.

When the doors slid apart, he found Orisa sitting on a chair with her face in her hands. "What is it?" she asked, her voice a bit softer than he had heard it lately.

"I wanted to discuss our next move with you," the captain said.

Orisa looked up at him. "It's obvious, isn't it? If there are three living informants, all we need to do is stake out their homes—and wait for the murderer to show up."

But she didn't look happy about the simplicity of their task. In fact, she looked miserable.

What's more, Kirk knew why. If Dornic was telling the truth, the Draqqi they were going to protect were cowards and traitors . . . people who bought their conveniences with the lives of their fellow prisoners.

"Helping scum like Aavo . . . it seems like we're fighting on the wrong side," he observed.

Orisa sighed. "This Sanda was a friend to my people at Sadj Monh. A hero. And we're going to arrest him."

"For the sake of the peace talks," the captain noted. "He's still an Iach'tu, remember—and it's still important that we keep this quiet."

But that wasn't his only reason. "Besides," he said, "we can't let him claim another life."

"Even a life like Aavo's?" she asked.

"Even that one," Kirk asserted. "It's not up to us to judge people, Orisa. It's not up to us to decide who lives and who dies."

"It isn't justice," she rasped, her eyes angry and red-rimmed.

"Maybe not," he conceded. "But it's our duty . . . not just as officers, but as people. There's a killer out there—and he has to be stopped."

Orisa didn't say she agreed with the captain. However, she helped him map out what they had to do.

Before they were finished, Uhura contacted Kirk via ship's intercom. "I have a message from the Draqqi government," she said.

"Go ahead," the captain told her.

"They say Heenin Vonakh is dead, sir."

Kirk sighed. That left only two informants for them to protect.

Nes Aavo's house was clearly the dwelling of a wealthy man.

It was a series of light blue arches with plenty of windows—especially on the side that faced the shifting green waters of Tuyatt Bay. On the other three sides, it was surrounded by tall, auburn-colored trees, which gave Aavo privacy without sacrificing esthetics.

Kirk, Orisa, and a handful of Draqqi security personnel hid themselves among the shrubs in the hills above Aavo's estate, equipped with phasers and provisions. Then they began their vigil.

Aavo was the bait—and they were the trap. In order to keep the trap intact, they had refrained from telling the bait that they were there—or, for that matter, how they had come to the conclusion that he might be the murderer's next target.

Of course, the killer might have opted to strike at Lurt Rebbis instead, but Rebbis's house was being watched as well. Either way, Kirk and Orisa would have their man before long.

Not for the first time, the captain felt out of place. But he had taken an oath to serve the Federation, whether he was ensconced in the center seat of a starship or crouched behind a bush with a phaser in his hand . . . and serve he would.

Day eventually yielded to a splendid bloody dusk, and nothing happened. Then, as the stars were beginning to assert themselves in a darkening sky, Kirk saw an animal about the size of a squirrel dart away from Aavo's house.

Animals didn't move that way for no reason—he knew that from his boyhood in Iowa. Gesturing for Orisa to follow him, the captain hunkered down and made his way down the slope.

Halfway to the ring of trees, he heard the sound of something shattering. A window, he thought. Somehow, the murderer had gotten past them and made it to his destination.

Their fifty-fifty chance had paid off—but Aavo might not live to applaud their decision.

His heart pumping hard in his chest, Kirk slipped through the trees and saw a series of tiny, irregularly shaped pools glistening on the ground. It took him a moment to realize he was looking at shards of glass.

"That way," he told Orisa, pointing with his phaser.

The window frame still contained splinters of glass, but the captain located a splinterless spot and vaulted through the opening. He found himself in a small, unoccupied room with another doorway at its far end.

Beyond the threshold, there were voices. One was harsh, the other scared. Kirk could hear the latter voice rising in pitch.

Before it could reach a crescendo, the captain darted into the next room. Orisa was right behind him, her phaser in hand.

However, they only saw one figure in the room—that of Aavo. He was standing near a second doorway, nearly as pale as Mani Begron had been.

Too late, Kirk realized where the murderer was.

"Drop your weapons," said a voice from behind him.

The captain did as he was asked. Orisa hesitated, then did the same, her phaser clattering on the floor.

"Now turn around," the voice instructed them.

Again, they complied—and saw someone standing beside the door. He was a tall, rangy figure with the green eyes and pale gold hair of a Draq . . . and he had a Klingon disruptor in his hand.

"Contact the others," he snapped. "Tell them to stay where they are."

"You don't have to do this," Kirk told him.

"*Tell* them," the murderer insisted.

Orisa took out her communications set and ordered her men to keep their distance. Then she put the device away.

"It doesn't matter," she told the murderer. "You're surrounded. You'll never get out of here."

The figure grunted. "Don't you think I know that?"

The captain wanted to keep him talking, so he said the first thing that came to mind. "You're the Iach'tu, aren't you? The one who worked in the camp at Sadj Monh?"

The murderer nodded, his eyes flitting from Kirk and Orisa to his prey and back again. "I'm Sanda," he confirmed.

"Why are you doing this?" Kirk asked. "To avenge yourself on the people who put you in prison?"

Sanda's mouth twisted into a scowl. "When Aavo and the others exposed me, they didn't just deprive me of my freedom—I could perhaps have forgiven them for that. They also deprived the other prisoners of the help I might have given them . . . and that, I can never forgive."

"Everyone thought you were dead," the captain told him. "When your transport was attacked. . . ."

"The Draqqi underground knew who I was," the Iach'tu replied. "But I couldn't join them, for obvious reasons."

"So what did you do?" Kirk asked. "Where did you go?"

"I worked on merchant ships for years and years," Sanda told him. "I bided my time, waiting until the time was right for me to pay back my enemies. Then the moment came . . . and I acted."

He leveled his weapon at Aavo. Seeing it, the Draq screamed and tried to screw himself into the wall.

"No!" Orisa insisted, taking a half-step forward. "What's past is past. You can't change what happened."

She sounded sincere. However, Kirk knew that she didn't necessarily believe the sentiment herself.

Sanda shook his head. "I'm not listening to you. For all I know, you were a sympathizer too."

He turned his disruptor on Aavo again. Kirk was about to make a desperate play for the weapon when someone else walked into the room through the other doorway.

It was a Draqqi child—a boy no more than ten years old. He looked around with big blue eyes, wondering what he had stumbled into. Then, before anyone else could react, Aavo grabbed the child and hugged him to his chest.

"Please," he told Sanda, "spare his life! He's my only son!"

But it was clear to Kirk that Aavo wasn't concerned about the boy. He was just using the child as a shield, knowing it was unlikely that Sanda would kill the son to get at the father.

The captain felt dirty just being in the same room with Aavo. Judging by Orisa's expression, she had much the same reaction.

"Send the boy out of the room," Sanda snarled.

Aavo didn't do it. He just stood there, wide-eyed, clutching the child to him like life itself.

Sanda stared at the boy, the muscles working in his jaw. For a moment, Kirk thought the Iach'tu might shoot anyway. Then he splayed his fingers and let his disruptor fall to the floor.

"I wouldn't want to hurt Estheen's son," Sanda said solemnly. "Nor will I hurt the man who somehow saved him from Sadj Monh . . . no matter what else he may have done in his lifetime."

Both the captain and Orisa took the opportunity to kneel and recover their phasers. Then Orisa took out her comm set and called for her Draqqi to enter the house.

Seeing that he was safe, Aavo released the child. The boy's expression turned curious . . . and he took a step toward Sanda.

"How did you know my mother?" he asked.

The Iach'tu could have told him. But then, that would have involved his letting the boy know what scum Aavo was, and that he wasn't the child's real father. So instead Sanda replied, "I was a guard in the camp where your mother was held prisoner."

Suddenly, out of the corner of his eye, Kirk saw Aavo go for Sanda's weapon. He knew what the Draq was going to do with it, too—make sure that the Iach'tu didn't reveal the skeleton in Aavo's closet.

But the captain was faster than the informer. As Aavo picked up the disruptor, Kirk grabbed his wrist and took it from him.

Sanda didn't comment on what Aavo had tried to do. He just looked at the boy and said, "Everyone loved your mother. You should know that. We just had different ways of showing it."

The child studied him for a while. Then he nodded, as if he understood. And maybe he did, the captain reflected.

Just then, Orisa's Draqqi entered the room, eyes alert, phasers at the ready. They relaxed a bit when they saw that the situation was under control.

"Come on," Orisa told the Iach'tu, but not with great eagerness. "It's time to go."

Frowning, Sanda allowed the security personnel to escort him out of the room. Kirk watched him leave, then glanced at Orisa.

She looked drained. He didn't blame her.

"You know," the captain, "he's going to need someone to speak on his behalf. Someone who knows what the camps were like."

Orisa nodded. "I'll do that. Gladly." She looked back at him. "You were right, James. I didn't want justice. I wanted revenge."

"So did Sanda," he noted. "But he found the same thing you did— that it was a bit more complicated than he had imagined."

It always is, Kirk added inwardly. If he had doubted that even a little, the truth of it had been brought home to him with renewed fury.

"I need some air," Orisa told him, just a hint of the woman she used to be shining in her dark, exotic eyes. "Would you care to join me?"

The captain smiled. "As long as there are no bridges around. I don't much like bridges."

She smiled too, though it was clear that she was out of practice. "No bridges," she assured him. "I promise."

Captain Will Decker
U.S.S. Enterprise

"I respect an officer who is prepared to admit ignorance and ask a question rather than one who, out of pride, will blunder blindly forward."

Captain Jean-Luc Picard, *Star Trek: The Next Generation*

DIANE DUANE

At first glance, the idea of doing a story about Will Decker as captain of the *Enterprise* might strike you as odd. After all, in the first motion picture he was captain for a matter of minutes, before losing the center seat to Jim Kirk.

Still, Kirk recommended Decker for the position, so there must have been something to the man, something in his nature that allowed Kirk to trust him with his ship and crew.

In the following story, Diane explores a captain's love affair with his ship, and his affection for the crew. You get an insight into the refit and how everything pieces together.

By now it is obvious that *Star Trek* authors are also fans, and they like things to be tidy and orderly. Note how the April story set the stage for the events depicted in the episode "Conscience of the King." Other elements in stories throughout this volume either foreshadow events we have come to know and love or speculate how certain things got established in the *Star Trek* universe.

Diane hasn't written in this universe for a while, mostly because she's been busy crafting tales in her own worlds or visiting other people's universes. The Ireland-based writer is enjoying renewed interest in her Young Wizards series of novels since they are usually found on bookstore displays with the sign, "If you liked Harry Potter, we suggest you try . . ." And we second the recommendation.

Night Whispers

He sat there in the center seat and looked at the viewscreen. It was
blank.

Will Decker sighed, for about the thirtieth time that day, and
tapped the control on the arm of the center seat. "Scotty . . ."

"Still nothing?" said Scotty's voice, from somewhere down in the
bowels of engineering.

"Nothing."

"It's a' this bloody redundant circuitry," Scotty said, sighing too.
"Sometimes I think it should be made redundant in the old sense of
the word."

"Look, Scotty," Will said. "Why don't you knock off for the night?
It's probably some obscure command buried in that new LCARS systems that's causing the trouble. We'll get the computer to help us do a
track-and-trace on the circuitry in the morning, maybe get a better
handle on the image-versus-sound problem."

"If you're tryin' to tell me that that dim heap of wires can get a better handle on this problem than I can—"

"Never," Will said. "Perish the thought. But you're worn out, Scotty: finally solving that damned intermix problem has to have added a few gray hairs."

"Aye, well, 'solved' is a dangerous word. We'll see how it runs when we throw the switch in a few weeks," Scotty said, "and all the other integrated systems are running too. Mind you, I wouldn't say no to another month's worth of simulations."

Will smiled. That was Scotty to the bone, always reluctant to risk the machinery itself until the simulations were perfect. *We should be grateful he wasn't looking over the Creator's shoulder at the start of things,* Will thought; *we'd still be waiting for the Bang while Scotty ran just one more test cycle on the Cosmic Egg. . . .*

"Well enough," Scotty said. "What about you?"

"What about what?"

"Beggin' the captain's pardon, but it's well into what would be gamma shift, if we were running shifts yet, and you're due for a wee bit o' downtime yourself, I'd say."

"No," Will said, standing up and stretching. "I'll take a turn around before I go off."

"I thought Doctor Chapel had a word with you about all these late nights you've been doing," Scotty said, rather reproachfully.

So much for medical confidentiality, Will thought. But this ship had always more routinely functioned as a family than as one of the more narrowly defined sorts of organization—and in families, tales got told. "Well," Will said, "I might just see her too before I go off. See how sickbay's looking now that the physical imaging hardware's finally in."

"Had a look at that myself earlier," Scotty said. "It's a bonny piece of design, the new imaging center."

"So Christine said yesterday. I'll have a look at it. Meanwhile, Scotty, go get some rest. The screen and the sensor array will keep till tomorrow. It's not like anything's going to sneak up and attack us in spacedock."

Scotty chuckled at that. "Aye lad, well enough. But get your sleep too. I want to get the viewscreen sorted out in the morning . . . no good having all these sensors and still having to send someone out to stand on the hull with a camera to see what's there. . . ." And a pause. "Now there's a thought. If the external sensor interface was—"

"Scotty."

"No, lad, listen, if the gamma-welding lads jostled the—"

"Scotty. Go to bed. That is an order. *This is your Captain speaking!!*"

A snort. "There you go pullin' rank on your elders again, you young whelp. It's all the Academy's fault, they . . ."

Will laughed and punched the communicator button. The link went dead.

He sat back in the center seat and let out another long breath, looking at the screen that, even if it were working properly, wouldn't show him much, except for the surrounding structure of spacedock and the great globed jewel of Earth underneath it. Maybe Scotty was right to tease him about the hours he'd been spending aboard *Enterprise* since the refit started. But it was rare enough for a ship's captain to have such an opportunity—to see the ship all the way through from her reconception as an upgraded vessel, through the refit itself, and out the other side. Will would know his new ship as few captains ever had the leisure to . . . and when things went wrong later, he would be in a unique position to do something about them.

Meanwhile, Will's main job was dealing with the day-to-day frustrations of a refit that always presented problems no one had suspected. The frustrations receded, though, in the evenings, when the ship emptied out. Evenings were the best time—the time when Will had time to wander around, getting to know the ship, listening to the echoes, wondering what new ones would replace them when the refit was done.

Echoes . . . They had been on his mind, during this process; more lately than in the earliest stages, when they had stripped *Enterprise*'s skin off her and begun the serious reshaping of her most basic structural members. Then he had felt more like a surgeon overseeing a desperately radical rebuild of an unconscious patient: pulling the "chest cavity" of her secondary hull apart and increasing its length by half, while increasing the size of all the contained organs and adding a few new ones; chopping the nacelle "legs" off at midthigh and attaching newer, longer ones; increasing the capacity of her primary-hull "skull" by thirty percent and installing bigger, newer brains (and an equivalent amount of empty deck- and other space, for unlike the way human brains were arranged these days, *Enterprise*'s redesigners wanted to leave her room to expand in hardware as well as software). It had been a harrowing period, including a three-month stretch when there was no part of her that held the vacuum out, a long cold time when *Enterprise*'s skeleton shone spidery, bare, and baleful in the starlight, and in his little bunkie in the spacedock facility Will would wake up in the night shivering, for no good reason. But when they put her hull back on, and pressurized and warmed and reinstalled the interiors; when there were corridors again, and rooms; then, when Will had first started prowling these corridors late at night, he had started to hear the whisper of old voices.

At first he had resented them. But Will had swiftly put the resentment aside. Over the years, that had become his particular talent— the art of dealing with the raw hand the universe dealt him, and not getting too upset about it until after a given crisis was over and there was leisure for that kind of thing. Captains could not afford to nurse grudges or throw tantrums. Too many lives usually depended on the captain for such indulgences of temper, and between times they also looked bad . . . and summoned up ghosts better left resting, especially in Will's case. He knew how miraculous it was that he had been given this command at all, considering his father's final tour of duty in Starfleet. Fortunately, Command had not—this time—been so vindictive or blinkered as to judge the son by the father. And also . . . Kirk had been plugging for him. That by itself had probably made the difference.

Not that the man's influence could not be felt here, inevitably, all through the refit. Will stood up and stretched, looking around the bridge at the new computer interfaces, the new paneling and screens . . . and still it was as if the impress of Kirk's personality lay deep, soaked right into the substructures of the reshaped hull, into the gamma-welded metal of *Enterprise*'s infrastructure. There was no denying the history that had been made here. Will had spent much time going through her logs while in the pre-deconstruction stages, the time when everyone looked at the ship to evaluate the stresses she had been through, when the initial 3-D imaging of her present hull and skeleton were being done preparatory to the strip-down stages. Will had been thorough, had spent a long time insisting that certain details be checked—the results of the stresses inflicted on the ship at Eminiar 7, in Tholian space, in the encounter with the Gorn, in so many others; brushes with Romulan plasma weaponry in the Neutral Zone, with this powerful alien tractor beam or that holding field, the one that had looked like a god's giant hand. . . .

But more than mere physical details had come up in the logs. There had been the voices—stressed, outraged, triumphant, defiant, dejected, thoughtful, amused, afraid: the voices of *Enterprise* command crew, caught by the bridge recording devices over five years. And even now the memories, in the quiet dogwatches of the night, sometimes spoke surprisingly loudly—Red-Alert alarms howling at dangers the ship had seemed to survive almost by miracle; voices raised in anger, in surprise, occasionally in wonder; ". . . we will not kill today." . . . "Get these things off my bridge!" . . . "Would it really have hurt us just to burn a little incense?" . . . "Decker, no!" . . .

Will shook his head, and the echoes receded. There were nights when they were so strong they drowned out the sound of his own breathing. *An overactive imagination . . . ?* he thought as he left the bridge, listening to the sound the lift doors now made when they closed, and noting with approval that the annoying squeak that had been coming from one of the hydraulic units had now been repaired. "Deck 12," he said, and the lift scooted along sideways briefly on its way to the main lift shaft.

Maybe not precisely overactive, Will thought. But this ship had so much history with her old crew, a truly astonishing group of people. Easy to feel overshadowed, sometimes, by so much experience, so many experiences. He knew he would have his own chances to make history with this ship: years of chances, if Command was kind to him, and he didn't screw up. That fear was his particular shadow to fight with for the moment . . . and to that fear, evenings made no difference. Any small mistake made now might turn into a bigger one later, and he would be blamed for it: and his career would be over. There were too many people in Starfleet for whom the name Decker was still poison.

The lift stopped, opened. Will stepped out and heard voices coming toward him down the hallway, ones he immediately recognized. He grinned a little as they came around the curve of the corridor toward him. It was the specialized engineering team delegated by Scotty to work on the weapons systems: Wirth, Hanlon, Torsten, and Odanga, known casually to some of the other engineering people as "the Ineffables" for their tendency to speak to one another almost exclusively in technological terminology so abstruse as to make even Scotty shake his head. The Ineffables might speak to lesser beings, such as their captain, in English, but it was apparent that this cost them some strain.

"Captain," said Wirth as Will came around the corner, and the others behind him nodded courteously to Decker.

They looked dog-tired, the whole lot of them; haggard. "Thought you folks should have been off hours ago," Will said.

"Oh, you know how it is, Captain. It got . . . interesting." Wirth smiled at him, and Will grimaced. The gunnery team's work had become much more than usually "interesting" with the installation of the new gunnery conduits that sourced their power directly from the warp engines. The original specs had suggested "heretofore impossible" increases in phaser output due to the new design. Will (and the gunnery team) suspected that the word "heretofore" could be safely dropped from the description, because no one had been able to get the damned things to work even in simulations once they had to interact with the ship's warp engine *in situ*. Will had found himself once too often crawling up the butt end of a Jefferies tube alive with the raw energies of the universe and cursing all the "paper engineers" in the world, the ones convinced that everything would inevitably run smoothly as long as both sides of all the equations balanced. Those were the people who were going to be responsible for sending the *Enterprise* out into her new life with weaponry that was going to have to be "run in" on live mission time.

"It's not *too* bad though, Sir," said Torsten, pushing away the wisp of blond hair that seemed perpetually to be falling in front of her eyes. "Now that we're getting close to launch . . . a *lot* of people are finding things more 'interesting' than they have been. Not just the installation problems." She grinned at him. "It's just exciting. A lot of extra time going in, all over the place. Those crazy guys down on the computing team, even the furnishings and fittings people . . ."

Will grinned. "Well, okay, but don't try to tell Fleet I made you do it. But the phasers . . ." He shook his head. "Is this system *ever* going to work?" Will said, possibly sounding a little more desperate than he meant to.

Wirth shrugged. "In my depressive moments, I think maybe on the Greek kalends, sometime. But one way or another, we'll get 'em going for you, Sir."

Will clapped him on the shoulder and headed away. "Good man . . . I appreciate it. You people go get some sleep, now!"

"You do that too, Sir. . . ."

Their chatter resumed as they headed for the lift, making for the transporter room, and Will smiled at the sound as the lift doors cut it off. He had few words for how intensely pleased he was that his people were as concerned about this ship's readiness as he was. Weaponry in particular was something of an issue for Will. Not that Fleet's purposes were not peaceful . . . but peace was sometimes best achieved and maintained by carrying a very big selection of very big sticks which could be set for "brandish" or "clobber" as necessary. This one, though, would apparently be a while before it was ready to clobber anything. *We could have gotten this sorted out a long time ago,* he thought. *If only, as Scotty says, we were running shifts. . . .*

Unfortunately, Starfleet was taking the leisurely approach to *Enterprise*'s refit. To Will's annoyance, they had some justification for this: most of the "dedicated" construction crews were busy at the main spacedock facility on the other side of the orbital facilities' path around Earth, deep in work on *Yorktown* and *Congo*, two new ships at a much earlier stage of development. This made Will grouse sometimes to his refit staff, but there was no point in it. He had tried to get Fleet to understand the importance of having this ship ready in the minimum possible time, but they were simply not seeing things his way. "What if something *happens?*" he had said to Admiral Nogura, knowing that he had nothing but a hunch to go on; and Nogura had told him in that bland way of his that there was no reason for alarm, that there were plenty of other ships in Starfleet in case "something should happen" . . . and that Will should get on with his work and stop bothering him. All very avuncular and jolly, in Nogura's usual manner: but the message was sharp.

So Will went back to his ship, understanding the subcontext—that Matt Decker's son had better not get caught showing any significant eccentricity—and got on with work. Everyone else had as well. The kind of report he had just now from the gunnery people, who had been receiving most of his attention these past few days until the sensor and viewing systems had started to act up, had been routinely duplicated elsewhere . . . dedication, exercised to nearly insane levels by people who were proud to be working on this ship and were determined to do their best for her. Will had heard often enough before about the obsessiveness of the computer installation crew, down there working themselves to pieces all the hours that God sent; he had certainly initialed enough of their overtime manifests, and with pleasure, since they deserved them. Those computers were *Enterprise*'s nervous system, more and more important with every passing day to the ship's function. Already many, many more functions were handled by them than had ever been handled on a starship of this class . . . but that was inevitable, as the ships themselves became endlessly more intricate, the product of billions of man-hours of labor in terms of design and installation. *Must go down and see those folks,* Will thought. *First things first, though . . .*

He swung down the corridor toward sickbay. The new facility had a wider, airier, roomier design than the last one, as much for psychological reasons as ease of care and access, so Christine Chapel had told him during another of these late nights. She too was determined to understand her new facility completely, and to be complete in mastery of it by the time the ship went active and was likely to start routinely presenting her with patients. She had already been receiving them, of course, ever since *Enterprise's* keel was "sealed over" again and she went airtight. Any naval construction site has a certain "budgeted" number of accidents—even (though this was less frequently discussed) an expected number of construction-related deaths, though Decker thanked the Great Bird fairly frequently that there had been none of these yet—and Fleet saw no reason why injuries should be treated off-site when the ship had a perfectly good sickbay even partially in place. Christine, for her own part, agreed; transit time to other facilities would imperil the survival chances of the seriously injured. And she plainly intended to keep any serious casualties from going more serious, or fatal, on her watch. She had been spending more time down here than was probably strictly necessary, getting sickbay readier than it would normally have been at this stage of things.

The sickbay doors parted for him. He glanced around. "A bit stressed, Captain," said the mild voice from the next room.

"You don't need the machines to tell you that," Will said.

"No, but you walked through the scan field," Doctor Chapel said, and came through the glass doors from her office. "The blood pressure again. You haven't been working out."

Will snorted. "I've been doing bench presses with a two-million-ton starship," he said. "Should do something for my abdominals eventually, if nothing else. How are things shaking down in your neighborhood?"

"No complaints."

He smiled in disbelief at *that* one, standing in the midst of sickbay and looking around. Chapel had gone some ways beyond the original consultation documents which McCoy had provided, shifting equipment around and insisting on the addition of some extremely new and expensive items to the design; additions that had taken some fancy footwork to implement, and some quiet favors done up in the more senior ends of engineering and in the Surgeon General's office. But everything had eventually gone as Christine had wanted it, despite the budget overruns. It helped to have Scotty chewing on the upper-ups from one side, and on the other, McCoy descending from one of many other consultations to exercise his usual tact and discretion on the SG in an unscheduled lunchtime "meeting." Will very much wished he had imagery and sound on *that* encounter.

" 'Blood pressure,' " Will said to Doctor Chapel. "You must not have had a lot of time to evaluate that data thoroughly."

"Don't try to wriggle out," she said. "And on the contrary: I had all I needed. I've been seeing how hard I can push this creature." Doctor Chapel patted the wall behind which lived the managing computer for the medical scanning hardware and software. There was a tremendous amount of computing power in there, since it had become plain that there were advantages to keeping the sickbay computing resources as independent as possible from the ship's "main" ones. McCoy had been militating for similar design "splits" which would ensure sickbay did not lose its power when the rest of the ship did, for example during battle situations: but this was a more involved issue, one which might not be resolved in this refit.

"And is it satisfying your requirements?" Will said.

"So far."

"But seriously, you read me down the hall? Might be some confidentiality issues there."

"If the people using it weren't responsible," Christine said, "yes. Not that anyone of that description is ever going to work in here, not if *I* can help it." She sighed. "Now about your b.p. . . ."

"Christine, please," Will said, "I'm going to bed, honest. And I told you I stopped putting salt on things. It's even starting to taste strange to me, now."

"Good."

"And as soon as I look in on the computer people—"

"Not *right* to bed, then." She gave him another of those potentially grim looks.

"Just half an hour more, honest. I might ask what *you're* doing here so late."

"Oh, well . . ." The grimness fell off her expression, and a shade of smile crept in. "Tell them all they should go to bed, too."

"It was on my mind. I'm going to sneak up and surprise them; their work habits are starting to pass into legend. And what about you? All work and no play . . ."

Doctor Chapel grinned at him. "Will," she said, "what makes you think this isn't play? All these lovely toys . . . You in particular should understand."

He had to laugh at that. "Okay, right," he said. "I'm going down to 16 . . . then to bed. Don't make me send some poor ensign for you."

She snorted. "Get out of here," Doctor Chapel said, "before I find some interesting new elective surgery to perform on you."

Will chuckled, and headed out.

Deck 16 was where the computer core lay, and Will took the turbo-lift nearest to sickbay and headed down that way. The lift system was presently being "polished" and debugged on the starboard side be-tween decks 11 and 20, after some interior flaws in the tubes became evident, so that this lift would not deliver him right down the hall from the core as the fully functional one would: Will would have to walk a few hundred meters to get where he was going.

The lift doors opened, and Will stepped out. The doors closed be-hind him, and he stood there for a moment. Silence, and the echoes: the whisper of voices from a long time ago . . .

Will walked through the silence and the faint, far-off sound of the voices. They were mostly benevolent, down here, for this was part of

Scotty's realm, and most of the echoes had the accent of the Glasgow shipyards. "They canna take the strain . . ." he could hear Scotty grousing. But somehow "they" always did. He trailed a hand along one corridor wall as he went, remembering, with slight amusement, the dream he'd had a couple of weeks ago in which he'd done just this, and the wall had absently pushed back against his hand, like a cat being stroked. . . .

All of a sudden the spirit of mischief woke up in him. *I'm just going to have a little look at what they're doing,* he thought, *before I go in there. Pull the "omniscient captain" number on them a little. They deserve a laugh.*

Will hung a right at the next corridor junction and headed off down that corridor to one of the ancillary computer access/control facilities that served the core. There were seven of these dotted around the ship on various decks, places where engineering or computer staff could get a "look" at the operating systems and runtime parameters of the computer control network. The multiple facilities were an indicator of the way the net itself had now been decentralized, in response to events in old *Enterprise*'s history when one or another invading force had temporarily mastered the ship by mastering her computer. Will had approved heartily of the idea of making this kind of stunt more difficult by restructuring the system so that it was both holographic in nature and multiply redundant, with the heuristic parameters set to take away control from any "rogue" part of the network, analyze the roguery, and self-firewall against it while attempting to resume control of the hostilely abstracted functions. It meant the system was much more complex than it had been, but Will was willing to accept that problem in trade for not having the ship's computers routinely taken over by alien beings with alien agendas.

Now he leaned toward the access pad by the door and let it read his iris patterns; the door cheeped obediently and opened for him. Will slipped in, waited till the door was secure, and then went over to the freestanding console in the middle of the room and began touching it here and there, activating its linkage into the main "trunk" of the many-branched tree of the new LCARS console coordination system. It was the first implementation of this system on a starship, still experimental and still much too buggy for Scotty's liking; but one of *Enterprise*'s jobs in her new incarnation would be to work the bugs out of it so that the rest of Starfleet could get it implemented. Self-configuring control consoles would be worth whatever trouble they cost, once they were up and running.

Will watched the console come alive with bands of color under his hands, in this particular mode indicating the activity in the computer core. They were installing more new memory down there, if they were on schedule—and Will suspected they were. He cleared the console and tapped it to bring up the graphical representation of the areas of the computer which were being worked with at the moment.

It showed him a pie chart representing quiescent memory, memory in use, memory being altered; 45 percent, that last, with quiescent down to 10 at the moment. *No kidding they're busy*, Will thought, slightly surprised: this was not exactly a configuration that suggested they were about to start winding down for the night. *They must have found something structural that was conflicting with the main system.* Maybe even the problem that had been causing the bridge displays to go down. *That would make Scotty happy. . . .*

Will touched the console again, instructing it to go "one level down" and show him what interactions were taking place inside the machine at the LCARS language level—the actual programming instructions. The console went briefly dark; then a sleet of characters, alphanumerics, and the various specialty symbols that had been added to the LCARS programming languages started running down the panel.

Will squinted at these, waiting for them to start making sense. It was a habit about which Scotty teased him, but then Scotty could read this language as effortlessly as a composer reading a score and hearing the music in his head. Will, though he was growing increasingly fluent in LCARScript, still took a few moments each time before he could start "hearing" the meaning of the instructions. Now he

watched the language slide down the console, letting his eyes go a little unfocused, and it all started to make sense. Yes, they were restructuring active memory, more or less from the bottom up: a very elegant
construction, this, it could make things run a little faster if they . . .

Will stopped short. There was at least one instruction there that
made no sense at all. *That* one looked like it would stop a memory implementation dead in its tracks. It would modify everything else that
came before it, too. *And why would anyone . . . ?*

Will swallowed, seeing another pattern run by that he recognized.
That was a comms call. The master memory management program
was being instructed to wait for a communication from outside the
system. One of the other in-ship nodes, perhaps, or something from
comms proper, maybe even from the main communications board on
the bridge. Yes, that was its "address" inside the *Enterprise* system.
There shouldn't be any calls like that in normal memory, Will thought.
What the heck does this . . . ?

His heart seized inside him.

It's not like anyone's going to attack her in Spacedock. . . .

Oh, really?

His first impulse was to go down there with a security detach-
ment—throw whoever was down there at the moment straight into
the shiny new brig first, and ask questions later. But Will made himself hold still and just breathe for a moment, and think. *What good
would that do? We need some questions answered first. Who are they?
What have they been doing? For how long? And why?*

He smacked the controls harder than necessary, "moving" the readout of the work being done over to one side, and touching the cleared
display to bring up a "new instructions" structure. Will was sweating,
but it was no longer the cold sweat of fear. He was angry now, a useful
state for him, one he could manage and use as fuel for what he needed
to do. He ran an inquiry "root" down into another node of the *Enterprise*'s computer brain, sealing the inquiry to his ID information and
iris pattern, and also sealing it away from the work presently being
done in the core: to anyone down there, this research would be invis-

ible. Will then called up the personnel information for the *Enterprise* reconstruction team.

It was a massive list of names and histories, for the man-hours involved in this refit were well up into the millions. *Computer crew* . . . The names came up: a hundred thirty-four people of various species, some done with their work, some not yet scheduled to start. The present crew involved in memory installation and structure numbered fifty-four. All of these were officially scheduled off-shift now until 0800 Greenwich, the meridian *Enterprise* used while in orbit with the spacedock. But the computer recognized that two of the computer crew had not logged off at end of shift; their names turned up bold in the list.

MALIANI, ROBERT, ENSIGN/COMPSPC
DORWINIAN, ELWE, LIEUTENANT/COMPSPC

Will touched their names, and their expanded personnel files came up, with pictures. Maliani was a handsome, high-cheekboned young man, almost certainly of Italian extraction with a name like that; born in Milwaukee, educated in the Sao Paolo suburbs, entered academy in 2365, completed basic three-year matriculation specializing in electronics and computer heuristics, first "apprentice" assignment *U.S.S. Intrepid* computer refit, "journeyman" assignment *U.S.S. Morgarten*, new main computer installation, blah, blah, blah . . . Five or six complex long-term jobs, now, with various commendations, good work reports from previous team leaders and line commanders . . .

Will smiled grimly. *Good work reports,* he thought, and noticed a tendency among Maliani's previous team leaders to commend the ensign for a willingness to do overtime. *So that no one will think it unusual when you do it now?* . . . He turned his attention to Dorwinian. She was a tall willowy young woman, an Elthan to judge by the short-shorn silvery hair, born on 14 Corvacis, one of the Elthene Affiliate worlds; very good looking, too, with those big oblique golden eyes. She had gone through routine education in an Elthene early-latency program, accelerated acceptance to the secondary/symposial level, then into Starfleet Academy at the minimum acceptance age: completed the three-year matriculation in two and a half years, again with a specialty in heuristics. Then the initial installation on *Morgarten,* and others on *Burundi, Gita, Al-Burak, Nesvadba* . . . Dorwinian had several commendations of her own, mostly for problem solving in difficult circumstances; otherwise nothing out of the ordinary . . .

The fact that these two bright young people were here at all was evidence that both had passed the usual Starfleet security checks. But such checks could never be completely exhaustive. Will studied their pictures. Both Maliani and Dorwinian were a bit dark-complected: a Mediterranean olive-skinned look in Maliani's case, the standard Elthene duskiness in Dorwinian's. Taken separately, it wouldn't have meant much. But here were the two of them, together alone, late at night, doing work that Will was finding more suspect by the moment . . . and the coincidence seemed less coincidental. *Cosmetic alteration has its limits,* he thought. *If you're going to immerse operatives deep, better disguise them as little as possible. . . .*

Assuming I'm right. Let's find out.

Will swallowed, and hit the comms button. "Sickbay."

"Doctor Chapel," she said. "Come on, Will, you *promised.* . . ."

"It's not about that," he said. "I have a question for you."

Christine caught the tension in his voice immediately. "What's the matter?"

"How far *can* that scanner of yours scan?"

"Well, I'm still working on that. But readings get fuzzy around the edges, at distance. Are you not feeling well? I could come down with a normal medical tricorder. . . ."

"No! I don't want any activity down here yet. I need a reading from where you are."

"On you?"

"No. The computer crew who're working late."

"What's the matter with them?"

He was sensitive enough to possible charges of paranoia, even with

Christine, that he wouldn't say it out loud yet. "You take a look," Will said, "and you tell me."

There was a brief silence at the other end. "Just a moment," Doctor Chapel said. Will could hear her stepping over to the control console for the bed scanner. "Hmm," she said then. "Where are they, ex-actly?"

"Deck 16," he said, "the computer core. That's as close as I can tell you at the moment. Don't try to pinpoint it. Exclude one area: node chamber twelve."

"Hmm," she said again. "All right. Hang on."

More silence. "I see them," Christine said then. "What did you want to know, specifically?"

"I just want you to look them over."

"Don't want to give me a hint?"

"No."

"You really must begin," Doctor Chapel said softly, "to trust your chief medical officer. Since I will be doing your physical and mental evaluations for a good long while . . ."

Will opened his mouth, then closed it again. No, not even after *that* accurately placed a barb was he going to respond. At the same time, he allowed himself a small grim grin. This woman had spent too much time around McCoy not to have caught something of his man-agement style.

Another pause. "This thing is just about at its maximum range," Doctor Chapel said. "And they both seem normal enough. One human, from Earth I would guess, not seeing atypical drift in the 'nor-mal' temperature. One—Elthan, would it be? Running a little cooler."

Will's sweat went cold again. *Paranoia* . . . The thought of the irra-tionality he so feared swept over him and made him shiver. *Just a crazy idea* . . . All right, so this one had done no harm. *Except to sud-denly make you distrust, without reason, two innocent crew members,* said that uncertain part of his mind again. *How many more times will this happen? How many of your crew will you treat unjustly?*

*Are you really up to this job? Maybe the suspicious types at Starfleet are
right after all. . . .*

"Now that's interesting," Christine said suddenly.

"What is?" Will could hardly be more interested now.

"A pair of little energy signatures down there," said Christine, "one
associated with each of your people."

"Translator implants," Will said.

"No," said Christine, sounding much more interested . . . and suddenly sounding suspicious, too. "Not at all. A different frequency."

Will's eyes widened. "What are they for?"

"Good question. Each one's set a little differently. You know, they
might—"

"Might what?"

"*Ssh.*"

He kept himself quiet, though it was hard. "Now that is interesting," Chapel said softly. "441 hertz . . ."

"What?"

"The human body 'broadcasts' bio-electricity," Christine said. "Did
you know? It's one of the things our scanners read. Your human down
there—"

"Ensign Maliani."

"He? She?"

"He."

"I thought so, but I didn't want to guess . . . fine structural readings
are fuzzy at this range. That little device inside him is broadcasting at
441. Your other one's at 480; that's right for an Elthene, but . . ."

"But if Elthenes broadcast at that frequency naturally . . ."

". . . then why would they need a device to do it?" Christine said. A
moment's pause. "I'm telling my scanner to block those
frequencies. . . ."

Silence. Will held his breath.

More silence yet.

"Christine. . . ." he said after a moment.

He heard her breathe out sharply. "465," she said.

"Not human, then."

"Neither of them," Doctor Chapel said, "no."

"Then *what are they?*"

"I've got to coax this thing, Will," she said, briefly sounding rather fierce. "Don't bother me for a moment."

He held his peace with difficulty. *Not human.* They had indeed slipped through Starfleet's safety net. And they had been playing with the most important system on his ship for months. *And it took me this long to catch them. The damage they've almost certainly done—*

"Those little devices," Christine said, then, surprisingly conversationally, "will be interesting to examine, later. They very effectively fog the genuine vital signs riding underneath them, while substituting different ones, seamlessly, to Fleet-type med scanners. Fascinating . . ."

It occurred to Decker that McCoy was not the only member of *Enterprise's* old crew to which Christine might have been overexposed. "And the real vital signs?" he said.

"Temperature's running around 104. Bone density's heavy, about 16 percent heavier than human, 19 percent heavier than Elthene. I think I'm seeing trilobal spleens, though I'm not sure. Not that I need to be, when I'm reading cyanoglobin like this." The humor in her voice was definitely grim now.

"*Romulans,*" Will whispered.

"They could be mistaken for Vulcans," Christine said, "by someone less well acquainted with the subtle differences between the two species." The humor was getting angry. "But they couldn't have been mistaken for human or Elthene by anyone who actually touched them rather than just running a scanner over them. Damn it, how many of us touch our clients, anymore?—or feel their foreheads to see if they're running hot? Not enough, it looks like." That was McCoy's annoyance, there, well adapted. "Will, stay where you are and I'll call security."

"No!" Will said, staring down at the two pictures that looked back at him, slightly smiling, from the console. "Not yet."

"*What?* They're doing God only knows what to the ship's computers, and you don't want to—"

"I don't *want* God to be the only one who knows," Will said. "I want to know too! Christine, this ship has to be ready to go places shortly. To undo whatever they've been doing down there, we need to find out what it *is.*"

"How? They're not going to tell you."

"They have to have left traces of what they've done in the code."

"Uh huh. In the clear, do you think?"

"Of course not. And not in English, either . . ."

"And you read Romulan, do you?"

Will considered for a moment. "There are ways around that," he said. "Look, your computers are mostly separate from the main system. I want you to wall them off completely except for the connection to this node."

"All right," she said, "but you'd better give me a few minutes. I'm still getting the hang of how to do that right."

"Make sure it's right this time," Will said softly, and killed comms for the moment.

The silence was loud, and in it he could hear the whispering. For the moment, though, Will paid no attention. It was not old problems he needed to think about, but a new one, and his own. *When I find out what they're doing—assuming that I can*, said one of the less confident voices in the back of his head: he frowned. *What do I do with them then?* There was always the intelligence officer's favorite solution to the discovery of an embedded enemy asset: leave it in place, and give it the "mushroom treatment"—keep it in the dark and feed it "unrecycled waste."

But these two have had the run of any number of starships' computers now, Will thought. *It's all very well to leave an asset in place when no lives are at risk. This case is different. Too many lives depend on those ships' computers working . . . and this one's. Better to be safe and uproot these two mushrooms right now.*

"Captain," said Christine's voice.

"Ready."

"So am I," said Doctor Chapel. "Double-check the connection from your side."

Will did. It was secure. "Good," he said. "I'll hook into your universal translator system from here when I need it. You've got the non-implant version running for the medical beds—"

"Yes, but I'm warning you, the interface is cranky. It still has a lot of trouble with idiom."

"I don't think I'll need it to be six-sigma precise," Will said. "Wish me luck: I'm going to do some digging around. I may be some while. . . ."

"Are you armed?" Doctor Chapel said.

Will grinned. "The usual number of arms and legs," he said, "and my brains."

"Let me know if you need something a little less organic," Doctor Chapel said. "And I'm watching your pulse."

"Thanks." He cut off comms again and turned his attention back to the console.

The amount of data through which he was going to have to sort was daunting: millions of man-hours of code. But he had an advantage. As both captain and senior officer in charge of refit, Will had access to the master code templates which were stored in the spacedock facility's own master computers, the "original version" of the computer software and memory management routines that were to be loaded into *Enterprise* and tailored to her. Now he touched the console here and there, opening his accesses to the spacedock computers, leaning close to let the panel see his iris again. He would tell the system to compare the templates against everything currently in *Enterprise*'s memory, and show him only material that differed from the originals. There would still be massive amounts of it, but from that point he could start narrowing the search. . . .

Will checked the integrity of the wall between his node and the work being done down in the core; then gave the system his instructions, and leaned there on the console to wait for the comparison to finish and display its results. It would take a while.

He was still angry, but managing it. *My ship. My ship. How* dare
they! Yet under the anger ran a little thin thread of pride that, as far as
Will could tell, the Romulans had not bothered to try to sabotage one
of the other ships a-building, but *this* one. Those ships were merely
nascent. *This* ship had a life. She *was* somebody . . . somebody they
hated . . . and they were determined to do away with her.

We'll see about that, Will thought.

A short time later the console cheeped softly, and Decker looked
thoughtfully at the "pie graph" it displayed for him—a big blue disk, a
smaller red-burning tranche—and whistled softly. Something like 40
percent of the code originally installed had already been altered
somehow. That would have happened anyway in the normal course of
things, as code was tailored to systems forced to work together in new
and sometimes unexpected configurations.

Will would have died of old age any number of times if he'd tried
reading through that much code. But there was more than one way to
swing a cat, as his father had always said, and fortunately Will knew
fairly well in what direction to swing it. "Computer," he said softly.
"Delimiter statement. Display percentage of code altered while one or
both of the following personnel have been on duty: Ensign Maliani,
Lieutenant Dorwinian."

"Working," the computer said as softly. After a few moments the
disk and tranche displayed on the console burned dimmer, and the
tranche subdivided itself into a large slice of about five-sixths the original size, and a smaller one of one-sixth, which burned a brighter red.

That was better, but still an awful lot of material to go through.
Will breathed out, looked at it, turning over in his mind something
else that was of concern. *Those comms calls in the code I was looking at
before . .* He touched the console again, brought up one or two ex-
cerpts of that material. Not all those comms calls were to other ad-
ministrative nodes in the ship's computer network. Some of them
appeared to be to nodes outside *Enterprise.*

The absolute nerve of them, Will thought, flushing hot and cold
again. *They were sending messages out, probably about their work,*

*through our own system. Certainly coded. Probably to their handler . . .
reporting progress, asking for new instructions. And the brilliance of it;
their messages to their handlers masquerading as our own.*

He frowned at the console. On a whim, Will touched one control,
and let the computer feed him live sound from down in the computer
core.

Someone was humming as they worked: a soft, unconcerned sound.
A second tone added itself to the first, a fourth higher; an odd har-
mony, if the listener hadn't known about Elthene multiple intona-
tion. Will knew about it, though, and smiled slightly at the
completeness of the role being played here, of which cosmetic alteration was literally only the surface. *Surgery on her larynx, too. Too bad
she'll have gone to all that trouble for nothing.*

"Computer," he said. "With the exception of areas presently being
accessed or referenced, examine all code in this last sample for nonstandard content."

"Define 'nonstandard.' "

"Comment material. Also communications calls to and from other
nodes and/or systems."

"Working." After a moment's silence, another much smaller, slim-
mer tranche displayed itself, burning red.

"Display code. No, stop," Will said then. "Analyze selected code
for evidence of cipher algorithms, single- or multiple-element satchel
ciphers, or other encryption."

"Working." He held his breath again.

"No result."

Impossible. Will bit his lip, tempted to tell the computer to do the
analysis again; but that would be useless.

But wait a minute. "Rerun analysis," he said, "by same-time or near-
time sections, using letter or phoneme distribution based on standard
Romulan dialect, expressed using Modern Roman characters."

"Working," said the computer. There was a long pause.

Will held his breath.

"Sixty percent positive," said the computer.

Eureka! "State parameters for percentage of positive."

"Letter/phoneme distribution not invariable. More than 20 percent variation in suspected same-word or similar-word or -group content."

That would be likely enough, especially if the "private" coded messages were written in one or more of the Romulan subdialects. Or it might have to do with the limitations of the universal translator's Romulan-language data, which understandably lacked the widest desirable vocabulary and idiom, since there had been so little official contact between the two species. But the basic translator hardware had the grammar and syntax down all right: that had been an absolute requirement for the subspace-radio-negotiated treaty that had ended the First Romulan War so long ago and established the boundaries for the Neutral Zone.

He swallowed; now came the worst question. "Is the cipher breakable?"

A long pause. "Affirmative," the computer said, "using on-file nonstandard additional 'legacy' decryption routines installed during last command."

He realized what that meant, and could have fallen down and hugged the console, or whatever nameless computer technicians had recognized those old routines in the old *Enterprise* computers' programming for what they were and had preserved them, "off to one side" as it were, in the new installation. The Vulcan who had been responsible for writing and installing those routines in the first place had been more than merely a genius in the mathematics of both computer systems and cryptography generally; this was a ghost that Will didn't mind haunting his ship, not at *all.* "Estimate of decryption time."

"Five hours, twenty-three minutes."

Not good enough. "Recompute estimate," he said, touching the console here and there, " using *Enterprise's* entire processing capacity except for that specifically excluded in previous instructions."

A moment's silence. "Twelve minutes, forty seconds."

It was going to have to do. "Computer," Will said, "begin decryption of patterned/ciphered sequences. Arrange ciphered sequences in time earliest to latest. Priority processing for sequences with portions which also occur in other sequences. Report on progress. Report when complete."

"Working," the computer said, and fell silent.

Will stood there, wishing there were a chair in here . . . leaning on the console, listening to the minutes ticking by, and to his heartbeat. He thought suddenly of the likeness of this quiet struggle to the combat Kirk had had first with the Romulans long ago: nothing face to face, everything remote, move matching move across the darkness, a business of anticipation, uncertainty, feeling your way in the dark . . . and waiting. He waited now, and for once the whispering was silent, the voices waiting with him. Only the faint humming came from elsewhere in the deck, and someone's casual voice said, "Pass me that solid, will you?"

"Of a certainty. How do you proceed?"

"It's going fine. Another twenty minutes, half an hour maybe . . . then we may as well knock off for the night."

"*Idiom is a problem . . .*" Not for him, Decker thought, wry. "Progress," he said softly.

"Working. Thirty percent complete."

"Type of cipher."

"Switched-packet satchel, compressed, alternating-character type."

He whistled again. It was a "hard" cipher, and would probably not have been detected unless someone got suspicious of just these two people . . . and what were the odds on that? But ships called *Enterprise* carried their own luck with them, and handed it off sometimes to their captains . . . as Will was now discovering, to his delight. It was the ultimate accolade, the one that no money could buy, no mere Starfleet assignment could guarantee. *She* would wake up to you and make you part of that unique symbiosis . . . or else she wouldn't. *If we survive this,* Will thought, stroking the console idly, *we're going to get along famously, you and I. . . .*

"Progress."

"Sixty percent."

He stood there trying not to count seconds or heartbeats. *And I will always do right by you*, Will thought. *No surrenders . . . no retreats. No alien species is going to take you away from me and run you halfway to another galaxy. You belong to me now. . . .*

It took what seemed like a very long time before the computer spoke up again. "Analysis complete," it said.

"Display results," Will said, and bent over the console.

The results were all expressed in text. Will breathed out slowly at that. *No voices to fake . . .* His luck was still running, so far: but there was no telling how long it would hold. The messages were spotty, incomplete, the syntax of them mangled: again and again the computer had inserted ##### in the translation, indicating it reckoned its chances as less than fifty-fifty that it knew what a word was. Looking at all the other words, Will began to sweat at the thought that the computer might be wrong in its evaluation of some of those words, too. Yet for the time being he had no choice but to trust the universal translator algorithms stored in Christine's end of the computer. *They were good enough to get a treaty signed*, Will thought, *and there were additions later, too, out of the online instructions from when Kirk and Scotty stole the cloaking device—Scotty told me so, told me he passed them on to Uhura for incorporation into the translator. It'll be good enough.*

It'll have to be good enough. . . .

Will swallowed again and took a few deep breaths as he read down the text of the many, many messages. They were short. Both sides of this conversation were terse, probably not wanting to artificially inflate the size of the standard-text messages in which these encrypted missives were encapsulated. PROGRESS REPORT UNSATISFACTORY, said one of them, a statement which just about summed up Will's feeling about this whole business. ##### INSUFFICIENT ##### TIME FRAME ##### UNSCHEDULED CHANGES. *Does that mean they're working too fast, or not fast enough? Or that the Enterprise won't be ready as fast as they wish it would be?* It was the only other thing on which Will thought he was likely to agree with these people.

He scanned on down the messages. ##### SATISFACTORY, said the next one. And the next. ##### ALTERATIONS ##### IN-SERTED ROUTINES EXCELLENT, said another. CONTINUE ##### CAUTION REGARDING SECURITY ##### . COMMUNI-CATIONS TEST SUCCESSFUL, TEST ROUTINE CORRECTLY IMPLEMENTED, ##### TRIGGERED.

Will kept reading. This was more than enough evidence to keep these people in the pokey until their ears grew back—assuming that their genetic heritage could reassert itself that far through the surgery, implants, and other disguising procedures that had been used on them. But there was too little information on what he really wanted, the details about the sabotage—

Aha, Will thought then. *My own fault.* "Computer," he said, "re-arrange the decrypted messages, pairing remote demand and local reply side by side. Oldest to newest."

The display blanked itself, then complied. Will bent to his reading again. There were still plenty of uncertainties in the translation, and nothing could be done about those, but he was beginning to see what was going on. One of the places the original Romulan "treaty" trans-lation algorithms had been strongest was computer terminology, be-cause otherwise the two sides could not have coordinated their communications sufficiently to get each other to understand the treaty's terms in the first place. Now that strength was standing Will in good stead, and serving to betray his enemies. And in an additional irony, since the language of computers had moved so far ahead on both sides since the time of the treaty negotiations a century ago, to make themselves understood to their handler, the spies aboard the *Enterprise* had been forced to choose between coining new words to explain what they were doing, and using Terran ones with Romulan noun affixes. Being in a hurry, and not being linguists, they had cho-sen the latter. . . .

Will was grinning harder now as he read. Even in as delicate a job as this was, bureaucracy had been rearing its ugly head. SCHEDULE ##### PRESSURE FROM SENATE INTELLIGENCE COMMITTEE, said one of the later messages; Will hoped desperately that, if nothing else, the translator program was right about the renderings of the words for "intelligence" and "committee," two terms usually otherwise mutually exclusive in his opinion. REPORT PROGRESS ADVANCED SCHEDULE SOONEST. And at the end of that message, a word that had not been translated, because it was recognizably part of a proper name: TR'HRIENTEH. And the same word, at the end of another message a little further along; and also at the end of a third one, almost at the end of the sequence.

Will grinned wolfishly. *A spymaster who starts to sign his messages,* he thought. *How careless can you get? Or how arrogant.* Yet arrogance could be part of the Romulan mindset, Will knew, especially when faced with what seemed a stupid or unworthy enemy. And this time, it had blinded its owner in a way which made Will's job much easier.

The "handler's" terseness was mostly matched by that of his two spies. "7387" and "3364" was how they referred to themselves in their responses. There was no way to tell which of them was which, and Will wasn't sure, at the moment, that it mattered. MEMORY RESTRUCTURING ##### ACCORDING TO PLAN, SCHEDULED ##### DELAYED DUE TO COMPUTER TEAM INTERFERENCE, RESCHEDULED FOR ##### THREE DAYS. And then, near the end, a message that made the hair stand up on the back of Will's neck: FINAL PHASE COMPLETE, RUNNING CHECKS, CHECKS COMPLETE ##### FORTY-FIVE HOURS LOCAL, FINAL LOCKDOWN AND ENCRYPTION SCHEDULED IN FIFTY HOURS LOCAL—

That message, outgoing from the spies, was dated yesterday morning, eleven hundred Greenwich. *One more day,* Will thought, sweating, *and they would have sealed their sabotage routines into permanent memory, encrypted and disguised as normal machine language . . . and we might never have known until some day out in space, when everything started to go wrong . . . if it was indeed designed to "go wrong" slowly, and not in some immediate and irreparable way like overloading the warp engines. . . .*

But I wouldn't do that, Will thought, *if I were a Romulan . . . not unless I had no choice. I'd try to get my hands on the ship first . . . and if I couldn't do that, I'd blow her to hell. Especially this ship, which they hate. . . .* And the Romulans would not be insensitive to the blow such destruction would be to the Federation, and the propaganda coup for them, if the *Enterprise* were to be lost with all hands. . . .

But that's all conjecture, Will thought. *I need better data.*

He looked down at the messages from the spies' handler . . . and the idea came to him. It was dangerous. It was possibly foolhardy. But he had come too far now not to try it. *Tr'Hrienteh,* Will thought, *whoever you are, you're about to send another message. . . .*

"Computer," Will said softly. "Composing message."

"Ready," said the computer.

"Senate Intelligence committee re-formed after suicides," said Decker. "Schedule now queried in all particulars. Complete project summary required soonest, highest possible priority. Tr'Hrienteh. Finished," he said to the computer.

"Message complete."

"Encrypt using the decryption algorithm used to decode the previous messages," Will said. "Encapsulate code in a message derived from logically arranged sections of earlier 'encapsulating' messages. Match context and improvise where necessary. Time-stamp new message in agreement with previous message transit times and transmit to destination address of previous received messages."

"Working," said the computer. After a few moments' silence, it said, "Complete. Transmitted."

Will leaned against the console again, listening to the audio from the computer core. There was nothing he could do, now, but wait.

Down there he heard Dorwinian humming again, a different melody this time, but still perfectly tritonal, a sequence of major chords. "Gonna be glad to be done with this for the night," said Maliani after a moment.

"I also," said Dorwinian, "will seek my sleeping place with pleasure."

Will swallowed. There was another long, long pause. Then he
heard a soft chirp, and a rustle as of someone turning to look at another console.

"Got a message here from my mom," said Maliani then. He
sounded a little bemused.

"I thought you said you had not expected such," said Dorwinian.
"These are not her usual hours. . . ."

"I hadn't," said Maliani. "Hmmm . . ."

There was another of those long silences, presumably while Dorwinian read what Maliani had received from his "mom." "Sounds
kind of urgent," he said. "I guess I'd better take care of it. . . ."

"We are almost done here," said Dorwinian casually; "pausing to
make a reply now will not put us behind schedule."

"I guess not . . ." Maliani said. "Computer . . ."

"Working."

"Keypad mode . . ."

"Done."

Will could hear nothing for the moment. "Computer," he said to
his own console. "Intercept message when sent. Prevent transmission.
Reroute to this console, decrypt, and translate."

"Prevention of transmission impossible under present main comms
programming routines," said the computer. "Reroute and translation
will be executed on send."

Will held still for a moment and thought about that. It meant that
one last message would go out to their masters from these spies before
they went "off the air" . . . and the odds were good that Romulan
High Command would eventually guess what had caused them to
send this last report. But by the time it reached the Romulans, subspace delays being what they were between here and the empire, their
agents would be permanently out of the loop as far as *Enterprise* was
concerned. *They won't try anything like this again,* Will thought. *Which,
as far as Romulans are concerned, simply means they'll make sure their*

next ruse is much more deeply buried than this one. In the long run, we
may have cause to be sorry about that.

But meantime, I'm going to make it plain that you don't mess around
with Enterprise *and get away with it.*

All he could do for the moment, though, was wait. After what must
only have been about ten minutes, but seemed more like ten hours,
Will heard Maliani say, "There—"

There was another pause. "Is that reply to her complete enough, do
you think?"

"It should be plenty," said Maliani, and laughed a little. "All the recent news is there . . . and if I sent much more than that, she'd start
complaining that I was up past my bedtime."

A couple of soft incidental sounds. "There," said Maliani. "Now we
can finish up here. Want to stop by the dock commissary for a snack
after we go off?"

"Indeed my pouch has been growling somewhat," said Devanian.
"Let us do so. . . ."

"Message received," said the computer. "Decrypted. Translated."

It displayed it on the console, and Will read swiftly down it.

Oh . . . my . . . God, he thought. Here it all was, the history of the
two Romulan agents' work—set out in ten broad subsections, with
apologies for not being able to give more detail, but the committee
had in the past expressed impatience with too much emphasis being
put on the technical explanations. Every one of *Enterprise's* major
computer-operated systems had been compromised to greater or lesser
degree, with the intent of disabling *Enterprise* "on command" at a
time when Romulan vessels planted in a given area would be available to take her captive and force her across the Neutral Zone into
Romulan space. Locations of the implementations to each system
were then briefly described. The only ship's system spared this treatment so far, the report said, was the warp drive system, which could
not yet be compromised because the warp intermix formulae had not
yet been finalized. However, as soon as they were, the operatives had
left in place a "logic bomb" which could be triggered to activate while

the ship was underway. This would critically overload the warp drive by accelerating the antimatter feed at some crucial moment, ideally when the phasers were (according to the controversial new design) drawing power from the warp engines while charging or during combat. The resulting warp crisis would be assumed to have been caused by a phaser malfunction . . . if there was even time to assess what had happened, before the ship blew. Final adjustments to the programming were now being made; the two operatives expected to be in place here for some time before Starfleet moved them on to work on other ships. Orders for these new ships were awaited, now that this team had fulfilled its primary mission of revenge for the harms done the empire by *Enterprise* in the past.

Glory to the empire . . .

The report was signed only with the two operatives' numbers.

Will straightened up. "Save this message," he said. "Send a copy immediately to Admiral Nogura's office: flag it triply most urgent."

"Warning: this instruction will cause the admiral to be awakened if he is on sleep cycle," said the computer.

Will grinned. "Ask me if I care. Execute."

"Done," said the computer. "Initial instruction serves no purpose."

"All too true," Will said. He ran his hands through his hair, stretched once, and turned toward the door. Time for the captain to pay them a visit and tell them what a good job they've been doing, he thought.

If he had a problem, it was that there was no armory on this deck. "Computer," Will said as he stood in the doorway. "Scan computer core for weapons."

There was a pause. "No conventional weapons detected," it said. "One tricorder. One nonstandard sensing device."

Meaning one of them is carrying something that reads like a tricorder, Will thought. *But then they also read as a human and an Elthan, too, until Christine interfered. . . .*

Never mind. "Decker to sickbay," he said softly.

"Captain?"

"I'm locking down the accesses to the computer core, except for one," Will said. "Security detail, computer core access C. Ten minutes."

"They'll be there in five," she said. "Out."

He straightened up. His back was killing him, and his heart was starting to pound . . . and he was going to *enjoy* this.

Will made his way out of the node room and slowly, casually, down the hallway to the C access to the core. Just before coming to the access, he paused, stretched once or twice more; he had been standing in the same position, nearly, for a long time. . . .

Right.

He went through the door. As it slipped aside for him, he glanced around him casually, as if he had no idea where the two crew members were, then "spotted" them over by one of the main read-in consoles. "Aha," he said. "There you are."

"Captain?" They had been seated at the console. Now both of them stood as he ambled toward them. *Very good,* Will thought. *That may make this next part easier. . . .*

He strolled idly along toward Maliani and Dorwinian, doing his best to look like a captain who had been working hard all day and was up well past his bedtime: a little soft around the edges, and completely off his guard. The two of them watched him come with expressions that were, to put it mildly, neutral. *The one place their training's fallen down a little,* he thought. *They don't know how to fake being comfortable with a senior officer . . . because they would never be comfortable with one of their own, not really. And because I am the enemy . . .*

"At ease!" Will said, as he came along toward them, smiling. "I thought before I went off, I'd come down and see how you folks were doing. You the last two left down here?"

"Yes, Sir," said Dorwinian. "We have been completing some of the memory inset programming. . . ."

"Don't get all technical on me now," said Will easily, leaning past them and peering at the console they were working at. Naturally there was no sign of the message he knew had just been sent. "My brains are all full of gunnery at the moment: you've heard about the problems we've been having. . . ."

"Yes, Sir, the Ineffables mentioned it to our team a few days ago, at lunch," Maliani said. "Not our problem, fortunately. . . ."

"No," Will said, "but you have enough here to keep you busy, it looks like." He turned around and actually leaned backwards on the console, which caused them to look at him a little oddly. "I just wanted to let you know how much I appreciate your hard work. Everybody keeps telling me about the crazy computer people, how you work all hours of the night . . . and now I see it's true."

Maliani and Dorwinian exchanged a look. "You know how it is, Captain," he said. "You get busy . . . other things, less important things, can wait. There were a few loose ends we wanted to tidy up."

"It is our pleasure to serve," said Dorwinian.

"Yes," said Will softly. "Mine too." He stood up and put a hand on each of their shoulders, and turned them around to walk away with him from the console. A little bemused, they came with him, as good crew members would. "And you know," he said, "when everything's said and done, there's only one thing to say on that subject." He looked from one to the other of the young, dark, handsome, slightly confused faces as they walked away from the consoles and up the steps to the "walkway" level which led to the door; he heard the little sound outside.

"*Tr'Hrienteh,*" Will said.

Both their eyes went wide.

In the next second, Maliani lashed out with one elbow, with deadly force, at Will's head. But Will's head was not there anymore: it was about two feet lower, as he bent down and threw himself sideways into Maliani's side. All three of them went down together, for as he hit the floor, Will had also scissored his legs around Dorwinian's, tripping and toppling her. The next second he had bounced to his feet again, between them and that console: whatever happened in the next few minutes, they would not touch it again.

Maliani scrambled up into a crouch. Dorwinian scrambled up too, and burst away toward the door.

It shot open to reveal Christine Chapel standing there. Without the slightest hesitation Doctor Chapel straight-armed the charging "Elthan" right in the sternum. The woman staggered back, her arms flying up, and Christine stepped in and stuck a hypospray straight into the space directly under her right ribs. Down Dorwinian went, like a sack of potatoes.

Christine looked past her, chucked that hypospray over her shoulder, and came up with another one, looking most meaningfully at "Maliani."

He looked at Will, then at Chapel. He took a step or two toward her—and then stopped, hearing behind her the thunder of footsteps running, the security detail coming at speed down the corridor.

"Maliani" looked up at the ceiling . . . and then crumpled to his knees.

"Doctor Chapel!" Decker said as the security people came in and filled the room, picking up the woman who lay prone in the doorway.

Chapel hurried forward . . . but as she did, Maliani fell forward on his face. Christine had her medical tricorder out, was running it over him. Then she shook her head.

"Neurotoxin," she said. "His EEG's flat already." She looked up regretfully. "Could be anything from the old-fashioned hollow tooth to an implant with a pressure pump. I'm sorry, Captain. . . ."

"Never mind," Will said. "The other one didn't have a chance . . . nice job, Doctor." He glanced at the security people and said, "You'd better get her down to sickbay and restrain her so that the doctor can remove whatever her friend used. I have a feeling Starfleet security is going to have a lot of questions to ask her. . . ."

The security people carried Dorwinian out. Will stood there, breathing hard, and looked up at Chapel with amusement.

"You were watching my pulse, weren't you?" he said.

"Far be it from me to miss a cue," Christine said. "So now what?"

The comms board in the computer core whistled. Will had to

smile. "Nothing happens for hours and hours," he said, "and then everything happens at once. . . ." He went over to the board, touched it to life, half afraid it would be Admiral Nogura.

"What're you still doin' up, lad?" Scotty's voice said, outraged.

"Oh, nothing," Decker said. "Really, nothing, Scotty . . ."

"Good," said Scotty, "because now you'll have some somethin' to do." He sounded both alarmed and pleased.

"What?"

"I'm just tellin' you, lad. My comm goes off five minutes ago, and who is it but Admiral Nogura—" *Oh lord,* Will thought, *here it comes.* "—blatherin' on about the daftest thing you ever heard at three in the morning. And what should it be but some great big cloud of no one knows what, comin' toward Earth—"

Will blinked. "A *cloud?*"

"The damn thing's half an AU across if it's an inch, he said, and it's coming straight toward us. At extreme sensor range yet, a week or ten days away at the speed it's making. But no one knows what the great beastie is or what it's made of, and guess what ship is the one best positioned to go make rendezvous with the thing?"

"Oh, *Scotty*—!" Will was torn between terror, fury, and sheer delight.

"Aye, and if you haven't been to bed yet, you won't be for a while, for Nogura's putting the tail end of the refit on shift rotations as of right this minute; that ship'll be full of people right out to the skin in less than half an hour." He laughed. "You were right, Sir: not that he'll admit it, and you'd be wise not to rub it in. We've got enough work ahead of us to get your great big lassie ready to go."

Will gulped. Until this moment, everything about the refit had been slightly unreal, almost like a dream, like something happening to someone else. But that time was over now. This was the awakening. Finally he and *Enterprise* would be free together, out in the world that they had both been born for—in *Enterprise's* case, reborn for. They would venture out into the universe, into the great unknown, to begin together a long career of service and adventure, at last . . . safe at last from anyone who might try to separate Will Decker from his new command.

"Get yourself over here, Scotty," Will said. "I need you. *She* needs you. And the computers are all screwed up; we've got some nasty stuff to dig out of them in a hurry."

"Ach, what have you been *doin'* to them, Captain?"

Will laughed. "Better get over here and see," he said. He killed the connection and went off to start preparing his new ship for her first journey.

The door closed behind him, and if the captain of the *Enterprise* once more heard behind him the voices whispering, the echoes, he paid them no mind. . . .

Captain Spock
U.S.S. Enterprise

"You've never voiced it, but you've always thought that logic was the best basis on which to build command."

Dr. Leonard H. McCoy, *Star Trek*

A. C. CRISPIN

In 1999, *Star Trek* fans were treated to the event they have waited decades for: the marriage of Spock. The debate has usually been over to whom he was best paired, but most fans seemed content to have him wind up with Saavik. The story of their betrothal and marriage was recounted in *Vulcan's Heart* by Susan Schwartz and Josepha Sherman . . . but the early days of the couple's relationship remain a mystery. When exactly did they began to notice one another as potential partners?

In addition to laying the groundwork for *Vulcan's Heart*, Crispin also continued some of the themes established in Carolyn Clowes's *The Pandora Principle*.

A.C., no stranger to Vulcans, also explores Spock's comment in *Star Trek II* that he is content to command a training mission. Of all the captains in this book, he may be the best suited to teach command strategy. Having served with Pike, Kirk, and Decker, Spock also worked alongside Picard and can distill their varying styles into easy-to-digest portions.

Crispin burst onto the scene with *Yesterday's Son*, making her the Trek author in this volume of the longest standing. She has followed that with *Time for Yesterday*, *The Eyes of the Beholders*, and the *Star Trek* hardcover bestseller, *Sarek*. In addition, Crispin created the Star-Bridge Academy series of novels. She also paid a visit to the Galaxy Far Far Away, when she wrote the Han Solo prequel, a trilogy about the life of our favorite rogue and smuggler in his pre-*A New Hope* days. She even visited the world of V in three volumes.

These days, Crispin is working away on new projects and divides her time between writing and acting as Science Fiction and Fantasy Writers of America vice president.

Just Another Little Training Cruise

Twin beams of concentrated energy lashed out at the *Enterprise* like the taloned paws of a great predator, engulfing the starship in a white blaze of light that, for a moment, rivaled the glory of the stars on the viewscreen. The bridge crew cried out and ducked as the energy demolished what remained of their shields, cutting deeply into the ship's hull. A rapid series of explosions shook the science station, the helm, and navigation. The stench of burned insulation and slagged computers filled the air, accompanied by thick, choking smoke. Bodies crashed to the deck, then lay still, covered with blood, several horribly burned.

In the aftermath, silence prevailed, broken only by soft gasps that sounded suspiciously like sobs.

"Lights," Captain Spock ordered. "Activate blowers."

The lights came up, and the smoke that filled the bridge was quickly sucked away. The crew of trainees picked themselves off the deck, their faces strained and pale. Spock saw tears on one young ensign's face. When he realized that Spock was regarding him, the young man hastily scrubbed his sooty face with his sleeve. The Starfleet officers who had been mixed in among the trainee crew climbed to their feet and began brushing themselves off, mopping off artificial blood and burned "flesh."

Spock stood at the door of the simulation chamber, watching these cadets he'd trained struggle with the grim realization that someday they might face just such a situation in real life. One trainee, an Andorian, marched up to the Vulcan, his blue features flushed indigo beneath his mop of fluffy white hair. "Captain Spock!" he said, his tone barely civil. "Request permission to speak, Sir!"

Spock nodded, and led the way out of the chamber to the corridor. "Permission granted, Cadet Theron. What is it?"

Theron pulled himself up stiffly. "Captain, with all due respect, I protest the way this test was conducted! As Trainee Captain, I followed every Starfleet regulation to the letter. And yet they fired on my ship and destroyed her . . . with no provocation! This was not a fair test of my command ability!"

Spock raised an eyebrow. "Cadet Theron, the *Kobayashi Maru* exercise does not test a candidate's retention of Starfleet regulations. Instead it allows the instructors and the candidates themselves to examine trainee reaction to stress, to what the humans term a 'no-win' scenario. Starfleet officers must learn to face the possibility of defeat—even of total destruction. It has been our observation that this test allows candidates to realize, sometimes for the first time, that life as a Starfleet officer can be dangerous and requires individuals of strong character. In my opinion, you acquitted yourself well in your command role, Cadet. We will discuss your performance in more depth during your official debriefing. I have scheduled you for 0900 hours tomorrow."

Theron paused, obviously taken aback by Spock's words. The Vulcan was not known for handing out accolades lightly. He searched for a reply, but found none, and fell back on trainee protocol. "Very well, Sir, I shall be there."

Spock nodded. "Dismissed, Cadet."

Theron turned and walked away, slightly favoring his left leg. The final explosion had flung him from his command seat, because he'd forgotten to activate his restraint system. Spock made a mental note to mention that tomorrow during the evaluation.

Cadets filed past him, mostly silent, a few muttering to each other. Spock made appointments with all of them for their evaluations, then stood alone in the corridor, watching the last of them leave. He had an appointment, and she was most unlikely to be late. She . . .

A step sounded behind him, even as a voice spoke in Vulcan. "Their faces are always the same, my teacher."

Spock turned to find Cadet Saavik approaching him. She wore a Starfleet cadet's red and buff jumpsuit, her long dark hair swept up and secured neatly, as regulation decreed. "The test is not an easy one, Saavikam," he replied, in the same language. "All those who would command a starship must learn to face difficult, even impossible, situations."

"I fail to see the logic in training cadets to become familiar with defeat, Mr. Spock," she said, raising an eyebrow at him.

Spock raised his eyebrow in turn. "It is my belief that victory can, at times, be snatched from the jaws of defeat, to borrow a human idiom. I have seen it done . . . more than once."

"By James T. Kirk," she said, and it was not a question.

"Indeed."

"The admiral is known throughout Starfleet for his . . . resourcefulness . . . under such circumstances," Saavik admitted. "Someday I hope to be able to meet him."

"The admiral frequently conducts personal inspections of graduating classes, Saavikam. It is likely you will encounter him then."

Saavik nodded. "I am content to wait, my teacher. Being here at Starfleet Academy is . . . the fulfillment of a long-standing goal. I learned . . . much . . . my first year here. One of the most important things I learned is that I still have things to learn. Especially about interacting with the other cadets."

Spock nodded. "Indeed. The life of a Starfleet cadet is challenging. The *Kobayashi Maru* simulation is but one challenge cadets must face."

Saavik walked over to peer into the simulation chamber. Her nostrils contracted slightly as she took in the rank smells of burned insulation and cloned blood. Spock watched her, then added, "You will understand more of the reasoning behind the test when you finish your training and take it yourself, Saavikam."

"I do not plan to take the test," she said, levelly.

"Why?"

She hesitated, clearly searching for words. Finally, she replied, "When I hear them speak of the test, I consider myself fortunate to be in training as a science officer. I have no wish to become a line officer."

Spock raised an eyebrow. "Is that why you chose to pursue science officer training? Because you did not wish a command of your own?"

When she did not reply immediately, Spock held his silence, knowing that she would answer in her own time. And her answer was likely to end in a question for him. For all of their long association, Saavik had been asking him questions.

The Vulcan had been Saavik's mentor, her guide, ever since he'd found her, naked, starving, and feral, on the Romulan planetoid known as Hellguard. He'd led a rescue mission of Vulcans who had learned that kidnapped Vulcans had been brought to that desolate place as part of a Romulan "experiment." The captive Vulcans had been forced to mate with Romulans, to produce children of shared ancestry. What the Romulans had intended for those children, nobody knew. The experiment, whatever it had involved, was abandoned by the Romulans. The children had been discarded, left to starve and slaughter each other for a few scraps of food. Spock had managed to communicate with the child Saavik, had convinced her to trust him. Then he'd brought the savage, fiercely intelligent youngster away from that desolate planetoid and overseen her education. Because of him, she learned to speak properly, received an education, and, eventually, was accepted into Starfleet Academy.

Since he'd first rescued her, Saavik had regarded her Vulcan mentor with near-reverence. The cadet had never made any effort to trace any of her Vulcan relatives, though gene-testing would have provided her with proof of her ancestry. Instead, she had looked to Spock for companionship. It had been his approval that counted. He was her teacher, and she honored him as she did no other living being.

Finally, she nodded—a short, economical motion. "Correct. I have no wish for command. I do not consider myself suited for it."

"Saavik . . . please explain your reasoning. While you have been a student here at Starfleet Academy, your performance has been . . . above average, even for a Vulcan. Your test scores indicate that you would make a commendable line officer."

Saavik's expression hardened, and there was a glint of . . . what? Stubbornness? Defensiveness? in her eyes. "Mr. Spock, from what I have heard of the *Kobayashi Maru* test, I have no wish to experience an examination designed to provoke officer candidates into illogical and irrational behavior." Her dark eyes met his. "I understand that you did not take the test yourself, my teacher."

Spock nodded. "You are correct in that. Because I started out as a science officer, I did not have to take the test."

"Then how did you become a line officer, my teacher?"

"A field promotion, while serving under Captain Christopher Pike," Spock replied. A sudden memory of Pike as he'd last seen him on Talos IV filled his mind—young, strong, and handsome once more, striding eagerly towards lovely Vina. That had been sixteen standard years ago. Was Pike still alive? Communications with Talos IV were still proscribed, so there was no way to know.

"I am off duty for the remainder of the day, Saavikam," Spock said. "Have you thought about what you would like to do this afternoon?"

Saavik nodded, her dark eyes suddenly betraying eagerness. "I have, my teacher. I should like to go back to the Valley of Death, and run."

Spock nodded. "Very well. I shall change and gather our supplies, and meet you at the HQ transporter unit in ten minutes."

"Very well, my teacher." There was a note of eagerness in Saavik's voice that was most . . . agreeable, Spock noted. Since he had become one of Starfleet Academy's head instructors, he hadn't had enough time to spend with his protégée. It was . . . pleasant . . . to know that Saavik still desired his company.

Two hours later, Spock and Saavik raced together down a rocky ravine, beneath the light of the westering sun. Both were clad in sleeveless shirts and light trousers, wearing boots and small backpacks. They had been running for over an hour, glad of the chance to exercise in the desert. Spock could not help contrasting this Terran wasteland with the vast deserts of Vulcan. The ground was similar, rocky, with little vegetation, the soil thin and sandy. But he could never have imagined himself on Vulcan—the air was thick and heavy, and the temperature, which could prove deadly to an unprotected human, seemed to him quite pleasant. The gravity was lighter, and the difference made his flying feet feel light.

By the time they halted, the sun had dropped beneath the horizon, and a cool breeze stirred the air. Spock sat down on a convenient rock, as did Saavik, to watch the brilliant colors of sunset. They were beautiful, vivid crimson and orange, shading to violet and purple . . . but as the minutes passed, Spock found himself watching Saavik as much as he did the sky. Her hair had loosened from its moorings, and part of it tumbled down past one cheek and spilled across her shoulder. Spock regarded her averted profile. Her face was rounded, but it was the rounding of a woman now, not that of a child. Her body was sturdy and fit, but, for the first time, he realized that she would never pass for a young man now, not even in dim light. The child he had helped to raise was gone, and a woman sat there on the rock, her face flushed from the exercise, her dark eyes alight as she drank in the beauty of the desert, the sunset.

Feeling his gaze upon her, she turned, and Spock glanced away, then, realizing for the first time that the breeze was chilly, reached into his knapsack for his jacket. He did not look back at her until he had pulled it on. Taking out his water bottle, he took a sip, musing that on Vulcan, such behavior would be judged self-indulgent. Vulcans prided themselves on being able to cover long distances in harsh land with little in the way of food or water.

Saavik had also pulled on her jacket. Being half Romulan, she was not as sensitive to the cold as he was, but now that the sun was well down, even a human might have been tempted to cover up bare arms.

They shared food: oranges and Vulcan kalafruit, flatbread and a handful of almonds apiece. They ate in silence. Spock listened to the sounds of the nocturnal desert life, hearing the soft slither of scales gliding across sand from a snake hunting some distance away, then picking up a scritching sound that was probably its prey—some small rodent, most likely. A nightbird called mournfully.

"Saavikam," Spock said. "There is something I would like to discuss further."

"Yes, my teacher?"

"I would like to ask why you believe you would not make a suitable line officer."

Saavik did not turn to regard him. He could make out her profile against the last, fading lightness in the western sky. Finally she said, "I have learned to work with the humans. Tolerate their illogic." She paused, shook her head. "No, more than tolerate. I have learned that they do many things well, even if they do not use logic as we do to analyze their situations and arrive at conclusions. Humans are not the problem they used to be for me during my first year."

Spock nodded. He'd seen Saavik's reports from her first year as a Starfleet cadet.

"But the others, the Andorians, the Caitans . . . the Tellarites . . . especially the Tellarites! They are, if anything, even worse than the humans! They are totally governed by illogical emotions. They act on impulse, without reasoning. It is most . . . taxing . . . when I must work with them, during labs, for example. One Tellarite female made an extremely offensive comment to me when I—" she broke off, then shook her head. "There is no purpose to be served by going into that. Suffice it to say that I doubt my own ability to command illogical beings. We are taught in Starfleet that good commanders must have empathy, must be able to see many sides to a question. I see only the logical side to questions. I will be much better off working with scientists than I would trying to command humans and other humanoid species."

Spock nodded. "I appreciate your candor," he said. "However, I believe you may be, as the humans say, 'selling yourself short,' Saavikam. I urge you to reconsider your decision." He took a bite of flatbread. After he had chewed and swallowed it, he changed the subject. "There is a training cruise coming up next week. I shall be gone for two months."

Saavik turned to face him in the darkness. There was no moon, but he could make out her form clearly enough in the starlight, though not her expression. Her voice sounded . . . amused. "I know, my teacher. I shall be on that cruise."

Spock raised an eyebrow. "You rated first in your class?"

He could discern excitement in her voice, despite her careful control. "Yes, I did. They announced the ratings today. As is traditional, I have thus been offered the chance to spend semester break on a Starfleet vessel, accompanying the upperclassmen. It will be my first time to actually serve aboard a vessel."

"I see . . ." Spock said. He found the thought of seeing Saavik every day for weeks to be pleasant, yet unsettling. For a moment he wondered why that thought should occur to him, then dismissed it as illogical. The Vulcan busied himself gathering up his knapsack and taking out his communicator. It was time to contact the transporter tech at Starfleet HQ. "I am sure you will serve well, Saavikam."

"Nothing would please me more, my teacher," she said softly, looking up at the heavens. "To be back among the stars . . ."

"Yes," Spock said. "I know."

Tail swinging lazily back and forth, Rrelthiz stood before the viewport in the giant spacedock, gazing out at the enormous starship that would be her home for the next two months. In design, it was very different from a Carreon vessel. Her people's ships were thick in the middle, tapering towards one end, and on the other, a jutting, sickle-shaped prow. This vessel, the *Enterprise*, had two slender nacelles above a large, central disc that was topped with a small, protruding "bubble."

Hearing footsteps behind her, Rrelthiz hastily raised her tail, then grasped it and secured it to the loop that hung from her belt. If an unwary humanoid were to step on it, it would break off, causing her great pain, and taking many seasons to grow back. Her tail, like the rest of her, was slender, black-skinned, and striped with neon blue.

Carreons were an amphibian race that had only recently applied for membership in the United Federation of Planets. Rrelthiz, like all her species, stood only shoulder-high to the average human. She had a slender body, a lean muzzle, and dexterous clawed fingers. She wore no clothing save a belt around her middle, festooned with little storage pockets, plus her tail-guard loop. Her feet, like her hands, bore seven slender, taloned digits.

A deep, resonant voice came from behind her, speaking in her own language. "Greetings, daughter. Having second thoughts?"

Rrelthiz turned to face her nest-father, the envoy from Carreon. Bbalsho was peering at her anxiously, his lidless blue eyes, the same color as his stripes, darting back and forth between his child and the human-built vessel. "Spending half a season with a crew of aliens . . ." he added. "You will be the first of our people to actually live with other species. It will require a great adjustment."

Rrelthiz drew herself up, refusing to allow her nervousness to show. "Nest-father, this is a wonderful opportunity for one of our people, to be invited to travel aboard a Federation starship as an observer. Captain Spock's crew is diverse—I will be able to meet and speak with Andorians, Tellarites, a Caitan, and a Vulcan cadet, as I understand it. If we are to join the Federation, we need better understanding of the species we will be dealing with, is that not so?"

Bbalsho made a sound halfway between a hiss and a sigh that signaled resignation. "It is so, my daughter. But it will require many . . . adjustments in the way you live. Even enduring discomfort, I fear."

"I am aware of that, and am prepared to endure, nest-father. As a Healer, I am sure I will learn much that will benefit our people on this voyage. And when I return, I shall be able to assist you and the other Carreon diplomats as you work to understand and communicate with these people in our trade negotiations. The knowledge I will gain will surely help us in our application to join the Federation."

Her nest-father's throat sac inflated, and he hummed for a moment, sending the sac pulsing. Rrelthiz knew that this was a sign that he was cogitating, and did not interrupt his thoughts. Finally, Bbalsho spoke again. "Daughter, your observations will indeed benefit our world. Our people have had only limited exposure to other species. Their mental processes and mores are difficult to apprehend. I trust that you will be able to make the adjustment. The environment will be difficult for you."

"They have assured me that I will be able to program my cabin to my own comfort, nest-father. And when I must do my observations, or mingle with the crew, I will be careful to keep my skin supple. I have improved on the emollient I devised before our mission to Earth. The new one will protect our skin for nearly twice as long as the one I originally formulated."

Bbalsho cocked his head at his daughter. "Ah, that indeed is good hearing, Rrelthiz!" He pressed the skin of his own spindly, black-skinned arm, and winced. "I need another application. This dry environment can be . . . damaging."

Rrelthiz reached out, took his hand, then touched the skin above his bony wrist experimentally. "You have been negligent, nest-father. You are in dire need of a refreshing mud soak. As the team's physician, I order you to return to the ship immediately and rest in the mud baths until the evening meal. I shall bring you some of my new emollient. I have added a hormonal supplement and various bio-extracts that greatly increase its effectiveness."

Bbalsho gazed at his daughter appreciatively. "You were always clever, my child. I shall do as you say."

"Good, nest-father. I will beam over to our ship soon, do not worry."

"Very well."

Bbalsho turned and left, tail carefully secured against mishap, his steps slow and dogged. *His skin is tight over his joints,* Rrelthiz realized, with concern. *Tomorrow I shall make sure to give the entire mission staff a last checkup, and to dictate complete notes for my replacement, so she will have my new formula when she arrives from Carreon.*

Moments after Bbalsho left the observation lounge, another figure entered. Rrelthiz recognized the tall humanoid from news-vids, though she had never met him before. She made her species's "greeting to those who are honored" bow. "Captain Spock!"

"Healer Rrelthiz," the Vulcan said, holding up his hand, fingers spread. "Peace and long life. They told me you were here."

"Yes, I wanted to gaze upon the ship," Rrelthiz said, gesturing at the viewport. "Such a famous vessel. It honors me much that I will be permitted to travel aboard a ship prominent in Federation history."

Spock inclined his head. "We will be honored to host you, Healer. I shall be pleased to take you on a personal tour the day we embark."

"That, Captain Spock, would be most gracious. Our people are eager to learn much about your Federation, and the member species. What will be our mission . . . if speak of it you may?"

The Vulcan made a slight dismissive motion. "It is by no means classified, Healer Rrelthiz. We have been assigned to map a section of space that is new to us, but far from the Romulan Neutral Zone, or the Klingon Empire. I am expecting no . . . incidents."

"Shhhhh . . ." Rrelthiz hissed, in appreciation. "There are times when lack of incident is to be appreciated, Captain. My people have a saying, 'Embrace boredom. Soon enough one will yearn for it.' "

Spock raised an eyebrow, and his mouth quirked slightly. *Signs of what? Amusement? Discomfort? Did I say something wrong, or something funny?* Rrelthiz wondered. She was still not astute at reading humanoid facial expression. She expected to be much better at it when she returned from this voyage. "My human cadets would do well to learn the merit of that saying, Healer. Humans seem to seek out excitement and incident . . . often to their detriment."

"I am eager to meet and speak with your cadets, Captain."

"I shall introduce you to the crew during our tour. Such a cultural exchange can be only beneficial."

Rrelthiz gestured her thanks, her motion graceful and formal. "Captain Spock, I have heard of the Vulcan reverence for Infinite Diversity in Infinite Combinations. I thank you, and look forward to our voyage."

"As do I, Healer," the Captain said. "We embark in two days. You will find that you may adjust your cabin controls for your comfort. Also . . . please be prepared to provide our engineer and medical staff with any Carreon nutritional needs, so they can be programmed into the ship's food synthesizers."

"I shall do so, Captain," Rrelthiz said. "Your concern is most gracious."

With a final nod, the Vulcan excused himself and left the lounge. Rrelthiz turned back to gaze at the *Enterprise*, feeling a surge of mingled anticipation and apprehension. Despite her brave words to her nest-father and Spock, she was worried. *What if something goes wrong? The honor of my species will be resting upon me. It is a great responsibility. Am I ready for it? What if I become ill? No one aboard knows anything about treating my kind. What if I make some kind of irreparable social blunder? I could cause a diplomatic incident. . . .*

"Nest-Goddess," she whispered softly, "help me to bring honor to my people. Help me be strong, help me be wise. . . ."

Spock stood on the engineering deck of the *Enterprise*, regarding the gaggle of white-coated Starfleet technicians with a raised eyebrow. "Mr. Rollins, with all due respect, forty-eight hours is not an extensive testing period in which to determine the efficacy of new food synthesizer programming and equipment. Food and water are essential to life support. I question your logic in installing new equipment when we are setting out on an extended training cruise."

The head technician, Rollins, shook his head. "But Captain Spock, this equipment isn't really new. We've just added a few new wrinkles to the existing synthesizers. We've made them more efficient and given them greater variety. Your trainee crew consists of a higher than average percentage of nonhuman cadets. This will be a perfect opportunity for them to enjoy a variety of their own native dishes, instead of having to be content with rations."

Spock fixed the balding human with a skeptical look. "Mr. Rollins, I would prefer to test new equipment during a shorter, shakedown cruise. Not a two-month mapping mission. We will have to rely on the synthesizers for this voyage. . . . We are not going to be carrying a galley crew. Logic dictates that you select another ship to test your 'new wrinkles.' "

"Captain Spock . . ." Rollins hesitated. "Tell you what, let me prove to you that the revamped synthesizers work just as well—as a matter of fact, much better—than the old ones. Eat your evening meal aboard ship tonight, and request the synthesizer to prepare any kind of Vulcan food you'd like. If you're not pleased with the results, we'll put your old synthesizers back before you ship out tomorrow."

Spock hesitated in turn, considering. Finally he nodded. "Very well, Mr. Rollins. I shall do as you suggest."

The Vulcan was busy for the next few hours, overseeing the final preparations for the cruise. His trainees were beaming aboard to spend tonight in their new quarters, and the corridors were filled with bustling, chattering youngsters, excited to be aboard the legendary vessel.

Finally, he finished the last of his preliminary checks and keyed the intercom. A voice responded almost immediately. "Cadet Saavik here."

Spock addressed her in Vulcan, so she would know immediately that this was not an official dialogue. "Good evening, Saavikam. I must test the new food synthesizer equipment tonight, so I wondered . . . are you available to join me for dinner in my cabin?"

"That would be agreeable, my teacher," she responded, immediately.

"At 1900 hours, then? What would you prefer for your meal? You may choose anything you wish, the technicians tell me. Even Vulcan cuisine."

"Really? That will be . . . interesting."

Saavik had been to Vulcan only a few times, but she had professed to enjoy the food when she was there. When Spock had first rescued her, she'd eaten meat, but as soon as she realized that her mentor, and his people, did not, she had adopted Vulcan food ethics. Good Vulcan cuisine was not easy to come by on Earth. Humans tended not to appreciate it.

"I'll have *t'miirq* soup, braised anwoa sprouts on wafer-toast . . . and iced Vulcan fruits. Is that enough of a test?"

"That should be sufficiently challenging, yes. I shall see you then."

During the next two hours, Spock found himself actually anticipating the evening. Lately his and his protégée's schedules had not been conducive to spending much time together. It was . . . refreshing . . . to speak his native tongue with a good listener. He found himself standing before his closet, staring in at the duty uniforms neatly hung there, the dress uniform beside them. And his Vulcan clothing. *Tonight we will eat the food of my homeworld*, he thought, reaching for one of his black robes. *It seems appropriate to dress for the occasion.*

Minutes later, when he heard the door chime, he said immediately, in Vulcan, "Enter."

The door slid open, to reveal Saavik, also clad in Vulcan garb. She wore a dark red tunic and trousers. Her hair was pulled back, but not pinned up. A silvery earring hung from her left earlobe, glimmering faintly in the light of the many candles. The cadet's eyes widened as she took in the traditional table settings and the elegant repast spread before her. Soft music from a Vulcan harpist made a barely heard accompaniment.

"Be welcome to my table," Spock said, formally, seating her.

She glanced up at him, and a faint smile touched her mouth. "The blessings of logic upon this house," she replied. "Thank you for your hospitality, my teacher." They ate, sampling each dish, and, despite his apprehensions, Spock was impressed. "I shall inform Technician Rollins that his new synthesizers are working well," he said. "More braised sprouts?"

"Thank you, I will," she replied, helping herself. "This is as well prepared as that restaurant near the Vulcan consulate in San Francisco."

"Indeed," Spock said. "I must agree." He gazed appreciatively at Saavik, thinking that the informal hairstyle was more esthetically pleasing than pinning her hair up tightly. Her freed tresses softly brushed her shoulders, shining with good health. The curve of her revealed ear was delicate, like the shell of a *veren*. . . .

He realized that he had been staring only when she turned to regard him, her eyebrow going up. "What is it?" she asked. "Is something wrong, my teacher?"

Spock blinked, then looked down at his plate. "Nothing at all, Saavikam," he replied. "I believe it is time to serve the iced fruits."

When she started to get up, he motioned her back. "Please . . . allow me. This was my invitation."

Again that faint smile touched her mouth, and was gone, almost before he could be sure he saw it. "Very well," she said softly.

After the fruits had been served, Spock cast about for a subject, because suddenly the silence seemed almost . . . loud. "Were you aware that we will be hosting a Carreon on this cruise, Saavikam?"

She nodded. "Yes, I met Rrelthiz today. We chatted for a while, and she asked if she could interview me. She's particularly interested in meeting the nonhuman cadets. Her people have been relatively isolated prior to Federation first contact, and she's fascinated by all the different species."

"Did she seem to be settling in well?"

"Yes, I believe so."

Spock nodded, satisfied. "More fruit, Saavikam?"

"This, the formal part of my interview, is concluded," Rrelthiz said. "I thank you, Cadet Saavik, for your cooperation." With a stab of her taloned forefinger, she shut off her recording device. "There! As the humans would speak, 'that is that.' "

Saavik nodded at the alien, thinking that, while the formal part of Rrelthiz's interview might be over, the alien was almost certainly not done asking questions. *Rrelthiz asks a great many questions . . . nearly as many as I ask my teacher,* Saavik realized. *I am fortunate that Mr. Spock has so much patience with questions. . . .* The Starfleet cadet sat cross-legged on a cushion in the *Enterprise's* observation lounge, and Rrelthiz sat beside her. As both interviewer and interviewee relaxed, the Carreon reclined on another cushion. Her oiled skin shone faintly in the dimmed illumination. The huge viewport was filled with slowly moving stars, shining steadily because there was no atmosphere here to make them twinkle. In space one could make out the colors of those stars . . . red, white, yellow, blue-white. . . .

The *Enterprise* was two weeks into her mapping mission, and so far the work had proceeded without incident. Some of the cadets were beginning to chafe at the unvarying routine, and Spock and the other senior crew members had had to quash more than one rowdy party. But their mission was on schedule, which was the important thing.

Rrelthiz stared out the viewport for a long time, then suddenly raised her arm, her taloned digit pointing. "There, I can see it!"

Saavik turned around. "Your home star?"

"Yes, it must be, the little yellow star it is, left of the star the Federation catalogues call Procyon. Shhhh . . ." she sighed. "In my native words, we call her Ailannq . . . the Bright Mother. . . . I miss her, and I miss my world. Humans call this feeling to be sick of home, yes?"

"Homesick," Saavik corrected absently. She squinted, thinking that Carreon vision must be excellent. Finally, by using her peripheral vision, she was able to make it out.

"Friend Saavik, which of all those is your home star?"

The cadet hesitated. "Rrelthiz, I have no home star. I was raised on a world that does not, for all practical purposes, exist now. It was a terrible place. I am glad that it is dead and gone." *Rrelthiz is easy to talk to,* she realized. *I have mentioned Hellguard to perhaps three people in my entire life. . . .* "I watched my home planet die and rejoiced to see it destroyed. In doing so, I regained my honor."

"Honor is an important concept to my people, too," Rrelthiz said. "We believe in honor, and revenge . . . and, when we have committed a wrong, we believe in reparation."

She almost sounds Romulan, Saavik thought.

The little Carreon put out her taloned hand, rested it on Saavik's fingers. Her flesh was cool, almost chilly, and rather damp. "Friend Saavik, sorry indeed I feel to make you speak of such a place. Please accept my apologies."

Saavik shook her head. "It is of no matter, and no apologies are needed, Rrelthiz. I wished to speak of it to you, so I did. Besides . . . Vulcan and Earth have become my home now. I am content."

Saavik realized that was literally true. She was indeed more . . . content . . . than she had been in a long time. It was a pleasure to be able to see her mentor every day, to have him tutor her privately, answer her unending questions, and even to be able to play chess several nights each week. Thinking about playing chess with Spock made her frown slightly. She glanced over at Rrelthiz. "Something . . . odd . . . happened last night."

The little alien gazed at her out of neon-blue eyes. "Odd? What was that, Saavik?"

"I defeated Mr. Spock at chess."

"Is that the first time you have ever done so?"

"No," Saavik said. "But it is the first time I have done so in only ten moves. His game was definitely off. I wonder if he was feeling well."

"Perhaps he should see Doctor Mukaro," Rrelthiz suggested. "I have been in sickbay most days, reviewing material on all of the species who are serving aboard ship, and we have chatted several times. He seems like a good Healer, competent physician, and kind. He tells me this will be his last voyage, that he will be . . . what is the word . . . resigning . . . no, that is not it. . . ."

"Retiring?"

"Yes, that is it. But about Mr. Spock . . . health check, he has had one recently?"

Saavik shook her head. "He tends to avoid them, as do I." *And no wonder,* she thought, *considering Doctor McCoy's penchant for asking personal questions . . . illogical ones.* "Last night I asked him whether he was well, and he said he was . . . and then congratulated me on playing exceptionally well. Except . . . that was not true. I played no better than I do most of the times we play together."

"Perhaps the captain was distracted," Rrelthiz. "Missing his home, his family? Is he mated?"

Saavik shook her head. "He has a mother and father, cousins, but no . . . he has no close family. And no mate."

"How odd," Rrelthiz said. "Unless . . . are you and he old enough to be mated, friend Saavik? Or does sexual maturity among Vulcans come late in life, as it does for some species?"

Spock and I? Mates? The thought shocked her, until Saavik realized that this was just another instance of Rrelthiz innocently mixing up Standard syntax. Universal translators were not foolproof. For some reason her face grew hot, and she spoke with more than a touch of asperity. "Captain Spock is certainly of sufficient maturity to have taken a mate," she said curtly. "As am I, I suppose."

Rrelthiz was studying her in the dimness. "My question . . . it made you uncomfortable? Something offensive, I said? I am sorry—"

"No, you said nothing wrong," Saavik said, studying the toes of her Starfleet-issue boots. "I . . . I do not know why the captain has no mate. I have never asked him." *And why not, when I have asked so many other questions?* she wondered. *Some of them quite personal indeed. Why have we never discussed that subject? Why do I feel that I would rather discuss almost anything else in the universe—including my childhood on Hellguard—than that subject? Most illogical!*

"And you, friend Saavik?"

Saavik was finally able to look at the Carreon. "I have no mate because I was not raised on Vulcan, and thus was not betrothed at a young age, as many Vulcan children are."

"Do you regret that?"

Saavik allowed herself a small smile. "Not at all, friend Rrelthiz. If I ever choose to mate, I shall want to do the choosing myself. Besides . . . my career in Starfleet is of primary importance to me now, and for many years to come." She quickly changed the subject. "Your hand . . . what happened?" she asked, looking down at Rrelthiz's fingers and pointing to a synth-flesh "bandage" that glimmered pale against the alien's black skin.

"Another accident," the Talaerian said. "These days I am subject to clumsiness, I fear. Sliding doors to my quarters yesterday nearly lost me my tail." She smoothed the whiplike appendage gingerly, and Saavik saw it bore a slight kink. "Then this morning I was experimenting with the food synthesizers and foolishly did not realize that requested items came already encased in containers. I was holding a glass beaker in the unit when I activated it. The beaker broke and cut my hand. It is not serious. Just one of a series of small accidents that have plagued me as I attempt to adjust to the different kinds of technology used by your Federation, as well as the higher gravity aboard ship."

Saavik nodded. "I remember the first time Mr. Spock showed me a synthesizer, and I realized I could eat whenever I wished. I made myself quite ill." *And Spock took care of me. . . .* Hastily, she turned her mind away from thoughts of the past. "Friend Rrelthiz . . . have you ever played chess?"

"No, Saavik, but learning is of much value and pleasure. Teach me?"

"Certainly."

"Sir, the duty roster for your signature . . ."

Hearing a note of strain in the Trainee Yeoman's voice, Spock glanced up at the young man. Cadet Goldman was obviously in distress . . . eyes glazed, his jaw working, a sheen of sweat making his face glisten in the bridge lights. "Cadet?" Spock said. "You do not appear well."

Goldman shook his head, obviously struggling to maintain his demeanor. "Captain, I'm sorry . . . I suddenly . . . feel sick . . . as if . . ." He grimaced, then turned away, clapping his hand over his mouth. He staggered toward the bridge doors, but tripped on the step and landed on his knees, vomiting.

The Vulcan slapped the intercom. "Sickbay, Doctor Mukaro to the bridge."

"Captain?" an uncertain young voice responded, "I'm sorry, Sir, the doctor is . . . indisposed. He's sick, Sir."

"Send a med-tech to the bridge immediately, then," Spock said, heading for the retching trainee. He supported the young man as he heaved, and the bridge crew of human cadets milled around, distressed, some gagging softly in sympathy. Only Saavik had the presence of mind to run a tricorder over Goldman. She shook her head. "His temperature is at a dangerous level for a human, Captain," she said. "He needs immediate treatment."

The bridge doors slid open, and the young med-tech rushed in, medical kit in hand. Despite her youth, she was efficient, administering a hypospray, then overseeing Goldman being carried out on a litter. The cadet was moaning, barely conscious, doubled up with cramps.

As soon as Goldman was on his way to sickbay and Spock had summoned the cleaning equipment, he turned to the young med-tech, whose ebony features were tight with anxiety. "Nurse Nbanga, a cadet said that Doctor Mukaro had also been taken ill?"

"Yes, Captain Spock. Sir, his symptoms are identical," she replied.

"Then we must consider that they have been afflicted with the same illness," Spock said. "Please report to me on their status. Notify me if any additional cases occur."

"Aye, Captain."

As the Nurse left the bridge, Spock stood gazing after her, and his dark eyes were troubled.

Over the next six hours, twenty-five more cases turned up, and the rate of illness was increasing. Spock summoned Saavik, whom he'd appointed acting science officer, and Doctor Rrelthiz, who was now the closest thing the ship contained to a certified physician, to Doctor Mukaro's office for a briefing. After Nurse Nbanga had filled them in on the rapid spread of the condition and its severity, the Vulcan reviewed the medical data. "These med-scan readings do not correlate to any known human illness," he said, as he finished the report. "The onset is so sudden, and so violent."

Saavik raised an eyebrow. "A sudden onset. Could we be dealing with a poison, rather than a viral agent? Something introduced into the food or water? We have new synthesizers. Could someone have tampered with them during their installation? Introduced a slow-acting poison? Could this be sabotage?"

Spock shook his head. "That was the first thing I checked. Logic dictated that since Starfleet had just installed new synthesizer equipment, a malfunction—either deliberate or accidental—was a possibility. With that in mind, Chief Engineer Jaansen and I ran complete diagnostics on all of the new equipment as soon as Goldman collapsed. The synthesizers are functioning normally. We checked for any anomalous chemicals and found nothing."

Nbanga nodded. "Captain, I wondered the same thing. If it is a poison, it's not one in the Federation database. My scans detect no alien chemicals in the systems of the victims."

Spock steepled his fingers and his expression was grave. "Let us hypothesize for the moment that we are dealing with a disease, then. Have you been able to isolate any kind of contagion vector?"

"No, Sir. People have been taken ill on different decks, at different times, and, while some of them were in physical proximity to each other, at least two cadets who had been off duty in their quarters, asleep, came down sick. I can't account for the spread, Captain."

"What is Doctor Mukaro's condition?"

"We're doing everything we can, Sir, but it's worsening steadily." She hesitated. "For any kind of severe intestinal disorder, the elderly are at greater risk. Dehydration and exhaustion can prove life-threatening, especially in older people."

"Is the doctor conscious?"

"On and off, Captain, but his fever is so high he's not lucid."

Spock ran his eyes down the roster of those who had been taken sick, and then raised an eyebrow. "All of these people are human," he said. "Not a single nonhuman has been affected."

Nbanga's eyes widened. "That's right! How could I have not realized?"

"Nurse Nbanga, you have been occupied," Spock said, noting the trainee's stricken expression. "Any condition with such a swift onset requires concentrated study. Caring for violently ill people leaves little time for analysis." He turned to Rrelthiz. "Doctor Rrelthiz, can you take over medical testing and analysis for Nurse Nbanga, leaving her free to supervise her medical techs? Cadet Saavik will assist you. If this condition is indeed only contracted by humans, then we shall need to mobilize the nonhuman crew members."

The little alien inclined her head. "Honored I will be to help in any way possible, Captain. This is so distressing! Is it possible the mission should be aborted, so traveling to better facilities will be possible?"

"I will be contacting Starfleet Command," Spock said, and Saavik looked up at the grim note in his voice. "However, Doctor Rrelthiz, Starfleet regulations do not permit us to dock at any Starbase or go into orbit around any Federation world until we have eliminated the possibility of an unknown pathogen."

Rrelthiz waved her slender, taloned hands in distress. "But . . . surely they can send help!"

"Doctor, we are four days' travel from the nearest Starbase." He paused. "We cannot count on outside help to solve this problem. Logic dictates we must spare no effort to find the cause and cure ourselves."

The Vulcan left Saavik and Rrelthiz poring over the readouts in the medical lab, while Nurse Nbanga bustled around, ordering her med-techs to set up pallets on the decks. As he headed for the turbolift, he rounded a corner to see one of the senior crew members, Chief Engineer Jaansen, staggering towards sickbay. Spock managed to catch him before he could fall, then paged sickbay for a medical team.

When he reached the bridge, he found that half the crew there were now nonhumans. Checking in with Nurse Nbanga, she told him that another five cases had been admitted in the past half hour.

Spock looked over at the cadet who was manning the communicator. "Cadet Theron," he ordered, "Contact Starbase 5."

Four hours later, Saavik straightened up, shaking her head. "This is not accomplishing anything. The data are contradictory. Perhaps it would help to interview the victims, try to identify an environmental reason for the onset."

"Agreed," Rrelthiz said, hissing in what Saavik had come to realize was distress. "Some of these readouts . . . something about them . . ." she hissed again. "Something that I cannot put my digits upon! But it is there, dancing in my forebrain."

Saavik understood what the little alien was trying to say. "I know. I'll be back soon," she said, taking her tricorder and heading for the door leading into sickbay.

The door slid aside, and Saavik stepped through it into a nightmare. The deck was crowded with pallets, and the sounds of moaning and retching filled the air. Saavik took an involuntary step back, and it took all the Vulcan discipline she'd learned not to react. Despite the earnest efforts of the med-techs and the cleaning equipment, the deck beneath her feet was damp and the smell . . . Saavik swallowed, breathed through her mouth, and began walking.

"Nurse Nbanga . . ." Saavik said, seeing the young woman's back, as she stood beside one of the diagnostic beds, "I wish to—"

Nbanga swung around, and Saavik stopped in midword. The

nurse's dark features were streaked with tears, and it was clear she was about to break down completely. "What is it?" Saavik asked.

The trainee sobbed, then tried to regain her composure, swiping at her face. "It's . . . it's . . ." she gulped, then gestured at the figure on the bed. As Saavik stepped around her, she straightened her shoulders, then took a deep breath, then pulled the silvery sheet up over Doctor Mukaro's still features.

"He's gone," she said, struggling for control. "He was such a nice man. I tried, but he just went downhill so fast. . . ."

"I am sure you did everything you could, Nurse," Saavik said, searching her memory for the appropriate human phrases.

"I need to tell Captain Spock," Nbanga muttered. "What are we going to do? Six of my med-techs are sick, now. I had to request non-human trainees to fill in for them, and they don't know anything about caring for sick humans. Sickbay is full. We're going to have to start putting them on blankets in the corridor."

Saavik gazed around at the chaos. Only three human med-techs were left. The nonhuman "recruits" stood in the middle of the room, clearly uncomfortable with their new roles. Four burly Tellarites, plus an Andorian and a Vulcan. "Go and speak to the captain," she told Nbanga. "I shall oversee setting up additional pallets, as you suggest."

Nbanga gave her a grateful glance. "Thank you, Saavik. I'll be back in just a few minutes."

Saavik watched her leave, then stood there, summoning her resolve. *If Spock can command Tellarites, so can I. . . .*

She strode over to the group, then beckoned to the human med-techs to join them. The humans were obviously on the verge of exhaustion. Saavik regarded them. "These trainees will be helping you. I am assigning two trainees to each of you. Instruct them in what to do, then supervise them. When you can, get some rest."

"Just a moment," one of the Tellarite females spoke up. "Who put a second-year in charge here? We're upperclass. One of us should be giving the orders, Vulcan."

"I will take charge," the Tellarite male said to the female. "I out-rank you in cadet standing."

"It is not logical to argue," the Vulcan trainee said. "We have our duty."

"Vulcans!" sneered the Andorian. "Why don't you use logic to fig-ure out what's gone wrong here?"

The third Tellarite snorted loudly. "You two have no idea how this should be organized. I, on the other hand . . ."

"*Quiet,*" Saavik said, not loudly, but in a tone that stopped the big alien as though he'd been punched in his snout. "We are going to work together to get through this crisis. The captain has appointed me acting science officer, since Lieutenant Kelly collapsed. That means I am in charge of duty assignments here. You two," she pointed at the first Tellarite and the Andorian, "go with med-tech . . ." she peered at the nametag, "Robinson. You two," she pointed at the Vul-can and the second Tellarite, "go with technician Greentree. And you two," she pointed at the remaining two Tellarites, "will assist technician Yamamoto. Any questions?"

The biggest of the female Tellarites bristled at her and opened her mouth. Saavik carefully didn't look at her. "Good, then. I know Cap-tain Spock will appreciate your willingness to assist. I shall be sure to mention your names when I report to him. Your crewmates need you. Dismissed."

For a second, none of them moved, and Saavik thought it wasn't going to work. Then, slowly, they dispersed, each with their assigned tech. Saavik watched them go, and could hardly believe it. *Tellarites, giving up on an argument? I must have said something right. . . .*

Grabbing her tricorder, she went looking for cadets that were still capable of speaking, determined to find out exactly what each of them had been doing before he or she had fallen ill. As she spoke to cadets, Saavik kept an eye on the work crews and was pleased to see that each of the aliens was working diligently to assist the human med-techs. . . .

*　*　*

An hour and a half hour later, Spock faced the strained young faces across the table in the *Enterprise's* briefing room and knew without asking that there was more bad news. "Nurse Nbanga?"

"Captain, there's been another death, Sir," she said. "Cadet Mikala Martinez. I . . . she . . ." she shook her head and fell silent.

"Understood, Nurse Nbanga," Spock said. "What is the total number of cases now?"

"As of ten minutes ago, we had 158 down sick. Six are in critical condition, Sir," she reported.

"How are you progressing on treating the condition?"

"We've established procedures, and they are helping in some of the cases. The teams Saavik organized have been a big help."

Spock felt a momentary flare of pride. *I knew she had command ability. . . .*

"But Captain Spock, we're running low on medical supplies," she added. "By tomorrow, we'll be out of a lot of things."

The Vulcan glanced over at Rrelthiz. "Where is Cadet Saavik?"

"Unknown, Captain," the Talaerian said. "Her planning was to interview cadets that were capable of speaking, trying to trace behaviors that might—"

The door slid open, and Saavik stood in the doorway, tricorder in hand. Despite her attempt at control, her excitement was plain. "Captain!" she said. "Permission to speak?"

Spock nodded. "What have you found, Cadet?"

"Sir, I believe the food synthesizers have been contaminated by some biological agent," she said. "In each case I interviewed, the one thing they had in common was that they had eaten within the last hour before becoming ill. Reaction times varied from an hour to ten minutes. The synthesizers are functioning normally; yes, at least the equipment is. But whatever has been introduced into them—and, as you noted earlier, Sir, it is not chemical—humans are reacting to it violently."

Spock remembered Technician Rollins assuring him that the new synthesizers would be perfectly safe, and felt a most un-Vulcan-like urge to seek out Rollins when they returned to Earth, then force him to eat some of the contaminated food. *Illogical,* he reprimanded himself. *It is possible that this contagion has nothing to do with the new equipment. Concentrate on the problem at hand. What is my best course? What would James T. Kirk do?*

The answer came immediately. *Jim would see to the safety of the crew, then search for a cure.*

Spock regarded Saavik gravely, then nodded. "Good work, Cadet Saavik." She nodded back at him, her dark eyes shining, and he knew how much his praise had meant to her.

The Vulcan activated the "all ship" on the intercom. "This is the captain speaking," he said. "We have reason to believe the food synthesizers may have become contaminated. No human is to eat or drink anything but stored rations or water until further notice. I repeat . . . consume only emergency rations and water until further notice."

He flipped another switch. "Spock here. Send a team to the emergency rations locker, and instruct them to pass out emergency rations and water in accordance with standard emergency procedure. Alert security to post armed guards over the locker. Instruct all trainees to remain calm. Spock out."

Depressing yet another switch, he said, "Captain Spock here. Who is currently in charge of engineering?"

"Sir, I am," a voice replied. "Cadet Garrul, Sir."

"Cadet Garrul, please report immediately to the briefing room. Spock out."

While they were waiting for the Tellarite cadet to arrive, Spock examined the data Saavik had collected. When he looked up, he said, "Commendable deduction, Cadet Saavik. I find no flaw in your logic. I note that your data indicate that all of the stricken humans had consumed synthesized versions of animal protein." He turned to Nbanga, "Nurse, have you eaten in the past day?"

"Yes, Captain, I have. But, Sir . . . I am a vegetarian. A strict one."

"Ah," Spock said. "That may account for why the Vulcans have remained unaffected. Or it is possible that our contagion is one that only attacks humans. Some Tellarites and Andorians consume animal protein. Doctor Rrelthiz, please concentrate on the proteins in the synthesizer during your next tests."

"I shall, Captain Spock."

The door slid aside, and the Tellarite trotted into the briefing room. "Cadet Garrul reporting, Captain!"

Spock waved him to a seat. "Cadet Garrul, we have reason to believe that the new synthesizers are responsible for the illness that has struck the humans aboard. I will be assigning Cadet Saavik and Doctor Rrelthiz to work with you in an attempt to determine what has caused this—and to eliminate it." He glanced over at Nbanga. "Nurse, have any cases recovered naturally?"

"No, Sir, not one."

"Very well. Cadets, Dr. Rrelthiz . . . the *Enterprise* has sufficient emergency rations and water to last for three days. I have been instructed by Starfleet Command that a rescue ship, manned by nonhuman medical personnel, will be dispatched from Starbase 5 in approximately three hours. We have been ordered to rendezvous with them in two and a half days. In order to reduce the risk of further cases, I hereby order all of the sick trainees, plus all nonessential human trainees, to be placed into stasis. Once in stasis, the progression of their illness will be halted. When we know that their cases have been arrested, we shall turn our attention to finding out what has caused this, and determining a cure."

Spock looked at each of the trainees in turn. "I know I can count on each of you to do your utmost to help your crewmates. Your dedication in this time of crisis will be noted in my official report. Cadet Garrul, please assemble a team of nonhuman engineering trainees to oversee the operation of the stasis units. I want Deck 2 sealed off, the temperature lowered to five degrees Centigrade, and microgravity implemented. We shall use Deck 2 to contain the bodies that have been placed in stasis. The cold will help maintain the hibernation state, and microgravity will permit us to 'layer' the hibernating trainees."

"Aye, Captain Spock."

Spock looked over at Saavik. "Cadet Saavik, prepare a list of nonessential human trainees. Once all of the sick cadets have been placed in stasis, begin with the ones that have not yet been affected."

"Yes, Captain Spock."

Spock looked at his "senior officers" one by one. "Carry on."

"Captain, there is a communication coming in from Starbase 5," the Andorian at the communications console said.

"Onscreen, Trainee Thiril."

"Yes, Sir."

Spock looked up to see Commander Tregarth on his viewscreen. "Captain Spock, the Starfleet medical vessel *Lancet* departed Starbase 5 twenty minutes ago. Are you under way?"

"Yes, Commander. We have had one more death, bringing total casualties to three. I have ordered most of my crew placed into hibernation, to arrest the progress of the condition and prevent more cases from occurring. We are running with a skeleton crew of mostly nonhumans, but so far we are proceeding on schedule."

"Good, Captain. Any idea what caused this outbreak?"

Spock quickly summarized their theory. "I have Doctor Rrelthiz and my acting science officer working to find out what has happened to the new synthesizers to cause this," he concluded. "So far, only the humans have been affected. Sending a nonhuman crew aboard the medical vessel was definitely indicated."

Tregarth hesitated, then grinned a bit sheepishly. "Well, it's not *entirely* a nonhuman crew, Captain Spock. There was one senior Starfleet medical officer who pulled rank and is aboard the *Lancet*, having come equipped with his own environmental suit and supplies of food and water."

Spock raised an eyebrow. "I do not even need to invoke logic to determine the officer's identity, Commander," he said. "How is Doctor McCoy?"

Tregarth grinned. "As cranky as ever, Captain. You'd better brace yourself for a tirade when you rendezvous with the *Lancet*."

"Of that, I have no doubt, Commander. Spock out."

The Vulcan rose from the captain's seat, turned the conn over to the senior trainee, then went below decks to check on the progress. "Stasis implementation is on schedule, Captain," Garrul reported. Spock activated one of the vid-pickups in the area he had designated, and saw the bodies of the trainees floating motionless. The lighting was dim, and the entire area had an eerie resemblance to a morgue. Spock shut off the picture. "Proceed, Cadet Garrul."

His next stop was the life-support area of engineering, where he found Saavik and Rrelthiz working over the diagnostic readouts for the food synthesizer. The Vulcan picked up a padd and set to work to help them analyze the data down to the most minute level.

The three nonhumans had been working for several hours when Saavik spoke up. "Captain Spock . . . look at this, please."

Spock put down his padd and came over to the station to gaze at the readouts the cadet had called up. One of the screens bore a strange genetic code, like nothing he'd ever seen before. "A protein-bonded code," he said. "Most unusual. I have never—"

"Where did that come from?" Rrelthiz broke in. Her tail slid free from its anchorage and began lashing violently, like an angry *le-matya*'s. "Friend Saavik, where did you find that?"

"You recognize that code, Doctor?" Spock said.

"Yes, recognize it I do . . . most unfortunately, Captain. Mutated Carreon DNA, combined in a most unusual way with proteins from your Federation synthesizers. We call it . . . a virbac organism. Not virus. Not bacteria. Something . . . in the middle. And this one . . . it is different. I have never seen its like before."

Spock looked over at Rrelthiz, who was visibly trembling as she stood there, tail whipping back and forth. "How could Carreon genetic material get into our new synthesizers?"

"Rrelthiz . . . your hand," Saavik said softly. "That day the beaker broke . . ."

The Carreon wrung her slender black digits and let out a sound somewhere between a wail of anguish and a hiss. There was such agony in her cry, such distress, that Spock moved towards her, his hand out. She skittered back, away from him, and began to speak, her Standard even more fractured than usual. "Sorry! So sorry, I am, terrible, my fault . . . cut my hand that day . . . the synthesizer activated . . . blood splashing, pushed the cancel . . . the synthesizer reassimilated the material . . . my blood . . . splashed everywhere . . . mixing with emollient, hormonally based, bio-extracts . . . combining with animal-based proteins. . . ."

Spock realized what she meant, despite her garbled words. "Doctor Rrelthiz . . . you are saying that when you programmed the synthesizer to produce your special skin emollient, you cut your hand on a beaker, and it bled? And then, when you pushed cancel, the synthesized material was reabsorbed back into the new systems . . . along with some of your blood?"

"Yes!" she hissed. "Fine Healer am I, betrayer of my oath! My blood caused this! I am to blame for all that has happened!" The little alien was hysterical with grief and guilt.

"Doctor Rrelthiz, there is no way you could have known," Spock said. "Do not blame yourself. This was an accident."

"The nutrients in the emollient must have somehow combined with the living cells, then over a period of a day or so, they mutated," Saavik said. "Rrelthiz, Spock is correct. Nobody could have predicted this."

"Three humans dead . . . my fault . . ." Rrelthiz was not listening. "I am responsible. And to think I was concerned for the possibility of my own illness. I have broken the Healer's most important rule—I have caused death, and terrible harm."

Quite suddenly, she stopped trembling, and her tail ceased its thrashing. "I am responsible. I must make reparation."

And then, with a swift, scuttling motion, she skittered past them and was out the door.

Saavik stared after her, and Spock saw her features twist in distress. "No!"

"What is it, Saavik?"

She shook her head, her eyes wide and frightened. Spock moved over until he was beside her. "Saavik . . . let me help. What is it?" Concerned, he put his hand on her shoulder.

Spock had touched Saavik only a few times during their association. Vulcan telepathy usually required physical contact, so his people tended to be wary of touching others—especially other telepaths. As his fingers rested against her shoulder, Spock was conscious of how easy it would be to do a true mindlink—even a bonding—with Saavik. He could feel the warmth of her skin beneath the fabric of her uniform.

Hastily, Spock lifted his hand, wondering whether Saavik had shared that moment of sudden physical and mental intimacy.

But she was too concerned about her friend to notice her mentor's reaction. "I must go after her," she whispered. "Carreon notions of honor are similar to Romulan ones. Rrelthiz sees only one path to her honor . . . but . . ." she swallowed, and suddenly looked very young, "but what if I fail? What if I say the wrong thing?"

Spock gazed at her, forcing control . . . and succeeding. "Saavikam, you are more than you know," he said, holding her eyes with his own. "You will not fail. You have learned a great deal on this voyage. You will say the right things, I know you will. Now . . . go."

Whatever Saavik saw in his eyes made her straighten her shoulders in determination. She gave him a faint, grateful smile. "Thank you, my teacher."

Then she was gone, out the door, and there was only the sound of her boots, running. . . .

Spock sat down in the seat he'd abandoned, his mind filled with that final image of Saavik . . . brave, determined . . . and grown up. *No longer a child. A female grown . . . of marriageable age . . . strong and intelligent . . . and beautiful . . .*

He stared at the doorway, and it was an effort to regain his equanimity. . . .

*   *   *

Saavik ran down the corridor, her heart pounding, forcing herself to think logically. *Where will she go to say good-bye to life, to make her "reparation?"* she wondered.

And then she knew . . .

The observation lounge appeared deserted, which was hardly surprising, given the circumstances. At first Saavik thought she'd been wrong in her deduction. But then she caught a faint shimmer of neon blue in the dimness.

She slipped into the lounge. "Rrelthiz," she said, quietly.

The little alien was crouching before the viewport, and there was something formal, ceremonial about her posture. Placed before her, on the carpet, was a long, slender object. It resembled a thin tube with a sharp, pointed end. In the starlight, it glittered silver and deadly.

"Friend Saavik," the Carreon said. "Please . . . go away. Respect me, and my customs."

Saavik drew a deep breath. "Rrelthiz, you cannot do this. I am your friend, and I will not allow you to make reparation for something that is not your fault."

"It is my fault. No denying that, friend Saavik. My blood, my fault."

"Rrelthiz, it was an accident. You intended no harm."

The Carreon reached out, picked up the weapon. "Reparations must be made. Honor ritual demands."

"Rrelthiz, *listen to me*," Saavik said, tightly. "I was raised Romulan. That world I told you about, the one I watched be destroyed, while I rejoiced? It was a Romulan colony. I was raised Romulan, on Hellguard. Then, later, they abandoned us, as a failed experiment. We had nothing, not food, not shelter. I killed my own kind in squabbles over a bit of food. I even . . ." she swallowed, her gorge rising at the memory, "I even *ate* my own kind, once, when it was that or starve. I killed . . . but . . ." she had to stop a moment, fighting for control. She could feel tears threaten at the memory, and forced them back, forced herself to stillness. "I have never spoken of this to a living soul, not even to my teacher. Are you listening, Rrelthiz?"

The little alien turned her head, the silver killing implement gleaming faintly amidst her dark, taloned digits. "Listening . . . yes, friend Saavik. But you should not—"

"Spock found me on Hellguard. I was more animal than anything, Rrelthiz, but I have since learned different ways. If I could learn, you can, too. Rrelthiz, your 'solution' will harm us all. We require your help. If you make your traditional reparation, you will hurt the trainees who are ill . . . because, logically, you are the one most capable of helping us to isolate a vaccine, or an antidote . . . some kind of cure for the poison."

Rrelthiz sat still, and Saavik plunged on. "Here in the Federation, we work together to solve problems. We don't leave our friends behind to struggle without us. We don't abandon people who need us in an empty pursuit of ritual 'honor.' Rrelthiz, my friend . . . we *need* you."

"You need me," Rrelthiz repeated, no inflection in her voice.

Her slender talons turned the ceremonial weapon over and over, and Saavik watched it, hardly daring to breathe. *What more can I say? What can I do? Should I try to restrain her?* But her respect for Rrelthiz's rights as a free, sentient being would preclude that. This was the Carreon's decision to make. . . .

"Friend Saavik . . . you do not blame me for this?" Rrelthiz asked, at last. "I am told that Vulcans cannot lie."

"I am only half Vulcan," Saavik reminded her. "But I am telling you the truth. I do not blame you. Nobody will. What happened . . . happened by chance. An unfortunate set of circumstances combining at the wrong time. Logically, you are not to blame, since there was no volition on your part. Rrelthiz, we need you. That, also, is the truth."

The weapon stilled in the slender talons. Saavik froze, bracing herself to see the Carreon die. Then, slowly, carefully, Rrelthiz laid the weapon down. "Very well, friend Saavik. If I am needed . . . let us go back to the lab. We have work to do."

* * *

"Captain Spock, we're being hailed by the *Lancet*, Sir. We'll be in visual range in five minutes."

"Onscreen, Trainee."

The *Enterprise*'s viewscreen filled with familiar, craggy features. "Spock! What's this I hear about you playing doctor and finding a cure for this bug?"

Spock raised an eyebrow. "Doctor McCoy. What a pleasant surprise."

"Don't give me that innocent look—" McCoy broke off, grinning. "You found the cure? I guess all that Vulcan logic is good for something . . . occasionally."

"It was a group effort, Doctor," Spock said. "Doctor Rrelthiz, Cadet Saavik, and myself. I am having the formula transmitted to your ship, and ask your help in preparing sufficient quantities to treat my crew."

"I'll inform Captain Therenn," McCoy said. "It's good to see you, Spock, even under these circumstances."

Spock nodded. "Agreed, Doctor. It is good to see you, too."

After the transmission had been broken, Spock looked over at the science station, where Saavik was busily putting the finishing touches on the formula for the cure before transmitting it. He'd succeeded in regaining his former demeanor with his protégée, but the Vulcan could not, try as he might, forget that moment in engineering. *She is still so young,* he thought. *Saavik is barely beginning her career. She will not be ready to think about taking a bondmate for a long time . . . perhaps years. . . .*

The Vulcan leaned back in the captain's seat and let out his breath, allowing himself to relax for the first time since this crisis had begun. *Patience,* he counseled himself. *Only time will tell what will happen. . . .*

He closed his eyes. . . .

"Captain . . ." came a familiar voice, close to him.

Spock sat up straight and regarded the trainee. "Yes, Cadet Saavik?"

"Sir, I want you to know that during the past few days, I've been thinking about what you said . . . and I've decided to switch over to command training, as well as science. I will lose a year, having to catch up, but I think I understand what you were trying to tell me before. I can command, Sir. I have learned to work with aliens, as well as humans."

Spock raised an eyebrow at her. "Really, Saavikam," he said, quietly, speaking in Vulcan, but allowing a glint of humor to surface. "And what about the *Kobayashi Maru* test?"

Saavik returned the glint and raised her own eyebrow back at her mentor. "I am not concerned, my teacher. After all . . . how could the *Kobayashi Maru* be any worse than the past week? I endured that . . . I can endure the *Kobayashi Maru*. I have learned . . . much."

Spock looked at her, and his voice was very soft, very serious. "Indeed, Saavikam . . ." he said quietly. "We have both learned . . . much . . . on this voyage."

Captain John Harriman
U.S.S. Enterprise-B

" . . . a starship captain is not manufactured — he, or she, is born from inside — from the character of the individual. . . ."

Sirna Kolrami, *Star Trek: The Next Generation*

PETER DAVID

The self-proclaimed "writer of stuff" has the distinction of being the only author who has written original material to feature John Harriman, the seemingly hapless captain of the *Enterprise*-B. As introduced in *Star Trek Generations*, Harriman appeared unable to handle the stress of an emergency during a short cruise for the new starship. He was clearly in over his head which seemed designed to show the different shades of being a starship captain, with Harriman looking the poorer compared to either Kirk or Picard.

David rehabilitated Harriman in *The Captain's Daughter* and returns to continue burnishing the captain's legacy. After all, he is a captain of the *Enterprise*, and they are, as a class, a cut above the rest of Starfleet's finest. Additionally, David takes a look at the Romulan mind, a race he has not used much in his countless novels scattered throughout the *Star Trek* universe.

In addition, David created the *Star Trek New Frontier* series of novels, which have been well received and will be back in the fall of 2000 with the first *New Frontier* trilogy.

When not writing *Star Trek*, Peter writes a weekly column in *The Comics Buyer's Guide*, plus the monthly adventures of *Captain Marvel* (Marvel), *Soulsearcher and Company* (Claypool), *Spyboy* (Dark Horse), *Supergirl*, and *Young Justice* (DC Comics). He somehow also finds time to write other novels and has written the occasional screenplay for films and television.

An avid New York Mets fan, David resides on Long Island.

Shakedown

Rokan the Relentless, the greatest questioner in all of the Tal Shiar, was not a morning person.

That was why the renowned Romulan examiner—he who had broken the will of Zeblon the Formidable of Tellar, he who had reduced Gul Shenob, Cardassian strongman and slaughterer of billions, to tears—that was why Rokan left standing instructions never to be rousted from bed before at least 1100 hours. No exceptions, no two ways, nothing to be discussed. Rokan despised the sensation of blinking sleep from his eyes, or having to make some sort of coherent sense before at least two cups of steaming *glakh* had been poured down his throat.

Having demands made of him first thing in the morning . . . well, it simply did not suit his style. And to Rokan, style was a very important consideration. Rokan did not ask for much from the Romulan government to which he gave so much, but this, this was one of his few immutable laws: leave him alone in the morning.

Which was why he was so incensed when he found himself being rousted from a sound sleep at a time which he knew, instinctively, was far too early to have demands put upon him.

"Rokan," came a low voice again, practically in his ear. "Rokan, we have need of you."

Rokan blinked several times, trying to focus on the soon-to-be-dead man looking down at him. He knew the little bastard instantly; his name was Berza, and he was third or fourth in command on the praetor's vessel *Talon*. "Rokan?" said Berza, squinting, trying to determine whether or not Rokan was actually awake.

"I hear you," Rokan said, making no effort to hide his displeasure. "You know my strict instructions."

"It is not up to me," Berza said. "The orders came from above."

"Orders. What orders?" Rokan hauled himself to sitting, rubbing the vestiges of sleep from his eyes.

"We have a new prisoner. My superiors desire that you begin working on him immediately."

Rokan considered it a moment. "When was this prisoner taken?"

"A short while ago."

"Species?"

"Human. A Starfleet captain."

"Ah." Rokan stroked his chin thoughtfully. "And it is your desire that I question him about Starfleet's plans for the outer rim invasion."

"Yes, Sir."

"Very well." He thought a bit more and then, in a conspiratorial voice, he said, "I have need of your assistance, Berza."

Berza was clearly flattered to be a part of the Great Man's plans. "Whatever I can do to serve, Rokan. I have long desired to aid an examiner in his great mission. Tell me what to do, and I shall be your servant."

"Very well. Here it is, then: bring the human to an examining room."

"He is already there."

"Excellent. Then turn off all the lights . . . and leave him there."

"In the darkness?"

"Yes," affirmed Rokan. "He is to remain there, with no effort made at communication, for the next . . ." He checked his chronometer. "Four hours. During that time, you see, the dread of what is to happen to him will build, greater and greater, in his head. It will escalate to such heights that by the time the true examination begins, his imagination will have weakened his will tremendously, and our task will be that much easier."

"Brilliant," breathed Berza.

"Do not," Rokan said with much gravity in his tone, "let me down, Berza."

"I will not, Rokan," Berza assured him. He turned on his heel and walked out.

Rokan settled back onto his pillow and, with a smile of contentment, went back to sleep.

His first view of Captain John Harriman was somewhat less than impressive.

Rokan naturally made sure that the lights in the room came up full, hard and abruptly, giving Harriman no time to shield his eyes. The result was exactly what he expected; Harriman blinked furiously against the incandescence in his face. He would undoubtedly have raised his arm reflexively to block the light out, but his hands were tied securely to the armrests. So he had no choice but to slam his eyelids shut in pain and then open them slowly, by measures. He squinted at Rokan and frowned.

Rokan was aware that he should not underestimate this Harriman, particularly since he himself wasn't especially threatening at first sight. He was middle-aged, which was an impressive enough feat for a Romulan. His people had a fearsomely high mortality rate, with the primary cause of death being the traditional dagger in the back. His hair was thinning on the top, graying on the sides, and his eyebrows were thick and dark. His most telling feature was his eyes, which could harden to a flinty grayness when he was truly angry. At the moment, though, they were cool and placid. Even friendly. It always helped to give a subject the impression that somehow he was going to be on the subject's side. A ludicrous notion, of course, but those in dire straits were always eager for the slightest hint of alliance, from anyone.

Harriman had a pale complexion, a long, narrow face, and thick brown hair. He looked young and nervous, but to his credit he made an effort to cover it when his vision focused on Rokan. Rokan held no notes. There was no need for it. He had gone over Harriman's file before setting foot in the room and had memorized it instantly. It was one of his more minor, but useful, talents.

"So," he said calmly, "you are my latest client."

"Client?" Harriman looked at him uncomprehendingly. But then he smiled grimly. "Is that the Romulan term for 'prisoner' these days?"

"Not the Romulan term. Just mine." There was a chair directly opposite Harriman, and Rokan sat in it. He looked very much at home. "Besides, I do not think of you as a prisoner. I think of you as a resource."

"A resource that you keep locked up in a chair," said Harriman sarcastically.

"What can I say? I value my resources." He leaned forward and smiled. "Do you know why you are here?"

"I know why you're here."

There was feistiness in him. Rokan approved. Lately the only ones whom he had had the opportunity to examine had been other Romulans, suspected of treachery or in some other way acting in opposition to the interests of the government. And when they saw him, they tended to crack almost immediately, since they were familiar with his reputation. The human, however, did not know him. That meant that he could maintain his bravado for a time longer and provide a bit more of a challenge to Rokan.

"Do you? And why don't you tell me why I'm here?"

He expected that the human would not reply. That would be a nonsensical tactic, of course. Rokan knew perfectly well what he and the *Talon* were doing out there. The human could not possibly have any information that he, Rokan, did not have. But the pathetic human would undoubtedly view whatever meager information he did possess as some sort of strength, or bargaining point. He would not simply spout off, but instead try to play a game of dueling knowledge.

So Rokan was rather surprised when Harriman said immediately, "You're on your way to a Romulan incursion."

"Are we?" His eyebrows lifted, all innocence.

"Yes. Your people have made a series of strikes against several outer rim colonies," Harriman told him. "And your intelligence forces have told you that Starfleet is sending a number of ships as part of a counteroffensive."

Rokan's surprise dissipated. He even felt a twinge of admiration for the captain. The ploy was obvious: he was trying to get Rokan to confirm or deny, by even the most minute of changes in expression, his suppositions. The attacks on the outer rim colonies were something that, naturally enough, Starfleet was aware of. But his guesses about Romulan intelligence reports were simply that: guesses. Still, Rokan liked his spunk.

"Have they told us that?" Rokan inquired.

Harriman nodded. "And your people are desperate to know our plans, ship movements, and the like."

"But that hasn't explained why this vessel was going, under cover of cloak," pointed out Rokan.

With a shrug, as if sharing common knowledge, Harriman said, "Your kind always moves under cloak since you are, at heart, cowards, and wish to go about your business unobserved."

If the words were intended to get a rise out of Rokan, they did not succeed. He didn't respond to the obvious bait.

"Obviously," continued Harriman, "you're an interrogator of some sort. You're probably being transported to the outer rim to pump prisoners there for information. I'm merely a side trip."

"Oh, don't think so little of yourself, Captain," Rokan said in a faintly scolding voice. "With your capture, you have suddenly become the focus of this outing. You are, after all, a starship captain. . . ."

"And as a starship captain, you well know, I've been trained to resist all forms of interrogations and probes. You'll find nothing out from me."

"Oh, I doubt that," Rokan said softly. He rose from the chair and began to circle Harriman. "For one thing, you are a most unusual starship captain. John Harriman, CO of the starship *Enterprise.* A vessel name with a long and illustrious history . . . until you came along, that is. This is actually somewhat opportune for me. You can explain a name I've heard in reference to your vessel: *The Flying Dutchman.* Why would it be called that, I wonder."

Harriman's lips thinned. He made no reply.

"My, you've grown silent so quickly, Captain. Does it have something to do with your vessel's alternative name . . . the Death Ship? After all, the great James T. Kirk survived all manners of threats, including several at our hands. The man seemed unkillable . . . until he was on a ship five minutes with you."

"I've made my peace with that," Harriman told him flatly. "I did enough soul-searching, enough mental flogging, on that score already. You can't get to me that way."

"I'm not trying to 'get to you,' Captain. We're simply chatting, that is all. Chatting about your predecessor . . . although you certainly did put the 'decease' in 'predecessor,' didn't you?" Rokan laughed softly at that. "And then there's your command itself. It helped that your father is a powerful admiral. John Harriman, Senior . . . 'Blackjack' Harriman, they call him. Quite the legend, isn't he?"

"I don't have to defend my command, or my position in Starfleet, to you," Harriman said. He didn't seem the least bit rattled. Good. Rokan didn't want it to be too easy.

"No, you don't. You most certainly do not. Still . . . you do have a lot to live up to, don't you?" He sighed, shook his head. "The legendary Captain Kirk. The legendary Blackjack Harriman. The compulsion to be legendary must be rather overwhelming. Tell me,

Captain . . . is that why you took command of the landing party that brought you here?"

"We received a distress signal," said Harriman. "A vessel was in trouble. A type of freighter that I had served aboard in my youth. I was the best qualified to lead the landing party."

It was exactly the response that Rokan was hoping for. Harriman was already feeling a knee-jerk compulsion to defend himself and his decisions to Rokan. That could only benefit Rokan in the long term.

"Indeed. And how were you to know that it was a dummy ship, eh? That the trap would snap shut and you would be captured. Aren't you curious as to the fate of the rest of your landing party?"

"I'm assuming that either they got away or you killed them."

"You seem rather sanguine about it."

Harriman said nothing.

Rokan was having trouble getting a fix on Harriman. He spoke when there was no reason to do so, and he closed his mouth equally arbitrarily. "Perhaps you do not wish to let on that you are concerned. You feel that any such worries may be used against you."

"Harriman, John. Rank, Captain. Serial number 38324–27JO9."

"Ah." Rokan was amused at that. "Suddenly you fall back upon your name, rank, and serial number."

"Look, I'm not going to tell you anything," Harriman said, "so if that's your plan, you might as well drop it right now."

"Perhaps I don't desire to learn anything. Perhaps we intend to use you for a hostage exchange."

"Starfleet does not bargain with terrorists."

"I tend to think you're wrong about that. We'll find out. In the meantime . . ." and he smiled and sat down once more. "Let's talk."

"We've been talking."

"Yes, but I thought we'd best narrow the field of conversation a bit. That we should speak specifically of troop movements and such. You see, Captain, you were correct: my associates and I are indeed most interested in whatever Starfleet might have in mind in regards to the outer rim worlds."

"That," Harriman replied, full of confidence as if he were pleased that the conversation had taken the turn that it had, "is none of your concern."

"Nor are the rim worlds your concern," replied Rokan. "We know that the worlds were colonized specifically to serve as spy bases against the Romulan Empire."

"Nonsense. They're just colony worlds, that's all."

"Colony worlds that just so happen to sit on the border of the Neutral Zone. Captain," and Rokan shook his head sadly, as if scolding a child, "we are not stupid. We know how the Federation operates. We know of your spy missions. Or do you think we've forgotten how the great Captain Kirk himself was responsible for stealing the secrets of our cloaking device years ago? He came in the night, absconded with the technology, and his first officer kidnapped one of our officers."

"It wasn't like that," said Harriman. "That incident . . ."

"That incident was precisely as I described it," retorted Rokan. "If you believe otherwise, you are a fool. But I suspect you know the truth, and are merely a liar."

"And you would be the one honest Romulan in the Romulan Empire?" Harriman asked sarcastically.

Rokan smiled. "I? I never lie. I have far too much style for that."

"Style." Harriman snorted. "Is that what torturers are noted for?"

"A torturer?" Rokan looked stricken. "You wrong me, Captain, deeply. I am not a torturer. I simply ask questions. My little questions are designed to encourage you to answer."

"And if they don't do the job," replied Harriman, "then you haul in assorted torture devices, or pump me full of drugs, or do whatever it takes to get me to 'cooperate.' "

Rokan began to circle once more. "Is that what you want, Captain? Torture devices? Drugs? Perhaps the fact is that you want to cooperate. You know that you do not have the strength of character to resist even the most mild of challenges. Oh, but if you are subjected to drugs or 'devices,' then you can toss aside any concern over personal responsibility. You can tell yourself that there was nothing you can do. And won't that be simpler, less of a problem? Wouldn't you like that?"

"You don't know anything that I would and would not like," shot back Harriman. Then, as if realizing that he sounded a bit more plaintive than he should have, he drew himself up and said, "Harriman, John. Rank, Captain. Serial number 38324-27JO9."

"Very impressive," said Rokan, unimpressed. "Do you have problems with personal responsibility, Captain?"

"I have problems with being tied to a chair. If you'd care to do something about that, that would be fine."

"Very well. Let us discuss the seemingly infinite human capacity for self-delusion. In your case, that would refer to your claims that you have 'made peace' with the loss of Captain Kirk. Or your concerns that you were given command purely because of your powerful father. And then there was the disgraceful incident where you killed one of your own crew women—one Demora Sulu—even though she was naked and unarmed. That was certainly one of the high points of your stellar career."

"You seem to know a great deal about my stellar career," Harriman said. "That being the case, you'd know that Demora Sulu was actually unharmed. That what I killed was a berserk clone of her. One should not always take things at face value, Rokan. They are not always what they appear to be."

"Oh, I have always believed that. Just as I do not take your protests of your self-satisfaction to be anything other than that: mere protests. When I look at you, Captain, do you know what I see?"

"No. Nor do I care."

Rokan advanced on him, brought his face right up close. "What I see," continued Rokan, "is a weak . . . pathetic . . . posturing . . . uncertain little fool who is completely out of his depth. Who knows that he has no business in command of a starship. Who is desperately trying to prove himself to his crew, his father, himself, and continues to fail over and over again. A man who, from the moment he allowed his vessel to be taken out of dry dock before it was fully prepared to go, has been on a constant treadmill of futility. Running and running after something approaching self-esteem, and never coming close to catching up."

"Harriman, John. Rank, captain. Serial num—"

"—ber 38324–27J09," Rokan completed for him. "You live your life in fear, Captain. Terrified that you're going to be found out. That the depth of your uncertainty, your confusion, your inadequacy is going to be brought to the forefront. Frightened that you are going to wind up letting yourself and Starfleet down at a point where the stakes are so high, they will never recover. Tell me, Captain: did your main qualification for taking charge of the landing party consist of the fact that you don't particularly care whether you live or die? What harm is there in taking the point, after all, if your own safety is irrelevant to you?"

Harriman's voice was low and husky. "You think you know me. You know nothing about me. I know you, though."

"Do you." Rokan was amused. "And what do you know? Of me?"

"You're not young, for starters," Harriman said. "Maybe that's why you hate me so much. Because I remind you of young upstarts coming in behind you."

"I don't hate you. I do not care about you one way or the other."

But Harriman didn't seem to care what Rokan had just said. "Look at you. Hair gray, reflexes not what they once were. You don't see that many old Romulans around. The reason for that is obvious: young men like me, pushing you aside, determined to show everyone that they can do the job better than you can. And who knows, maybe they can."

"I am the praetor's finest examiner," Rokan said with a hint of pride. "He has every confidence in me to break even the strongest, most stubborn of minds . . . which yours, I should point out, most definitely is not."

"That's what he tells you, and that's what you may think. But there are always others who think they can do better. Others who feel that you're antiquated, your methods slow and dull. Young men who display a singular lack of the 'style' you consider so important. They don't care about style. They don't care about posturing. They care simply about getting the job done. Where you do the job with a rapier, they'll simply come in with an ax and hack away until they get what they want. And they do the job quickly, efficiently, and brutally, but it's done nevertheless. And it angers you because you see that as crude and unappealing, but you're also afraid of them because you know that they are the wave of the future."

"What you describe will never be the way of the Romulan examiner," Rokan snapped. "That is simply nonsense."

"You're old, Rokan. Old and weak, and we both know it." There was a look of insufferable smugness on Harriman's face. "And the others know it, too. You practice an unforgiving art, Rokan, in an unforgiving society. And that rapier you wield isn't going to mean much when you get the ax squarely in your back, now, is it."

Rokan smiled thinly, displaying his gleaming teeth. "Is that the best you can do, Captain? Do you truly think that you can undercut my confidence, lay me low, with such pathetic thrusts? Distressing, Captain, most distressing. I had hoped for better from Starfleet than that."

"That's the difference between us, I suppose," Harriman replied. "I had no particular hope for a Romulan examiner. An insufferable pig who fancies himself an artist of analyzing his 'victim.' That's what I expected, and that's what I got. That's the most laughable thing of all. Even the young ones who follow you . . . they're going to be no different. Not really."

"You're wrong," Rokan said, and then wished he hadn't spoken. He said nothing further immediately, realizing that speaking out of turn was unwise. The fact that he had nearly done so was a bit surprising to him. It was not the sort of slip he generally made. *Getting old and foolish* came to his mind, and then he immediately pushed it away. That was not a path down which he wanted to walk.

"Am I? Am I wrong?"

Rokan forced a smile, and hoped it didn't look as forced as it actually was. "You're endeavoring to play my own game, Captain. You should not make such efforts, for I am afraid that you're not especially good at it."

"You're afraid. I'll give you that much."

The taunt had no effect on him. This time, his mental defenses more solidly in place, he was able to brush aside the jape and see it as no more than exactly what it was: a juvenile attempt at throwing him off his game.

But Harriman hadn't stopped talking. "Every time you take on a new assignment, it increases the stakes for you. Because sooner or later, you're going to fail. And when you do fail, then those who are waiting behind you are going to exploit that failure for all it's worth. So when you start on each new victim, there's a stink of fear hanging on you. I can smell it from here."

"Can you?" Suddenly Harriman seemed far less amusing than he had before. "And are you quite certain it's not your own fear you're smelling? The stench of your bravado as it rots within you?"

Harriman smiled widely then, and there was not the slightest fear on his face as he said, "Harriman, John. Rank, captain. Serial number 38324-27J09."

Rokan did not like the way this conversation was going. Harriman was wrong, dead wrong, as far as Rokan was concerned. He did not worry about the young fools who would have killed to enjoy his rank and privileges. They were of no consequence. And yes, he was getting older, but age had done nothing to diminish his skills. Despite all of Harriman's pathetic insinuations to the contrary, Rokan was in control.

It was about time that he took that control in a more indisputable fashion.

Which was precisely what he did.

The conversation they had had up until that point amounted to little more than a preliminary bout compared to what followed.

Despite the fact that he had not had all that much time to study it, Rokan's knowledge of Harriman's record bordered on encyclopedic.

He used that knowledge, combined with his observations and suppositions about Harriman's psyche, to begin the session in earnest.

He poked, he prodded, he sliced and diced. As minutes rolled into hour and hours piled upon themselves, Rokan proceeded to ask Harriman about everything . . . except what he truly wanted to know about. He inquired about Harriman's childhood, about his education, his relationships with his parents, the most treasured keepsake from his childhood, the first time he had taken a test in Starfleet Academy, the first time he had loved a woman, the first friend he had ever lost. On and on, a detailed and unyielding investigation of one life. Not a single question had anything to do with troop movements or the schedules under which Starfleet vessels might be operating.

Sometimes Harriman replied. Sometimes he said nothing. Most times he fell back upon name, rank, and serial number. Perversely, those were the responses that Rokan treasured the most. When Harriman was silent, it meant that he was thinking about what was said. Rokan didn't want Harriman thinking; he wanted him compliant, obedient. When Harriman tried to reply in some way, it meant that he was rallying and trying to put up some sort of defense. It was only when Harriman fell back on the rote answer—name, rank, serial number—that Rokan knew that Harriman simply had no idea what to do. At those times Harriman didn't think, couldn't think, and sought refuge in the mundane and predictable.

Rokan also knew that he was blessed with far greater stamina than Harriman. Even an aged Romulan (Aged! Ridiculous. He hadn't lost a step in the passing years; he was all that he ever was!) was still more durable, in better condition, than a young Terran, even under the best of conditions. And these were certainly not conditions that favored Harriman. The evidence of the stress became more pronounced with each passing hour. For a time Harriman was sweating more and more profusely, so much so that his uniform shirt was visibly sticking to his chest. He was starting to look a bit paler, and the cockiness in his manner was slowly dissipating. Ever so slowly, it was being re-

placed by something that Rokan recognized all too well: creeping desperation.

"You *do* think you're going to be rescued. That Starfleet will en-
deavor to arrange your release," Rokan said after many hours and ten
successive replies that began, "Harriman, John." This time the more
wan-looking Harriman said, "I already told you: Starfleet doesn't bargain with terrorists. I don't expect to be rescued."

"Commendable. Commendable. Indeed, why should you be rescued, when it comes down to it? I mean, you haven't exactly covered
yourself in glory, have you? Perhaps the braintrust of Starfleet will
breathe a collective sigh of relief, glad to be rid of you once and for
all."

Harriman glared at him, but a brief shadow seemed to flicker behind his eyes. It was what Rokan had been seeking for some time: the
first seeds of doubt.

"Nothing to say to that, Captain?"

"It's not a remark worth dignifying with a response."

"Indeed." Rokan smiled at that. "Indeed."

And then Harriman laughed.

"Is there something particularly amusing, Captain?" inquired
Rokan solicitously.

"Well, yes. Yes, I'd say there is. You are, after all, out here by yourself. Your government sent you out with no escort; just this single vessel. What will you do, I wonder, if a rescue is mounted? Perhaps your
government cares less about what happens to you than Starfleet does
what happens to me. I mean, my capture—and the procedures involved in that situation—are all covered by regs. But you . . . hell,
Rokan, maybe your government sent you out with a minimal crew
specifically in the hopes that you would be captured and they
wouldn't have to worry about you."

Now it was Rokan who laughed, a bit more hollowly than Harriman, though. "If my government desired to rid itself of me, it
would simply do so. An elaborate ruse or scheme would not be required."

"How comforting that must be for you," Harriman said sarcastically.

Rokan hit him.

It was not a move that was entirely without forethought. Rokan preferred to keep his clients confused, off-center. Make them believe that he was going to act in one way, and then do something else entirely. The blow wasn't intended to have impact in and of itself so much as it was intended to startle Harriman, make him uncertain of what was to come next.

Harriman's head snapped to the side, caught unawares as he was. Then slowly he looked back up to Rokan and smiled again. "A hit. A palpable hit," he said. "Did I strike a nerve, Rokan?" Rokan's impulse was to hit him again, but he restrained it. The last thing he wanted to do was give Harriman any hope or notion whatsoever that he, Harriman, was gaining any sort of upper hand.

"I will credit you this, Captain," Rokan said after a brief period of thought. "You have moved me in directions that I rather would not have gone. You can take some small measure of pride in that, I suppose. Unfortunately, it will not bode well for you, either."

"Threats? Now you're threatening me, Rokan? Is this how the great Romulan examiner accomplishes his aims? By threats?" He laughed hoarsely. "I've heard a good deal of talk from you, Romulan. A lot of talk, and a slap on the face that wouldn't have hurt a five-year-old. Maybe you could pack a punch as a younger man, but now . . . you impotent old—"

Rokan struck again, this time far harder. The upsetting thing was, this wasn't calculated, and he knew it. Harriman had provoked him and he had responded, and that was singularly, screamingly unprofessional.

The side of Harriman's face where the blow had landed was red and inflamed, but Harriman didn't seem to care.

"You," Rokan said softly, "are overreaching yourself, Captain, just as you always have. You aspire to qualities that you do not have. You think I cannot break you. You are very wrong. I had hoped that you would realize just how limited your options are. Unfortunately, you do not seem to be a particularly bright individual. Not one of the better candidates that the academy vomited up from its maw of scholarship . . . although I suspect you already know that. I had wanted to refrain from using drugs or mechanical devices upon you. There's no . . ." He sighed in a rather forlorn way. "There's no style to such resources. No elegance. I prefer mind against mind, rather than battering one mind into submission. Furthermore, purely on a practical level, such treatments can damage the mind of the client severely. And since we have further uses to which we can put you, that would be unfortunate. I loathe the notion of wasting material."

Harriman's eyes narrowed. It seemed as if he wanted to believe that, somehow, Rokan was lying to him. For if he knew the truth, comprehended the scope of what Rokan knew, then it just might be that his entire determination to resist would crumble. "Further uses? What are you . . . talking about . . . ?"

Rokan laughed derisively. He was beginning to enjoy this session once more. There had been a point there where his determination had flagged, where he felt momentary lapses in confidence. But that was bound to happen from time to time. In order for a truly great examiner to accomplish his goals, sometimes he had to allow himself to get "close" to the mindset of his client. If the client was an uncertain, tentative individual, that closeness could begin to infest the examiner with his own doubts. It was simply one of the hazards of the profession and, for a brief time there, Rokan had forgotten that. Now, though, he approached the situation with renewed confidence. For now it was becoming time to separate, as it was, the examiner from the examined. To remind Harriman of, indeed, just how hopeless his situation was, and how he was caught up in something that was far more devastating, far more complex, than anything he might have imagined.

"Are you under the impression you're the only Starfleet officer we've ever captured and questioned?" said Rokan with a carefully constructed sneer. "It's happened several times . . . and we've always returned such prisoners, or 'allowed' them to escape. But once they were ours . . . they stayed ours."

"You're lying," Harriman said furiously. Rokan was quite pleased at Harriman's display of temper. It showed that he was getting closer, and that Harriman's control and confidence were utterly slipping away. "You're lying!" he said again. "What are you saying, that there's . . . there's some sort of Romulan sleeper agents in Starfleet? That's absurd! You could never do that to any Starfleet officer. You can—"

Rokan's voice went low and menacing. "Do not, Captain, presume to tell me my business. Do not presume to tell me what we are and are not capable of accomplishing. I would not tell you your business. I would not tell you how far you could push a starship before the engines gave out and the warp core collapsed upon itself. Do not, therefore, think that you can tell me just how far the human mind can be pushed before it likewise collapses in upon itself and becomes nothing more than malleable clay for us to reshape however we please."

He then turned and walked out of the room. Berza was standing there, apparently waiting for him. "How may I be of service, Examiner?" he said formally.

"My kit. In my quarters. Bring it to me," said Rokan.

Berza thumped his fist against his chest in salute, pivoted on his heel, and vanished down the corridor. Barely a minute later, he returned carrying a simple, nondescript gray case, which he handed over to Rokan.

"Prepare the chair also," said Rokan.

Berza looked surprised. "Do you expect that will be needed, Examiner?"

"Do I expect it? No. But I anticipate it. Expect nothing, anticipate everything. However, I also anticipate that within two hours, the drugs will have done their work sufficiently that the chair will not be required."

"Yes, Examiner," said Berza, saluting once more. He headed off down the hallway to carry out Rokan's instructions while Rokan re-entered the room. He was pleased to see that Harriman was watching him enter, rather than simply staring off into space. It indicated to Rokan that Harriman was no longer making any pretense that what Rokan said and did was of no interest to him. Clearly, Harriman was worried.

He had every reason to be.

There was a small table nearby, upon which Rokan placed the case. He ran his hands lovingly around the edges of the case, making sure that Harriman's attention was fully upon his actions. "This," he said reverently, "was handed down to me by my teacher in the arts of examination."

"Handed down? Or did you kill him to get it?"

Rokan did not even deign to respond. Instead he opened the case to display an assortment of spray hypos and mixes for assorted potions. They were kept perfectly immobile in slots that had been carved in the packing to contain them. His hand floated above them as he decided which to avail himself of first. "Do you have any preferences, Captain?"

"It won't do you any good," said Harriman. "In Starfleet we're conditioned to resist all manner of mind tampering. So it doesn't matter what you pump into my veins. I'm still not going to tell you anything."

"Oh, I doubt that, Captain. I doubt that very much. However, if you have no stated preferences," and he reached for one hypo, "then I suppose I'll just have to improvise."

He carefully extracted the hypo from the case and moments later the contents were hissing into Harriman's shoulder. Rokan was pleased, or perhaps a little disappointed, to see that Harriman was not squirming or trying to resist. There had been other occasions, other clients, who had writhed furiously in their chairs as if they had some remote hope of avoiding their fate. Harriman, however, did not resort to such theatrical and futile endeavors. "Such stoicism in one so young," murmured Rokan. Harriman still said nothing as the drug flooded into his system.

Rokan waited an appropriate amount of time for the drug to take its effect. Outwardly, Harriman showed no sign of anything happening, but Rokan was far too practiced to settle for any obvious signs. He could see it in Harriman's eyes. There was a steady clouding over, which Harriman then forcibly tried to shake off. He licked his lips, which was quite common since this particular drug caused a degree of dehydration. His head lolled slightly, and he forcibly brought it around, trying to keep his focus on where he was and what was around him.

"Now then, Captain," Rokan said conversationally, "I want you to tell me about the troop movements your Starfleet has planned for the rim colonies."

"Go . . . to hell," Harriman managed to say.

With a disappointed sigh, Rokan said, "Now, now, Captain . . . that attitude really isn't going to get you anywhere." He held a recorder to Harriman's mouth and said, "I want you to tell me the positions of every starship in the quadrant. The names of their commanders, their firepower . . . everything. I know it's a good deal to ask for off the top of your head, so I will naturally forgive you any gaps in your memory. But I am seeking some aid."

"Harriman . . . John . . . rank . . ."

Rokan made a dismissive wave. "That's quite enough of that," he said, not trying to keep the testiness from his voice. "You don't seem to understand, Captain. I'm on your side."

"My . . . side . . . ?" Harriman looked at him with eyes that had a flare of life to them for a moment, but then started to lose their focus once more.

"You are running out of time, for my superiors are not infinitely patient. I, of course, am. I could do this all day. But they insist on immediate results, and they will not wait indefinitely. The drugs that I am placing into your system will eventually work their way out of you. You will be left unharmed by their passing. Before that happens, though, you must tell me what I need to know. If you do not do so, I shall have to use more formidable means of obtaining the information. Means that will leave a more lasting effect upon you. That will be most unfortunate for you."

"For you . . . too. . . ." Harriman's voice sounded thick, each word formed with effort. "You like to think . . . you've outwitted . . . outsmarted people . . . make you feel . . . superior . . . instead of what you are . . . which is nothing. . . ."

"Your opinion is duly noted," Rokan said archly. "Now . . . the names of the ships, please. . . ."

"Go . . . to hell. . . ."

Rokan sighed. This was going to take longer than he had thought.

The chime at the door angered Rokan, and he crossed to it quickly. Berza was standing there, the equipment that Rokan had requested floating next to him on a small antigrav lift. "Well?" Berza said. He was keeping the respectful tone in his voice, but it was clear that he was meant to convey an attitude of impatience. "It has been three hours since you administered the drugs. You said you would require no more than two. . . ."

"I know what I said," said Rokan. There was more testiness in his tone than he would have liked. "I was there when I said it."

"Am I to understand that Harriman has not yet told us what we wish to know?"

Rokan cast an annoyed look in Harriman's direction. "You understand correctly," he finally admitted.

"Perhaps you did not administer the drugs in sufficient quantity to . . ."

Rokan's angry gaze snapped back at Berza. "I know precisely how much to administer, and in what quantity. I have been doing this job since before you were born, Berza. Do you dare to question . . . ?"

"No. No," said Berza, but there was mildness in his tone that for some reason almost drove Rokan to distraction. "I do not question." But the questioning was there all the same, in his attitude if not in his words. "Please understand, Rokan, that if it were up to me, I could wait all day, all week. But those above me . . ."

"Yes, yes, yes," said Rokan impatiently. "There are always those above, aren't there?" He considered the situation a moment, and then gestured to the equipment and said, "Bring it in." Without waiting to make sure that his order was carried out, Rokan went back to Harriman and knelt down next to him.

Harriman barely appeared conscious. Rokan had not stopped with the initial drugs that he had administered. He had pumped still more into Harriman's veins when the initial dosages had proved insufficient. And still, damn him, Harriman had resisted. Rokan would not have thought it possible. Yes, he knew about Starfleet training. Moreover, he understood Harriman's overwhelming need to prove something to himself. He was certain that he had read and understood Harriman's psych profile correctly. He had a desperate need to be a hero, to succeed at something. Harriman fancied himself a captain in the mold of James Kirk, and he was probably of the opinion that Kirk would not have succumbed, no matter what the torture. Kirk had been built up to such legendary status that simply holding on to that image alone was enough—incredibly—to keep Harriman going.

Every time that Rokan was certain Harriman couldn't last much longer, he somehow rallied. It was amazing. No . . . it was more than amazing. It was damned inconvenient, was what it was.

"John," Rokan said urgently, going for the more familiar, intimate name rather than the formal rank. "John, can you hear me?"

Harriman didn't respond at first, and Rokan thought that he had passed out again. But then, slowly, Harriman raised his head. He stared in Rokan's general direction, but didn't seem to be focusing on him. His hair was matted down with sweat.

"John," Rokan said again. "John . . . can you hear me."

"Can . . . hear you, Dad. . . ."

Rokan couldn't quite believe his luck. If Harriman was disassociating, Rokan could make use of that. "I'm glad you can hear me, Son. Son . . . can you help me with something . . . ?"

"Sure, Dad . . ." Harriman sounded as if he was speaking from a million miles away.

"I'm on the way to help with the rim colonies . . . and I don't recall the names of the other vessels we're supposed to rendezvous with . . . can you tell me . . . ?"

"Suuure," Harriman said. He coughed several times, and then nodded. "Sure . . . anything you say, Sir."

Rokan brought the recorder up to Harriman's face. Harriman didn't even notice it was there. "What are they?"

"There's . . . three . . ."

"Three ships."

"Vulcan ship . . . Myas . . ."

Rokan hadn't heard of it, but it might be a newly commissioned vessel. "Myas, yes, and the others . . ."

"Oh . . . oh, that's the second one that will arrive. The first is . . . is . . ." He frowned, trying to recall, and then his face cleared. "Right . . . the first is the starship . . . Kiss . . . and the third is . . . the Limeball . . ."

Rokan blinked in surprise. What an odd crop of names Starfleet was coming up with. "So the ships are Kiss . . . Myas . . . Limeball . . ."

"Say it faster, Dad . . . so you won't forget . . ."

He did.

Then his face darkened in fury as Harriman began to laugh.

As Harriman, from the depths of his torture, howled with amusement over his cleverness, Rokan—precisely, methodically—checked over the large, elaborate equipment that was positioned next to Harriman.

"Have you enjoyed what passed for your witticism, Captain?" he demanded.

"You should learn to laugh more, Rokan . . ." Harriman managed to say. "You'll live longer."

"Thank you for your advice, Captain," said Rokan. "I shall give it the same weight and consideration that you have given mine."

Harriman didn't appear to be listening to him. Instead he was eyeing the device that Rokan had nearly finished setting up. "Nice chair . . . good . . . I needed . . . a trim . . . leave the sideburns . . . all right?"

Rokan sighed heavily. "Captain . . . I should salute your fortitude, I imagine. Praise you for your unwillingness to bend. You have resisted my efforts thus far, and for that alone, you should be commended. Were this a fairer universe . . . a universe where gallantry was always rewarded . . . then at this point you would be congratulated, freed, and permitted to go on your way without further incident. Unfortunately, that is not the universe in which we are living. I am giving you one last opportunity, Captain. It is insane for you to keep holding back as you have been. If you tell us what we wish to know, you have a chance at saving your mind."

Harriman didn't reply immediately, and Rokan realized that Harriman's efforts at lucidity mere moments before had taken more out of him than Rokan had at first suspected. Despite his bravado, he was barely stringing himself together. The equipment would sever that string, and that would be unfortunate. "You can end this before it's too late. Please . . . I am asking you, as one who has gained some measure of respect for you . . . cooperate. Now. There will be no more opportunities."

"Harriman. John. Rank . . . Captain. Ser—"

"Oh, shut up," Rokan said, his patience gone. He adjusted readings on the large chairlike device positioned next to Harriman. "Would you like to know what this is, Captain? Would you like to know what your stubbornness has earned you?"

Harriman said nothing. Rokan, without fear of any precipitous move on Harriman's part, undid the restraints. For a moment, the dazed captain looked as if he was about to make some sort of strike against Rokan, clearly not willing to waste the unexpected opportunity that had been presented him. But he couldn't move. The drugs had been far too devastating. He couldn't so much as lift a hand against Rokan, as the Romulan had known would be the case. The Romulan, for his part, had considerable resources of strength of his own. With no effort at all, he hauled Harriman out of the chair into which he'd been bound and transferred him to the newly arrived equipment. Harriman managed a grunt of protest, but it did no good at all as Rokan strapped him in. As he did so, he said with no air of hurry, "This is actually a Klingon invention. We acquired it during our period of shared technology. They call it a mind-sifter . . . or mind-ripper, if you will. It will tell me what I desire to know. Unfortunately, if used at sufficient strength, it will empty your mind of everything presently in there. It will turn you into a vegetable. I would not like to see you turned into a vegetable."

"I'm not afraid of you," Harriman told him defiantly, with as much strength as he could muster . . . which didn't seem to be much.

"Unfortunately for you," sighed Rokan, "whether you fear me or not, dear fellow, is entirely beside the point." He touched a switch and the mind sifter hummed to life.

"Is this where you give me one more chance to tell you what you want to know?" asked Harriman.

"No. No, that time has passed, I fear. This is where you tell me everything. It won't matter whether it's relevant or not. You will tell me. You won't be able to help yourself. You will empty your mind of its knowledge with such eagerness that you will not be able to contain it even if you want to."

He activated the machine, setting it to the lowest level, and Harriman stiffened. His eyes widened, his jaw set, Harriman still appeared as if he was determined to try and keep resisting. "Fight if you wish, Captain. It doesn't matter anymore what you do."

Harriman snarled inarticulate defiance. The very air around his head began to glow as a surge of energy sent the mind-sifter stabbing more deeply into his mind. Pulling from the innermost depths of his will power, Harriman managed to say, "Why don't . . . we see . . . how much you . . . can take . . . from this. . . ."

"Are you suggesting I submit myself to the mind-sifter as well? See whether my stamina is on par with your own?"

Harriman managed a nod.

Rokan laughed. "Why, Captain . . . you truly *are* a funny fellow. Now . . . the troop movements . . ."

"Harriman . . . John . . . Rank . . . Capt—"

He brought it up to level two. Level two was enough to force an Orion into shrieks of agony.

Harriman cried out, and then sunk his teeth into his lower lip with such ferocity that blood streamed down his chin, and then for no discernible reason started singing, at the top of his lungs, the "Whiffenpoof Song." No information about troop movements or schedules or ships was forthcoming, however.

At level three, which was enough to reduce an adult Vulcan to racking sobs of anguish, Harriman screamed about the astrophysics exam that he had cheated on during his third year at the academy without ever having been caught, and he cried out the name of the first girl he had made love to, and he apologized for having killed Captain Kirk, and for wetting the bed until the age of eight, and he still didn't tell Rokan what he wanted to know.

At level four, he cracked.

And Rokan had been right. Harriman didn't simply come up with the information; he flung it from him as if it were cancerous cells devouring him alive. He screamed the names of the ships, he howled the rendezvous times, he vomited up (metaphorically) the number of crew members in the roster, he bellowed the amount of weaponry each ship was carrying right down to the last photon torpedo, he even sobbed about a torrid evening he'd spent with the first officer of one of the vessels after which he'd tried repeatedly to contact her again but she'd displayed no interest whatsoever. . . .

His tears mixed with the blood on his face, and when Rokan turned off the machine, Harriman sagged like a reanimated corpse that had just had the life force sucked from it. It was as if the only thing keeping him going was the pain, and when that was gone, there was nothing for him. His head lolled to one side, and he uttered indistinct noises that might have been his father's name or might simply have been little more than baby jabber.

Rokan sighed heavily as he finished powering down the mind-sifter. He barely glanced at the drool now trickling from Harriman's mouth. "Believe it or not, Captain," he said, not unkindly, "you were fortunate. One more level . . . and there would have been nothing left to you at all. At the moment, however, all you are feeling is lone-liness . . . emptiness . . . but don't worry. We've fixed others, as I told you. Sleeper agents, who are reprogrammed, made back into Starfleet officers . . . on the surface. But deep within their psyche, they are loyal Romulan agents. They do not know it, nor have we activated any such . . . yet. But we will at the right time . . . and you will be one of them, Harriman. We will have the chance to work together again, you and I. . . ."

And that was the point where Harriman really, truly impressed him beyond anything he'd seen before. For Harriman apparently pulled upon reserves that Rokan wouldn't have dreamed possible. He actu-ally managed to turn glassy eyes and to whisper, with a voice like one already dead, "Lying . . . no . . . no agents . . ."

"Oh?" sneered Rokan. "Ask Admirals Wetzler and Pattison . . . and Captain Wills . . . and Commander Bridges. They might have very different stories to tell. Oh, but that's right," he said with mock solic-itousness, "by the time we release you . . . you won't remember any of this. What do you say to that, my dear, heroic Captain?"

"Two . . . words . . ." he said, as if calling from beyond the grave.

"Oh, really. And what would those two words be?"

"End program."

But those words were not spoken like a dead man. Rather they were said in a strong, powerful, vibrant tone, and even as he spoke, Harriman sat up, and there was a blazing fire in his eyes.

Rokan took a step back, uncomprehending.

And the interrogation room vanished around him.

The Romulan stared around in confusion. All around him was darkness, with glowing squares outlining the wall, floor, and ceiling.

"I . . . I don't . . . what is . . . ?" His mind had frozen up, unable to process the information that was being handed it.

Harriman was wiping the trickling blood from his chin, standing there and looking absolutely none the worse for wear. As he did so, the door hissed open behind him. Rokan was about to shout for help, when he saw four Starfleet security officers enter. The door itself was further back than the door to the interrogation room had been, and beyond it was not the corridor of a Romulan ship, but instead a white bulkhead with the logo of Starfleet etched upon it. Speechlessly, he looked back to Harriman.

"Brand new technology," Harriman said, taking in the room with a gesture. "It's called a holochamber. It generates hard-light computer images. Just places at the moment, although eventually it'll be sophisticated enough to create simulacrums of sentient beings, so I'm told. We've got the prototype here on the *Enterprise*. Field-testing it, as it were. But they think that someday they'll be standard issue on starships. What will they think of next, eh?"

"I . . . I don't understand. . . ." Rokan stammered. Then, stepping in behind the guards came a man with a very familiar face. "Berza—!" he called out.

Berza just smiled and shook his head.

"Ah. You mean Lieutenant Patrick O'Shea. Lieutenant, take a bow." O'Shea obediently bowed as Harriman continued, "O'Shea's one of our better spies. He looks rather good as a Romulan, wouldn't you say? Most cooperative in getting us word of your ship's location and disabling your vessel so that we were able to capture it, quickly and painlessly . . . all while you slumbered peacefully away, since— apparently—you're not much of a morning person. So you were captured unaware. Then we kept you unconscious in sickbay until we decided what to do with you. O'Shea had caught wind of your 'sleeper agent' program but couldn't get any specifics on it. So we arranged this little show," and he gestured around him once more, "to get the information out of you."

"You . . . you were in control all the time!" said an infuriated Rokan. "The entire time you were simply toying with me! A cheap, insidious Federation trick!"

Harriman smiled thinly and said, "I warned you, Rokan, did I not? In Starfleet, we play fair. Remember what I said? 'One should not always take things at face value. They are not always what they appear to be.' " Harriman's smile widened and he said, "I like to think that even the late Captain Kirk would have approved. Besides, that wasn't toying with you, Rokan. That wasn't a cheap trick. That was . . . style. I thought you would appreciate it. Well, Rokan? You've had a good deal to say until now. At a loss for words?"

And Rokan, with a snarl, spat out, "Rokan. Rank: High Examiner. Imperial registration number 257—"

He was still rattling it off as Harriman walked out of the room, laughing softly to himself.

Captain Rachel Garrett
U.S.S. Enterprise-C

"For a ship and crew to function well, it always starts with the captain. You set the tone."

Minuet, *Star Trek: The Next Generation*

ROBERT GREENBERGER

As with John Harriman, little is known about Rachel Garrett. Her one appearance was in the now-classic "Yesterday's *Enterprise*" episode of *The Next Generation*. It should be noted that at the time Garrett commanded the *Enterprise*-C, Jean-Luc Picard was commanding the *Stargazer*, and it appears they had never previously met, a sign of how large the Federation and Starfleet had grown.

Some biographical material showed up in the *Star Trek: Starship Creator* program, and Bob, wanting to be neat like his colleagues, appended some of those details here. What's clear is that Garrett must have been quite the captain to command a crew loyal enough that they were willing to go back through the rift and face certain death. How did she treat them, was the question Bob first posed for himself when sitting to write this story.

By the time you read this, Bob will be a Producer at Gist Communications, after sixteen years at DC Comics. However, as time passed, he added to his freelance credits, which include several well-received collaborations in the *Star Trek* universe, and the solo novel *The Romulan Stratagem*. He has penned a few short stories set outside of *Star Trek* and will next contribute to a collection of spacefaring stories, due within the next year.

A bigger Mets fans than Peter David, Bob also serves as the Statistician to the Federal League, a fantasy baseball team he shares with Mike Friedman.

Bob wants to acknowledge the contributions of Inge Heyer, data analyst at the Space Telescope Science Institute, in making sure the science is right.

Hour of Fire

"We plan to honeymoon on Risa. I don't know how Mike swung it, but he's gotten us this wee cottage right on the shore." Aine McAvennie, a young blonde woman, was just taking her seat in the rec room when the captain entered. Leaning over toward her friend David Vinson, a dark man with white hair and ready grin, she added, "He can be such a romantic."

"Romantics are a nice breed," Vinson agreed.

In another corner of the room, Engineer's Mate Fletcher Chu-Fong listened as his taller partner, Ivan Cohen, completed a story. They stood to leave the room, spotted their commanding officer, and nodded in greeting. Chu-Fong, burly yet handsome, shook his head in confusion. "You can breed romantics?"

Cohen sauntered by, replying, "Check down in hydroponics, I think they're on special this week."

At the food processor, Polly Luttrull considered her options. Behind her, lab technician Coron fidgeted impatiently. The Bolian hated waiting behind Luttrull, who could never make up her mind. "Try the fish," he suggested through gritted teeth, his blue skin darkening.

"Fish might be good," Luttrull considered. "Of course, the processors don't always get it right. Braised or broiled?"

"Dead," the Bolian snapped. He then realized who was behind him in line, noted her relaxed composure, and quickly changed from consternation to something placid. "Good afternoon, Captain."

"Good afternoon, Ensign," she replied without much inflection.

"Would you prefer to go ahead of us?" Coron asked, not so gently pushing Luttrull before him. The tactical officer began to protest but recognized the voice declining the invitation. Blushing, she quickly ordered the fish—broiled with Martian spices.

Rachel Garrett, captain of the U.S.S. Enterprise-C, patiently waited for Coron to make his own selection before it was her turn. Her deep brown eyes scanned the room carefully, trying not to stare. Her ears were straining to grab pieces of conversations in the rec room.

"Can't believe Alfonzo won the parrises squares match."

"And then I slapped him and walked home."

"I'm telling you, the elections were fixed."

"Swap shifts with me so I can see the presentation with Katie?"

Garrett settled for a sandwich, salad, and rich coffee. It was becoming her routine midday meal, but that fact had not registered with her.

Taking her seat at an empty table, near the room's rear, Garrett absently picked up the coffee and took a sip. She never noticed the person joining her until the trim form settled into the seat.

"You've got that look again."

Garrett looked over at Chief Engineer Cat Singh, perhaps the only member of the command crew perpetually on the move. With a belated gesture, she belatedly invited the younger woman to join her and together they looked around the room.

"And what look is that, Cat?" Garrett ran a hand through her thick, shoulder-length hair. It forced her to refocus and pay attention to her closest friend among the crew.

"The one that says you're never satisfied. I see it often enough during inspection," the engineer good-naturedly grumbled. She started in on her hot and sour soup.

Garrett narrowed her eyes a bit, focusing on her closest comrade aboard the starship. "Well, Luttrull is right, the food processors can't make a decent fish." The captain let out a deep sigh. "Listen to them." She paused a moment, letting the ambient noise wash over them. People gossiping about relationships, someone complaining about being caught in an error, someone else missing home.

"No one's anxious. We've been together for six months already. I'll admit, Starfleet keeps us doing these milk runs, all worthwhile duties I grant you, but no one seems ready to be challenged. They're . . . complacent." She frowned before attacking her sandwich.

"You make that sound like a bad thing."

Garrett frowned a moment and replied, "It might be. Shouldn't they want something . . . more?"

"Does their captain show that same desire?" Singh looked at her with bright eyes and a bit of a smile. Garrett looked at her blankly.

"You're the leader," the engineer continued. "You act complacent, they act complacent. Trust me, when I'm in action down below, my crew hops to it. Try it sometime."

The captain nodded in thought.

"I like being among the crew. I want them at ease when I'm present, but maybe they . . . maybe I . . . have been too at ease."

Singh grinned. "And as chief engineer I thank you for that. After what some captains put their ships through, I like this. I can modify the engines until they whisper. I've gotten warp efficiency past the 100 percent mark more than once."

Garrett nodded in appreciation, finishing her salad. "Good. Never know when I'll need it. Think the crew is over 100 percent?" All she got in reply was a roll of Singh's shoulders.

After another sip, the captain shook her head as if to clear her dark thoughts and then asked, "Any trouble from that nearby binary?"

"Okay, we'll change the subject," Singh said agreeably. "Nothing out of the ordinary. Usual fluctuations along the electromagnetic spectrum, but it hasn't hurt the engines. Really think we'll find a usable world out this way?"

Draining the cup, Garrett stood up, Singh right beside her. As they moved to recycle the remnants of their meal, the captain shrugged. "Hopefully. The Warin need more space for their growing population, and we've been asked to find them a world. Survey ships indicate this sector shows some promise."

The pair walked out of the rec room and continued down the corridor toward a turbolift. With the shift underway, the corridors were quieter; the few crew seen were moving about with purpose. All slowed to greet the captain, and she responded in kind, impressing herself with the number of names she could summon from memory. "It's getting a little tougher for the Federation to grow. After all, we have other governments with claims to this quadrant of space and that hems us in just a bit. Thankfully, most are keeping to themselves, but others like to rattle their sabers now and then. Look at the Klingons. Still making noises about war despite the long years we've discussed peaceful cooperation. Sometimes I think they forget what happened at Camp Khitomer."

"Spoken like a true diplomat," Singh teased. "It's why you left Qo'noS, right?"

Garrett replied with a shrug of her own.

Singh keyed the turbolift and they entered the small space. The engineer directed them toward the bridge and then, with a laugh, said, "Just another mission for the *Enterprise*, wasn't it?"

The words caught Garrett by surprise, burrowing deep and touching a nerve. "The *Enterprise* is the most storied name in Starfleet history, and I read through every captain's log entry I could find from April to Harriman. You should hear the pride in their voices when discussing their ships . . . their crews. You'd think they never dropped out of warp, hurtling from adventure to adventure."

"Of course, it was a different era," Singh noted. "Everything must have seemed new to them."

The doors snapped open, and the watch officer, Lieutenant Carmona, stood up and announced, "Captain on the bridge."

"There are countless captains over the years to compare myself with," Garrett observed, just as she strode from the turbolift to her command chair. Singh lingered on the upper deck, studying the large monitor displays. To her left was a giant schematic of the *Enterprise* itself, all telltales indicating things were operational. The captain settled into the chair and surveyed her crew. She knew them all, at least by name, and was satisfied that all was quiet. This was what she asked for, after all. It was Garrett who petitioned Starfleet to relieve her of her diplomatic assignment to the Klingon Empire and return her to active duty. She felt the call of the stars, the unknown. What surprised her was how quickly they granted the request; she was even more surprised by the name of the ship she was assigned.

The *Ambassador*-class ship was the first to bear the name *Enterprise* in a while, but she knew it was inevitable. After all, a ship with such a famous history needed to be part of the fleet, as much for public relations as for crew morale. There was some comfort to be gained by knowing an *Enterprise* was patrolling the Federation and some pride in serving aboard the vessel.

"Status, Mr. Carmona?"

The olive-skinned officer crisply replied, "We're following the course suggested by the Warin. However, we're passing close to a binary star system, which is producing unusual effects. Nothing we can't navigate through, but it makes things a little tricky the further out we look."

The captain nodded and looked at the overhead display directly behind her, reading the amount of output in each waveband generated by the neutron star. At Starfleet Academy she specialized in history and diplomacy, but as an officer she had had to recall her science lessons on more than one occasion.

"Mr. Hemachandra, some background on this system, please."

Nelson Hemachandra, an older officer, finished consulting something at the science station, then turned and looked at his captain. "I'll try not to bore you, Captain," he began brightly. "A pulsar and a subgiant star form the binary system we're approaching. None of those planets can sustain life, given the amount of radiation being thrown off by the two. I would hope you're not planning to have us travel between them."

She grinned. "Wouldn't think of it. So, why the odd readings?"

"The neutron star has the stronger gravity and is 'stealing' gas from the outer layers of the subgiant," the officer continued in a dull tone. "The process of the material being attracted by the neutron star, settling in a disk surrounding it, and eventually hitting the surface is called 'accretion.' "

"Thank you, I do recall that much," Garrett said coolly.

Hemachandra nodded, suitably chastened. "Whenever enough gas from the cooler subgiant has accumulated on the hot neutron star, it burns it off in a pulse reaction—hence the name 'pulsar.' Between the two stars we're getting readings all over the spectrum."

"I see. Thank you. Helm, belay that order to fly between the stars," Garrett said.

At first McAvennie seemed startled by the order, then realized the intended humor. "Aye, Sir," she replied.

"Helm, what's out there?" Garrett asked, returning her attention to the forward screen.

Aine McAvennie looked over her shoulder with bright eyes. "I can't be certain, Sir. All sensors indicate routine space debris, gas, and lots of nothing. Target solar system is a day away at maximum warp."

"Understood. Steady as she goes, Mr. McAvennie. Cat, go back below and make sure these rapid pulses won't compromise the warp core. You promised me 100 percent, and I want it all. We're a long way from home, and I want no problems."

"No problems, aye," Singh replied and returned to turbolift.

The next three hours passed by slowly. Garrett remained in the center seat, reading reports on padds rather than sitting in her ready room, alone. She made an effort to engage her bridge crew in conversation, keeping things from growing too silent. Nelson Hemachandra was the oldest among them, a lieutenant who had served on six other ships before requesting a fresh start on the *Enterprise*. She trusted his experience and liked his keen interest in non-Terran musical forms. After all, during her time on Qo'noS, she grew to appreciate their operas. McAvennie was on her second star rotation but was hoping to transfer to Earth, assigned to Starfleet Command so she could marry her fiancé, currently an adjutant to Commodore Sarin. Carmona was the artist in the group, completing one canvas after another according to replicator reports, but he was too shy to show any of them. He was a competent first officer, and Garrett respected his privacy but had hoped he'd feel more comfortable after all these months together. Thithta, at communications, said he asked for the *Enterprise*, wanting to serve on a ship with such a famous pedigree, and Garrett couldn't help but agree. After all, she had to stifle her surprised exclamation when Admiral Lavin gave her new orders nearly a year earlier. In all, Garrett appreciated her bridge crew, complacent or not.

"I'm telling you that the maneuverability of the *Constellation*-class ship makes it better for deep space exploration," Carmona argued. "The four nacelle design gives it added thrust."

McAvennie rolled her eyes and replied, "If that's so, why are there so few of them doing just that? In fact, the *Excelsior* design, being larger, makes more sense to use when leaving Federation territory."

"Maybe, but which craft are they building today? That should help solve this little dilemma of ours."

"Actually," Thithta, the Andorian communications officer, injected quietly, "both classes are down to just two a year. They're already designing the next class of ship. . . ."

His words were cut off by the proximity alert. Nearly a dozen bodies reacted simultaneously, bodies turned to their stations, hands running over control panels. The silence was immediate.

Garrett's eyes went wide for a moment; then she set her chin and focused on the information streaming in from all stations. Everyone was hunched over their station, calling out without turning.

"Close-range sensors detect three vessels, twenty thousand kilometers off the starboard bow," Polly Luttrull announced from tactical, located to Garrett's left. "Approaching at warp 2 and slowing."

"Configuration unrecognizable," added Hemachandra at the science console behind the captain.

"No communications signal from the ships," said Thithta.

"Full stop. Yellow Alert," Garrett snapped, feeling her pulse rise. "Shields and weapons on standby, but let's not appear hostile. Thithta, standard hails using first contact protocols. Lieutenant Luttrull, how'd they sneak up on us?"

Shaking her tightly coiled brown hair, Luttrull said without turning around, "Haven't a clue, Sir. The sensors aren't at 100 percent thanks to the binary, and it seems our efficiency is down more than we thought as we get closer."

Hemachandra stood forward, leaning over the railing, fingers interlaced. "I believe the alien ships may have used the binary's energy against us."

"Explain," Garrett ordered, not taking her eyes off the viewscreen.

"The neutron star's bursts will give off radiation mostly in the short or high-energy wavelengths, X rays mostly, while the subgiant is very bright in the optical and longer or infrared and radio wavelengths. This pair covers most of the spectrum, which would mask their approach on our sensors."

"And they came at us from the opposite side of the stars," Luttrull added. "Somehow they detected our presence and must have been waiting for us."

"Okay," Garrett agreed growing cautious, "but to welcome us or not?"

"Sorry about that, Captain," Carmona said from ops. "My fault for not noticing that sooner." The first officer then sent inquiries to their astrometrics lab in an effort to find where these ships may have originated.

Garrett frowned, ignoring the comment and hating the limitations the binary imposed on her ship and crew. Pushing the thought aside, she ordered, "Mr. Hemachandra, get me everything you can glean from those ships. Are they built for speed or war?"

"I'm on it," he replied, bending deeper over his readouts. Garrett stared at the main viewer, looking at one of the alien vessels, getting control of her breathing. All data indicated each was roughly the same size as the *Enterprise*, maybe a little larger. It seemed composed of five vertical pods, held together with a latticework of struts and supports. The pods were in a deep orange while the support structure was in a dark purple, with bright white lights running up and down.

"Nothing comes close," Carmona admitted. "Astrometrics reports no lifesigns within two dozen light-years of our position. Definitely a first contact occasion. My first."

"Only Mr. Hemachandra can claim experience with that, I believe," the captain said, forcing her voice to remain calm. If Singh was right, and they took their cues from her, now was the time to exude professionalism.

"Did it turn out all right?" Luttrull asked.

"It didn't help that the captain was a Tellarite." The science officer laughed. "But fortunately the Calix were so interested in trade rights they chose not to notice."

The captain felt the adrenaline running through her like an electric charge, and it made her tighten her grip on the armrests. She was about to make her first contact with a new species and was determined not to make any errors. Garrett felt ready for the encounter, considering all her training at Starfleet and experience with other races, especially the belligerent Klingons.

"All three vessels are releasing . . . something . . . from their hulls," Luttrull said, her voice rising in anticipation. "Sensors are working better at close range so we should have data in a second. Probes maybe. Apparently not weapons, from their energy signatures." The orange devices were smaller versions of the pods, without struts and with a single engine exhaust.

"No reply to any hail," Thithta said in his soft lisp.

"Put it on automatic and start looking for signals. What's controlling the probes? Is one ship controlling the probes or all three? Any intership chatter we can monitor with the translator?" Garrett asked.

"No lifesigns on the probes," the dark-skinned Hemachandra offered. He started to add something; then his attention was distracted by a signal on his console. "The lead ship is scanning us," he announced. "Nothing overly invasive. May I return the gesture?"

Garrett shook her head, saying, "Not yet. I want nothing misinterpreted." The information was coming in at a rapid pace, and Garrett soaked up each piece, placing it on her mental table. Pieces to a puzzle, picture unknown.

"Luttrull, what are the probes doing?"

The tactical officer paused, running the information twice and then projecting it on the viewscreen closest to the main viewer. It showed the *Enterprise* in blue, the three alien ships in red, and the smaller probes in yellow. The probes were all in motion, scattering before the *Enterprise*, while the three other ships, further back, were spreading apart, slowly. Garrett studied the view, looking for a threat, uncertain of their formation. She frowned with concentration.

Then, suddenly, two of the ships shot past the *Enterprise* at twice their previous speed. The probes remained, and the captain wasn't sure what to make of it. She studied the tactical display, as did most of the bridge crew.

"Nothing hostile in that move, don't you think?" the first officer said.

"No change in the probes' power signatures," Luttrull offered.

"Then it wasn't hostile," Garrett agreed with a small smile. Certainly not like any first contact she recalled studying. Maybe they communicated through physical action rather than verbal communication, she considered. The ships continued to spread further apart on the screen, forcing Garrett to look for a pattern, trying to see trouble before it began.

"Helm, ahead one-quarter impulse," Garrett commanded after a few more silent seconds. "Let's keep our eyes and ears open, gentlemen. We haven't a clue what this all means, so we proceed slowly and cautiously."

The starship moved forward, closing in on the probes, which continued to float about, seemingly aimless in the distance. On the bridge, everyone stayed silent, uncertain of what was to happen when they engaged the probes. The tactical display showed the two vessels having slowed down and starting to turn.

"Are they coming back?" Hemachandra asked.

"Certainly not at ramming speed," Luttrull offered.

"Nelson," Garrett inquired, "what did the survey ships say about nearest life-forms?"

Always prepared, the science officer didn't need to consult the computer but said, "This entire area was declared devoid of sentient life-forms when the survey was prepared twenty years ago."

"A lot can happen in twenty years," McAvennie murmured.

"The food processors could *never* make fish properly," Luttrull teased.

"Eyes front," Garrett quietly commanded. Over the next minute, no one said anything as all personnel watched their own stations, stealing glances at the tactical display. The probes continued to spread out, in no discernable pattern, while the alien ships also spread apart in no obvious pattern. Garrett kept the *Enterprise* moving forward, seeing no reason to stop. Still, she tried to think beyond her training, approach the situation from an alien perspective.

Finally, they were among the probes, and still nothing changed. Some were now on both sides of the sleek starship, none registering any change in power or radio signal. The captain heard a few audible exhalations among those who held their breath.

"Captain, the alien ships are moving closer," Luttrull reported.

"Any other changes?"

"None," the tactical officer said, but was cut off by Thithta.

"The radio signal has changed. It's now coming from all three ships to the probes. Captain, it's like they're synchronizing. . . ."

Garrett quickly noted the tactical display and uttered a curse. She never stopped to watch the integration of alien probe and alien ship. Instead, she had only focused on the ships. The *Enterprise* was surrounded and vulnerable. "Red Alert," she snapped, mentally reprimanding herself.

Red lighting replaced the daytime hue, and a klaxon sounded on every deck. Garrett barely noted that the turbolift doors quickly opened as support personnel scrambled to man all the stations. It had always been a rule that every bridge station be manned by trained personnel during emergencies. They were specifically capable of handling multiple duties in case of injuries.

All idle chatter had stopped the moment the Red Alert sounded, and the tension on the bridge was getting thick. The unknown always had that effect on a crew, Starfleet's counselors had reported. Garrett certainly agreed, having faced the unknown on more than one occasion on both the *Gandhi* and the *Endeavour*. The latter had her patrolling the Romulan Neutral Zone after the now-famous Tomed Incident. It made the crew so jumpy, Starfleet changed its orders and rotated crews every four months to keep the officers sharp.

"All decks report ready," Thithta announced.

"Good," Carmona replied. "Phasers hot, all torpedo tubes loaded."

"Preliminary targeting?" Luttrull asked.

Garrett bit her lip for a brief moment. What was it K'mpec told her on Qo'noS? *Ignore nothing; everything was a potential threat.*

"Phasers on the probes, torpedoes on the ships."

"Aye, Sir," she replied.

"Thithta, what's going on?" Garrett asked, struggling to sound calm.

"Synchronization . . ." the Andorian began, but the aliens sprang to action at that moment. Bright blue energy suddenly emitted from the three ships to the probes. Like water buckets passed from hand to hand in an old-fashioned fire brigade, the blue light went from probe to probe until suddenly the pattern became obvious.

"A web," Luttrull said. "Caught like a fly."

"Or a Tholian," Carmona added. "Damn. We should have seen it."

"Energy reads as some form of charged plasma," Hemachandra said. "Not a pattern I've seen before."

"Singh to bridge," came a voice over the comm system. "Whatever those aliens unleashed is doing a number on the warp core. We couldn't generate a warp bubble if you doubled my salary."

Garrett grimaced. "Any damage to the core itself?"

"Containment fields are holding steady, but there's too much interference to try to initiate warp."

"Understood. Make sure everything down there is monitored and please make certain the weapons remain on-line. They're the priority."

"I can't make warp, but we can keep the phasers warm and ready."

"Finally some good news. Bridge out." Garrett rose from the command seat and began to walk around the lower section of the bridge. Her gaze barely wavered from the tactical display, while stealing glances at the ops and helm stations before her. She took another step, toward the science console on the upper ring of the bridge, when the ship was rocked and she lost her balance. Falling hard on her left hip, she stifled a cry of pain. Scrambling to her feet, Garrett saw she wasn't alone. It was a hard enough jolt that half the crew was also getting back to their feet.

Hemachandra, who had remained in his chair, was already studying the readouts. "They literally charged the entire area of the web with raw energy. The web interior generated feedback, causing the stabilizers to short out for a moment before the backups came on-line."

"The probes are moving, coming closer," Luttrull called out, catching Garrett's attention.

"Tightening the web, unlike the Tholian way," the captain muttered. "Projection of time until they touch the shields."

The tactical officer paused a moment and finally said, "Thirty-two minutes, six seconds."

"Nelson, when that kind of energy touches the shields . . . ?"

He looked directly into her brown eyes, the expression saying more than the word. "Boom." Hemachandra elaborated. "The reaction of our shield harmonics and that much naked plasma will cause overloads to just about every system you can name. We'd be dead in space and easy pickings for these aliens."

"Options. Everyone speak up," she invited.

"Phasers," Luttrull snapped immediately.

"I agree," Carmona said.

"Standard diplomacy doesn't appear to be working, so we need another approach," McAvennie added.

Garrett retook her seat, checked the ship schematic behind her for damage reports, and was pleased to see minimal trouble. She tried to channel the adrenaline flow, using it to stay focused. "Okay, target the forward probe. Fire on my command. Nelson, Thithta, watch the energy and radio signatures. See if we do any damage." Everyone agreed. For the first time since taking command of the starship, she gave the order every captain anticipated—and feared: "Fire."

Scarlet beams leapt across the viewscreen as the phaser array let loose its first volley. They struck the probe dead-on, but didn't appear to pierce the construct or interrupt the plasma flow. Instead, the added phaser energy in the already charged area of space in which the starship was trapped caused a ripple. The ship shuddered slightly. "No damage," Hemachandra said quietly.

The disappointment among the crew was palpable, and Garrett sunk deep into her cushioned seat. She wasn't going to panic, wasn't going to act rashly. Staring at some of the supernumerary crew in their buff and red jumpsuits or maroon duty jackets, the captain realized she didn't know them all. They were faces without names, and she was expected to put her trust into them. Well, she wanted command, Garrett reminded herself.

Shaking off the disappointment, she looked at the screen. The probes were slightly obscured by the brilliant blue of the plasma. Garrett then noticed the dull throbbing beneath her boots. The ship itself was feeling the effects of the tightening web, and things were only going to get rockier.

Thithta half rose from his seat, a hand toggling a control. "Static in subspace increasing."

Garrett rubbed a thumb across her chin, mind racing through options. She was dimly aware of Thithta's comment. Then her eyes snapped into focus.

"We may not understand the radio signals between ship and probe, but can you try to jam them—disrupt the connection and maybe break the web?" She looked intently at her communications officer. The Andorian nodded back.

"Mr. Hemachandra, your opinion?" the captain asked, a snap back in her voice.

"If he can find the right frequency, then there is a chance."

"Agreed," the captain said. Standing, she leaned over the helmsman's chair. "Mr. McAvennie, plot us a course 217 mark 5. We'll be going at full impulse. Mr. Luttrull, target probes one, three, and seven," the captain said, indicating the probes to the left of the viewscreen. "Use the deflector dish to enhance the signal. Bridge to engineering."

"Singh, here."

"Cat, it's going to get bumpier. What's impulse like?"

"Just fine."

"Keep it that way. Out. Okay, Mr. McAvennie, we're about to go for a ride. Pick a safe course away from the aliens."

McAvennie's hands hesitated for a second, then had the course entered. "Course laid in," she confirmed.

Garrett nodded. "Thithta, now!"

The Andorian flicked two fingers at controls, activating the proposed frequency. Unlike their last attempt, there was nothing to watch on the viewer. Not a sound. It appeared that nothing was happening, and Garrett silently counted the seconds. On a screen to the right of the viewer, a countdown silently ticked off the time remaining.

The ship shook violently, spilling the command crew from their chairs. Alert comm signals rang throughout the bridge, and the shuddering seemed unending. Garrett staggered to her knees, looking at her ripped pants leg; a trickle of blood ran from her thigh. Looking about her, she watched the blue energy start vibrating, flickering in and out of synch with the probes. Loose plasma snaked and actually seemed to destroy two probes, breaking the web for good.

"Full impulse, now!" she cried.

McAvennie, from her knees, pushed the controls and held tight as the ship bucked and then seemed to surge forward. She regained her chair and checked the readouts. Quickly, the Irish woman turned to the captain and smiled.

Within seconds, the ship was upon the gaping space and moving past it. Stray plasma continued to stream without direction, and such unchecked energy wreaked havoc with the *Enterprise*'s shields. Tendrils, which had earlier destroyed the alien probes, now whipped across the shields. While the actual contact was exceptionally brief, that much raw power coming into contact with the starship's shields caused major turbulence. It didn't take long for the crew to feel the sustained impact. Once again, the deck plates seemed to disappear, and people were thrown more wildly than before. As feared, systems began to overload, and first one, then three, then four consoles around the bridge sparked. Smoke billowed around them, turning the bridge into a red-hued hell.

Cries and curses were mixed with the alarm sirens, and all Garrett could discern were bodies falling and boots running on wherever the deck ended up. She had wrapped an arm around the base of the command chair and held on for dear life, ignoring her own pain. There was no question that this was going to be a costly maneuver, but she couldn't begin to imagine the damage to crew and ship.

Fans finally kicked into action, sucking the smoke away as fire suppression systems came on line. Some things still worked, Garrett decided grimly. Risking movement, the captain regained her feet and first looked about the bridge. A smooth operation was turned into a charnel house.

Carmona, her first officer, was slumped over ops, blood deepening his duty jacket.

McAvennie was curled under the smoking helm, sparks from a cable dancing around her bloody hair.

And Luttrull lay on the deck, ten feet from tactical, her neck at the wrong angle.

Garrett swallowed hard and called out, "Thithta, get medics up here!" There was no confirming reply, and the captain slowly turned around. Thithta was either dead or unconscious: Garrett couldn't tell. Steeling herself for the worst, she continued to survey her bridge. Hemachandra was alive but was nursing a sore arm, possibly broken. The older man appeared dazed, probably in shock. Some of the crew she didn't know were also dead, but thankfully not all.

Hitting her chair communicator, she called, "Sickbay, bridge. We have dead and wounded. Send a priority team."

"Casado, bridge. Acknowledged." The CMO was certainly busy, but the bridge staff took priority over all other areas, including engineering and weapons.

Finally, the captain forced herself to look at the tactical display on the main viewer, and through the thinning smoke she saw that the damaged *Enterprise* was moving away from the disrupted energy web, but the alien ships were also breaking formation. The fight was not over.

She walked stiffly to ops, which was still functioning. Carefully, but without hesitation, she moved Carmona's body to the deck and sat at the console. Wiping his blood away with her right sleeve, Garrett slaved helm's controls to the station. The captain slowed the ship's movement and refined the course, away from the alien vessels and moving directly away from the pulsar in an effort to clear their sensors. While she wanted to mourn, first Garrett needed to assess the status of her ship and crew. It felt like her time on the *Gandhi* all over again, but this time she didn't have to step in for a dead captain and face down the Cardassians. No, this was her ship, and she'd be damned if this were to become another *Kobayashi Maru*, another no-win scenario.

Garrett took a moment to get a feel for her ship and could tell something was wrong.

"Engineering, report."

"Singh here. That thing packed quite the wallop. Impulse is sluggish, and I'm tracking down the problem. Inertial dampers are shot, and we're running on the backups. Can you give me some repair time?"

"Don't think so, Cat. Looks like our neighbors are staying on our tail. Out." Okay, she thought, could have been worse. So much fluctuating energy in the area, from the binary and the plasma, things could have been much worse. Priority now is to get back to Federation territory without the aliens following. The last thing she wanted was a first contact not only to go badly but to invite hostile aliens into Federation space. Some legacy that would be.

"Captain."

It was a voice she didn't recognize and it took her a moment to look up. A handsome young man looked back. Clear eyes, no apparent injuries despite the smoke-darkened cadet jumpsuit. He stood on the bridge's upper ring and was fronting two others. "Cadet Richard Castillo, ma'am."

"Cadet?"

"What are your orders?" He had an intense look, seemingly unafraid of what was happening around him. The others had similar intent expressions, but Castillo exuded confidence, something she needed.

"Of course. Castillo, take tactical. You . . ."

"Maria Stachow."

". . . Stachow, take ops. And you . . ."

"John Nee, Captain."

". . . Nee, of course. Relieve Thithta at communications."

A chorus of ayes resounded, and the trio was in motion. The turbolift doors finally snapped open, and medical personnel came streaming in. Nee beckoned a doctor to the ailing Andorian while he grabbed the receiving earpiece.

"I need status, people. Stachow, give me distance from the alien vessels and best possible speed." Once again, she pictured her anxiety as a fine laser beam searing away all distractions.

Castillo had been studying the board in front of him, clearly his first time at that station. "The plasma web is shutting itself down with the alien ships no longer in position to control it. The remaining probes seem to be dead in space. The aliens themselves are closing, matching our full impulse."

"Hemachandra, what's out there?"

The science officer was already scanning the area so his response was quick and precise, something that gave Garrett unexpected comfort. "Plasma is dissipating, and this whole region is clearing up. We can maneuver freely."

"We've been running the automatic hails all this time and still no response," Nee reported. "If they're communicating intership, I can't find the signal."

Garrett rubbed her aching leg, waving off a corpsman, pointing to the bodies before her. "Stop transmitting. We tried it by the book, but now we have to handle it another way." She sat in her command chair and gave herself a deep breath to think. Clearly, home is the destination, but not with three ships in pursuit. *Enterprise* was hurt and couldn't possibly outfight them, and help was too far away.

"Captain to engineering."

"Singh here."

"Do I have full weapons?"

"Right now."

"Warp speed?"

"Give me an hour."

"Who am I to argue with my personal miracle worker?" she said with a slight smile. "Okay. Can we cut that time down?"

"Probably."

"Okay. I've got an idea. Keep someone nursing the dampers. I'll need them. Out. Okay, gentlemen, time to make a stand." She stood, walking around debris from the damaged consoles, avoiding the blood her officers left near their posts.

"Castillo, I need phasers at their finest calibration. I want pinprick precision, and target the underbellies of the alien vessels. Aim for the weakest spots, support struts, exhaust ports, whatever you can find. Tie in with Hemachandra's science sensors."

"Aye, Sir," the voice replied. It sounded strong and eager, matching her own feeling. The captain needed a strong crew right now and that's what she was getting.

"Stachow, I want to execute a heading with as much control as you can master. The helm may be slow and impulse will be complaining the whole time but don't deviate. First, let's go to 217 mark 42, then increase x-axis plus ten thousand meters, spiraling upward counter-clockwise."

"Aye, Captain," the blonde replied. Her fingers moved with ease; she had obviously had recent time at the station. All the better, Garrett thought.

"Castillo," she called behind her, "what are our friends up to?"

He paused, reading the tactical sensors. "Still approaching at full impulse. They may be trying to herd us toward the binary, let all that radiation fry what's left of the ship's systems."

"Are they within phaser range?"

Another pause, this one shorter. "One minute."

Her new bridge crew snapped to work, pausing only once or twice to find a control or fine-tune a command. Before committing the ship to fresh action, she gave everyone precious seconds to acclimate themselves. She knew it was a risk with hostile vessels nearby, but she also felt it was necessary. The moments would allow them to focus their thinking on the task at hand and not be entirely reactive, which could lead to mental errors. Garrett walked to the upper ring, checking on the crew there. Near the environmental controls, she put a comforting hand on an ensign being treated for a head wound. Andrew Norrie, a doctor she recognized, looked up with a stunned expression as he pulled a covering over the dead body of another crew member. If she lost this many on the bridge, what would the total casualty count be? She didn't dare ask aloud. Time enough later for a body count, she thought with a small shudder.

The bridge continued to be bathed in crimson lighting, but at least the acrid smoke was barely noticeable. Maybe she had become accustomed to it. No, she noticed then, the environmental controls were still intact and working.

The ship seemed to handling its new course well, giving her confidence to feed the rest of the instructions to her new helmsman. Dire communications on the overhead speakers had also died down, and Nee seemed to be handling the calls well. In fact, he seemed almost relaxed at the post, as if he were meant to serve there.

Stachow nodded as Garrett reeled off additional course information and then checked to make sure Castillo had the phasers targeted to her specifications. He looked at her with an apologetic grin, saying, "I only took the basic courses on tactical, Sir. Didn't even test on them during training cruises. Usually sat at the helm."

"That's all right, Castillo," Garrett replied, returning the smile. "You'll get a chance to sit there another time. Right now, you're my gunnery officer. You do know which are the firing controls?"

"Yes, Ma'am," he replied emphatically.

"Good. Okay, Stachow, stand by for my mark. Captain to the crew," Garrett said, addressing the speakers above her. "I've asked a lot of this ship in the course of our confrontation. I'm asking for a little more right now. Secure your positions. The next few minutes could get rough." Garrett studied the tactical display, still showing the blue starship being stalked by the red vessels. They were coming closer in a recognizable attack position, almost comforting in its familiarity.

She walked over to the helm, leaned over the ensign's shoulder and said, "Go."

The starship seemed to groan in complaint as it began to increase speed. On the main viewer, it appeared they were moving in a circle. Garrett had kept the viewscreen locked onto a forward view, so as the ship moved, the alien vessels came and went off the screen. Watching the readouts on the tactical screen, she checked the distance between the *Enterprise* and its adversaries; the gap between them narrowed, and she admired that the alien ships didn't slow despite the *Enterprise's* unusual movement. In the captain's mind, there was a magic number when it would be safe to release Castillo to do his part. Finally, the numbers ticked down and she bit her lower lip to steady herself, ignoring the pain from a bruise.

"Castillo, fire now."

Without responding, normally a breach of protocol, he stabbed the phaser firing controls and used his left hand to constantly adjust the targeting. Red phaser beams were seen striking the aliens' own screens. However, with each contact, their screens were clearly illuminated and seemed to crackle with energy. Perhaps they were vulnerable after all.

"Hemachandra, what do you read?"

"Their shield matrix does not seem as versatile as ours. They are weakening, but since I haven't managed proper scans, I can't begin to guess what kind of damage we're causing."

With some satisfaction, Garrett watched the tactical display and saw how her one ship was keeping three alien attackers at bay. They seemed unable or unwilling to fire their version of phasers, and their speed was dropping.

"Captain, they're breaking off, but two are trying to converge on our port nacelle," Castillo called out.

"Stachow, bring us about 145 degrees. Castillo, arm photon torpedo, lead vessel."

"Aye, Sir," both replied, twenty fingers moving rapidly.

"Fire," she commanded after a brief pause. For a change, she heard something: the torpedo being launched. Garrett watched it on the tactical readout. Counting to herself, the captain watched as the torpedo reached the vessel and exploded at the count of eight, apparently shattering its shields. Or overloaded them, as coruscating energy crackled around the ship—so much so that the companion vessel veered off.

Before moving away, though, it unleashed its own firepower, a blinding white bolt of energy that crackled against the *Enterprise's* shields and once more rocked the deck. No one fell, this time, for which the battered Garrett was thankful.

"One vessel incapacitated," Hemachandra reported. "All energy readings are dropping off the scale. They won't be causing anyone trouble now."

"Good shot, Castillo; sure you haven't done this before?"

"Certain of it," he replied with a broad smile. He refused to take his eyes off the station, which didn't surprise the captain. Confident as he was, it was all new to him and he was fighting nerves. She recognized it from when she had to assume command herself, when the *Gandhi's* captain was killed during an exchange with the Cardassians. She recalled the nerves, the adrenaline, and the outright fear that she had to fight while trying to stay focused on getting out alive.

"Singh to bridge! Captain, we have system failures throughout the ship. ODN junctures are shorting out. We've got everything bypassed but we've taken a beating. We'll be limping all the way home at this rate." Garrett had never heard Cat sound so troubled, and that in itself was a warning.

"Understood. Do what you can to hold us together. We still have two ships out there ready to do battle. Out." Her rising spirits reversed course.

Turning to her new command crew, the captain wasn't sure what she felt. It wasn't confidence, nor was it fear. So far they handled her orders just fine even if they took longer to execute commands than she wanted. Still, they fought through the carnage and rose to the occasion. Just what she had hoped for, what, days ago? A quick look at the chronometer shocked her: it had just been hours before when she sat in the rec room. And since they first encountered the aliens? Maybe an hour, probably less.

"What do they want?" she asked aloud.

"Got me," Castillo ventured. He kept whatever else was on his mind to himself.

"Without saying so, they are clearly protecting this sector of space," Hemachandra said. "Maybe their method of communication can't be translated."

"Could be," Garrett said, thoughtfully. "Castillo, status of the other vessels?"

"Functional but keeping their distance. The other one has moved out of range and is being protected by the others."

"These three came without warning. Any way to determine if there are more nearby?"

Hemachandra scowled at his science console. "No way, Captain. We didn't see these three when we were operating at peak performance. With the binary radiation interfering with the sensors, plus all the new energy unleashed in the area, it's still a mess out there."

Snapping her fingers, Garrett stood up and walked to the tactical display. Tracing a path with her forefinger, she stared for a moment.

"Stachow, plot us a course, back to the Federation but as evasive and erratic as can be for the first parsec. Castillo, rig five photon torpedoes with timers. I want them to go off five seconds apart, dispersion pattern Sierra."

She moved from the screen back around the upper ring, pausing at the science station. Hemachandra looked up at her, a questioning look on his weathered face. She smiled, leaning her uninjured hip against the bulkhead. "If we can't tell where they came from, we may create enough spatial interference to mask our path back to the Federation." He nodded in appreciation of her strategy, which gave her additional confidence.

"Photon torpedoes ready," Castillo called out.

"Course plotted, I think," Stachow added. The captain smiled and moved down toward helm, checking over the plot. Garrett adjusted two course corrections and patted Stachow's shoulder. "Not bad for a beginner," she complimented.

"Singh, bridge. We'll need warp speed shortly. What do you have for me?"

A pause and then the engineer replied, "I can give you warp 6, nothing better, and only for a short while. Will it do?"

"In a pinch. Stand by." Garrett resumed her seat, looking around the entire bridge. Everyone was at work, no one showing any hesitation in getting his or her jobs done. Damage control parties were already refitting the damaged helm console. She'd have to wrap this up and then get down to sickbay for the grisly body count. No question Garrett had been avoiding contacting CMO Casado, and the news must be bad since he had not called the bridge during the entire battle or come up with the others. It would make for a long trip home.

"Okay, crew. Let's go home. Stachow, execute the course. Castillo, launch the torpedoes in ten seconds and then give me a wide dispersal phaser barrage. Let's scare the aliens into hesitating as long as possible."

The *Enterprise* leapt into warp, more smoothly than the captain had hoped for. The view on the forward screen distorted as the warp bubble changed space. Rear phasers shot beam after beam as torpedoes streaked away from the ship. It was a sudden burst of activity that gave the captain a feeling of accomplishment. Battered or not, the starship was not going down without a fight.

"Alien vessels trying pursuit, going to warp," Castillo said from tactical. "We've got a good head start and they seem to be faltering past warp 4." A few seconds passed in silence and then he added, "Gaining ground and the evasive course has them confused. They're heading 14 degrees away from our present position."

"Not bad, but still close enough to find us with sensors. Keep it up, Mr. Stachow, Mr. Castillo. Look sharp in case reinforcements turn up."

For the next ten minutes, space was quiet. The stars distorted on the viewer as the starship traveled at seemingly impossible speed. The tactical board had to be reconfigured to indicate the vast distance now between the alien ships and the *Enterprise*. No other aliens appeared on the still-fuzzy sensor scans. Garrett could tell by simple feel that the ship was struggling at warp 6 but didn't dare lessen speed so quickly.

Ten minutes became fifteen, fifteen became thirty, and finally Garrett allowed herself to relax. She rose from the command seat and patted her officers on the shoulder. "Good work," she said quietly. "And thank you."

Looking around at the grinning Hemachandra, Garrett realized with finality that the danger was over.

"Bring us to Yellow Alert, shields down. Reduce speed to warp 3 and let's assess the damage. Damage-control teams take priority. Mr. Nee, contact Starfleet. I'd like permission to get repairs at the nearest facility. Feed them our sensor logs for the last two hours. Finally, Mr. Castillo, launch several warning buoys. Work with Mr. Nee on a universal message. I want this sector off-limits to Federation vessels until we better know what's going on out here."

Everyone acknowledged the commands and set about their work. She looked among them with a mixture of pride and regret. She was going to miss those who gave their lives just a short while ago. Garrett hoped they would rest easy knowing the ship was in capable hands. The crew lived up to her hopes.

"Captain," Castillo said.

She turned and looked at him, his face all serious.

"I agreed with Mr. Carmona. The *Constellation* ships are better for deep space. I did research on them at the academy." He paused a moment. "I thought you should know."

She looked at him, trying to recall the context. Finally, she gave him a small smile. "When we get back to base, the first round of drinks will be on me," she said, the first happy tone in her voice since Red Alert sounded. Her crew broke into smiles and watched as she strode off the bridge. Stepping inside the turbolift, she turned command over to Hemachandra, her highest ranking officer left on duty, and ordered the lift to sickbay.

Hours later, the shift changed once more, and the captain found herself seated in a different rec room, fussing over her typical sandwich. It just wasn't right anymore, and she pushed the plate away. Joining her were Singh and Casado. Both officers were clearly exhausted, having done their part to keep the *Enterprise* running. Casado, a seasoned medical officer, was solemn, given the work just completed. Neither said a word as the captain dithered over the plate.

"I've appointed Nelson as acting first officer until we get home," the captain said quietly. "His first task will be organizing the memorial services. God, what will I say to those families?"

Everyone at the table fell silent for a few moments.

"The buzz is different," Singh noted.

Garrett looked up. "What do you mean?" She strained her ears and caught pieces of conversations.

"I fell out of the Jefferies tube, right on top of Aria. Talk about your compromising positions."

"I must have set a dozen bones in under an hour."

"Could you see us spiral? Flawless. Just flawless."

"I'll miss Junior. She was a great bunkmate."

After a minute, Garrett returned to her drink, nodding in agreement with the chief engineer.

"Next mission will be different, you'll see," Cat added. "Guess the Warin will have to wait for a new colony world a little longer."

"You're right," the captain admitted. She was still coping with the loss of twenty-seven crew members and the serious injuries to another fifty-three—a sizeable percentage of her crew. "I got what I asked for, though. I got to see what they were made of and I like them. I think this won't be the only encounter that will help us live up to the *Enterprise* name."

"You mean being seen as a maverick?" Doctor Casado asked.

"No, Esteban," Garrett sighed. "April, Pike, Kirk—all did things as needed. We remember when they broke the rules, but they also served with distinction. And more than the captains, the crews were exemplary. I want the same reputation."

"Well, you've certainly gotten further along than poor Harriman," Singh said.

"Que?" asked the doctor.

"Poor John Harriman," Singh explained. "Captain of the *Enterprise*-B, lost a piece of his ship and Captain James T. Kirk, all during its first voyage," Singh said, wiping her mouth with a napkin. "Now that's a legacy to live down."

Garrett, who didn't necessarily like Harriman's history, suddenly felt obligated to defend her predecessor. "He recovered nicely, don't you think? Handled the Melkot problem pretty well and certainly deserved the Zee-Magnees Prize."

"Maybe," the engineer said with a wicked smile. "Still, pretty dumb to let a starship leave dock without being fully prepped. At least you had the sense to leave Mars with a full complement."

Garrett looked wistfully around the room and finally said, "Well, if I can't learn from history, and avoid those mistakes, then I don't deserve this command . . . or this crew." With that, she stood and began to walk from table to table, making contact with her people. Patting a shoulder here, answering a question at a few tables, and listening to their concerns. If they followed her lead, then they were going to be a crew that spoke to one another, and worked together.

Singh turned to Casado, who had helped himself to the untouched sandwich, and happily said, "Pretty good captain, don't you think?"

Captain Jean-Luc Picard
U.S.S. Enterprise-D

"I mean you're acting like you know exactly which way to go . . . but you're only guessing. Do you do this all the time?"

Dr. Beverly Crusher, *Star Trek: The Next Generation*

JOHN VORNHOLT

Rank, the saying goes, has its privileges. John Vornholt chose to set the following story in a quaint little getaway known as The Captain's Table. No one is certain where it is, but it is for the exclusive use of ship captains. The price of admission is a story. The concept was introduced in a series of *Star Trek* novels some years back and makes a return appearance here.

Captain Picard, current commander of the *Enterprise*-E, upholds the legacy of those who preceded him. He also has had the rare opportunity to fight alongside both Kirk and Spock, something the other captains never had the chance to experience.

John has chosen to concentrate on a little-explored aspect of Picard's personality, his dealings with youth. While no longer a youth himself, John has written numerous young adult novels including *How to Sneak into the Girl's Locker Room* and several nonfiction books. An accomplished playwright, John has several plays to his credit and has even performed on stage before turning full-time to writing. He has several *Star Trek* adventures to his credit, plus scripts for a wide variety of animated television programs.

Currently a resident of Arizona, John is rather happy with the notion that he's getting to write adventures to quicken a reader's blood much the way pulp heroes such as Doc Savage inspired him in his own youth.

The Captain and the King

Mmmm. Thank you, Cap, this is delightful. After tasting this ex-cellent Pinot Noir—quite a rare vintage for a Delacroix—I will be honored to recount a tale. I see many comrades and allies here tonight, but no Andorians. That's a pity, because it would be nice to have an Andorian's perspective on these events. Or perhaps that's as it should be, under the circumstances I can speak a bit more freely—

"And no one can call you a liar!" crowed a voice from the back of the dimly lit tavern, to much laughter.

True. But this much is also true: next to the Klingons, no race in the Federation has a more warlike history than our tall, blue-skinned comrades, the Andorians. Like humans, they are prone to fighting awful civil wars, so they depend upon a strong central government—a hereditary monarchy. It's been repressive at times, but it's held them together. They had a long reign of peace under a ruler named Collev, who died recently.

"Good riddance," growled a hard-bitten, green-skinned Orion. "That Collev was nothing but an old brigand."

Perhaps, but he made the shuttles run on time. Both Collev and his son and successor, Bregev, died in the same shuttlecraft accident. Or was it an accident? That's another story for another storyteller, but I'm sure many of you remember the harsh words and accusations that followed Collev's death. The Andorians have achieved peace again, but few of you know how that peace was obtained . . . and at what cost.

My involvement began when the *Enterprise* was sent to mediate and show the colors. With no clear-cut successor to Collev, two armed camps quickly formed. The Red Sash were renegades from the military who supported a general with uncertain bloodlines. The Absolutists were the old guard who supported Collev; without his family, to rally around, they were worried about staying in power.

Both sides were capable of devastating a whole planet, so a certain mixture of tact and firmness was necessary. Since Andorians are impressed by force, the *Enterprise* was chosen to go. I was a mediator, but I also had a message: if the Andorians started a civil war, they faced expulsion from the Federation.

"So they sent Captain Jean-Luc Picard, a well-known hero," said a Ferengi captain. "Smart."

Both sides were intractable, and I just tried to keep them talking. Neither one of them was an exemplar of virtue—the Red Sash were renegades with a history of terrorism, and the Absolutists wanted to keep their power and privilege at any cost. At least, both of them had a totalitarian bent.

My first officer and I took long walks in the streets of Andoria, discussing how to end the impasse. The capital city, Laibok, is a magnificent place with cockeyed buildings and towering doorways, all built with a complete disregard for symmetry. The doors are built for the lofty Andorians and their antennae, and their sloping houses reminded me of ramshackle cottages in the French countryside. I certainly didn't want to see any of this unique architecture destroyed by a pointless war.

On our walk, Commander Riker and I entered a bazaar, chockful of exotic clothes, food, and trade goods. I can still remember that pungent perfume the Andorians cherish—there were barrels of the stuff. One booth offered rather garish portraits of King Collev and many of his predecessors. One of them in particular intrigued me, because the king was so young and handsome-looking, while the others were all somber and aged. The silver frame had a latinum plaque that bore the words "King Thurl of Greater Andoria."

"Is that what he looked like?" asked Riker with surprise. "Awfully young."

"He was king just before Collev," rasped a voice behind us. We turned to see an old woman with wrinkled blue skin and antennae which drooped over her lofty forehead. Her hair was as white as a nova. "I can get you an autographed copy—if he's still signing them."

"Still signing them?" I asked. "Do you mean that King Thurl is still alive?"

"Ex-King Thurl. He abdicated while he was quite young . . . just after that likeness was made."

"Why?" asked Riker.

The shopkeeper shrugged her bony shoulders. "He was bought off. You are aware, aren't you, that our marriages involve four partners, and family connections get rather complicated? The royal family is actually a ragtag collection of families related by marriage—some wealthy, some not. Thurl wasn't rich, but his bloodlines were impeccable from all four parents. Collev had plenty of money but commoners in his family. So Thurl sold his throne for riches beyond imagining, although he's had to enjoy his wealth in exile. A sad exile, I would imagine."

"Do you like the monarchy?" I asked.

"Like it?" The Andorian spat on the dusty floor of the bazaar. "I like having a strong ruler and social order, but I also want to have some say in these matters. The problem with a monarchy is that there is no way to remove a bad king . . . except as we saw with Collev."

"You don't think his death was an accident?" asked Riker.

"Shhhh!" hissed the old woman. "We don't say such things in public." Loudly she demanded, "Do you want a royal portrait or not?"

I scratched my chin and gazed at the young king's portrait. "How old would Thurl be now?"

"About your age, I should imagine."

Riker looked at me and smiled. "If his bloodlines were impeccable back then, they're probably still impeccable."

That was exactly what I was thinking. At our next meeting with representatives of the Red Sash and the Absolutists, the bickering started all over again. I realized there was no way either of these stubborn parties would agree to the other choosing a king. It was time to suggest a third party acceptable to both.

When I suggested Thurl, both sides were in shock, because neither one could immediately produce a reason to dismiss it. My staff had even come up with precedents in Andorian history where deposed kings had come back to reclaim the throne. It took some arm-twisting, but both sides finally agreed to put Thurl back on the throne. Both got something they wanted in return—the Red Sash received a full pardon for their crimes, and the Absolutists got to keep their privileged positions.

As neither side trusted the other, they asked us to fetch Thurl from his exile on Pacifica and bring him to the coronation. Understand, this was quite a pleasant exile—on an ocean planet that many consider to be one of the most beautiful in the Federation. Thurl and his family had been living in ease and splendor for decades, and I really wondered how eager he would be to jump into the fire.

I needn't have worried. When our shuttlecraft landed on his private island, Thurl himself met us at the landing pad. He was a towering, robust man with a great shock of white hair. "Captain Picard!" he said magnanimously. "This is a great day for Andoria, our people, and my family."

After Thurl showed us around his estate, he served us afternoon tea in a courtyard surrounded by a lush garden. Lavendar bougainvillea grew everywhere, and I could smell jasmine and native flowers I didn't know—it reminded me of Tahiti. We met Thurl's family—two wives, a co-husband, and two children. One would think that a family with four adults would have numerous children, but Andorian females seldom bear more than one child in their lives. His two wives wept openly at the prospect of leaving their paradise for the capital. But it was his oldest son, Prince Yevan, who was the most vociferous.

"I refuse to go," declared the young prince, who was about seventeen years old. The youth was tall and slim, with a disdainful curl to his lip. "I don't want to leave my friends and my school. I've never even been to Andoria—why should I want to *live* there? Remember, Father, the last time you went to Andoria, they treated you shabbily. This is a dubious offer at best, and we don't need all these headaches and responsibilities. For what? We have everything we need right here, with our friends and business associates."

"He's right," said the youngest wife, sniffling through her tears. "And don't forget the danger . . . the court intrigue. What do you think happened to Collev?"

Thurl's cheeks filled with rage, and his blue skin turned a mottled shade of purple. I thought he would explode at his family, but his shoulders finally slumped in resignation.

His voice rasped, "I would expect concern from my spouses, but the selfishness of my eldest son is painful. I know . . . it's my fault that Yevan is spoiled and has no purpose in life, no sense of loyalty. What else could he learn in this pampered existence? It's true, I was treated shabbily when I was king, but I was young and foolish. I bought this paradise for you with my own shame and cowardice. . . . It seems I must keep paying."

The once and future king sighed, and his antennae seemed to droop. "It's been a high price, much higher than I anticipated. I've watched upheaval and change on my homeworld from a distance, helpless to do anything. I always knew I had made a mistake leaving the throne, and I chanted for an opportunity to redeem myself. My chants have been answered, and now it's my duty to help my people . . . to avert a civil war. There's a power vacuum and a vacuum in my heart, and I plan to fill both of them."

"Father!" said Yevan with exasperation. "You're good at making the speeches—you'll do fine at that—but think of the rest of us! Do we really have to be uprooted?"

"I'm sorry, Captain Picard," said Thurl, mustering some of his old dignity. "I'm sorry you had to see this family quarrel. We Andorians are a passionate people, even those of us in exile, and we don't like change. But change comes anyway, usually at the expense of comfort."

I cleared my throat and tried to speak softly, with an air of neutrality. "Everyone has signed the accords and agreed on you. There are no outstanding issues. We're all very appreciative that you agreed to reclaim the throne, because it *did* avert a crisis."

"My pleasure," answered Thurl, jutting his chin. "I think I'm wise enough to be king now. If my family wishes me to go home alone, then so be it. Now I can leave that much sooner, since I only have to pack for *one*. If you'll excuse me, Captain Picard, I'd like to take a last swim in the ocean. I'll miss these warm, lustrous waters."

"Can I swim with you, Father?" asked Prince Yevan, offering an olive branch of peace.

"I think not, Son. I wish to be alone." Thurl walked down the steps toward the beach, already removing his silky garments. "Show Captain Picard and his party to the gallery—I think he'll appreciate our modest collections. Captain, shall we say three hours until departure?"

"That will be fine, Sir."

It could have been much longer until departure, as far as I was concerned. Thurl's gallery was incredible—first editions of Bolian star maps, hand-carved Vulcan lyres, Klingon knives, artwork of impeccable taste from all over the galaxy. Despite opposition from his own family, I began to feel good about the selection of Thurl as king. He seemed an intelligent being, sadder but wiser after his exile, and he was motivated to do a good job.

Most of my crew had returned to the *Enterprise*, but I was still poking around the gallery when I heard a commotion outside in the corridor. I was about to stick my head out, when Prince Yevan charged into the room, looking for me. He had a wild, frightened gleam in his eyes, and I heard someone wailing in another part of the house.

"My father—" rasped the youth. "He's dead."

"What? How?" I sputtered.

"Drowned in the ocean." Yevan shook his head inconsolably. "They just found his body. He swam on that beach every day . . . hundreds of times. How could this happen?"

"We'll investigate," I promised, not knowing what else to say.

"No," muttered Yevan, replacing his grief with steely resolve. "There's no point—accident or murder, it's all the same. But I do insist that my father receive a proper royal funeral. The Valley of Sorrows is a remote wilderness on Andoria, where the royal remains are left to be consumed by wild animals, called *kritkraws*. Even if he can't be king, he can be honored as a king with the rending ceremony."

"We'll do what we can," I answered, "but my primary concern is to negotiate a peaceful transition to power for the next ruler. I need to contact the Absolutists and the Red Sash."

The young Andorian shouted, "*No!* You came here to drag my father out of his comfortable retirement—to put him in harm's way—so you owe him this much respect. You will take charge of his body, Captain Picard, and return him to Andoria for the rending. I will go with you, to make sure you do."

With that, the youth turned on his heel and marched away. I admit, I've never gotten along famously with young people—most of them are rude, spoiled, and demanding. Yevan was all of these and more. But I let him go without saying a word, forgiving his outburst as grief.

I tapped my combadge. "Picard to *Enterprise*."

"Riker here," answered a familiar voice. "I was just about to call you, Sir."

"I hope you have better news than I do, Number One. Thurl is dead—drowned in the ocean."

I heard a low whistle. "That's bad, Sir. It may explain why there are three Andorian warships trying to hide from us in the asteroid belt."

"Can you tell which camp they're in?"

"No, both sides have warships like this—*Spirit* class. They'd be a match for us."

I lowered my voice and strode away from the door. "Transport a medteam to my coordinates. Tell them to be equipped to handle a body. In fact, tell them to bring enough materials to handle two bodies."

"Yes, Sir," answered Riker, knowing when not to ask questions.

Within the hour, our medteam had taken over Thurl's body from the local authorities. After a brief autopsy, they confirmed that he had drowned. We couldn't tell whether it was an accident or not, and we didn't have time for a full investigation. Thurl's body was placed in a stasis container and brought to the lovely courtyard, where the entire household could pay their last respects.

Spouses, friends, and servants wept openly, but Prince Yevan seemed preternaturally stoic. He was intent upon seeing that his father was given royal treatment, even though the king's first reign had been brief and his second nonexistent.

I sidled up to the prince and said, "Can I see you in private?"

"Right now?" asked the youth impatiently

"It's urgent."

Yevan finally agreed to meet me in a small anteroom behind a curtain, which was perfect for my purposes. "What's so urgent, Captain Picard?" he demanded.

"Please wear this communicator badge." I pinned the badge on him and tapped my own. "Sequence one, energize. Duck your head, please."

Yevan yelped as his body dematerialized, along with mine. We rematerialized on the small transporter platform at the rear of my shuttlecraft, the one I had stepped off several hours earlier. The young Andorian glared at me. "What is the meaning of this?"

"Just trying to carry out your orders." I dashed down the aisle and slid into the pilot's chair. "Have a seat, we're leaving immediately."

"But my father's body is out there in the courtyard!"

"I'm afraid not," I answered. "It's there, behind the seats."

Yevan leaned over the last row of seats and pulled up a tarp. Under the tarp was a stasis container identical to the one lying in the courtyard, the one over which the entire household was weeping. Gingerly he touched the sides and felt cold sinew under the shroud.

"Captain, this is outrageous!" he snapped. "You've made a mockery of our customs!"

"I've done no such thing," I answered. "Now sit down, or you'll be knocked off your feet."

I ignited the thrusters, and the young Andorian stumbled into a seat just as the shuttlecraft lifted off the ground. He kept jabbering and complaining, but I ignored him while I carefully checked my instruments. I wanted to make sure nobody was following us or had paid undue attention to our departure. As we left Pacifica's atmosphere, I was satisfied that no ships were on our tail.

"All right, let me explain," I said. "I had a feeling that your house was being watched, maybe from people inside. I wanted everyone to think that your father's body, and you, were being taken to the *Enterprise*, not this little shuttlecraft. On this ship, we can come and go from Andoria as we please, without raising any suspicion. It will make the rending ceremony easier."

"I suppose so," murmured the prince. "But why couldn't you tell me in advance?"

"Because you had to disappear without a trace. I couldn't risk that you would say something."

"Why?"

I gritted my teeth, dreading this moment. "I mediated the new accords, so I know every word that's in them. The right of ascension is spelled out there for future generations, so Andorians can have a peaceful transition of power from now on. After Thurl's death, it's clearly spelled out that *you* are the rightful heir to the throne. You're next in line."

The young Andorian looked stricken with fear and anger in equal measure. "*What!* You would do this without my permission? And I'm next in line for what—assassination?"

"After Andorians crown a king, it's rare for him to be assassinated," I answered. "And nobody can hurt you if they don't know where you are. I'm sorry that you weren't consulted, but you're about to pay the price for your privileged life. You knew you were the son of a king. Or did you think all Andorians lived in such luxury?"

He stammered something, but I kept going. "Yevan, after meeting you, I don't expect you to rule your people and their vast empire. But I do want to keep you alive until we can work out some arrangement for a new ruler. Then you'll be free to sell your throne, like your father did."

"Captain Picard!" he said, his voice breaking. For the first time since we had met, tears formed in the young Andorian's pale eyes. "I never knew until today how much giving up the throne pained my father. We would see Collev on the news at some dreary dedication or meeting, and my father would laugh and say that could have been *him*. I thought my father was wildly successful . . . a carefree rogue. Now I find that he thought himself a failure. What if he did it himself . . . what if the drowning—"

"Don't think about that," I answered, feeling remorse at my bluntness. This young person had just lost one of his four parents, but it was clear that he felt a stronger bond with Thurl than the others. His carefree existence had ended with a thud, and his life was probably in danger. I realized that I should go easy on Yevan, irritating though he may have been.

"What does a king do?" he asked.

I shrugged. "I've never been a king, but I've been a captain for a long time, and I think they're similar. You can have the best advisors in the world, but at some point a decision arises that no one can make but you. Lives are often hanging in the balance; time is running short. That's why they need a king or a captain, to make the hard decisions."

I looked at my sensors, worried that I had just made a poor decision, but no one seemed to be following us. "If you're in charge, you're always a target," I went on. "Always the one to shoulder the blame. In addition it requires a great deal of courage to make decisions that affect the lives of others. And you won't always be thanked for it. Sometimes you'll make the wrong decision, and it will haunt you forever."

"Why do it then?" asked Yevan. "Why put yourself through all that?"

"You can do a lot of good for people," I answered simply. "Of course, the question arises as to why a person would choose that path to begin with. It's not always a choice. If your father had remained king, you would have been raised to be king. From the time you were a child, you would have known it was your destiny. Many officers in Starfleet are like that, descended from generations of admirals and captains. Other people just crave power, and they'll get it any way they can. Collev probably fell into that category."

"I suppose so," agreed Yevan. "You don't sound as if you came from a Starfleet tradition."

"Me? No. Some of us take a job and find out we have a knack for leadership along the way. No matter how you come to it, the best part is the good you can do for people. Right now you're in a position to do tremendous good, Yevan. You might be able to avert a war."

The youth scoffed. "I don't even understand why they're fighting. No matter who's in charge, including me or my father, the Andorians will just end up with another dictator. I've lived on Pacifica, and studied on Earth, and I've been exposed to democracy. Why do we cling to this outdated form of government?"

"Fear of change," I answered. "I talked to a few common citizens on Andoria, and I think they would embrace democracy, if given a chance. But the Federation can't impose a form of government on a member planet—they have to do it themselves. The people who have the power will always resist giving it up."

"Well, not me," declared Yevan, folding his arms and closing his eyes. "I could have all the power my world offers, but I don't want it.

I have a nice life already, and when we're done with the rending, I'm going back to it. Wake me up when we get there, Captain Picard."

"Aye, Sir," I muttered under my breath. For someone who didn't want to be royalty, Yevan had a regal way about him.

Thank you, Cap, for filling my wine glass. My throat was getting quite parched. If I still have your attention, Captains, let me go on with my tale.

The voyage in the shuttlecraft proved uneventful—after locking the autopilot on course I even let the lad take a watch, so I could get some sleep. By arrangement with my first officer, I wasn't to be contacted as long as they were keeping the Andorians busy and the ruse was working. Our official story was that Prince Yevan was aboard the *Enterprise*, too, and that we would be delayed in departure. As long as the *Enterprise* was in orbit around Pacifica, I felt the ship was safe from attack.

During the journey, I tried to think of ways to salvage the situation, but they all involved making Yevan king. I wasn't sure whether I wanted to thrust him into that position, or impose *him* upon his long-suffering people. I resolved to finish our funeral and get the lad to safety before worrying about the future.

At least he proved useful deciphering our Andorian maps, and he was able to find a remote mountain range named for the *kritkraws*. All I knew was that it was on the northernmost continent of Andoria, far removed from population centers.

On reentry, we sneaked behind the vapor trails of a freighter to avoid detection, and we kept low. I must say I did a good job piloting the shuttle through those remote fjords and mist-shrouded peaks. This was a glittering, snow-crusted wilderness with no settlements. Where the mist cleared below us, I could see animal tracks in the snow. The icy blue trees looked like starfish washed up on a brilliant white beach.

I had a navigator who had never been here either, but Yevan did a commendable job following the maps. With only a few half-remembered stories about his grandfather's funeral to guide him, he led us in a fairly direct route into the heart of the mountain range. Still I wondered if we would ever find the legendary Valley of Sorrows in the unending wasteland and thick fog.

"Are there any landmarks?" I asked doubtfully.

"People were here not too long ago for Collev's rending," answered Yevan. "If we could find some sign of that—a road or a camp—we would know where to set down."

I peered down at shrouds of misty clouds, broken only by glimpses of frozen wilderness. "Does it make that much difference where we land?"

"Yes, it does," snapped Yevan. "And we must bear my father by hand to the Valley of Sorrows." His pale eyes narrowed. "No transporters."

"You're quite the traditionalist, except when it comes to following your father's example. He wanted to be king to prevent a war, but you don't care about that."

Yevan snorted a laugh. "Come on, Captain Picard. Do you really think *I* would make a good king? Do you want to come to work for me as my secretary of defense? Or my chief ambassador?"

"My loyalties are spoken for," I answered. "As to whether you would make a good king or not, I don't know. I don't think *you* know."

The boy scowled and turned away from me to gaze out the window. He suddenly blinked in amazement and scooted forward in his seat. "Did you see *that?* It looked like a lean-to in the snow! Down there . . . near that big tree."

"Where?" I asked, peering into a sparkling white landscape of shimmering snow, blue trees, and a pervasive white fog. Not seeing anything, I doubled back around and made another pass over the same area. As if by a miracle, the clouds parted long enough for me to see a small patch of beige canvas under the frozen boughs.

Using my sensors to guide me, I swooped through the layer of fog and glided into a meadow between two peaks. The trees were sparse enough for me to avoid them, but I didn't know how much snow there was until we plowed into it, burying the shuttlecraft in a huge drift. We looked out the window at the curtain of white which engulfed us.

"Nice landing," muttered Yevan. "Now how do we get out?"

"Venting some hot air should melt the snow," I answered, keeping my temper with the young Andorian. "While we wait, we can put on our jackets and gloves." Our cold-weather gear was of civilian design, stripped of Starfleet insignias.

It took a while to melt the snow around the shuttlecraft and dress ourselves for the cold, but we managed to push the hatch open and claw our way through the drift. With considerable effort, we finally reached snow that was packed firmly enough for us to stand on. I rose unsteadily to my feet, and the cold wind plucked at my face with a million tiny tentacles.

I gazed around at fog-shrouded foothills and twisted blue trees, but couldn't tell one direction from another. Snow hung heavily on the tree boughs, and it also hung in the air, swirling in the sharp wind. Unreal silence graced this stark wilderness, making it seem like a vast tomb. Prince Yevan looked more thoughtful than usual, and I realized that this was the first time he had ever set foot on his homeworld. I wanted to ask him how he felt about it, but he turned swiftly and trudged off.

"The lean-to is this way," he said without explanantion.

In deep snow, a long-legged Andorian travels much faster than a human, I can tell you. I was trailing several meters behind Yevan when a pungent smell—like greasy wet fur—shot through the rarfied air. I whirled in the direction of the wind just in time to see a pack of dark figures burst from beneath a tree. The beasts came charging toward us, loping easily over the pristine snow.

"Yevan!" I shouted, but my words were shredded by the wind. The animals kept coming closer—from a distance, they looked like shaggy wildebeests. As they drew closer, they looked more like wild boars with curling tusks and fangs, plus long legs. I drew my phaser pistol from my holster.

"No, Captain! You mustn't shoot them!" I turned to see Yevan charging me from behind, trying to deflect my phaser. I fended off his clumsy move and dumped him in the snow; then I heard frantic panting and snarling to my right. I turned to see the first creature no more than ten meters away, closing fast and lowering his massive tusks. I aimed to fire, but Yevan jumped to his feet and ran in front of me, yelling at the beasts in a language I didn't recognize.

His crazy act kept me from shooting, and it also surprised our attackers, who scattered as the tall Andorian ran among them, waving his hands and shouting. Now they looked like herd animals scared by a predator as they circled us and reformed in a pack fifty meters away. Yevan continued to regale them, shouting one phrase over and over again. Remarkably, the animals seemed to be listening.

"Are you speaking to them?" I asked. "They're *kritkraws*, right?"

"Yes on both counts," he panted. "It's part of the Rending Chant, telling them why we're here."

"And you think they understand?"

"They're keeping their distance, aren't they?" He ignored me as he continued to shout into the wind in an ancient tongue, sounding very much like the monarch of this lonely wilderness. After a long while, the *kritkraws* loped behind a massive blue tree, where they were out of sight but within striking distance.

I stepped in front of the lad. "Can we leave your father here?"

"No, Captain Picard, because there's an altar where we're supposed to leave the fallen king." Yevan pointed in the direction we'd been walking; then he drew a deep breath. "But I suppose we should go back and get him—there's no reason to make the trip twice."

"That was quite brave what you did back there," I told him evenly. "But if you ever attack me again, I'll make sure you're bound and gagged for the rest of the trip."

Yevan rose to his full height and smiled. "You know, Captain Picard, if you had your wish, *I* would be the supreme ruler of this planet. I could have you imprisoned for life or fed to the *kritkraws* with a nod of my head. Think about that . . . absolute power. Do you see me with that?"

I looked squarely at him. "I know what power is, and you may not be as callow as you think you are. You could grow into the job, like I did. As your father found out, there's always somebody willing to take power from you. He also found out that the only ignominy lies in not even trying to use that power wisely."

"Let's get the real king," muttered the lad, trudging back through our footprints. "By the way, if you had shot a *kritkraw*—even stunned it—the others would have gone into a frenzy. There'd be nothing left of us by now."

"We need to communicate better," I grumbled, but he was already stomping away.

Thurl was a large Andorian, so his body was ungainly as well as heavy, and we struggled with that container for hours through deep snow, swirling ice crystals, and dense fog. The trees were like mountains themselves—towering blue pyramids covered in snow, which dropped like fluffy bombs every few seconds. I was in the rear and kept cautious watch over the *kritkraws* that were following us; I resorted to a tricorder hanging from my neck whenever they were out of my sight.

The *kritkraws* were out there all right, and growing in numbers. They were up to about twenty now, and there wasn't enough of Thurl's meager remains to feed them all.

Yevan plowed ahead, paying no attention to our pursuers or me. By walking in his footprints, I was able to keep up, but I didn't have a clue where we were going. I don't know how he knew where to go, because he was no more familiar with this land than I. Yet he trudged onward with single-minded purpose. The oppressive silence and prickly wind kept me alert, although I was more concerned about the darkness; it descended swiftly, turning the white forest into a gloomy shadowland.

I took out a handheld light and strapped it to my shoulder, but the beam barely pierced the thick fog, lighting only a few meters ahead of us. Andoria had no moon, but the stars came out in full glory, as glimpsed through intermittent patches of clearness. Still Yevan trudged onward, and I followed, wondering if both of us had taken leave of our senses. The setting and the cold, misty night both had the quality of a dream.

In the fading light we saw it—the tattered remnants of a beige tarp, stretched across some poles to form a shabby lean-to. Dragging the body across the snow, we rushed toward the weathered canvas as if it were real shelter in this frozen wilderness. Halfway there, the daylight fled completely, the snow turned into driven sleet, and the temperature seemed to drop ten more degrees.

"This is the place," said Yevan with satisfaction, although I didn't see anything that looked like an altar. "We can leave him here."

I dropped the legs of the corpse and dashed under what little shelter the lean-to offered. It was hardly better than hiding under a tree. The youth crawled in after me and removed his hat, letting his antennae uncurl to their full length. He sat cross-legged in the dim pool of light from our lanterns and looked earnestly at me. "I must chant. You can sit there, but please don't disturb me."

"Go ahead." Sitting quietly and drinking from my canteen was all that interested me at the moment.

As Yevan chanted in the old tongue, I heard the growls outside the lean-to. I started to draw my phaser, but the lad flashed me a stern look. Nevertheless, I stayed on guard as the *kritkraws* ripped apart the body lying only a few meters away from us. Yevan's strong chanting seemed to add to the unreal noises cutting through the fog on that foreboding night.

Finally the lad finished his ceremony, and the *kritkraws* stopped sniffing around the lean-to and went away. He looked at me with tears in his eyes and said, "He would have appreciated this gesture. Thank you, Captain Picard, for bringing us here."

I shivered and rubbed my arms. "Do we have to spend the night out here?"

"No, although some would." He crawled past me and exited at the opposite end, away from where we had left his father. I followed after him, my hand never far from my phaser pistol. Neither one of us looked to see what remained of the container we had dragged such a distance.

Now it was extrememly dark and cold outside, and we pushed our aching muscles to get back to the shuttlecraft. At least we could retrace our footprints in the snow and know exactly where we were going. Once again, I was aware of the *kritkraws* following our trail, and this time Yevan was aware of them, too. Several times he barked his chant into the wind, but I wasn't sure that words alone would keep the beasts at bay.

In our urgency, maybe we both sensed that something else was out there, following us . . . watching us. I didn't know for sure until the red beam of a phaser shot from the thick fog and punched into a nearby tree, eliciting a howl of rage.

"Picard!" snapped Yevan. "I told you not to fire at them!"

"It wasn't *me!*" I insisted.

We looked around, but no culprit stepped forward to admit to the crime. Suddenly a spread of phaser beams streaked over our heads, and we dove into the snow. But the unknown assailants weren't shooting at us—they were shooting at the *kritkraws*, and hitting them, judging by the howls. Within seconds, we were surrounded by growling, snarling shapes, darting nervously in the fog. I tried to pick them out with my light, but I only got glimpses of them.

Then I remembered what Yevan had said about them going into a frenzy, and I lifted my weapon just as the first one charged out of the mist. I fired blindly at the *kritkraw*, not hitting it until it was nearly on top of me. The unconscious animal flew past, its tusks centimeters from my chest, and its legs spun me around. As I fell to my knees, I saw another one dashing through the mist, and I shot again. I hit it, but more dark shapes were massing in the gloom.

When they charged, even Yevan was forced to shoot, and we were soon standing back to back, sweeping the dark fog with phaser beams. The lad shouted, "Someone deliberately set them upon us!"

Wounded *kritkraws* yelped as they fell, but others massed behind them, flashing through the snow like demons glimpsed in dim smoke.

With frenzied snorts, six *kritkraws* thundered toward us at once, tusks and fur flying. We felled the first row, but more came behind them, leaping over their fallen comrades.

I may have promised no transporters, but I didn't promise to die. I tapped my combadge and shouted, "Picard to shuttlecraft, execute sequence one!"

Yevan crouched down behind me, still firing at the maddened beasts. Our bodies disappeared just as the herd stampeded over our position. When we materialized on the shuttlecraft, my relief quickly turned to dismay, because four Andorians sat in our cramped cockpit, their weapons trained upon us.

"Why couldn't you have the decency to die an accidental death?" asked a female intruder. "Drop your weapons."

Yevan looked at me, waiting to see what I would do, but the female said, "Don't be foolish. We've got a squadron outside and ships all over the area. Drop your weapons."

I did as I was told, and Yevan followed suit. There was something about her righteous bearing that I recognized. "Red Sash?"

"Very good, Captain Picard," said the female, rising to her feet. "I am called Jandara."

"Did you kill my father?" demanded Yevan.

"No. And we didn't kill Collev or Bregev, although it appears certain that we'll have to kill *you.*" She whispered to her underlings, two of whom gathered up our phasers and crawled out the hatch into the swirling wind.

"Why kill anyone?" I asked. "This is Prince Yevan, the successor to the throne—chosen by your own leaders."

"That's all a moot point now," said Jandara. "A faction of the Absolutists have thrown all those accords down a black hole. They're the ones who killed Thurl, probably Collev, too. Didn't you hear that there's a coronation tomorrow—to crown the grand counsel, Levak, as king? We're massing our troops, getting ready to attack the coronation."

"Levak!" exclaimed Yevan with a derisive laugh. "That old fraud? His claims have been dismissed countless times."

"Not anymore. The Absolutists obviously prefer him to *you.*"

I sputtered in anger, "Don't . . . don't do this! You can't throw away weeks of negotiations to start a war."

"We didn't start it!" snapped Jandara.

"Let me handle this, Captain," said Yevan in a dismissive tone of voice. He smiled and mustered all of his considerable charm for the Andorian woman. "Jandara, who do *you* want to see on the throne?"

"Why, General Hargrev, of course."

Yevan nodded sympathetically. "That sounds like a good choice to me. So allow me to take the throne for a brief time; then I'll proclaim the general my successor—and abdicate. This is what my father did, and it's what I'll be happy to do. I'm just a playboy, right, Captain Picard? I've shown no interest in ruling Andoria, although you've tried to talk me into it."

"That's true," I grumbled, wondering how far he would take this.

"Just let me show up tomorrow," said Yevan, "and you and your cronies will be in power in no time. Without firing a shot." He held out his hands and smiled cheerfully, as if he were bred to make deals like this. "Of course, it will cost you some latinum. After that, perhaps you and I can take a trip together to discuss other arrangements we could make—marriages and such, to cement our bonds."

Jandara stared intently at him, then she leaned over the console and hit a comm panel. "Did you get that, Sir?"

"Yes, I did," answered an authoritative voice. "Don't kill them, but bring them to my headquarters."

In due time, we met inside an underground bunker with General Hargrev himself, a legendary figure who had remained in hiding all through my mediations with the Red Sash. Even now, he was unprepossessing for an Andorian leader—short, rather rotund, and balding. He had an intensity about his eyes, however, which brooked no interference. I wasn't about to give him any, because I wasn't doing much of the talking.

Yevan held court. "I really welcome this chance to meet you, General Hargrev," he began, "because I've wondered how to turn this windfall to my advantage. I don't want the throne—I've never set foot on Andoria until today, and I don't feel much loyalty toward her. Look at the videologs of the shuttlecraft, and you'll see Captain Picard trying to talk me into it. But I don't want all the headaches—let's leave that to someone who will do a better job. Like you."

The general looked doubtful over the idea that he could seize power so easily. "And you won't betray me? Because if you do, young prince, I will feed you to the *kritkraws* . . . while you're still alive."

"I'll be king for a day," claimed Yevan. "Just long enough to sign a couple of proclamations. And you'll be making a deposit to my personal account on Pacifica. I would say a million bars of latinum—"

"A million!" gasped General Hargrev. "You drive a hard bargain."

"It's all to make your life easier. Think of it, General—absolute power! I've thought of it, and Captain Picard and I have talked about it. But that's not for me—let wiser heads prevail." The young Andorian bowed to our captor.

"And what should we do with this meddling human?" General Hargrev scowled at me.

"Oh, he has to come along to legitimize the transition in the eyes of the Federation." Yevan looked at me as if I were an insect. "He'll cooperate, because he mediated the accords which gave my father, then me, the throne. Captain Picard made all of this possible."

I grumbled under my breath, unable to refute this. At least we weren't being executed, which was probably our only other option. I was, however, disappointed that Yevan had sold out so quickly. Apparently, nothing I had said had made any impression on him.

Under cover of darkness, hidden away in a freighter, we stole back to the capitol city of Laibok. I wanted to contact the Federation, the *Enterprise*, anybody, but I had to let Yevan play his hand. His solution, as onerous as it was, would at least avert a war. But I worried for future generations of Andorians; unless the transition of power became more civil, they would eventually face a war.

Yevan and I were kept under heavy guard, and I fought the temptation to talk to him. He had made his decision, and he was in a position to carry it out. Without any warning, we were ordered onto a transporter platform. Seconds later, we beamed into a great hall that was filled with Andorian dignitaries and a scattering of diplomats from around the Federation.

Our Red Sash escorts surrounded us, their weapons protecting us from the guards who started forward. "What is the meaning of this?" shouted a robed dignitary on the podium.

Jaranda stepped forward and pointed at Yevan with pride. "This is Prince Yevan, son of Thurl, true successor to the throne! We demand that you stop your illegal coronation and recognize him. By your own accords, Yevan is the true successor—not that pretender, Levak."

"But Yevan is dead!" shouted someone.

"No, he's not. This is Yevan!" countered Jaranda.

There was considerable murmuring in the crowd, and more than a few Federation dignitaries were staring at me. I hated to condone these unruly proceedings, but I had to speak the truth. "I'm Captain Jean-Luc Picard," I began, "and I mediated the new accords. By full consensus, Yevan is the next in line to the throne, and I will swear that *this* is Prince Yevan. He has been in my company since his father's death."

Despite my testimony, the crowded hall looked as if it would erupt in fighting. In one corner of the room, I could see someone dressed in regal robes—probably Levak; he was mustering a squad of soldiers. The Red Sash formed ranks around us, and many of them appeared to be itching for a fight. Many members of the audience began to rush toward cover.

Yevan suddenly broke from our ranks and ran up to the podium, exposing himself to every weapon in the cavernous room. He pushed the old dignitary away and seized the speaker's stand, and his amplified voice boomed throughout the hall.

"Everyone!" he shouted. "Be calm! Sheathe your weapons! We have no reason to fight. The Andorian people are a great people, and we have shown that we are above petty violence. Let this be a day of reason and forgiveness, along with celebration!"

Now the panicky crowd began to applaud. When fighting didn't break out, most of them started returning to their seats. While no one was watching me, I slipped away into an alcove and tapped by combadge, hoping against hope that the *Enterprise* was in orbit. To my relief, I reached my first officer on the bridge.

Yevan waved his hands, quieting the crowd. "We have observers here from around the galaxy—let's prove to them that we Andorians can have a peaceful transition of power. I know that a small number of misguided people killed my father in order to install Counsel Lavek on the throne, but I won't seek revenge. I forgive you all. When I'm king, I will pardon you all!"

Now the vast hall was so quiet that I could hear breathing and feet shuffling. Spontaneously, a wave of applause and cheering broke out, and the gathered crowd chanted, "Crown him! Crown him! Long live King Yevan!"

The lad nodded solemnly and turned to face the robed dignitary he had pushed aside. The man opened a large scroll and began to read in a shaky voice, asking Yevan questions every so often. The youth answered in a ringing voice, as if he had trained all his life for this moment. Roars of acclaim met his every word, and the crowd was cheering lustily by the time the ceremony ended.

I thought the worst was over, but I could see the soldiers of the Red Sash pushing forward, waiting to see if Yevan would abdicate and put their man in place. Yevan held up his hands, indicating he had more to say, and the crowd hushed breathlessly.

"For my first royal decree," said Yevan, "I pardon everyone connected with the death of my father, King Collev, and Prince Bregev. Let the mistakes of the past stay in the past. For my second decree, I declare that we will have a vote of the people. This plebiscite will decide whether to keep the monarchy or to install a democracy with elected officials. If the people choose a democracy in which everyone has an equal voice, I will give up power and step down!"

"Traitor!" screamed Jaranda, lifting her weapon to fire. Her blue beam caught Yevan in the shoulder, spun him around, and dropped him to the stage.

I slapped my combadge and shouted, "Two to beam up! Direct to sickbay!"

I never saw the rest of the mayhem, but I heard that Jaranda and several Red Sash were killed that day. I was more concerned about my young friend, for whom I had developed considerable respect. I've rarely ever seen a more noble or courageous act than his.

It took two weeks in our sickbay to nurse King Yevan back to health, and he almost died. I sat with the lad every day, filling him in on the progress of the plebiscite. As we both hoped, democracy won by a landslide, and the common people had a joyous celebration in the streets.

"Do you see, Captain?" said Yevan from his bed. "I had no intentions of ever taking that job."

"I'm enormously proud of you," I replied. "Your people love you for what you've done—you could easily be elected the first president."

"Which is precisely why I'm never going back there." Yevan lay back and stared at the ceiling. "I gave up all that power and adulation once—I don't know if I could do it again. It's best to avoid temptation. But I'm glad I listened to you, Captain Picard. Like you said, I made the hard decision."

"You have my admiration." I patted him on his undamaged shoulder. "Did the Red Sash ever pay you all that latinum?"

"No, I knew they wouldn't." He nodded slowly to himself, his antennae bobbing. "At least we know it was only a small faction of Absolutists who killed my father, and they've confessed. I would hate to have both sides as my enemy. It's bad enough that I must stay in hiding for a while, with the Red Sash looking for revenge."

"We could protect you on Earth," I said. "Or aboard the *Enterprise*."

The young Andorian smiled with amusement. "You want to hide an Andorian among millions of humans? I don't think so. It's hard to hide an Andorian anywhere but Andoria, but I have resources at my disposal."

"If you ever need help, get word to me. I'll be there for you."

"And I for you, Captain." We shook hands—two comrades, two friends, two equals.

I don't know what Yevan is doing now, except that he's still in hiding. He sacrificed absolute power and a comfortable existence in order to give his people a democracy. Today the name of Prince Yevan is just a small footnote in history, but his selfless, courageous act made all the difference in the future of Andoria.

That's my story, proving that there is very little difference between a captain and a king.

Lightning Source UK Ltd.
Milton Keynes UK
UKOW041700210313

207980UK00001B/17/A